Final
Cut

Final Cut

A HOLLYWOOD MYSTERY

Marjorie McCown

CROOKED
LANE

NEW YORK

Published in the United States by Crooked Lane Books, an imprint of The Quick Brown Fox & Company LLC.

Crooked Lane Books and its logo are trademarks of The Quick Brown Fox & Company LLC.

Library of Congress Catalog-in-Publication data available upon request.

ISBN (hardcover): 978-1-63910-367-6
ISBN (ebook): 978-1-63910-368-3

Cover illustration by Paul Thurlby
Cover typography by Meghan Deist

Printed in the United States.

www.crookedlanebooks.com

Crooked Lane Books
34 West 27th St., 10th Floor
New York, NY 10001

First Edition: June 2023

10 9 8 7 6 5 4 3 2 1

For Ann Collette,
Extraordinary literary agent and
cherished friend.
Your wisdom and perseverance shone
a constant guiding light.
This book is yours as much as mine.

"A writer needs a pen, an artist needs a brush, but a filmmaker needs an army."

> —Orson Welles, Director/Actor/Writer/Producer

"Crewing and being on film sets is kind of like being in a carnival, with carnie folk."

> —Ben Mendelsohn, Actor

JUNE 21
8:10 PM

Joey felt frustrated that she was late getting back to the shoot. By this time, nearly an hour after wrap, most of the movie crew had packed up and gone home after what had been a long, discouraging day. As key costumer, Joey usually started the morning on set, then ended her day at one of the specialty shops that made clothing for the film, or one of a dozen other tasks that went with her job. But tonight was different.

She'd made the long drive back to the shooting location in Malibu because she wanted to talk to Courtney in person, and even though she wasn't looking forward to the conversation, she wished she'd made it back before wrap. The second AD hadn't answered her texts, and now Joey worried she'd missed the chance to do timely damage control, to smooth over the tension between them after their flare-up on set earlier that day. The hectic pace of the movie had everybody on edge, but their confrontation could threaten the costume department's entire working relationship with the assistant directors. If she couldn't talk to the second AD without starting a fight, it was game over.

Determined not to let that happen, Joey stopped by the wardrobe truck then headed straight to the AD trailer as soon as she got

1

back to location. She'd seen firsthand the problems that came from bad blood between departments.

On one of her first films, the costume supervisor had gotten into a feud with the transportation captain. After that, the wardrobe trailers were permanently parked in base camp Siberia, as far from the actors' trailers as possible. The time it took to travel those extra yards added up fast when you had to cover them many times each day. Then drivers suddenly became unavailable to do runs of any kind for the costume department, no matter the urgency. That might not sound like a big deal, but transpo can be a lifesaver when you're up against an impossible deadline by making an important pickup or drop-off when everybody in your department is too slammed with work to do it, which can happen several times a week on a busy film.

Getting on the wrong side of the AD department was even worse. Assistant directors are like air traffic controllers on a movie. Without them, everybody crashes into everybody else, literally and figuratively. Alienate the ADs and you're just asking for trouble.

The costume department already had enough problems on this movie between the lack of prep time, late casting, and a director with an ego as big as his box office grosses. Making an enemy of the second AD wasn't an option. The thought sent a shiver through Joey, and she picked up her pace.

When she didn't find Courtney in the AD trailer, she continued her circuit of the movie's base camp, asking everyone she passed if they'd seen the second AD.

"She was by the cafe set last I saw her, but that was a while ago," one of the grips said.

Joey headed for the Paradise Cove Cafe up by the beach. All the actors' trailers, nearest the set, were dark and locked up for the night. She tried the back door of the cafe, but that too was secured, so she peered through the windows. A single work light remained on, but there was no sign of anyone inside, the cafe apparently deserted now that the day's filming was done. The sun was low in the sky, dipping toward the ocean.

The longest day of the year, and that's exactly what it felt like to Joey.

She'd run out of places to look. Anxiety tugged at her. Her relationship with Courtney was complicated, like it is whenever your ex is dating somebody new. And she needed to be honest with herself about the way her personal feelings may have clouded their interactions.

With daylight dying over the water, she stepped onto the beach, hoping to feel a scrap of the serenity she always found in the natural rhythm of the breaking waves, like a favorite refrain, a golden oldie that just gets better with time.

At the water's edge, she noticed a pile of clothing, buffeted by the incoming tide scudding across the sand. Her first thought was that one of the extras had abandoned their costume, but that didn't make any sense. As the sun dropped out of the sky, she took a few steps closer to investigate, at the same time as a larger wave swept aside what she'd taken for coils of kelp swirling around that bundle of fabric.

Horror sliced through Joey like a scalpel; she stumbled and fell to her knees. Courtney Lisle lay motionless in the shallow water at the shoreline as the cold blue Pacific surf washed over her body.

FOURTEEN HOURS EARLIER

Chapter One

The first day of principal photography on a film is always a milestone in production, like opening night in the theater. After working mostly independently of each other for three months or more, all the different departments merge to become one big machine. No matter how many movies you've done, every new job is a blank slate. Each time, you ask yourself: Do I have what it takes to climb that mountain again, to create a new world out of whole cloth?

Put up or shut up time.

Joey slept poorly the night before, which was par for the course; but she couldn't shake the feeling of dread that dropped on her like a net as soon as she opened her eyes that morning. She'd had a bad feeling about this job from the start; she'd nearly passed on the movie for a number of reasons, both personal and professional. But the carrot of working so close to home was finally too tempting to resist.

The costume department had been prepping for months, but the schedule was rushed for a project so large and complex. Lots of special effects, stunts, and complicated costumes; lots of money and reputations on the line. Still, she felt her department was as ready as they could be, and her standards for readiness were high; so she tried to chalk up her misgivings to first day of shooting jitters. Later, she'd wonder if they'd been a premonition.

Just before sunrise, she pulled her car into the crew parking lot, about a mile south of base camp in Malibu. A shuttle van idled, waiting to ferry people to the set. It was empty save for the driver, whose head rested against his seat back. The teamsters were responsible for the setup of vehicles and equipment, so that all was ready for the shooting company when they got to work. They were the first in and last out every day, and most of them were expert at grabbing a few winks when they had the chance.

Joey gathered her purse and work satchel, then locked her car and pinned her keys to her waistband. She had keys to the costume offices and storage space for the movie as well as her personal keys, and this was the only sure way to keep them at hand throughout the day without losing them.

She trotted over to the van and pulled the side door open, startling the driver out of his catnap. A grizzled veteran in his late forties, he sat up with a frown until he saw who was climbing into his back seat.

"Joey Jessop! Girl, how you doin'?" A wolfish grin lit his face. "You are lookin' fine as ever, Sweet Cheeks."

Pete O'Neill was a relentless lech, and even though he was basically harmless, he could be tiresome, especially first thing in the morning.

"Pete, what a nice surprise," she said, trying to hide her true feelings. "I didn't see your name on the crew list."

"We ran three weeks over on the last job down in Louisiana; made it back in the nick of time to get on this one. Didn't want to miss out on a big show in LA, for a change."

"No kidding," she said. "This is the first job I've booked in the past four years that's shooting here. I'm thrilled to be sleeping in my own bed for the next six months."

"You coming off location, too?"

"I've been back here prepping this one for a while, but before that I was out of town shooting a Western."

"How'd that go?" He wiggled his eyebrows. "You meet a lot of hunky cowboys?"

She managed to keep from rolling her eyes. "It was an education."

"Never done a Western before, huh?" He gave her a knowing look. "Whole different animal."

"That's one way of putting it." Joey had been on dozens of location shoots, but the Western was a real eye-opener. From the wild temperature swings in the desert—25 degrees at night to over 100 in the afternoon—to the dust storm that took out their generators one day, or the flash flood that nearly trapped them in a box canyon on another, the experience had given her a fresh appreciation for the comfort of shooting on a studio back lot.

She stifled a yawn. "At least it was fast. Six-week shoot."

"Yeah?" His expression was skeptical. "Who was directing?"

"Clint Eastwood." She smiled as she pictured the director on set, watching the shot in progress on a handheld monitor. Despite the difficult conditions, Joey enjoyed working with him.

Pete nodded appreciatively. "That man's a class act, old school Hollywood."

"Yes, he is," she said. "A real filmmaker. We could use more like him in the business these days."

"You got that right." Pete checked his watch. "I don't think I'll be getting any more customers for a while, crew call's not for another hour. If you want, I'll run you up to base camp now."

"That'd be great." She slid the door closed. "I can use some quiet time before everybody gets here."

He dropped the van into gear. They turned north onto the Pacific Coast Highway as a pale watercolor wash of daylight began to spread across the ocean, sketching in the horizon line to the west. Joey took a deep breath, bracing herself for the nonstop activity the next sixteen hours would bring.

"Have you read the script for this one yet?" Pete glanced at her in the rearview mirror.

"Didn't have much choice," she said lightly.

"That bad?"

"Not my cup of tea. I'm not a big fan of comic book movies."

"'Bout all they make around here anymore," he said, "if you want to earn a decent living."

"Don't I know it."

The screenplay was 125 pages of special effects–driven gobble-dygook, but Joey had no doubt it would play well with the movie's crucial fourteen- to twenty-year-old target audience.

"I heard this one's about some new superhero." Pete caught her eye in the mirror again.

"It's actually the Legion of Phenomenals, based on some underground comics that have a big cult following. Nothing new, but they haven't been used in any movies so far."

"Why not just call it that, instead of *UMPP*?" He was asking about the working title for the movie. "Sounds like a noise you'd make if you got punched in the stomach."

She couldn't help smiling. "It's code for Untitled Marcus Pray Project. You know how paranoid the producers are. They're trying to keep the fanboys in the dark."

"Like that's going to stop them. The director'll probably be posting pictures on Instagram from the set, and the studio won't say boo to him." Pete leaned back to talk to her over his shoulder. "Marcus Pray's no Eastwood, even if he is a big dog in the business right now. I'm taking care of his trailer, and I got a mile-long list of special stuff that's gotta be on board for him and his *friends*." Pete gave the word a suggestive emphasis.

Marcus Pray was a powerful Hollywood hyphenate, a producer-director with a string of action-adventure blockbusters to his credit. This movie was sure to be another lucrative notch on his belt. Joey hadn't worked with him before, and some of the stories she'd heard made her think twice before she signed onto this job.

Pete winked at her in the mirror. "I hear Pray's got a lot of pretty little friends. Can you believe, they made me sign a special NDA, about how to work and act around that guy, like I haven't been doing this for twenty-five years? The second AD was real nasty about it too. She may be good-looking, but she's a bitch on wheels."

Joey was relieved to get to base camp and put a period on the conversation. She wasn't interested in dwelling on personalities or gossip; she wanted to concentrate on the work. Whatever the movie's shortcomings might be, she was excited to see it start coming to life on film.

As key costumer, she straddled the two worlds between the shooting crew on set and the prep crew back at the costume house who worked ahead of the shooting schedule to get the rest of the movie ready for camera.

On a big movie there can be hundreds of speaking roles and thousands of extras. There's never enough prep time to complete all those costumes before the first day of shooting. Some important speaking roles might not even be cast before principal photography begins. One film Joey shuddered to remember went on location two weeks before shooting was scheduled to start, with no one in the cast except the leading man.

The film was modern, so Joey struck an agreement with the best men's clothing store in town to open for her any time with a phone call. She also had vendors on standby in New York and LA to messenger clothing to their location in Tennessee at a moment's notice.

The deals for the supporting roles were signed just in time to fly the actors in on the weekend before cameras were set to roll. Then it was up to the costume department to gather, fit, and alter their clothing in slightly more than forty-eight hours. Even with Joey's careful preparations, they barely pulled it off and avoided breaking the cardinal rule of film: *No matter what: Never Hold Camera.*

If anyone asked, Joey would say the thing she liked best about her position was that the definition of a key costumer was so vague, the job could be customized for each project, limited only by the talents and skills of the person hired for the gig.

But she also loved being part of a team, working with talented people toward a common goal. Every day on every movie was different, so the work was never boring. Even when that variety meant big and sometimes unexpected challenges, solving them made the job that much more satisfying. She felt lucky to feel that way about her profession.

Base camp was just beginning to stir as she threaded her way through the hodgepodge of vehicles wedged into the parking lot of their first shooting location, Paradise Cove Cafe, a funky little restaurant with tables set up for diners right on the sand. The mechanical drone from generators and diesel engines all but drowned the gentler rumble of waves breaking on the beach only a few yards away.

Joey climbed the portable steps to the tailgate of the principal wardrobe truck, a converted fifty-three-foot semitrailer that served as the costume department's headquarters on location. Fixed double-tiered hanging racks for clothing lined both sides of the interior. A stackable washer/dryer sat up front beside a slightly elevated platform, aka the poop deck, a flex space fitted out with countertops and cupboards. That tiny piece of real estate had more uses than square feet: daily clerical work, impromptu fittings, costume alteration and repair, sometimes all of the above could be cycling through the poop deck at any given time.

A movie of this size required two wardrobe trailers, one for principal clothing, the second for background. Both trailers accompanied the shooting crew to every location, including the soundstages on the studio lot. In addition to clothing, the trucks were stocked with supplies and equipment such as safety pins, wardrobe tags, zippered clothing bags, laundry detergent, clothing steamers, sewing machines, digital printers for continuity photos the costumers would take on set, and a host of other items the crew might need at their fingertips during the workday.

"Awesome! You're early!" Zephyr Tomomatsu, the set costumer for both leading actresses, pounced as soon as Joey came in the sliding glass door at the back of the trailer. A waterspout of shocking red hair somehow harmonized with the vintage men's clothing she always wore. At twenty-eight, she was six years younger than Joey, though her irrepressible puppy dog energy often made that gap feel even bigger. But they'd worked together before, and Joey knew how capable she was. In fact, she'd recommended Zephyr for this job, a step up from her usual position of general set costumer.

But the look on her face dashed Joey's hopes for a little quiet time before the morning rush hit.

"Brooke's having a meltdown in her trailer. She doesn't want to wear the bikini. I tried to tell her she looks incredible, but she won't listen to me." Zephyr fixed her almond-shaped eyes on Joey. "Can you please, please talk to her?"

Brooke Austin Reynolds was a twenty-one-year-old actress who'd gained attention in a small but well-received independent movie before she was cast in this big-budget studio extravaganza. A beautiful young woman, she nevertheless wrestled with a raft of insecurities, mostly centering on her appearance. No matter how gorgeous or thin she looked to the rest of the world, the reflection she saw in the mirror always came up short and fat.

Zephyr leaned into her pitch. "You're the closest thing we have to an assistant designer, and Brooke respects your opinion. She told me she thinks you're smart and have great taste."

Joey shook her head in frustration. It was a tricky problem to address because logic didn't apply. There was no talking Brooke into seeing herself in a different light. Joey had learned that lesson years ago when she first came across the same situation with another lovely actress. Since then, she'd seen it too many times to have any illusions about a quick fix.

"Maybe we should wait for Dahlia. This should be her call."

Dahlia Raines was the costume designer, and though Joey was her right hand in most respects, coaxing actors to wear costumes already agreed to in the fittings was more properly part of the designer's job description.

"You know Brooke and Dahlia don't really get along." It was Zephyr's turn to shake her head. "Besides, we'll be lucky if she gets here by shooting call."

Reluctantly, Joey set down her bags. "I've got my phone. Text me right away if Dahlia shows."

"Will do," Zephyr said brightly. "Those jeans look amazing on you, by the way. I'd kill for your figure."

As she headed to Brooke's trailer, Joey tried to put herself in the actress's shoes. This was her first big job—an opportunity, but also a test that could trigger self-doubt, even in the healthiest psyche.

Joey didn't spend a lot of time thinking about her own looks, one way or the other, partly because she'd learned to detest the film industry's obsession with image. She understood some of that focus went with the territory, but in Hollywood the quest for physical perfection had become a cruel religion.

She liked to stay fit, but she wasn't compulsive about it, and she wore little makeup so she wouldn't have to bother with mascara for a six AM set call. For the same reason, she kept her dark blonde hair cut in a simple wash and wear bob.

But actresses, who spent their professional lives in front of a camera, didn't have the same freedom when it came to personal appearance. They were scrutinized, criticized, and judged every day by agents, casting directors, producers, other actors, and if they were successful, by the public at large. She had to keep all that in mind when she talked to Brooke if she wanted to help the young woman get past her insecurity about wearing the bikini.

She rapped on the door of Brooke's trailer and put a smile in her voice. "Brooke, it's Joey. May I come in?"

The door cracked open, and the actress peered through the narrow gap. "Are you by yourself?"

"Nobody here but us chickens."

Brooke stepped back and let the door swing open; Joey followed her inside. This trailer was smaller than the wardrobe trucks, and more of a traditional mobile home arrangement, with a sitting area and kitchenette up front, a bedroom and bathroom at the back, all comfortably furnished.

"I hear you're having some doubts about your costume." Joey wasn't going to beat around the bush but kept her attitude friendly and patient.

"I told Dahlia in the fitting I wasn't comfortable." Brooke was already fighting back tears.

"I remember," Joey said kindly. "But I thought you agreed to wear the bikini for this one dream sequence."

"She pressured me into it. I felt like I had to say yes, but I never felt okay about it. I thought maybe on the day it would be different." The tears finally spilled down Brooke's cheeks. "But I just can't."

"Sit down and let me fix you a cup of tea," Joey said.

She guided the girl to the love seat in the sitting area, then set about filling an electric kettle with water. The kitchen cupboards were stocked with cups and dishes, along with all kinds of snacks, teas, and protein drinks. She held up a box for Brooke's approval.

"Chamomile?"

The actress nodded. "Sure."

She didn't look any happier, but at least the tears had stopped.

"You know, we fit you with that pretty batik sarong." Joey poured hot water over the tea. "We sent the pictures to Marcus, and he said they looked fine."

She smiled and handed the steaming cup of tea to Brooke, thinking she had a compromise that might satisfy everybody. "Would you feel better if you could wear the sarong over the bikini? I'll talk to Dahlia about it, and if Marcus agrees, I'm sure it'll be okay with her."

Joey knew the sarong, a draped skirt of sheer cotton, would still show plenty of skin, especially when the actress was filmed splashing around in the surf. But it might give her some psychological armor and allow her to get comfortable on set without feeling so exposed.

Brooke took a sip of tea and gave a hesitant smile. "I think that could make all the difference."

Joey stayed until Brooke seemed calmer, chatting through another cup of chamomile, and as she walked back to the wardrobe trailer, she hoped they'd put the bikini issue to rest. There was always a chance Brooke might change her mind again before she made it to set, but Joey still sympathized with her.

This movie could be her big break, opening a world of opportunities, maybe launching her into the stratosphere of stardom. But Joey understood how those high stakes could make it even more difficult for an insecure young woman to display her body in front of the whole shooting company. That kind of vulnerability went deeper than the superficial discomfort of physical exposure.

Because within the movie industry, actors are commodities; in a very real way, they're products the studios sell to the public, and Joey knew that put a different sort of pressure on them than simply trying to do a job to the best of their ability. Success or failure rested on so many intangibles—like sex appeal, a must for most stars, but especially for an actress just getting started in film. Hollywood is even harsher to women that way, and their shelf life is half that of their male counterparts; nobody in the business even pretends otherwise. Joey could see Brooke was terrified about making a bad decision that could doom her fledgling career.

Back at the wardrobe trailers, the entire costume crew had shown up, and morning prep was in full swing. Background players were already lined up at the tailgate of the second trailer. Most would be given clothing to wear from the truck, items either purchased from stores or rental stock pulled from a costume house, all chosen weeks in advance by Dahlia, Joey, and a small crew of prep costumers.

In terms of its look, the movie was a mash-up of sci-fi-fantasy-meets-the-nineteen-eighties, a cost-cutting decision driven by the fact that the eighties were back in fashion and available retail. Even with that compromise, the costume budget (still a work in progress) hovered right around six million dollars. Most of that money was earmarked for construction of the elaborate superhero costumes. With fifteen characters to outfit in full comic book splendor, the bills piled up fast.

Joey gave Zephyr a thumbs up to let her know Brooke was on board with the bikini, then checked to make sure the other costumers had everything they needed. Once she was satisfied all was running smoothly, she moved to the background trailer to help assign clothing to the extras and check them once they were dressed.

The scene they were shooting that morning didn't advance the paper-thin plot, but it was crucial to upping the sex and beauty quotient of the movie. Specifically, the natural beauty of Southern California beaches paired with a teenage fantasy of the people who played there. The staff at PMBG Players had done a good job casting the background, and the costumers were able to work quickly, handing out bikinis and speedos to the Hollywood version of beach-going types, every one of them young, tanned, and smoking hot.

The next time Joey looked up from her work, an hour had passed. As she stood on the tailgate of the background trailer checking the last of the stragglers, she noticed Eli Logan, the first assistant director, deep in conversation with his second-in-command, Courtney Lisle. They looked too cozy to be discussing the day's shot list. Joey knew they were a couple, but when Courtney looped her arms around Eli's neck to plant a kiss on his mouth, she felt a pang of anguish that took her by surprise.

And Courtney didn't stop there. She glanced to be sure Joey was watching, then slid her hands down Eli's back to grab his butt, grinding her hips against him. The move was lusty and crude, Courtney marking her territory.

Joey forced herself to look away, then pivoted and hurried back inside the wardrobe trailer.

"Excuse me, am I approved to go to set?" called the curvy brunette dressed in a turquoise bikini who stood waiting by the tailgate.

"Hang on, I want to get you some sunglasses." Joey stumbled to the front of the trailer, then stopped to catch her breath. Until that moment, she'd convinced herself she was immune to any twinge of jealousy over her former boyfriend.

Even so, this was the biggest reason she nearly passed on the job: Eli was her ex, and after a year apart, she was still working through some difficult feelings about their relationship, mostly because of the way it ended. That hadn't been much of an issue till now because she'd had little direct contact with him during preproduction, aside from a few emails to schedule fittings for the principal actors.

But the first AD is the number two man in the command structure of a movie set. He's the overseer who coordinates all the departments, the one who keeps the day's work on schedule. Now that they were shooting, Joey would have to see Eli every day, and she began to understand that might prove more challenging than she'd realized. Especially if it meant watching him nuzzle his new girlfriend on a regular basis.

Throughout preproduction, she'd communicated more with Courtney, the second AD, about daily management details. Their interactions had been cooperative, but never anything close to friendly. Joey supposed that was normal under the circumstances since Courtney knew about her past relationship with Eli, but she also felt an aloofness from the second AD, a cold streak that seemed part of her nature. Joey didn't think they could ever be pals, even without Eli in the mix.

There was no mystery about Eli's attraction to Courtney. She was beautiful enough to be an actress. Even in work clothes, she had a classic glamour that brought to mind stars from the golden age of Hollywood, like Elizabeth Taylor and Ava Gardner. Joey shook her head impatiently and told herself to get back on track. That kind of distraction was the last thing she needed.

The costume crew broke three at a time to grab a walking breakfast from the catering truck. Joey always waited until the rest of the crew had eaten, but before she had a chance to go for food, Dahlia, the costume designer, breezed in and had to be briefed about the events of the morning.

The designer had an eye for the spotlight. With masses of curly blonde hair, she looked a bit like Stevie Nicks and tended to play that up with her own brand of devil-may-care chic. Well into her fifties, she was a head-turner in any crowd, even if she'd spoiled some of her God-given good looks with too much plastic surgery.

"Sounds perfect," she said about the decision to have Brooke wear her sarong. "That fabric is gorgeous, and it'll set her apart from the other babes on the beach."

"Do we need to run that by Marcus first?" Joey asked. "Or Eli, just so they know?"

Dahlia's attention strayed to a tall, elegant man with striking silver hair who walked by just then, headed toward the set. She flashed a killer smile, homing in on him like a heat-seeking missile.

"Bernard, *ciao, bello!*" She brushed both his cheeks with a quick kiss. "I'm so excited to be working with you!"

He greeted her politely and continued on his way.

"I can't believe Marcus snagged a cinematographer with Bernard Greene's pedigree to DP a comic book movie." Dahlia's curious gaze followed him. "But I guess even a guy with a shelf full of awards wants to work at home every now and then."

"What do you say about Brooke's sarong?" Joey asked again, trying to stay on point. "Do we need to get Marcus's approval?"

"Not at all." Dahlia waved the notion aside. "He was practically salivating over those fitting photos."

Joey breathed a sigh of relief: bikini problem solved. "The background came in looking good," she said. "I can have them line up if you want to check them yourself before they go to set."

"If you think they're camera ready, that's good enough for me."

This was Joey's first time working with Dahlia, and she appreciated the fact the designer was willing to delegate, then trust her crew to do the job. That wasn't always the case.

They went on to talk about plans for the remainder of the day. Once they got the first shot and the costumes were established (photographed for the first time), the rest of the day's filming would be in continuity, meaning no changes of wardrobe. At that point, Joey would break away from the shooting company and go about preparing for scenes that were coming up later in the schedule.

Before she knew it, the ADs were on the walkie-talkie calling actors to set. The set costumers were already up by the cafe, double-checking their kits and racks were properly stocked. They were responsible for making sure every costume was correct every time camera rolled, and for documenting each outfit with still photos and notes so that shots could be matched in the editing room during postproduction. That was especially important because many scenes in the movie would be filmed out of chronological order.

Joey had great respect for that job; a good set costumer was an invaluable member of the department, but she knew she'd never last in that position, tied to the set all day. Too much waiting around for camera and lighting adjustments, along with countless delays that cropped up. At the same time, you couldn't afford to let your guard down. Film is a fluid working situation, and there's always a mountain of detail to keep your eye on.

Joey preferred the prep work, racing ahead to get everything ready for camera: doing the research, choosing fabrics, overseeing clothing construction, pulling existing costumes from rental stock, and last, but definitely not least, fitting the actors.

She and Dahlia had started to make their way to set when the DGA trainee, low man on the totem pole in the AD department, came rushing over with a walkie-talkie in hand.

"They're calling for you on set," he said breathlessly.

"Me?" Joey asked.

"And her." He nodded at Dahlia. "Ms. Raines."

Dahlia frowned. "What do they want?"

Joey sprinted ahead without waiting to hear the answer. When the ADs call you to set on the walkie, you don't stop to ask why.

Chapter Two

A few yards from the set, Joey could hear Marcus Pray, the director, yelling.

"They're trying to ruin my movie!"

She rounded the corner to find Pray pacing back and forth on the sand in front of the cafe. Wiry and compact, his build was nothing special, but he always seemed to require more attention and space than a guy his size would need.

Brooke stood nearby with her head bowed, her face curtained by a wave of dark hair. Next to the actress, Zephyr looked stricken, as though she'd taken root at Brooke's side. Other crew members watched as the director fumed, their expressions ranging from confusion to dismay. Some exchanged inquisitive glances, several spoke together in low tones, an awkward captive audience. Nobody expected fireworks like this on the first day of shooting.

"When she comes onscreen, every man should start drooling!" Pray raised his arms and clapped his hands twice. "Let's take a vote: all the guys on set. How many of you'd want to sleep with this girl?"

Joey froze in shock when he pointed at Brooke. The rest of the crew looked around uneasily, trying to figure out how to respond. For many of them, this was their first day on the job, and no one seemed to feel brave enough to challenge the director, regardless of his behavior.

"Let's hear it, guys." Pray cupped a hand behind one ear and pointed to the prop master. "You, what's your vote?"

The prop master blinked and shook his head. "Count me out." He turned abruptly and jogged off toward base camp.

Some crew members looked like they wanted to follow his lead, but walking off the set with camera ready to roll was nothing less than mutiny.

Joey's mouth had gone dry, but she pulled herself together and stepped up to draw Pray's attention. "Marcus, if there's a costume problem, we can solve it."

He turned, zeroing in on her. "Wardrobe." He infused the word with scorn. "The *problem* is my leading lady looks like a nun. I can't see her body; you geniuses have her all covered up."

Joey tried not to flinch when he leaned close to her.

"Or maybe you'd like to trade places with Little Bo Peep over there." He let his eyes drift up and down, appraising her figure. "I'll bet you could rock that bikini."

Joey felt herself flush with embarrassment, too shaken to think clearly.

"Marcus, stop being a bloody jerk." Bernard Greene appeared at the edge of the crowd. Despite his dignified manner and that mane of silver hair, the grand master of cinematography looked ready to throw down. "Quit your showboating; let the crew get back to work."

"What makes you think you can talk to me like that on my own set?" Pray glared at him.

"The two Oscars I have at home give me an edge, I'd say," Greene replied. "If you want me to photograph this one, you'd better start behaving yourself."

Joey sucked in a breath. The military-style chain of command on a movie set means the director's word is law, especially when that director wields as much power in Hollywood as Marcus Pray. Greene's defiance was a major break with protocol, and it gave her the nerve to speak up again.

"Marcus, the sarong is only an option." Her heart hammered with tension, but she managed to keep her tone professional. "Dahlia thought it would help set Brooke apart from the other young women on the beach, but it is removable."

"Then get it off her!" he growled.

Greene shook his head in annoyance and stalked away. Joey wondered if they'd need to find a new DP before they even got the first shot.

She touched Brooke's arm gently, and the younger woman lifted her head. Tears washed trails of mascara down her cheeks. Compassion for the actress helped Joey set aside her own discomfort; she lowered her voice so only Brooke could hear.

"Listen to me; we'll do this together. Do we need to take a break and go back to your trailer?"

"No, let's get it over with," she whispered.

"Okay, here we go." Joey unfastened the clasp on the hip of the sarong and removed the delicate wisp of fabric. She could feel Brooke tremble like a trapped animal.

"Now we're talkin'." Pray ogled the young actress. "Stupid to hide that gorgeous figure."

Brooke wiped her cheeks, smearing mascara across her face.

"You didn't get hired for your acting chops, honey, so you better get used to showing your assets." He gestured impatiently. "Get her back into makeup while we finish lighting the scene."

By now, Joey's initial shock had curdled to disgust. But Pray was still in charge, and she had to think about Brooke's well-being, to get her off the set as quickly as possible. She put a hand on Zephyr's shoulder, cueing the costumer to follow. As the three women started back to base camp, Pray hurled a parting shot.

"Give her some more cleavage, while you're at it."

Joey seethed with indignation but kept her temper in check. Spouting off at the director in front of the company, however much he deserved it, would be counterproductive, inviting backlash not only for her, but for her department. She'd learned long ago to navigate the rough and tumble of a testosterone-heavy work environment, and it was a point of pride with Joey that she'd never quit a job before. But she'd also never run into the sort of deliberate cruelty Pray exhibited on set that day, and she thought that might be a deal breaker.

Near the outer edge of base camp, they met up with Dahlia, who didn't seem in any rush to join the shooting company at the beach.

"Everything okay?" she asked cautiously.

Zephyr opened her mouth to speak, but Joey silenced her with a look. Brooke was still shaky and didn't need to hear a recap of the incident.

"Go on with Brooke to the makeup trailer." Joey handed the sarong to Zephyr. "Then take this back to the principal truck."

Zephyr sent her a pleading look.

"It's going to be okay," she said and hoped she wasn't lying through her teeth. "We'll talk about it later."

"I guess we lost the sarong," Dahlia said lightly.

Joey could tell she didn't want to hear the details. "Less is more, according to our director."

"Brooke looked a little green around the gills."

"He didn't mince words," Joey said. "Tact doesn't seem to be part of his skill set."

Over Dahlia's shoulder, she saw the DGA trainee trotting toward them, holding his walkie-talkie aloft.

"Ms. Jessop!" he shouted. "The first wants to see you on set."

Joey's pulse jumped, but working with Eli was a fact of life for now. If she didn't get a grip on herself, she'd never make it through this shoot.

"I'll head to base camp to make sure Brooke's all right," Dahlia said with a wave. "Keep me posted about the mood on set. I'll check in with Marcus once he's stopped breathing fire."

Joey turned back toward the cafe, wondering if avoidance was Dahlia's standard method of conflict resolution. Not that she was judging; she understood the professional tightrope her boss had to walk.

Costume designer was a showy title but came with little juice in terms of the Hollywood power structure, for one simple reason: costumes don't sell tickets. Designers could develop clout through alliances with powerful people, but that influence was only bestowed or borrowed.

Those transactional relationships and the politics involved held no interest for Joey. She knew that meant she'd have a different career path from someone who enjoyed all the wheeling and dealing, but she'd made her peace with that.

She found Eli inside the cafe, watching as Bernard Greene supervised grips and electricians adjusting key lights for the actors. Stand-ins wearing clothing that matched the principals' costumes were positioned to determine placement and focus.

Eli spotted her as she came through the back entrance. The corners of his mouth turned up as he waved her over, but his smile didn't reach his eyes. Joey took a deep breath, trying to steady her nerves. They'd always worked well together, and she was determined to keep their personal history separate from this job.

She returned his careful smile and sat down next to him in a booth near the front of the cafe. "The trainee said you wanted to see me."

He leaned toward her to speak more quietly. "We've got another problem. Marcus isn't happy with the background."

Her heart sank and all thoughts of their past relationship evaporated. "He wants us to redress them?"

They'd used their best background stock for the scene when they handed out clothing the first time around that morning.

"No, he isn't happy with the women they sent. He wants us to call in Victoria's Secret models."

She stared at him. Eli's face looked drawn, and she couldn't help thinking the stress of the job was taking a toll on him already. He was too thin and needed a haircut; new strands of gray showed near his temples.

"You mean he wants them now, for this scene on the beach? Won't that cost a fortune?"

"And time we don't have to waste, but that's not my call. Courtney's on the phone with casting as we speak," he said.

"What about the guys? Does he want male models too?" She wasn't really worried about the men; they'd be easier to redress, but she had to know the full scope of what she was dealing with.

"He could care less about the guys. He's only interested in getting more hot women on camera."

Joey was floored by Pray's arrogance, thinking he could just snap his fingers and change plans that took days or even weeks to prepare. Not to mention his flagrant chauvinism, rejecting an entire slate of background women on a mean-spirited whim.

She puffed out her cheeks in frustration. "Can casting even book models of that caliber that fast?"

"I guess we'll find out. My question to you is, can you dress them?"

"How many are we talking about?"

"He's asked for fifty."

Twice the number of women they had dressed that morning.

Her mind raced ahead, working the problem. "We'll need someplace for them to change. We can't send fifty models to the honey wagons to dress."

The honey wagons were two trailers equipped with portable bathrooms for the shooting company, along with a couple of additional compartments that could be used as changing rooms for day players or extras. They were barely acceptable on a provisional basis and completely inadequate for the task of outfitting dozens of elite models.

"We'll get something rigged in one of the rooms we're not using inside the cafe," Eli said. "There're some offices and a storage room in back that could work. But I need to know if you have enough clothing."

"When will they be here?" Her brow puckered as she watched him intently.

"I can't answer that right now. As soon as casting can get them booked and out to Malibu."

A commotion on the other side of the room interrupted their discussion. The DP was losing patience with two of the grips who couldn't seem to get a light stand placed to his satisfaction.

"When I said two feet to the left, I meant camera left," Greene said, gesturing. "Come on, gentlemen, we need to pick up the tempo."

The grips moved to make the adjustment, but right at that moment, the power cut out. The cafe went dark except for a few weak shafts of daylight filtering through the windows. Joey nearly cursed aloud. What else could possibly go wrong?

"We need the gaffer on set," Eli barked into his walkie, calling for the head electrician. "We lost power in the cafe."

"Copy that. He's on his way," came the reply.

Eli glanced at Joey. "Are we good?"

She pressed her lips together and nodded, the only acceptable response. She wanted to talk to him about Pray's on-set tantrum, but they had more immediate problems, so that would have to wait.

Eli spoke into his walkie again. "I need the gaffer on set. Now."

Dismissed, Joey picked her way through the cafe, past the crowd of grips and electricians working to restore the power. She had to get back to base camp to make a count of the costumes they had on hand to dress the models, and then she had to figure out the quickest way to gather more. She was up against another cinematic rule of thumb: *Good. Fast. Cheap. Pick two.* One thing was certain: dressing fifty Victoria's Secret models on the fly wasn't going to be cheap.

The power popped on, then flickered and went off again, drawing a collective groan from everyone on set. To get to the exit, she had to squeeze past a ladder next to the problem light stand. By this time Greene had climbed up to make the adjustments himself. Without warning, one of the instruments flared in his hands. A blinding arc of electricity flashed across the room at the same instant a sharp jolt hit Joey like a truck.

Next thing she knew, she was lying on the floor, staring up at the ceiling of the cafe. She tried to raise her head, but that made her dizzy, so she lay back down again. A dense haze hung in the air, along with the smell of burnt meat. Three feet away, Bernard Greene sprawled flat on his back, both arms flung wide. Tendrils of smoke rose from his clothing, and he didn't seem to be breathing.

Chapter Three

The set medic performed CPR on Greene while Eli called for an ambulance. One of the grips helped Joey sit up, another gave her a bottle of water. An odd buzzing in her ears made it hard to hear, but at least her dizziness passed quickly, and she didn't have any pain. After a few minutes, she felt well enough to get to her feet without the helping hands offered by the grips, who'd kept an eye on her.

Greene was still unconscious but breathing now on his own. Joey's concern over his condition and her own narrow escape was clouded by her uncertainty about what had actually happened.

When the ambulance arrived, the EMTs loaded Greene onto a stretcher and carried him off the set. The medic advised Joey to go with them to the hospital for a thorough examination, but she refused. She'd have to be a lot worse off than she felt to spend the better part of the day sitting in an emergency room.

Eli and the gaffer watched as three electricians worked to dismantle the damaged light stand. Other crew members stood by waiting to hear from the first AD and his team about how the rest of the day would play out. Joey felt strangely gripped by the jittery mood on set. The blowout that injured the DP had pitched the whole company into a kind of churning confusion.

As time passed, her head finally cleared enough for her to realize nothing was going to happen until production made some decisions.

Apparently, that was going to take a while, so she headed back to the wardrobe trailers, still a little wobbly, but determined to stay busy. She needed to focus on something she could control.

"Are you okay?" Zephyr said when Joey came in through the tailgate door. "We tried to get to you, but they closed the set. Nobody's allowed up there until they know what went wrong."

"I think that's a good idea, don't you?" Joey put on a smile for the sake of her crew. "And I'm fine, thanks."

Zephyr gave her a doubtful look.

"Really, I'm okay," Joey said. "It's Bernard Greene we need to worry about."

"I won't go back up there until they can guarantee it's safe." Christine, one of the set costumers, was on the verge of tears. "You could have been—"

"Christine, calm down," Zephyr said sharply.

Joey kept her tone mild, trying to hide her own uneasiness. "I know they're working hard to figure out what happened, and they'll tell us as soon as they know something. Production doesn't want people getting hurt any more than we do."

"Should we call the union or OSHA?" Christine asked.

Joey shook her head. "I think we should sit tight until we have more information."

"Remember the DP who got shot on that Alec Baldwin movie?" Christine insisted. "And then there was poor Brandon Lee on *The Crow*."

"How about Vic Morrow and the two children who were killed on the set of *Twilight Zone*," Eduardo, the men's principal costumer, piped up. "When the director made a helicopter pilot fly too low in the shot."

"Nothing like that is going on here," Joey said firmly. "We're probably looking at some kind of mechanical problem, and that's certainly cause for concern, but until we know what the real issue is, let's not overreact."

"Maybe it's not exactly the same, but we all know accidents happen way too often on sets, and most of them don't make it into the news." Christine drew a shaky breath. "Production doesn't always pay enough attention to safety, especially when things aren't going well to start with."

Joey didn't necessarily disagree, but she didn't want to get bogged down in a gossipy confab that would whip up tension in the department. Her anxiety level was already jacked.

"I'm just saying, let's take a step back and see what happens," she said. "There'll be plenty of time to get our representatives involved if we need to."

Christine turned away, stiff with resentment, but she seemed willing to let the subject drop.

"Does anyone know where Dahlia is?" Joey asked.

"She's outside, on her phone," Eduardo replied. He took care of the two male leads, Fiske Larsen and Cameron Troy, breakout stars of a *Stranger Things* knockoff. "She didn't look happy; you might want to give her a minute."

"Thanks for the heads-up," Joey said. "Would you please text me when she's free? I'll be in the background trailer if anybody's looking for me."

Joey was relieved to find she had the second truck to herself. She wanted a task that kept her busy and didn't need a lot of thought. But it wasn't so easy to forget the image of Bernard lying unconscious as smoke rose from his clothing. In spite of the brave face she put on for her crew, she remembered only too well the sudden blow that slammed her to the floor before she knew what hit her.

Still, she had a job to do, and she was glad to have something useful to occupy her. Although she continued to feel a little foggy, she made quick work counting the available swimwear to fit the Victoria's Secret models; not enough there, but it was a start. With that information in hand, she got on the phone to the Studio Services departments of Barney's, Neiman's, and Saks, all lined up within blocks of each other along the Wilshire corridor in Beverly Hills.

Los Angeles is wired on all fronts to support the film industry— a company town in every sense of the word. Individual movies can set up accounts with various vendors and enjoy a level of service most customers never experience. Joey was able to request Studio Services staff at each of the stores pull a selection of swimsuits and accessories within guidelines she provided in terms of size, color, and style. The clothing was written up on memo so that a costumer or driver could pick up the merchandise and deliver it to the set. Whatever was used would be charged to the film; whatever was left over would be taken back to the stores. Returns were only a matter of checking off the paperwork.

Any clothing that was purchased automatically became the property of the movie's production company and stayed with the film, whether it ended up on camera or not. But this memo approval deal with the vendors cut down on labor and confusion throughout the fitting process, so that clothing could be borrowed for a period of time (about a week for any specific pull was the standard cap) until final selections were made. The arrangement benefited both sides of the transaction, the costume departments and the stores. It was an efficient way to avoid large volume purchases and returns continually being rung through the stores' sales systems, as well as the nightmare of accounting paperwork that would generate for the costumers.

Joey would have preferred to do the shopping herself rather than call the order in to Studio Services, but she was realistic. This would save her time on a day she had none to spare and solve the problem that fell in her lap when Marcus Pray decided to call in fifty fashion models at the last minute.

Early on, she learned the key to her job often lay in the ability to maneuver, to pull logistical rabbits out of hats. When faced with ridiculous deadlines, using ingenuity to cheat the clock became the goal, and any creativity that managed to creep into the process was a bonus.

But there were hundreds of decisions, both large and small, to be made every day. And sometimes the perfect button or length of fabric, or a lovely piece of vintage clothing discovered in a costume house was enough to spark a flash of satisfaction that reminded her why she'd chosen this profession.

Her phone vibrated in her pocket, and she pulled it out to find a text from Eli:

All crew members report to the cafe set for briefing.

Every bit of anxiety her swimsuit project had kept at bay came rushing back.

Dahlia stuck her head in the side door of the trailer. "I heard you were looking for me. Did you get the text from the ADs?"

"I was about to head over there."

Joey climbed down the stairs and the two women fell in step.

"Has anybody told you about the fifty Victoria's Secret models Marcus asked the ADs to call in?"

"Yes, the snippy little second gave me the word," Dahlia said. "How are we fixed for stock to fit them?"

"We have enough to dress about a dozen girls. I went ahead and called Studio Services at the usual suspects to get them started pulling clothes for us. I'll arrange a pickup once we know what the rest of today's going to look like."

"I hope production has the good sense to write off the day to insurance. How are you feeling, by the way?" Dahlia said. "I'm sorry I didn't think to ask till now. I heard you got a pretty bad jolt, along with poor Bernard."

Joey wasn't sure how she felt, but she didn't want to get into that with her boss. She lowered her voice as they stepped onto the set. "I'm fine."

The rest of the crew was already gathered in the cafe. Eli nodded to them when he saw Joey and Dahlia come in the back way. Joey thought she could see new lines of strain in his face, and she wondered how he was handling the fallout from the morning's on-set emergency.

Eli was a control freak, which was a big part of what made him good at his job. He'd worked in feature films for twenty years, built a solid reputation in a cutthroat industry. But in many ways, the drive to be in charge that served him at work kept him isolated personally, and Joey knew from experience he could be his own worst enemy.

Eli held up a hand to get the room's attention. "I'm sure everyone will be glad to know Bernard's awake and out of danger."

Joey felt relief wash over her as the company responded with a mixture of gasps and cheers.

"He wants to be back on set tomorrow morning, but I think we'll have to play that by ear. The important thing is, he's going to make a complete recovery. We got very lucky today."

"How about Joey?" one of the camera operators called out. "Is she okay?"

Joey blushed when Eli pointed to the back of the room. "Let's ask her." He raised his eyebrows. "How are you feeling, Joey?"

She started to answer, then had to clear her throat. "I'm doing fine, thanks."

"You go, girl!" the camera operator shouted.

Everybody laughed and clapped, which made her feel even more conspicuous, but she smiled and waved her thanks. She wondered if Eli would have said anything if the camera operator hadn't asked, then felt perturbed for having the thought. She'd worked too hard to let herself backslide emotionally.

Eli waited for things to quiet down, then continued. "I know we're all under the gun, feeling the pressure of a tight schedule; and I'm not saying this to single anybody out. Accidents happen, but this movie is busier than most, and if this morning showed us anything, it's that we need to maintain a very high level of vigilance to keep ourselves safe."

One of the carpenters raised his hand. "Do we know what happened?"

"We believe a ballast controlling the current through that instrument failed," Eli said. "The power outage may have aggravated the problem, we're not sure. But we've replaced the equipment and the issue's resolved."

A murmur of nervous chatter rippled through the crowd.

"Come talk to me if you have questions or doubts," Eli said. "But right now, I need you to regroup and get ready to continue with today's work."

"You mean we're going to shoot without the DP?" The prop master shook his head. "Why not push camera and give us the day to catch up? We could all use the extra prep time."

"Marcus doesn't want to lose the day," Eli said. "He's going to work directly with the camera crew."

"Lucky them," the prop master deadpanned.

"You're on payroll, and that means you owe my production company a full day's work."

All eyes turned to the back of the room where Marcus Pray stood, his expression cold and dark.

"I know more about camera work than most DPs, and if anybody has something to say about that, come talk to me; I'll be happy to sign your pink slip. Nobody's forcing you to work for top dollar on the biggest movie of the year." He turned to go. "Anybody who's staying, be ready for camera within the hour."

At the head of the room, Eli looked pained. Despite the tension between them, Joey's heart went out to him. He'd been trying to reassure the crew when Pray swooped in to squash that effort flat. But the first AD couldn't openly contradict the director if he wanted to stay on the job, and Joey knew Eli needed this job. In the past eighteen months, his once stellar reputation had taken a beating.

It started as a stopgap. That's what he said when he finally called her from Beaufort, South Carolina. A little bump of coke to get him through a string of tough days on a brutal location shoot. They were still together then, and she told him if he needed drugs to function, it was time to pack up and come home.

He laughed that off, said he'd be fine. But the pace never let up, and a few tough days turned into an endless grind. When Eli came home from that movie, he'd lost thirty pounds he couldn't spare, and his coke use was routine.

The first time he got fired, from a big sci-fi fantasy a week into shooting, he cleaned up long enough to land another job. He got booted even faster from that one, just three weeks into preproduction. Word was getting around by then, and work dried up completely.

Joey was frantic, worried he was killing himself along with his career. She gave him an ultimatum: either quit the drugs or she'd leave him. Eli promised he would, and he did try for a while, but he couldn't stick with it. He'd stay clean for a few weeks, then relapse and binge for days at a time.

After months of agony, Joey finally had enough. The trouble was, she made the mistake of telling Eli they were finished one night when he was high. He flew into a rage, and she had to lock herself in the bathroom and call 911. She waited for the cops while he trashed his apartment. As she crouched in the tub, hoping the flimsy builder-grade door would hold if he tried to break it down, she swore she'd never let anything like this happen to her again.

When the police arrived, they arrested Eli. In the end, he was charged with assaulting a police officer and resisting arrest, in addition to drug possession. He opted for residential rehab to avoid serious jail time, and to his credit, he'd been drug-free for a year now, working steadily again in film.

Joey was glad for him. He made his amends to her, and she formally accepted his apology. But their connection was broken; she could never consider sharing her life with him. And though his career seemed to be back on track, he was still on probation in the eyes of the industry. Another slip and he'd be blacklisted for good.

"That's all for now." Eli placed his palms together, saluting the company with the gesture. "Like I said, come see me with any concerns. And you heard the man: we want to be ready for camera in less than an hour."

Joey shook off her memories and snapped back to the present. She and Dahlia exchanged a look, then stepped up to talk to Eli.

"My darling, what's happening with the fifty Victoria's Secret models that Marcus needs for this scene? Are you planning to get them on camera today? Because it's going to take us a minute to dress them," Dahlia said sweetly.

He glanced around to make sure no one else was listening. "We're still trying to get as many as possible out here for Marcus to approve, but I'd say the chances of getting them on camera today are somewhere between slim and none. If we get a few establishing shots with Fiske, Cameron, and Brooke, that's about all we can hope for."

"Good to know," she said. "Keep us in the loop. Any girls he likes for camera need to see us today too."

"We're paying them to trek out here anyway, so we might as well get our money's worth," he said.

Joey thought it was a waste of time and money to hold up production to book high-priced models as glorified set dressing. But Pray was one of the executive producers, so he could do whatever he wanted until the studio was willing to say no to the eight-hundred-pound gorilla they'd put in charge of the show.

She walked with Dahlia back to base camp after the meeting. "I'll get a driver to pick up the clothes from Beverly Hills and bring them to set. Do you need me to stay to help fit the models?"

"Don't you have those two day players to fit back at the department this afternoon?" Dahlia asked.

"I do, but I can reschedule them if you want."

Joey hoped Dahlia wouldn't take her up on the offer. She needed a break from the negative energy that hovered over the shooting company like a cloud of poison gas. A few hours away would help clear her mind.

"If you're not up to fitting them after everything you've been through today, I completely understand." Dahlia stopped to look at her. "If you're feeling shaky, take the rest of the day off."

"I'd much rather stay busy."

She longed to escape the gloomy set, but she didn't want to sit home worrying about all the work they had to do; and she definitely didn't need time on her hands to think about what happened that morning.

"Then by all means, go do the fittings," Dahlia said. "I'll get Zephyr and Christine to help me with the models if any of them show. Or Eduardo; he's got a good eye, and it doesn't sound like they're going to be busy on set. Besides, if I can't fit a few pretty girls in bikinis, it's time to turn in my union card."

Dahlia's attitude about the models seemed a little relaxed to Joey. She didn't understand why the designer wasn't more upset that Pray rejected the twenty-five beautiful background women they dressed for the scene that morning. But she didn't have time to dwell on that now; it was almost noon, and she'd barely made a dent in her work list for the day.

Before she left for the fittings, Joey headed to transpo to schedule a driver for the run to Beverly Hills. As she made her way back to the wardrobe trailers to collect her belongings, a slender woman with dark hair and exceptionally good legs waved to her. Joey wondered if she was one of the Victoria's Secret models.

"Can I help you?" she said.

The woman smiled. "Maybe we can help each other." She extended her hand. Joey reached for it, then saw she was being offered a business card. She glanced at the printed information.

"Maggie Fuller." She looked up from the card. "What's *Popvibe*?"

"The website I work for."

"You're not one of the models casting sent over?"

"You flatter me." The woman's smile grew fixed; Joey saw she didn't appreciate the assumption in the least. "I'm a journalist, and I'd like to talk to you about the explosion on set this morning."

Joey stared at her in disbelief. "How did you find out about that?"

"Oh, please," Fuller said. "The whole town's talking about it. I've even seen photos texted from the set right after it happened." She took a step closer. "But don't worry, I'm not here to sensationalize the accident, *if* that's what it was. I'm more interested in whatever role Marcus Pray may have played in the incident."

Joey's fingers tightened around the business card. "What makes you say 'if that's what it was'?"

"Hey, paparazzi Barbie! I told you, this is a closed set!" Courtney, the second AD, came on the run.

Joey shaded her eyes, waiting for Courtney to catch up to them. Fuller stood her ground as well.

"I'm not here to chase celebrities," the reporter said. "And I have a journalistic right to hand out cards to anyone who might want to talk to me, on or off the record. Here you go, Ms. Lisle." She held out a card. "Take one, in case the spirit moves you."

Courtney batted the card away. "You've already been warned you're trespassing. If you don't leave now, I'll have you thrown off the property."

"You do that," Fuller shot back. "I'd love to have that photo op to go with the article I'll write about how this company is more committed to protecting its bottom line than safeguarding its employees."

Courtney thumbed her walkie-talkie. "Security, I need you over by transpo to get rid of a pest." She pointed at Fuller. "If you come around again, I'll have you arrested. You're nothing but a cheap rumormonger."

"My dear, I'm anything but cheap, and that malignant narcissist you're so devoted to is going to find out exactly what that means." Fuller sauntered off to meet the two uniformed security guards who jogged into view. She mimed holding a phone to her ear. "Call me," she said to Joey.

The security guards flanked her, and each took hold of an elbow. "Hi, boys," Fuller said. "What kept you?"

As the reporter was led away, Courtney rounded on Joey. "What did you say to her?"

"Nothing," Joey said, still stunned by Fuller's comments about the accident and Pray. "I thought she was one of the models."

Courtney glared at her. "Don't forget you signed an NDA when you did your deal. If you violate that, you're toast."

Joey bit back a sharp reply. "Duly noted, Courtney. Now, if you'll excuse me, I've got some fittings back at the costume department."

Courtney thumbed her walkie as she stalked away. "Eli, what's your twenty?"

Glad to be on the move, Joey checked in with the costumers at the wardrobe trailers and picked up her bags. She was on her way to catch a shuttle to crew parking when she realized she was starving.

The drive to the costume offices in North Hollywood would take over an hour in midday traffic, and she wouldn't have time to stop for lunch. It was worth a detour by craft service to pick up water and a snack to go.

One of the few constants on a union film set is access to food. Full meals are served every six hours by the caterers, and a separate craft service area near the set always has a spread. You'll never go hungry, but Crafty is usually stocked with grab-and-go items geared toward satisfying a salt or sugar craving, so Joey was happy to see plates of fresh fruit and veggies among the trays of food laid out across three portable banquet tables behind the cafe.

There was a big group gathered at the tables already. Joey figured the crew was on a break before shooting resumed. Most of them clustered around the starches and sweets, stress eating right out of the gate, apparently.

Not that anyone could blame them, she thought.

A pretty young woman was restocking ice chests with soft drinks and bottled water. She looked up with a smile when Joey approached.

"This fruit looks wonderful," Joey said, helping herself to a pear.

"I'm glad you think so." The girl wore her blonde hair in a single braid that trailed down her back. "Let me know if there's something you'd like that you don't see here." She held up a finger. "Except nuts. The director's allergic to tree nuts, so we aren't allowed to have them on set."

There was a gentle quality about her that made her seem child-like. Joey automatically looked around for someone working along-side her, thinking she shouldn't be left on her own with this crowd, many of them older men with an eye for the ladies.

"Everything you have here looks great." Joey bent to snag a bot-tle of water.

"That's good to hear. This is our first movie job, and we want to make sure everybody's happy." The girl held out her hand. "My name's Sam."

Joey had to juggle the snack items she'd collected to shake the girl's hand. "I'm Joey."

Sam gave her sweet smile again. "We both have boy names."

"I'm glad I caught you before you left." Courtney appeared at Joey's side and dove right in, all business. "Eli and I think we have to come up with a better way to present the background to Marcus. He needs to see them in costume ahead of time."

Joey was put off again by her manner, but let it slide for the moment.

"We can't dress them until the day of shooting," she said. "Production won't approve the cost for background pre-fits, unless Marcus wants to authorize the additional expense."

"That's not going to happen," Courtney said. "Eli and I decided you'll get them dressed on the day and we'll do a lineup for Marcus before they go to set."

What a recipe for disaster, Joey thought.

It was one thing to have Dahlia check out a lineup of background players, quite another to have Pray see them out of context. After his unforgivable treatment of Brooke and his arbitrary nixing of the background women that morning, Joey doubted he had the temperament or ability to evaluate them with the big picture in mind. By definition, extras were part of the backdrop for a scene, and redressing large numbers of them on a daily basis would be time-consuming and expensive.

"Wouldn't it be better," she said, "to let him look at them once they're dressed, on the set where they'll be photographed? In the meantime, you and Eli could make sure he's seen their head shots so he can weed out anybody who doesn't meet his standards. He didn't object to the clothes this morning; it was the people he wasn't happy with."

Joey was acutely aware that all chatter around them had ceased, and the crowd gathered at Crafty was hanging on every word as her disagreement with Courtney heated up.

"I guess I need to remind you that your job is to make sure Marcus gets what he wants on camera," Courtney said. "And my job is to make sure you do that in a way that accommodates him."

Joey felt her temper climb. "Are you telling me we don't get a say in how we do our job now?"

Courtney shook her head. "I'm not going to argue with you about this."

"You're absolutely right," Joey said. "We need to sit down with Eli, Dahlia, and our costume supervisor to work it out, because this decision could add thousands of dollars to our budget, in both materials and labor."

Courtney's walkie-talkie crackled to life. "What's your twenty?" Eli asking for her location.

"At Crafty talking to wardrobe. Coming your way." She started toward base camp, but not before she took a final swipe at Joey. "I know your history with Eli, so I can understand why you'd be resentful, but this is the second time today you've gotten testy with me. This is a long job, and I'm only going to say this once. Don't let your personal feelings cloud your judgment."

Chapter Four

Joey stared after Courtney, wondering if the woman had a point. A minute ago, she'd have sworn she'd say no to a background lineup for Pray, for the reasons she spelled out, no matter the messenger. Now she wasn't so sure. Would she have tried harder to work out a compromise with somebody else—as in, anybody who wasn't sleeping with her ex?

"I told you she was a bitch," a voice crooned softly in her ear.

She winced and turned to find Pete, the teamster, with a triumphant smirk on his face. She wanted to tell him to take a hike, and her expression said as much. His smile melted away, and he moved on without further comment. The rest of the crew had mercifully lost interest in the aftermath of the scene with Courtney.

A dark blue Dodge Ram pickup pulled in next to the craft service station, and Joey noticed Sam hurried to meet the truck.

"I'll get the stuff from the back, Daddy," she said.

"Leave those flats of water, Sammy. Just grab the bags."

"It's okay. They're not heavy," she replied cheerfully.

The flurry of activity roused Joey from brooding over her dustup with the second AD. Embarrassed, she waved to Sam, ready now to get on the road.

"Thanks for the fruit." She held up the pear. "This is just what I needed."

She nodded to the driver of the pickup. He wore classic Wayfarer sunglasses, and when he got out of the truck, he stood over six feet tall. His shoulders had begun to stoop with age, and he carried too much weight through the middle, but he was still powerfully built. She noticed he cradled his left arm next to his body.

"Aren't you the young lady who got hurt earlier in there?" He gestured to the cafe.

Joey would rather have ducked the question. She was still trying to process what had happened and didn't feel like talking about it with a stranger, but she didn't want to seem rude.

"Nothing serious," she said. "I just got the wind knocked out of me."

He pushed up the sunglasses, so they rested on his forehead. His pale blue eyes looked fierce with disapproval. "Can't say I know much about this kind of operation, but so far, I'm not impressed. A little slipshod, you ask me. I'm glad you're okay, miss."

"My name's Joey. I work in the costume department."

"Sounds like that'd be an interesting job." His eyes lost some of their heat. "I'm Stuart Campbell, and I guess you've met my daughter, Sammy."

"Good to meet you," Joey said. "I don't think I've ever seen a better craft service spread." She smiled. "I'm sure I'll see you both again soon."

Twenty minutes later, she drove through Malibu Canyon on her way to Left Coast Costumes in North Hollywood. Most of the independent costume companies that served the film industry were situated in the San Fernando Valley, known to locals simply as the Valley, as if there were no others worth mentioning. Several of the major studios—Universal, Warner Brothers, and Disney—each with its own large costume department, were headquartered there as well. Joey appreciated this user-friendly arrangement, which essentially provided a home base for the entire costume community.

She usually enjoyed the drive through the canyon; the scenery was so lush and unspoiled, she could almost forget the nearby urban scuffle of LA. But today her mood was a stark contrast to the buttery sunlight that warmed the slopes of the Santa Monica Mountains towering over the winding road. She couldn't stop thinking about the accident that sent Bernard Greene to the hospital and nearly put her out of commission.

But was "accident" the correct word? Maggie Fuller's pointed questions made her wonder. She couldn't think why anyone would want to sabotage the shoot, but she also couldn't believe somebody in the company texted pictures from the set right after the explosion.

How could she reassure her crew if she wasn't certain what really happened? It was her responsibility to set an example, but always with the costumers' welfare in mind. She kept an eye on her crew for signs of exhaustion, illness, depression, and on the rare occasion, substance abuse. But it was a fine line to walk, the difference between being a good leader or a pushy boss.

That balance was hard to find on the job because the film industry is a giant bureaucratic engine whose main purpose is to generate cash, lots of it, and fast. Time is money, after all. If pushing the pace caused a glitch that resulted in the odd human casualty here and there, Joey knew that was an acceptable outcome from the studios' corporate perspective, provided the profit/loss ratio ended up in the black.

Even if the explosion that morning was accidental, she had to admit Christine's point was legitimate. Production was often too willing to cut corners in favor of efficiency over safety.

Suddenly, a pair of squirrels darted into the road, chasing each other in a game of tag. Joey stomped on the brakes. The back end fishtailed, but her car held the road. Heart racing, she braked again more gently and pulled onto the shoulder. She peered through the windshield, glad to see the squirrels had made a safe escape. Then she leaned against the steering wheel, feeling faint.

This was her second near miss of the day, only this one was her fault. She'd been lucky: traffic through the canyon was sparse for the hour, and no one had been on her tail. After a careful look in the rearview mirror, she got back on the road and shelved her doubts about the movie for the time being. She needed her head in the game, focused on the work.

Joey's particular expertise, honed over a fifteen-year career, was as a made-to-order specialist. She was in charge of all the costume manufacture for the movie, clothing and accessories: hats, boots, shoes, gloves, whatever was needed. And because she usually worked on the biggest A-list feature films, that meant hundreds, if not thousands, of costumes for each movie. She had a pages-long to-do list every day.

Her job called for careful organization and an ability to prioritize. She tried to work at least two weeks ahead of the shooting schedule, though factors beyond her control sometimes made that impossible. Last-minute casting or changes to the schedule could, and often did, throw her plans into chaos, so she worked with an eye that looked ahead for any and all problems. Hope for the best but prepare for the worst.

"Speak of the devil," she said when a familiar number popped up on her Bluetooth.

Damir Novak was the eccentric genius who founded and ran a specialty costume house called Hammer and Tongs, cutting-edge experts in the construction of sophisticated fantasy props and costumes, a must-have vendor for any comic book movie.

She hit the button on her steering wheel to take the call. "I don't like talking on the phone while I'm driving, but I'll make an exception for you."

"As well you should. I have some helmets to show you. Any chance you'll be by today?"

Damir ran his business like his own private fiefdom, and his massive ego took some handling. If his work wasn't so spectacular, dealing with him wouldn't be worth the time and colossal expense. But it was, which made the investment necessary, and Joey admired the determination that fed his drive for perfection.

"I can't this afternoon," she said, "but I'll make sure I get there tomorrow. And I have a hypothetical I need to run by you, since we're on the phone."

"I'm listening."

"There's been talk about bringing some of the green screen special effects work forward on the schedule. If we needed the first complete costumes for Fiske and Brooke sooner than July twelfth, is that doable?"

"How much sooner?" Damir never sounded alarmed, even when he should.

"Say, in ten days."

"It's possible," he said. "Barely."

"How will that affect the cost?"

The costumes were already priced at more than $100,000 apiece, and that was without a rush charge.

"I'll have to get back to you on that," he said, "as soon as you can give me a definite date."

"Can't you give me a ballpark?"

"I can't quote accurate figures without a specific time line."

Joey was used to this dance, but she didn't have the patience for it today.

"Damir, I'm only looking for information so I can let the producers know what they're in for if they change the schedule."

"Tell them they'll be looking at significant additional charges for overtime labor."

Well duh, she wanted to say, but she could tell he wasn't going to budge.

"Okay, so we're clear: I'm not saying that we need to up the delivery date, not yet anyway. I'm only trying to suss out our options."

"Got it. The sooner we know, the better."

"Story of my life," she said.

She clicked off the call, already thinking about the costume fittings that would occupy her for the next few hours. She hoped they'd go smoothly and not take the entire afternoon. The day already felt like a marathon, and she still had so much to do.

As she turned onto Vanowen Street, she noticed the parking lot in front of Left Coast Costumes looked full. That would be just her luck today. There was a large parking lot behind the building that never filled up completely, but that alternative would cost her time she didn't have.

LCC, as it was known to everyone in the industry, was by far the biggest commercial costume house, not only in the city, but in the world. Its main claim to fame was a stock of hundreds of thousands of pieces of clothing from various periods in history available for rent. There were also storage facilities and offices for lease on a temporary basis that could serve as headquarters for even the largest movie costume departments.

The real bonus, however, was the variety of skilled artisans LCC employed who were on site to make or alter both men's and women's clothing, anything from an eighteenth-century ball gown to a Storm Trooper uniform. They also had one of the best shoemakers in town on staff, as well as milliners, glovemakers, and an in-house dyer. There was a supply store that carried everything from shoe polish to clothing steamers, and a small but exceptional fabric store where you could find certain kinds of cloth that hadn't been manufactured for fifty years. All conveniently situated under one roof.

The huge main building was a quarter-mile hike from one end to the other, which was the reason Joey wanted to park in front, where the offices and fitting rooms were located. She managed to snag the last free space. A half dozen scruffy-looking paparazzi hung out under a clump of shade trees that bordered the parking lot; not exactly unusual, but not something that happened every day, and she wondered who'd drawn the celebrity stalkers this far from their normal stomping grounds.

She hurried inside, texting the head cutter for the ladies' workroom and the men's head tailor, to let them know she was there, and her fittings were on schedule.

The receptionist waved as she came in the door. "I had to bump you to fitting room two."

A knot of people packed the reception area, and Joey felt her spirits lift when she spotted Ben Affleck at the center of the group, chatting affably with everyone.

"Joey! Small world!" Ben grinned and spread his arms. "You look great for someone who works too hard for her own good."

She stopped to give him a hug. "You're one to talk. You work harder than all the rest of us put together."

The year before, they'd spent twelve weeks in Georgia making a movie he wrote, produced, directed, and starred in. Joey took the job because it was set in the 1930s, one of her favorite periods. The shoot had been weeks of night work, mostly exteriors, and in no way easy, but Ben earned the crew's respect by standing shoulder-to-shoulder with them throughout. Despite his trouble with bad press in recent years, Joey found him to be one of the most generous and collaborative celebrities she'd ever worked with.

"Looks like you've got a posse waiting in the parking lot," she said. "If you don't want to run the gauntlet, there's a back way out of here. You could have your driver pick you up by the loading dock."

"Drove myself." He flashed the grin again and held up his car keys. "That'll teach me." He gave her shoulder a squeeze. "Be good."

"Call me on your next one," she said.

He wagged a finger at her. "Careful what you wish for."

She watched him through the glass of the front doors as the photographers surrounded him. She didn't feel sorry for him, or any celebrity, for that matter. It was part of the gig if you were lucky; but she also didn't envy that trade-off. Fame was the jackpot they chased until they caught it and found they had a tiger by the tail.

Chapter Five

Joey continued down the hall where *UMPP* had two big suites of offices. Bill Nichols, the costume supervisor, was holding down the fort. The rest of the department was deployed on other missions, pulling costumes from stock for upcoming scenes, or purchasing fabric and supplies.

"Hey there, you need any help with your fittings?" Bill said when she came in the door.

A fifty-something fireplug of solid muscle, Bill was at the top of his profession, with good reason. He was the keeper of the costume budget, no small task on its own. But even more important, he was a strategic planner, helping coordinate the work of the entire department.

"I'm okay," she said as she checked the clothing on her fitting rack. "But I'll always welcome your opinion if you want to kibitz."

He rolled his eyes. "I'm on my sixth iteration of the budget, so as much as I'd like to look at something besides numbers, if you're really okay, I'll pass."

She peered at him anxiously. "Anything new on Bernard's condition?"

Bill was information central and always had the latest updates.

"He's still in the hospital, so we'll see. No preliminary call sheet yet. I guess the ADs are waiting to hear if he'll be released today." He hesitated briefly. "How are you doing, I'd say is also a question."

"I'm fine." Joey shook her head impatiently. She wasn't going to get hung up again on doubts and suspicions, not while she was on the clock.

"Good to hear," he said briskly. "Just don't be a hero, okay?"

They'd worked together a number of times, and they respected and liked one another; Joey was glad to have him as an ally.

"No worries about that." She started to push the heavy rack through the doorway, strong-arming it over the threshold.

Bill frowned as he watched her struggle. "Hold on a second. There's somebody I want you to meet." He leaned back in his chair. "Hey, Malo? Leave the copies for now and give Joey a hand out here."

"No, I'm good," she said. "My first fitting's not for another half hour, so I've got plenty of time."

The mechanical thrum of a copy machine in another room ended abruptly, white noise Joey only noticed when it stopped. A young man with curly dark hair and Buddy Holly glasses popped out of one of the smaller offices in the suite. He had on skinny black jeans and a T-shirt with a picture of Our Lady of Guadalupe worn thin by many trips through the washer.

"This is Malo, our new PA. Malo, meet the queen of made-to-order in this town, Joey Jessop."

The boy ducked his head, and Joey could see he was blushing. "Nice to meet you."

"Don't be bashful," Bill said to Malo, then to Joey, "Before you got here, he was jabbering away about how he was looking forward to working with you." He threw an amused glance Malo's way. "Why don't you start showing him the ropes and use him in your fittings."

She eyed him narrowly. "You know as well as I do, he's not allowed to handle the clothing." She turned to Malo. "Nothing against you, but this is a union house and there's always somebody watching for violations. The company could be fined thousands of dollars if we get reported for a production assistant touching the costumes."

Bill waved her concern aside. "Let him take notes for you, take the fitting photos, print them out, and email them. The kid has some skills, and it'll do him good to see a real pro at work." He winked at them both. "And at the end of the day, if he happens to hang up a shirt or two when you're cleaning up in the privacy of the fitting room, nobody'll be the wiser."

Joey nodded to signal her agreement, annoyed she'd been cornered. But she didn't want to make the kid feel bad, either. She leaned into the task of pushing the fitting rack through the door.

"Here, let me." Malo launched himself across the room to help her.

She put up her hand like a traffic cop. "This is what I'm talking about. In the public areas, you can hold the door, but no touching the racks or clothing. *Capisce?*"

Yet soon enough, she appreciated the helper Bill forced on her.

Fittings are the real proving grounds when it comes to costume design. Joey learned early in her career that no matter how beautiful a sketch looks on paper, or how well clothes hang on a mannequin, you never know what's going to work for your movie until you see the costume on your actor.

Some fittings are easier than others. When she fit Cate Blanchett, every piece of clothing looked like a dream on the actress; Joey could see right away that Cate had an uncanny ability to inhabit the costumes and use them to flesh out her character.

Other times, it takes longer to find the right answers; then the fitting process can become a test of resourcefulness, patience, and sometimes endurance. Joey got an important lesson about that in a costume fitting for one of the first real movie stars she worked with, Tom Hanks. Daniel Orlandi was the costume designer for the film, and Joey was inspired by the way the talented designer and star collaborated like master craftsmen at their work bench during a fitting that lasted several hours. Joey took their example to heart and tried to carry the same commitment into every job.

But that afternoon at Left Coast Costumes she was off her game, and she knew it. Usually, she'd have no trouble organizing the fittings: arranging the clothing and accessories for both efficiency and visual impact was second nature to her. Today it felt like a chore.

As a rule, she'd chat with the actors to make them feel comfortable while they were measured and manhandled to produce clothing that not only fit them better than their own but helped bring their characters to life onscreen. At the same time, she'd be working with the dressmaker or tailor with an eye to every detail as alterations were pinned for each garment, each change was photographed, and every note was listed.

Today she was distracted. She couldn't stop thinking about the explosion, the worried faces of her crew, Marcus Pray's cruelty, Courtney Lisle's criticism, Maggie Fuller's accusations, all the questions she couldn't answer. She hobbled through the fittings, a shadow in her own skin, as though watching someone else go through the motions.

Malo picked up the slack. He made coffee for the actors, shot nicely staged photographs, took good notes, and kept everything organized. Three hours later they stood together in the middle of the room, all the costumes neatly hung and tagged with notes, ready to deliver to the workrooms. Joey smiled at him then, feeling grateful.

"I couldn't have done this today without you. Bill was right—you have real skills."

Malo ducked his head; this time his face was flushed by her praise. "You can tell that from this afternoon?"

"I could tell that in the first fifteen minutes, but you just kept impressing me."

"Cool." He smiled shyly. "Would you like me to get the fitting photos emailed to Dahlia?"

She laid a hand on his shoulder. "That would be awesome."

Joey left him to finish and headed upstairs to pick up some eighties punk rock research she'd requested from LCC's library.

"I didn't think I'd see you today." The research librarian smiled as she typed commands into her computer. She was a handsome woman of indeterminate age who knew everybody in the business and all the latest gossip.

Joey plopped in the big wooden chair next to her desk. "Wasn't sure I'd make it myself, and I've got to get back to the set."

"How's your DP doing?" the librarian asked sharply.

Joey wished she'd asked Malo to pick up the research. She knew this was only the beginning of the questions she'd have to field from the costume community, but she hadn't had the foresight to prepare herself.

"Bernard's going to be okay, from what I'm hearing," she replied. "But it's been a rough day for everybody on set."

"That's certainly the scuttlebutt." The librarian studied Joey over the rims of her half-glasses. "You think it was really an accident?"

"Why does everybody keep saying that?" Joey didn't want to have this discussion. She tried to avoid lending grist to the gossip mill, and she'd never gotten in trouble by keeping her mouth shut.

"Everybody knows your show's got big problems, along with the rumors flying about that pig of a director. He makes Donald Trump look like a pussycat." The librarian pursed her lips. "Pun intended."

Joey wasn't eager to defend Pray's behavior, but she didn't see the connection to the movie's problems. "Pray may be obnoxious, but he wouldn't want to sabotage his own film."

"I'm not saying it was him. The studio wants the focus on something besides their superstar director's indiscretions. If he wasn't such a moneymaker, they'd have cut him loose long before now. But this little incident provides some diversion, maybe even a delay in the schedule with insurance footing the bill."

Joey frowned. "You don't really believe that."

But she found she couldn't dismiss the idea, especially since it lined up with some of her own doubts. Pray represented hundreds of millions of dollars in box office profits for the studio. She knew that would buy him a lot of special consideration if he needed to be bailed out of a bad situation.

"The DP'd have to be in on it," the librarian said conversationally as she handed Joey a manila envelope full of color Xerox images. "The same way De Niro faked a broken toe to get insurance to pay for an extra week's prep on *A Bronx Tale*."

"Nobody faked what happened on set this morning," Joey said with more conviction than she felt.

Her head was starting to throb, and now all she wanted was to get out of the costume house and back to the set. The irony wasn't lost on her.

"Whatever you say." The librarian didn't seem persuaded. "Can I get you a cup of tea? I hate to be the one to tell you, but you don't look so good."

Joey was sure she looked miles better than she felt at that moment. This was only the first day of shooting, and every time she turned around, some new problem or worry popped up, like a vicious game of Whac-A-Mole.

On any other day, she would have spent a few minutes paging through the research she'd been given, making a point to show her appreciation for the work the librarian had done. Today she practically sprinted out of there without even glancing at the images she clutched in her hand.

Joey didn't put much stock in conspiracy theories, and she wasn't superstitious by nature, but this latest conversation rattled her. The movie had been an uphill slog from the start, almost as if it were cursed. She counted down the tally of problems they'd already faced for what felt like the umpteenth time.

Late casting wasted half their prep time, and without actors to build costumes for, it's hard to make much progress. An actress who'd been cast in a featured supporting role broke her leg water skiing and still hadn't been replaced. Several key locations fell through toward the end of preproduction, which led to major schedule changes just before the start of principal photography.

Recent script revisions called for additional action sequences that involved six of the superheroes, which meant additional stunts, additional costumes, additional expenses that hadn't been budgeted. Now they were biting their fingernails, hoping their order for another four hundred meters of Eurojersey (a fabric made exclusively in Italy) for all those extra superhero costumes could be filled before the Italian fabric mills shut down for the month of August, as they did every year.

That was only a partial list of the difficulties they'd had to deal with so far, but now Joey looked back on those logistical problems almost fondly. Why, oh why had she shrugged off every instinct that told her to steer clear of this one?

She checked in with Bill before she left for the set. Malo was out of the office, but she made a point to tell Bill the kid was a keeper.

"Thanks for giving him a chance," he said. "I have a good feeling about him too."

"Any more word from the ADs about Bernard or tomorrow's schedule?"

"Nothing yet," he said, "but let's touch base once you get to Malibu."

She considered mentioning her conversation with Courtney about lining up the background for Pray each day, but Bill had enough on his plate. With that in mind, she sent Courtney a text, trying for a neutral tone:

Headed back to set. Let's talk before wrap. I'd like to work things out with you. Thanks. Joey.

Traffic was the usual rush hour nightmare, a sea of brake lights creeping along in slow motion. Joey tried to console herself with the thought she'd be close to home at the end of the day, but she couldn't get past the anxiety that sat like a rock in her gut.

By the time she finally made it back to set, the shooting company had been wrapped for forty minutes. But the costume crew was still checking in a long line of background, exchanging their vouchers for clothing they'd been given that morning. No voucher, no paycheck was how that worked.

"They held these poor people all afternoon without using them," Zephyr said. "What a waste of a day."

"Didn't they shoot anything?" Joey asked.

"Pray spent most of the afternoon holed up in his trailer." Eduardo sucked in his cheeks and struck a pose, vamping a runway slouch. "Casting finally wrangled some models for him to approve."

Joey rubbed her eyes, anticipating the answer to her next question. "Did the ADs send the models over so Dahlia could look at them?"

"Not a one," Eduardo said. "I guess they were too busy 'auditioning.'" He framed the word with air quotes.

Zephyr frowned, jerking her head in the direction of the background still waiting in line. *Not in front of the kids, honey.*

"Where's Dahlia?" Joey asked, annoyed by the breakdown in communication.

"Oh, she went home hours ago." Eduardo again.

Joey pulled out her cell phone. No messages, nothing from Dahlia, and no reply from Courtney to Joey's earlier text.

"I've gotta talk to the ADs," she said. "Then I'll be back to help finish up."

She bounded out of the costume truck, nerves jangling, and headed toward the two-banger, a trailer divided like a duplex. One side served as the AD office, but the only one home was the DGA trainee, and the poor kid looked like his day had been even worse than hers.

"Courtney and Eli?" Joey said.

"I think Eli's talking to the gaffer. Courtney, I don't know. Haven't seen her for a while."

"Can you try to raise her on your walkie?"

He did, but the only response was static.

"She's around here someplace," he said, defeated.

Joey kept moving, determined to find the second AD. She had to fix things with Courtney, to salvage something positive from this wreck of a day.

The gaffer was on the electrics truck, supervising his crew as they packed up for the night. He shook his head when she asked.

"Haven't seen Courtney since wrap. Have you tried the AD trailer?"

Joey set off again, trying to keep her frustration in check as evening gathered around her. She pounded out a follow-up text:

Back at the set. Important that I speak with you tonight, before you leave.

She passed one of the grips on his way to the shuttle van. He gestured toward the beach when she asked if he'd seen Courtney.

"She was up by the cafe set, last I saw her, but that was a while ago." He shrugged apologetically.

It wasn't until much later that Joey was able to recall the next few hours with any clarity. Because within minutes, she made her way to the abandoned set, where she'd been lured by the fading light and the sound of waves sweeping across the sand. When, almost without thinking, she wandered out to the beach to watch the sun set over the ocean, and instead of the short time-out she hoped for at the close of a long hard day, she discovered Courtney's lifeless body lying in the surf.

Chapter Six

A full moon lit the waves breaking offshore as Joey climbed the steps to her narrow front porch. Normally the sight delighted her; this was why she'd chosen her home, a snug prefab bungalow just steps from the ocean, and why she put up with the commute from the west side of town that often tacked an extra hour to both ends of her workday.

But "normal" had gone by the wayside hours ago, when she crash-landed in an alternate universe where the unthinkable had become all too possible. At this point, she felt nothing; not shock, sadness, or even exhaustion, and certainly not delight.

The little gray and white cat that had shown up recently padded into the house, meowing for dinner. It was only then she realized she'd forgotten to shut the front door.

"Hey, baby girl." Joey clicked her tongue, and the cat followed her into the small galley kitchen.

She got a clean bowl from the dish rack by the sink and opened one of the cans of cat food she'd stocked in a cupboard. The cat meowed again as she set the bowl on the floor, and Joey felt soothed by the simple task, providing comfort to this small creature.

The cat had appeared three weeks before, a cute little animal with blue-gray fur and white paws that had two extra toes apiece. Joey since learned it was a genetic quirk prized by many cat lovers, like Ernest Hemingway, who'd kept a small herd of the polydactyl felines at his house in Key West.

"I still have to come up with a name for you," she said as she watched the cat wash her face with those big Minnie Mouse paws. "And I need to get somebody out here to install a cat door."

They'd been to the vet the week before to make sure the cat had no ID chip. When the scan came up clear, Joey told the doctor to go ahead with blood tests and the first round of vaccinations. But the experience had made the cat skittish. They had another appointment the following week for the second round of shots, and for the little girl to be spayed.

"I hate to think how you'll feel about me after that."

The cat gave a jaw-popping yawn in response and sashayed off to the sunroom, tiny tail waving like a flag. Joey was glad the little animal was making herself at home, but even that warm thought wasn't enough to keep her mind from the awful scene in Malibu.

The police wouldn't say how Courtney had died. Joey hadn't seen any blood or sign of serious injury, but she'd been too shocked to register much beyond the fact the young woman was unresponsive, her skin cold to the touch.

She couldn't remember running toward base camp screaming for help, only the look on Eli's face when she led him back to the beach. The next few hours were a blur of confused images: the arrival of the first responding sheriff's car, then emergency personnel, for the second time that day. Next came the investigators, detectives, and crime scene technicians; finally, the coroner.

A chill that had nothing to do with the temperature made her shiver. The police had questioned her for hours, the same questions over and over, questions she hadn't the faintest idea how to answer.

The cat meowed again to be let out. She tended to stick close to the small garden that surrounded the house, nestled among the succulents and native plantings. But she didn't seem ready to move indoors full time—thus the need for a cat door.

"Stay safe," Joey called softly, as the little one scooted back out into the night, though she might have been talking to herself.

She wandered aimlessly through the house. Though she lived in what was technically a trailer park, it was a far cry from the shabby encampments that term can bring to mind. The *New York Times* featured her small seaside community in their travel section, dubbing it "America's Most Glamorous Trailer Park," and the marketing team for the homeowners association pounced on the nickname. Houses here averaged in the mid-six-figure range but shared the coastline with mansions and estates valued up to fifty times more—by far the most economical way to own a piece of ocean front property in Southern California.

Her neighbors tended to be free-spirited creatives—musicians, interior and fashion designers, as well as at least one YouTube influencer who posted videos about the park that garnered her millions of followers. One middle-aged man she had a nodding acquaintance with was an artist who lived there under a pseudonym, famous for his iconoclastic pop-up installations all over the world.

Joey's clapboard bungalow was just under a thousand square feet, cozy but big enough for her needs, with an open concept living room and kitchen, a bedroom, bath, and sunroom she used as an office. A small service porch was equipped with a stackable washer/dryer combo and a wall of custom cupboards for additional storage.

Visual clutter made her claustrophobic, and she'd furnished the place with minimalist simplicity. She wanted to be able to put her feet up and read a book in comfort, but she didn't need more than one good chair and a love seat to cover her bases.

When she chose to entertain, her back patio served the purpose, where she'd installed a gas grill and prep counter. A mesquite wood dining table and chairs sat beneath a cedar pergola wrapped in vines of fragrant star jasmine.

But it was the Pacific, with its ever-changing moods, that provided the show-stopping backdrop, making her place a Lilliputian slice of paradise. Joey never tired of walking the shoreline, a healing meditation she counted on, a touchstone for her peace of mind.

Tonight, however, all that was moot. Lingering trauma created a kind of emotional vertigo she'd never experienced. The kitchen clock read 2:37, but that number felt meaningless. She knew she should rest, but she couldn't imagine lying in bed, allowing her thoughts to run rampant, or even worse, giving in to sleep where her subconscious would have free rein in her dreams.

She caught sight of her reflection in the mirror over her bedroom dresser, surprised to find she looked the same as always. Green eyes stared back at her, taking inventory: nose and mouth accounted for, and apparently unchanged, dark blonde hair streaked with highlights by the sun. Hard to believe she could feel so strange to herself but appear untouched, as if the figure in the mirror was another being altogether, like a clone with no emotional capacity.

She looked down at a picture that sat on the dresser showing her as a baby cradled in her mother's arms. Her father sat beside them, arm around his wife's shoulders. Both parents were smiling proudly, both younger than Joey was now. It was the only picture she had of the three of them together.

Visions from the death scene in Malibu suddenly swam before her eyes, blotting out the faces in the picture. The painful images burned through her numbness. Two people down in one day on a movie set, of all places; one dead, one critically injured, and nobody could tell them why. How was that even possible?

She was desperate for answers, but none would be coming that night. On impulse she snatched an afghan from the foot of her bed, then hurried out to the back patio. The only peace she could hope for might come from the murmur of the waves, the salt breeze off the water. She curled up in a tight ball on the outdoor sectional, wishing she'd wake up with the sun shining to discover this day was nothing but a bad dream.

A scrabble of claws on the flagstones told her she had company. She looked up to find the cat sitting in a patch of moonlight on the hearth of the small gas fireplace next to the sectional. Her big golden eyes were fixed on Joey.

"Thanks, I can use the moral support."

She picked up the remote fireplace starter and clicked it. The yellow flames were a comforting sight. The cat yawned and stretched her front legs out to warm her oversize paws by the fire.

"How do you feel about the name Bigfoot? I know it's not very feminine, but it does seem appropriate."

But the cat was already asleep, and Joey wasn't far behind, taken down by the twin demons, emotional and physical exhaustion.

When the thin light of false dawn woke her just before five in the morning, she lay still, feeling blank. Anxiety flickered at the edge of her awareness, but it took a minute or so for the events of the previous day to come flooding back. There'd be no more sleep for her; she'd do better to get up and get moving.

Bigfoot presented herself for breakfast and purred while she ate. Joey forced herself to finish her morning routine before she even looked at her phone.

Eli had sent a blanket text to the company:

Most of you know by now Courtney Lisle was found dead on set at the end of the day yesterday. The sheriff's dept. is investigating. They have closed our location and impounded our equipment while they proceed with their examination. We have no time frame for completion of this work. The studio is cooperating with the authorities and instructs the entire company to do the same. Production is suspended for the next two days pending decisions about what actions can and should be taken moving forward.

I will keep you updated as I receive information. Please contact me if you need to, especially if you are struggling with this news and need support. We are united in sorrow about the loss of our friend and colleague. In the coming days and weeks, I know we will find a fitting way to honor her memory. Be well and stay safe.

Bill Nichols had sent a similar message to all members of the costume department. He tacked on an addendum:

I'll be in the office today to continue working on the budget. I have verbal approval from the Unit Production Manager for our department to work if we choose. Compensation may be in the form of overtime reflected on future timecards. We have a lot of work to do, and this is an opportunity to make up ground, but the decision rests with each of you. No harm, no foul. Please be at the costume offices by 9:00 AM if you plan to work today.

The unit production manager was the studio's in-house watchdog on the film, charged with making sure each department stayed within its budget. Joey was surprised he agreed to the additional day for the costume department, but she also suspected Bill had struck a bargain. The back-and-forth negotiation with the studio about the costume budget had been going on for weeks, not unusual for a production of this size and complexity, but both sides were frustrated with the process. Bill may have promised the UPM he'd keep his nose to the financial grindstone if he could have the crew prepping alongside him.

Right away, Joey knew she'd go in to work. She was too upset to sit around with nothing to do. Chores didn't count; she'd never found any comfort or joy in housework. Besides, her desk at the costume office was piled with clerical work that needed tending, and she had vendors to visit to check on their progress. The routine of her job was exactly what she needed. She sent a text to Bill so he'd know to expect her, and another to Dahlia to see what she had in mind for the day.

"Knock, knock! I smell coffee." Gina Russo, her next-door neighbor, sailed into the kitchen on a cloud of patchouli, a tinfoil-covered plate in her hand. "I come bearing goodies. Thought you could use a treat."

Gina was a gifted baker, and Joey was sure the plate was stacked with one of her specialties, fudge brownies liberally laced with chopped walnuts and homegrown pot.

She wasn't in the mood for a neighborly chat, but she had to make an effort. "I've gotta get going if I want to beat the traffic, but I can take a minute. Help yourself to coffee."

Joey pocketed her phone and leaned in for a quick hug. She was fond of Gina, who'd become a friend over the past three years since Joey had moved into her house. But not the sort of friend she'd confide her deepest doubts and fears to, which today ran pretty deep.

The older woman had spent thirty years touring as a backup singer with Linda Ronstadt, James Taylor, and Jackson Browne. Then a few years ago, she started a side business making bent-wire jewelry she sculpted in intricate patterns—earrings, brooches, necklaces, bracelets. She put a few pieces up for sale online at Etsy and eBay, and they took off like gangbusters. Now she had her own website and couldn't make jewelry fast enough to keep up with the orders that flowed in from all over the world.

"I've been reading about what happened yesterday." Gina blew across the surface of her coffee, watching Joey over the rim of her cup. "How're you holding up?"

"What're they saying?" She felt her insides tighten, though she wasn't surprised the story was already fodder for the twenty-four-hour news cycle.

"Just that somebody died on your set. The cops aren't giving out much more than that, but Twitter's blowing up about it, and there's a story on *Deadline.com* about the trouble the studio's had in preproduction with delays and cost overruns on the movie. Some people are saying this'll shut the production down for good."

Joey closed her eyes. She wasn't happy about the news but thought that might be best for all concerned. Gina mistook her reaction for disappointment.

"Oh, honey, I'm sorry. We don't have to talk about that now." She ran a hand through her thick gray hair. "Me and my big mouth."

"No, it's fine. I didn't sleep very well, that's all." Joey tried to drum up a smile. "But thanks for stopping by with the treats."

"Can I fix you some breakfast?" Gina peered at her sympathetically. "You'll feel better if you eat."

Joey shook her head. "I wish I could, but I have to get to work."

"Really? I thought . . ." Gina gave her a curious look. "Never mind, I've gotta go walk Rocky, but I'll catch up with you later."

Rocky was her beloved Chihuahua-terrier mix who thought he was master of the universe. Gina waved on her way out the door.

"Wait until you get home to try the brownies. This batch is the bomb if I do say so myself."

Once the door closed on her neighbor, Joey fought the impulse to dive down the internet rabbit hole. The bits and pieces Gina mentioned only sharpened her appetite for more information. She'd started to unpack her laptop when her phone buzzed with a text from Dahlia:

Think I'll sit today out. Call if you need me. D xo

She felt a little envious that Dahlia could find a way to separate herself from the ongoing drama, but the text gave Joey the push she needed to get out the door. She could always troll the web from her nook at the office, and she was more likely to pick up some inside scoop if she was physically present at work.

By seven thirty she was on the road to North Hollywood. Most days, the marine layer that blanketed the coast kept the sun from burning through until noon. Joey didn't usually mind the pale overcast; it kept the mornings cool and dreamy, cushioned in mist. But today the gray skies only seemed gloomy, and she was glad to leave them behind as she made the turn off PCH to head inland through Topanga Canyon.

A call rang through on her Bluetooth. She didn't recognize the number that popped up on her console, but she answered on the second ring. "This is Joey."

"Ms. Jessop, this is Detective Corinne Blankenship, Los Angeles County Sheriff's Department."

The name didn't ring any bells. Blankenship wasn't one of the people who'd questioned her the night before, but something in the woman's no-nonsense tone made Joey's heart beat faster.

"Yes, ma'am, what can I do for you?"

"We have a few follow-up questions regarding the death of your colleague, Courtney Lisle. I wonder if you can come down to the department to speak with us this morning."

"You mean now?" Her resistance shot up. "I'm on my way to work."

"We'll do our best to expedite the process, but we do need you to come down here as soon as possible."

The night of questioning had seemed endless; Joey felt hollowed out by the ordeal. "I already told you people everything I know last night, more than once."

"I understand." Detective Blankenship was a study in patience. "But it's in everybody's best interest that you cooperate. I'm sure you want to help us complete this investigation and arrive at the proper conclusions."

What could she say to that? Especially when it was clear she had no choice in the matter.

"Where do you need me to come?"

The detective gave her an address in Monterey Park.

"I'm heading through Topanga Canyon." Joey gripped the wheel tighter. "I'll be there as soon as I can."

"Drive safe," Blankenship said and hung up.

Chapter Seven

"What was your personal relationship to Ms. Lisle?" Detective Blankenship asked.

Joey had been talking with her for half an hour before the detective lobbed this changeup. Till that point, the interview had been a replay of questions she'd answered the night before.

"We didn't have a personal relationship." Joey shifted in her seat, though she realized that telegraphed her discomfort.

Blankenship, mocha-skinned and fortyish, sat across the table from her in a small, windowless room. Joey was surprised to find the address the detective gave her belonged to the Homicide Bureau of the Los Angeles County Sheriff's Department, which answered one of the questions on her list: Courtney Lisle's death was being investigated as a murder.

That news was jarring enough, but Joey had never even been inside a police station before, and the stark institutional setting coupled with the detective's cool demeanor made her jumpy.

Blankenship continued to look at her impassively. "You never had any personal interaction with Ms. Lisle in the course of your professional association?"

"I didn't know her very well." Joey wasn't going to lie, but she wasn't going to volunteer a lot of extra information. "We'd never worked together before this job."

"What is your relationship to Eli Logan?"

"We're coworkers." She hesitated. "We've known each other for some time."

The detective nodded slowly. Her steady gaze was unnerving. She had a legal pad and pen sitting on the table in front of her, but she hadn't taken any notes. Joey wondered if the interview was being recorded.

"Were you aware that Mr. Logan and Ms. Lisle were in a romantic relationship?"

Joey felt a flush creep into her face. "Yes, I knew they were together."

"Did that bother you?"

"No." Just a small shading of the truth.

"Even though you and Mr. Logan used to be a couple."

She wondered who the detective had been talking to, not that it really mattered. The information wasn't hard to come by, but she began to feel even more uneasy about the direction of her questions.

"Eli and I haven't been together for a long time." She tried not to sound defensive.

"Was it an amicable split?"

"For the most part." Now she was skirting an outright lie. "I think breakups are always difficult, but Eli and I managed to put that behind us."

That was closer to the truth; Joey didn't want to cling to any dark history. The relationship with Eli had taught her some valuable lessons that would inform her choices for the rest of her life. She paid a price for the education, but she appreciated the insight, and she hoped he felt the same way.

"Then you had no trouble with the idea of working alongside him and his new girlfriend?"

"I gave that a fair amount of thought before I accepted the job."

Blankenship smiled faintly. "It's one thing to consider a situation in the abstract, but another to confront the reality, don't you think?"

"I suppose that's possible, but I think it can go either way. Sometimes things work out better than you expect." *Theoretically*, she thought, but didn't add.

"Is that how you felt about this situation? Because you still haven't answered my question. Was it difficult for you, working so closely with your former boyfriend and the new lady in his life?"

"No, I told you." Joey's impatience flared. "Eli and I are past all that. We've both moved on, and we're professionals. We work well together, and we take our jobs seriously."

"What about Ms. Lisle? Did she have the same professional standards?"

"I guess so." Joey knew the detective was baiting her, but this time she didn't bite. "Eli hired her as his second, and she seemed competent."

"Did you know before you started working with her that she and Mr. Logan had hooked up?"

Joey hated that expression and didn't try to hide her distaste. "Yes, I think I already mentioned, I knew Eli was seeing someone, and she'd be working on the movie."

"How did you hear about that?"

She sighed and closed her eyes. This was humiliating. "Eli called me; he wanted to tell me himself." She didn't think Blankenship needed to know the gesture was part of Eli's twelve-step program.

"That was thoughtful." The detective raised her eyebrows. "He sounds like a good guy."

"He is. That's why . . ." Joey shook her head in frustration. "I took the job because it's an important movie, and that's what I do. I thought about the decision carefully because of our past relationship, but when all is said and done, Eli and I respect each other. I want the best for him, and I know he feels the same about me."

She knew she was babbling. She pressed her lips together to stop the flow of words.

"You need a minute?" the detective said. "Glass of water, maybe?"

"No, I'm fine." Joey took a deep breath. "How did Courtney die?"

She'd been wanting to ask that question since they sat down at the table.

Blankenship leaned back in her chair. "How do you think she died?"

"I don't know." Joey frowned, feeling confused. "That's why I'm asking."

"You're the one who found her." The detective's tone grew sharp. "You didn't check to see if there was a reason she was lying unconscious in the water?"

They were back on familiar ground. Joey had already answered different versions of this question many times last night and also earlier in the session with Blankenship, but each time stirred up an array of ghastly images she'd rather forget.

"I thought it was more important to get help than try to figure out what was wrong with her."

"You had your cell phone. Why didn't you call nine-one-one?"

"I don't know." Joey groped for an answer but came up empty. "I think I was in shock."

"Crew members who saw you running from the beach say you were hysterical."

"I was scared." She looked down at the table, feeling a hot rush of shame. "Courtney was just lying there; I wasn't thinking straight."

"You didn't try to get some kind of response from her before you went for help?"

"I touched her." Joey cringed at the memory. "Her skin was cold, and I couldn't tell if she was breathing."

"Why not try CPR?"

"You want me to say I messed up? Okay, I messed up." Tears choked her, but Joey swallowed to keep them down. "I should have called for help from the beach, and maybe I should have tried to do CPR, but I ran. I'm sorry about that, but it doesn't change anything, does it?"

"No, it doesn't." Blankenship rapped her knuckles on the table twice. Joey wondered if it was a signal to whoever was listening in. "Maybe we should take a break." The detective pushed her chair back and stood up.

Joey felt drained, all the energy leached from her body. She needed to get out of this building, away from Blankenship and her implacable stare.

"How much longer is this going to take?" she asked.

"I have a few more questions."

"Then can we please just keep on with it?" she said quietly.

"Sure, if that's what you want."

The detective sat down again, then let the silence stretch out. Joey tried not to fidget, and she forced herself to maintain eye contact with Blankenship.

"Tell me about the texts you sent to Courtney yesterday," the detective finally said.

Joey had to think for a second; so much had happened in the past twenty-four hours.

Blankenship gave her a prompt. "You sent two texts about two hours apart, and you sounded quite anxious to speak with her in person before the end of the day."

"Oh, that." Joey shifted again in her chair. "She came to me yesterday morning with a request about the background players. I wanted to make sure we continued the discussion and worked out a compromise."

The detective looked skeptical. "The messages sounded more urgent than your explanation."

"It was important to resolve the issue. We needed to find a solution that worked for everybody before things got more complicated than necessary."

"You're saying your motive for the contact was strictly professional."

"Correct."

"You didn't have any sort of personal agenda?"

"Absolutely not." Joey clasped her hands in her lap to keep them still.

"You weren't upset by the PDA show she and Mr. Logan gave on set yesterday morning in front of the crew?"

Joey's mouth dropped open. How could Blankenship know about that? She thought she was the only one who noticed, or cared, about the dry hump Courtney staged for her benefit. But someone else saw it, along with her reaction, and then talked to the cops about it.

"What about the argument you and Courtney had later at craft service, again with a lot of the crew on hand?" Blankenship continued. "How did it make you feel when she called you out in front of your coworkers, accusing you of being resentful about her relationship with your ex?" The detective looked at Joey coolly. "I know I would have been angry about that."

Blankenship's eyes stayed on her face, waiting for a response. For the first time since the endless rounds of questions began the night before, Joey felt a pulse of real fear as it finally dawned on her the detective thought she might have done this horrible thing. She probably should have been more candid about the tension between Courtney and herself, but too late for that now. She took a moment to collect her thoughts before she answered this time, worried her voice would betray her.

"I'm very sorry Courtney's dead, but the last thing I wanted to do yesterday was have a conversation with her," she said evenly. "But my job required me to do exactly that, and that's why I texted her, to set a meeting to discuss the question of how to present the background to the director every day."

On the job, Joey was at her best in the clutch, known for her ability to stay calm when others hit the panic button. She often found it a useful skill, but she had to dig deep for it in this setting.

Blankenship continued to watch her closely. "Did you have the opportunity to see or speak with Ms. Lisle between the time you texted her and"—the detective made a rolling motion with her hand—"your discovery of her on the beach?"

"No, as I've said before, many times now, I was away from the set for most of the day, from around noon until after the shooting company wrapped."

"What were you doing during that time?"

"I had fittings scheduled at Left Coast Costumes in the Valley." She had to resist the urge to wipe her sweaty palms on her jeans. "Why do you keep asking the same questions? Do you think I had something to do with Courtney's death?"

The words were out before she could stop them.

"I don't think anything at this point." The detective's expression was unreadable. "I'm only looking for information."

"That's not how it feels on this side of the table." She knew it wasn't smart, but it felt good to blow off a little steam. She braced herself for a full court press, then Blankenship surprised her.

"Just doing my job, Ms. Jessop." The detective spread her hands. "I think we're done here for now. Thanks for your time."

Joey had to pull over five blocks from the Homicide Bureau when the adrenaline aftershock flooded her body. She was shaking too hard to drive. She rested her forehead on the steering wheel, struggling with a jumble of thoughts and emotions while she tried to compose herself.

She knew the sheriff's investigators were talking to everybody who worked on the movie. It was obvious she'd be of special interest as the person who found the body, as well as the ex of the victim's current boyfriend.

Eli would be in for the third degree too. She wondered how he'd handle the barrage of questions and suspicion at the same time he mourned for Courtney. He'd worked hard the past year to turn his life around, but now it occurred to her that all that stress could trigger a relapse.

As for her own circumstances, she'd been at the costume house, then on the truck with the other costumers, and then talked to a trail of coworkers on her way to the set. Plenty of people to vouch for her if it came to that, which it wouldn't.

Still, she needed to stay sharp. First Bernard, then Courtney. Was that a terrible coincidence, or an indication the whole company might be at risk?

She told herself that was crazy; she'd been listening to other people's wild speculations for the past two days. Who stood to benefit from those tragedies, anyway? If the studio wanted to torpedo the movie, there were easier and more subtle ways to do it within the complex mechanism of that giant bureaucracy.

But somehow, that logic didn't make her feel any better. Now she was champing at the bit to get to the office and catch up on the latest developments. She allowed herself a final shudder to shake out the heebie-jeebies before she dropped the car in gear and steered into the flow of traffic.

Chapter Eight

The sun was out with a vengeance when Joey pulled into the parking lot behind Left Coast Costumes. Shimmering waves of heat rippled off the blacktop surface, and the temperature hovered at a toasty 103 degrees. The Valley was always the hottest part of the city, one of several microclimates within the greater metropolitan area, and just one more reason she was willing to make the commute from the beach, where it was always twenty degrees cooler than North Hollywood, especially in the summertime.

She went in through the loading dock past the lineup of cages, no-frills spaces with concrete floors and chain-link walls (hence the name) available for rent to individual films. They served as storage areas, workstations, and makeshift fitting rooms during prep and often for the duration of production. Even when a movie shot out of town, a skeleton crew usually stayed back to feed the shooting company all the necessary clothing and equipment it couldn't get on location. A cage at LCC was essential for holding and staging those shipments. Another plus: the cages were located next to the in-house shipping department with its daily scheduled FedEx pickups and deliveries.

There were no windows, no natural light at all in this back area of the building, unless the loading dock doors stood open. The cages were filled with dozens of costumers at work on various films, organizing supplies, unpacking boxes, and rolling racks of clothing, and the noise generated by all that activity bounced around the cavernous space, creating an odd Tower of Babel effect.

A long row of folding chairs sat outside the largest of the cages. All of them were occupied by elderly men, waiting patiently. Through the chain-link walls Joey saw an assembly line of costumers fitting the white-haired extras in ecclesiastical garb she recognized from working on *Angels and Demons* near the beginning of her career. The sea of brilliant red and white vestments reminded her of a flock of exotic birds, which was apt in a way. The ceremonial garments transformed the old men into some of the most powerful figures in the Catholic hierarchy, cardinals of the Holy Roman Church.

Her friend, Kenn Smiley, waved to her. "Want to pitch in? We've got cardinals coming out the wazoo all day today." He placed a square red hat called a biretta on the gentleman he was fitting.

"Another Dan Brown adaptation?" she asked.

"Close enough." He adjusted the placement of the hat on the actor's head. "This one's based on a book called *The Fisherman's Tomb*. We could use your expertise."

The casual banter felt strange today, but she tried to keep up her end. "Looks to me like you've got it handled."

"What can I say?" He wiggled his eyebrows. "Crosses and cassocks, right up my alley."

She managed a smile. "I don't even want to know what that's supposed to mean."

Other friends waved and called to her as she made her way past the rest of the cages and into the main warehouse where the costume rental stock was housed. She didn't stop to visit, but nobody seemed to think twice about it. Everybody was busy, and time was always short. So far, the drama surrounding her movie appeared to be flying under the costume house radar.

"I've got a two-parter for you." Henry Burchette was a walking encyclopedia of film and theater history. Whenever a regional company called from the hinterlands to rent costumes for their production of *My Fair Lady*, *The Sound of Music*, or some other Broadway warhorse, Henry was the go-to guy at LCC to pull it together and send it off to them.

"Part One." Henry held both index fingers aloft for emphasis. "For what two movies did Olivia de Havilland win the Oscar for best actress?"

Joey couldn't remember how it started, but Henry always had a brainteaser for her, some vintage piece of movie trivia. She wasn't really up to socializing, but Henry was sensitive, and she wouldn't hurt his feelings for the world. She changed course to swing by his cubby.

Henry's tiny kingdom sat at the end of one of the massive triple-hung rails of costumes that reached to the rafters twenty-five feet overhead. A system of catwalks suspended high above the warehouse floor provided access to the upper tiers of clothing.

The pod he used for an office was fashioned from freestanding modular panels. It was crammed with a desk, an oversized chair, and a set of narrow bookshelves wedged together so that there was room for only one person, especially when that person was Henry, who tipped the scales somewhere north of three hundred pounds. The walls were covered with dozens of notes, sketches, and fabric samples that were tools of his trade. But he'd also devoted a corner to photos of his alter ego, Edith Headlights, a platinum-haired drag queen with a weakness for sequins and size fourteen spike heels.

Joey leaned to peer over Henry's shoulder at the latest addition to Edith's gallery. "I love that red dress with the feather trim."

"My latest creation." Henry batted his eyes. "It's hard for me to buy anything off the rack."

"I can see how that would be a problem in evening gowns." She smiled at him fondly. "I didn't know Olivia de Havilland ever won for best actress, let alone twice. I thought her only Oscar was for best supporting in *Gone with the Wind*."

"Which brings us to Part Two of our quiz." He rubbed his palms together with delight. "Who beat out Olivia de Havilland for the best supporting Oscar in 1940 when she was nominated for *Gone with the Wind*?"

"No idea." Joey hiked her shoulders. "I thought she won."

"I'll give you a hint. It was an actress from the same movie, and it was an historic win."

The light bulb went off. "Hattie McDaniel as Mammy." She held up her hand for a high-five.

Henry obliged, eyes shining with glee. "Olivia got best actress for *To Each His Own* in 1946 and *The Heiress* in 1949."

"I've never even heard of *To Each His Own*, but I should've thought of *The Heiress*."

"Did you know she only died in 2020?" He shook his head in wonder. "One hundred and four years old, lived in the same house in Paris since 1956."

She blew him a kiss. "Thanks, Henry, you're exactly what the doctor ordered today."

Joey continued up front to the *UMPP* offices feeling lighter, as though Henry had chased away some of the grim thoughts that followed her from the sheriff's Homicide Bureau.

Bill Nichols was already at his desk, looking frustrated as he talked on the phone. "If you don't want to pay for four helmets, you need to talk to the director and the stunt coordinator, because if second unit's shooting stunts for the sequence at the same time first unit's shooting the green screen special effects, we need enough to dress all those bodies."

He rocked back in his chair and tightened an imaginary noose around his neck while he listened to the person on the other end of the line. "Uh-huh, sure. No, I get it."

His expression was at odds with the agreeable tone he'd adopted. "I'll crunch the numbers one more time, but when you've got fifteen principal superheroes—that comes with some steep fixed costs. I've already cut our contingency to almost nothing."

He set the phone on his desktop and hit the speaker function. Gordon Pomeroy, the UPM, was saying, "I need you to work with me, Bill. We've got to find a way to shave another five hundred thousand off your budget."

Bill closed his eyes and propped his chin in his hands. "I'll see what I can do. Speak with you later, Gordon."

He picked up the phone to end the call, then tossed it across the desk. "Always a pleasure."

Joey glanced around the empty office. "Where is everybody?"

"Just you and me, kid." He rubbed his eyes. "And Malo. I told him he didn't need to come in today, but he wanted to when he heard you were going to be in the office." Bill sent her an indulgent smile. "You've got a new fan."

"Nobody else?" She was a little surprised, even though the approval to work had come on short notice.

"Nope, and frankly, I don't blame them. I'm beginning to wish I'd taken the day too. I could be lying by the pool instead of beating my head against the wall, trying to keep Gordon from stripping us bare." He stood up and crossed to the kitchen. "I'm so sick of having the same arguments on every movie."

He pulled an energy drink out of the fridge and held it up. "Want one?"

"No, thanks." One cup of coffee in the morning was all the caffeine she could handle, even on a good day; and this was as far from a good day as she'd had in a long time.

"How'd it go?" he asked.

Joey had called to let him know her change of plans when she was summoned to the sheriff's department.

"Little weird. I felt like I was in the hot seat," she said, remembering Detective Blankenship's impassive gaze. "But then, this whole thing is bizarre."

"Tell me about it." He went back to his desk, which was awash in piles of paper. "I've been buried in the budget all morning, so for a while, I forget." He shook his head. "Then it'll hit me, and I'm shocked all over again."

"I still can't wrap my mind around everything that happened yesterday." Joey felt a flutter of dread deep inside and looked at him, hoping for some sort of reassurance. "It doesn't seem quite real."

"Yeah, no matter how many terrible stories you see in the news, it's different when something happens in your own back yard."

Malo came bounding through the office door just then, loaded down with bags full of kitchen and office supplies.

"Back so soon?" Bill switched to an upbeat tone, signaling the need for a change of subject.

Malo set a large manila envelope on Bill's desk. "Production coordinator told me to give this to you right away," he said, then turned to Joey. "Good to see you today, Ms. Jessop."

She frowned in mock disapproval. "You make me feel like some old crone. We're coworkers, Malo. Call me Joey."

The young man beamed with pleasure. "Yes, ma'am."

"Worse and worse," she complained, but she smiled when she said it.

Malo moved into the kitchen. "I'll get this stuff unloaded, then I'm ready for another job."

Bill leaned back in his chair with a groan. "I want you to sit with me to plug some new numbers into the budget. It'll go faster if I read them off and you do the entry."

"You got it," Malo replied.

Joey needed to know how those numbers were changing. Tens of thousands of dollars were being spent every day, and she was responsible for a lot of that outlay.

"I heard you on the phone with Gordon," she said, trying to settle into work mode. "How can we possibly cut half a million dollars, especially with the script additions they made last week?"

"That's an easy one to answer: we can't." Bill took a gulp from the energy drink. "I can make a few adjustments, here and there." He set the bottle on his desk, frowning as he gazed at the viscous red liquid. "Or I could arbitrarily slash every line item and give him the figure he's asking for, but that would be a lie."

"You think they might shut us down?" Joey wasn't sure what she hoped for, but any clear answer would do. "I heard *Deadline* posted an article this morning about the problems we've had in preproduction. If the studio's looking for a reason, that gives them an excuse."

"That's not going to happen." Bill shook his head emphatically.

"How can you be so sure?"

"Because they're way too pregnant to abort."

She made a face. "You should watch that kind of talk, particularly at this moment in time."

"You're right, my bad." He tipped his head, granting her point. "I'm just saying, this movie's a tentpole."

Malo poked his head out of the kitchen. "What's a tentpole?"

"Ah, grasshopper." Bill gestured to a chair by his desk. "Come sit. Listen and learn."

Malo took a seat as Bill continued. "The studios rely on the blockbuster profits from these comic book operas to prop up their whole operation, which means they need this golden goose we're working on alive and well to balance their books." He looked at Joey. "To use a more PC metaphor."

"But that's good for us, right?" Malo asked.

"Except the business has become one-note," Joey said. "In this country, anyway. Used to be, there were other types of big movies to work on, period pieces like *Water for Elephants* or *Benjamin Button*."

She felt like she was telling a story about a make-believe land far, far away.

"We don't make movies like that here anymore?" Malo asked.

"The studios won't back them the way they used to," she replied. "If those movies get made here at all, they're strictly independent low-budget productions, and mostly they're made somewhere else."

"But why?" Malo persisted. "Those movies can't cost more to make than the superhero movies."

"Lots of reasons," Bill said. "The business model in Hollywood started changing in a big way around the early two thousands with runaway production, the bottom dropping out of the DVD market, the financial crash in oh eight." He shrugged. "The studios needed to expand their markets dramatically, and the only place to do that was overseas."

"Can we please wrap this up before I have to jump out a window?" Joey said. "It's all too depressing."

Bill stood and spread his arms like a carnival barker. "The studios' obsession with those emerging markets is the main reason we're stuck with the comic book franchises: no complicated stories or dialogue to follow, no cultural gaps that don't translate abroad."

He clapped Malo on the shoulder. "And because Hollywood still does action and special effects better than anyone else. Put that together with name recognition from the superhero brands, and it translates to big bucks, here and overseas. The formula that keeps the studio system viable in the twenty-first century."

"That's no guarantee they won't pull the plug on this one." Joey was still skeptical. "Other big movies have shut down over less. You'd think the studio would be worried stiff about liability after the day we had yesterday."

"Keep in mind, they've already sunk millions into this masterpiece-in-progress," Bill said with a wave at his computer screen. "And they're banking on it as next year's entry in the Fourth of July box office sweepstakes. So it's a superhero super-tentpole. That's job security, my friends." He sat back down at his desk. "Class dismissed."

Bill went back to crunching numbers while Malo entered the new figures into the computer, and Joey moved to her desk in a far corner of the room. Her nook was lined with cork boards where she'd tacked fabric samples and research images. A giant calendar that took up a lot of wall space laid out the shooting schedule with notations for costume fittings, due dates for the completion of man-ufactured items, and other significant deadlines.

This unexpected nugget of quiet time gave her the chance to catch up on clerical chores she usually had to shoehorn into her day, like bringing the construction bible up to date. By this point in the pro-cess, the bible, which provided a complete record of all the costumes being made for the movie, filled three bulging four-inch binders.

Each costume was documented with a sketch accompanied by samples of every fabric, trim, button, buckle, and zipper, plus the sources, style numbers, and prices for all purchased items. Notes about the makers of every piece of clothing were also included.

Tracking the work in that much detail was a huge time-suck, and absolutely essential. Changes in the screenplay or schedule, not to mention possible reshoots months down the road, could mean an item made at the start of production might eventually need to be remade or multiplied. If the information in the bible was incomplete, that task could become almost impossible.

But try as she might to concentrate on her work, Joey couldn't shake the anxiety that had dogged her since the interrogation that morning. Blankenship's cold stare, along with the detective's questions and insinuations, played on an endless loop in her mind, crowding out any thoughts about construction details, due dates, or the tiny bits of fabric arranged in piles across her desk.

An hour in, when she realized she'd transcribed notes for one character onto a different character's fact sheet, she knew it was time to make a choice. She could either let her fears control her, or she could try to get some answers to the questions she couldn't ignore.

She wasn't quite sure how to manage that, but Joey wasn't afraid to tackle a complex problem, even one she didn't know much about to start with. That was part of the reason she was so good at her job.

The first step was to gather as much information as possible. She knew the value of research; that was where every new project began. If nothing else, the accumulation of facts would make her feel as though she had a handle on the situation. *Knowledge is power* was one of her favorite mantras. The thought didn't exactly give her confidence, but it allowed her to feel less helpless.

She went online and began to read everything she could find about Courtney's death. It seemed the logical place to start. Most of the stories were basic and repetitive, adding little to what she already knew, until she clicked on a slightly offbeat piece that was part news article, part obituary from a small-town paper in Elk City, Oklahoma, posted on *local.com* that day:

Native Daughter Slain

Courtney Lisle, who grew up in Elk City, was killed yesterday in Los Angeles on the set of the movie where she worked as an Assistant Director. LA County Sheriffs have released few details, but say the investigation is ongoing. Ms. Lisle made her way to Hollywood after graduating from Oklahoma State University and found work almost at once in a demanding profession. With movie star looks that could have put her in front of the camera, Courtney chose a role behind the scenes to help craft the movies she worked on. Her ambition was to become a filmmaker in her own right, and she was on her way to achieving that goal when her life was cut short. Her twin brother, Caleb, says tenacity was the key to her success:

"Courtney was fearless. She wouldn't take 'no' for an answer. She didn't wait for some big break to come along; she believed you make your own luck. Once my sister set her sights on something, she was unstoppable."

In a twist of fate, Ms. Lisle was working for fellow Oklahoman and hometown hero Marcus Pray when she died. The renowned filmmaker is also a former Elk City resident. Courtney is survived by her parents, Benton and Gerilee Lisle, and her brother, Caleb. A memorial will be scheduled in the near future.

Joey sat back, goose bumps prickling her arms, and read the short item a second time. A strange coincidence that Courtney and Pray were from the same small city in Oklahoma. Or was it?

She looked up Courtney's résumé on IMDb, the Internet Movie Database, an industry mainstay listing the professional credits of nearly everybody working in film. In addition to *UMPP*, Courtney had worked on Pray's three previous movies. Joey wondered if chance had brought the two Elk City natives together in Hollywood, or if there was more to the story; not that it necessarily had any bearing on Courtney's death, but it would be good to know.

"Knowledge is power," she said aloud.

A wad of paper landed on her desk. "Earth to Joey."

Startled, she looked up.

"Didn't you hear the page?" Bill said.

As if on cue, a voice echoed over the PA system. "Joey Jessop, please come to reception. You have a visitor."

"I don't think I forgot an appointment." She glanced at the production calendar on the wall, then bobbed up from her chair. "Be right back."

She hurried up the hall. A group of costumers crowded around the front desk, arguing with the receptionist over fitting room privileges.

"You paged me?" Joey said.

The receptionist pointed to a tall, slender brunette standing near the front door, staring at the screen of her iPhone. Maggie Fuller looked up from her phone and held out her hand with a pleasant smile.

"Nice to see you again, Joey. Is there someplace we could talk more privately?"

"About what?" Joey gestured over her shoulder. "I'm in the middle of a project."

Only minutes before, she'd considered calling the number on the reporter's business card to finesse a few questions about Marcus Pray. Fuller seemed to have a particular interest in the director and Joey thought she might be able to use that to her advantage. But she felt a little spooked to have Fuller show up this way, almost as if she hoped to catch her off guard.

"I'd like to ask you some questions about what happened yesterday on your set," the reporter said, full voice. "I hear you're the one who found Courtney Lisle's body."

Everyone in the reception area turned to stare at them.

Joey felt as if she'd been slapped. "Who told you that?"

"And I know you and your ex-boyfriend have already been questioned by the sheriff's department about her murder," Fuller said.

Instinctively, Joey backed away.

Fuller stepped up and got in her face. "I just want to hear your side of things. This may be your only chance to get out ahead of the story before it breaks wide."

Joey spun and rushed down the hall, trying to outrun the feeling of walls closing in around her.

"You need to go on record before the studio hangs you out to dry," the reporter called after her. "This is a big story, Joey. You'll have to talk about it sooner or later."

Chapter Nine

Joey was up early the next morning. The confrontation with Fuller made her even more determined to try to get some answers herself and take charge of her own fate.

Overnight she'd thought long and hard about the entire situation with the movie, including her dislike for Marcus Pray and her reluctance to go on working for him. But she had to face the fact that she was a potential suspect in Courtney's murder, and until the investigation was over, she worried quitting the job would only draw more unwanted attention and possibly create suspicion about her reasons for leaving. That wouldn't do her any good with the police or professionally: she couldn't afford the appearance of a guilty conscience. The matter might be settled for her, anyway, if the temporary suspension of production turned into a permanent shutdown on the movie.

In the meantime, she needed to stay busy. The horror of Courtney's death and Bernard's accident was devastating, crippling if she allowed it to stop her. But that wasn't her nature; hard work and persistence had always been her most reliable tools, and she believed they'd serve her well now as she tried to dig up any information that might bring order back to her world.

That's why she holed up at home that morning, reading everything she could find online about the movie and its problems, especially the disastrous first day of shooting. The story got full play in all the industry publications, and briefer pieces appeared in some of the tabloids.

Once again, the reports were repetitive, like the articles about Courtney's death: short on facts, but often long on speculation. One of the more imaginative posts, on *themartinishot.com*, claimed *UMPP* had been the target of industrial espionage. The author gave no motive or source for the attack but promised to stick with the story. In other words, stay tuned for more improbable updates.

Disappointed with the results of her search, Joey poured herself a normally forbidden second cup of coffee, then went to the sunroom to get a pen and paper to make some notes. Bigfoot meowed at the back door, so Joey let her in and patted the kitchen counter next to her laptop.

"Come on up and keep me company. Looks like I'm going to be camped out here for a while."

The cat padded into the kitchen and vaulted gracefully to a spot on the counter where she could observe Joey without risking direct contact.

"Really?" she complained. "I get no credit for being your food source?"

Bigfoot gave a huge yawn, then turned in a circle and settled down for a nap. Joey went back to the computer and entered another Google search, looking for anything she might have missed relating to Courtney; but nothing of interest popped up, and she felt as though she'd played out that thread for now.

She sipped her coffee, doodling aimlessly on the pad of paper. Something about the hometown paper obit/testimonial she'd read the day before bothered her, although maybe "bothered" was the wrong word; struck her as odd was more like it. The tone of the article felt unusually personal and familiar.

She pulled up the item and read it through for the third time. Courtney's twin brother, Caleb, was liberally quoted, and there was that bit again about Courtney and Pray coming from the same little backwater town. She still wanted to know how the two of them began working together and made a note on her pad:

Call production office for contact info on twin brother, Caleb.

The twin had a lot to say about his sister's drive and ambition; he could probably fill in some blanks, if he was willing. But the production office was closed pending the official green light to get back up and running, so she'd have to wait on that. She took another sip of her coffee, thinking about how to proceed.

Despite his lofty status in the industry, Joey knew little about Pray's background. That might be worth a deep dive since she had the time. Plus, there'd be loads of material to sift through that could produce other threads to follow.

Starting with the basics, she skimmed Wikipedia and the carefully crafted details of the director's press release history. The teenage boy from Oklahoma who came to Los Angeles straight out of high school with twenty dollars in his pocket and a dream, a self-made power broker who climbed the ladder in Hollywood with record speed by virtue of talent and determination . . . blah, blah, blah.

She moved on to Pray's IMDb page. He already had a lengthy filmography for a producer-director still in his prime, and if the critical reception of his work left a lot to be desired, the commercial rewards were abundant. Most of his movies were major box office hits.

That kind of success came with a hefty downside, no matter who you were. But for someone as abrasive and arrogant as Pray, the odds of making enemies multiplied exponentially. Conflict always produced a digital trail, especially for the rich and famous.

She started spitballing, making notes on her pad. *Feuds? Professional? Personal?* There was nothing to indicate the troubles on the movie were tied directly to Pray, but context was always useful. At the very least, maybe she'd piece together a more complete picture of the temperamental director she was working for.

Rather notably for a man in his forties who'd been wildly successful in a glamourous, high-profile profession, Pray had never married. Wikipedia made no reference to former romantic partners, no dating history at all. That was a puzzler.

She thought over the interactions she'd witnessed between Pray and the women around him. She'd never seen him flirt or connect with anyone on a personal level. Even when he talked about Brooke's gorgeous figure, the comment was more of an insult, as if the actress was simply an object to be judged and ranked.

Remembering the ugly episode on set made Joey angry all over again. Nothing she'd seen led her to believe Pray had any respect for the women he worked with. If he carried the same attitude into his personal relationships, what would that look like? She shuddered, creeped out by that train of thought. Maybe she didn't want to know more about the man's love life, after all.

On impulse, she typed in a Google search: *Marcus Pray: sexual harassment/abuse.*

She felt a dark charge when several pages of hits popped up on her screen. But as she scrolled through the results, only a handful looked to be on point; and most of those referred to one specific incident. Nothing official or litigious, but the tabloid press had a field day when a young B-list actress blasted Pray in an interview. She claimed he treated her "with habitual disrespect" on set, and she went on to criticize "his pattern of portraying women as little more than sex objects on screen."

Her accusations went viral and Pray struck back. He enlisted crew members from the movie they worked on together to write an open letter to the media. They all signed the statement, smearing the actress as a publicity-hungry slut, a nightmare of tantrums and crude behavior on set.

And it worked. A decade before #MeToo was even a vibration in the ether, the twenty-three-year-old actress's career was ruined while Pray went virtually unscathed. If anything, it appeared his bad boy antics lent a raunchy luster to his image that made him even more admired by his teenage fanboy audience.

That was the sum total of negative press on Pray: not a hint of personal scandal that Joey could find, no matter how many ways she entered the search. She began combing through images, photos of the director at various industry events, award shows, film openings. A three-page spread in *The Hollywood Reporter* covered the ceremony when he got his star on the Walk of Fame.

He was photographed with lots of beautiful women, many of whom Joey recognized, though most appeared in professional settings. If they dated Pray, that detail didn't draw much public attention.

Once again, she was surprised by the lack of information; for someone as famous as Marcus Pray, "private life" was practically an oxymoron. The real mystery was how a person with such a massive media presence could keep his social track record under wraps.

Around three o'clock that afternoon, she came out of her internet trance long enough to check her phone. She had a couple of dozen text messages and a handful of missed calls, but the number that made her heart jump was Eli's. He had sent her a text at one o'clock:

Need to talk to you in person. Can you meet this afternoon? Guisados? Name the time.

He followed up with a phone call at one thirty when he'd left a terse voice mail: "Please call me when you get this."

She felt torn between curiosity and dread. Something important must have happened if he was asking her to meet him, at one of their favorite old hangouts, no less. That was strange enough on its own, but there was no point trying to figure it out, and she had to return his call.

"I've been avoiding my phone," she said when he answered.

"I guessed as much. I was almost ready to drive out there."

She was relieved he hadn't shown up unannounced. They'd spent a lot of time at her house in happier days: sunset walks by the ocean, quiet dinners on the patio, coffee together in the morning with the sun streaming in. She wasn't interested in resurrecting those memories.

"That's probably not a good idea, but I don't think I want to go out." She wasn't going to mention her research on Pray. "I'm lying low today."

"Are you okay?" He sounded genuinely concerned.

"I'm well enough." The online fishing expedition had absorbed her, but now the outside world crowded back in. "There's nothing physically wrong with me, anyway."

"*That* I understand better than you can probably imagine."

The sadness in his voice gave her pause; she'd been preoccupied by her own worries and hadn't given much thought to his feelings. After the slightest hesitation, she said, "I'm very sorry about Courtney."

"Thank you." He cleared his throat. "To be honest, I'm floundering. I don't want to impose, but I don't have many people I can talk to."

An excuse to avoid meeting him was on the tip of her tongue. "Guisados is fine," she said instead. "I can be there by four."

"Four it is, then." The gratitude in his voice was palpable. "I appreciate this, Joey."

She threw on a sweater and jumped in her car before she could change her mind. She was surprised he had reached out to her, but when he made his amends for the way his addiction had harmed her, she had wished him well and told him she'd support him in his commitment to stay drug-free. Even if he hadn't explicitly asked for that sort of help today, she'd feel like a hypocrite if she tried to weasel out of seeing him.

Guisados was a hole-in-the-wall taco joint on Caesar Chavez Avenue, which is what Sunset Boulevard becomes when it crosses into East LA. Tacos and quesadillas were the only items on the menu, but Guisados did them up right, with house-made corn tortillas and uniquely delicious fillings. An added benefit, from Joey's perspective, was the fact that it was off the beaten path. They'd be unlikely to run into anybody they knew in that part of town.

Eli had already claimed a table at the back of the small dining area when Joey got there. He was nursing a large horchata.

"Sorry, I didn't expect so much traffic coming east this time of day." Her eyes flitted around the crowded restaurant, scanning the other customers. "There was a big backup on the one-ten interchange."

She was relieved to confirm there were no familiar faces. Sitting down to eat with her ex was enough of a challenge; she didn't feel like making small talk with friends.

"No problem." Eli stood and gave her an awkward peck on the cheek. He looked tired, but otherwise okay, all things considered. He was better dressed than she was, in a crisp white shirt and linen jacket. "Why don't you sit down to hold the table, and I'll get in line. You going to have the usual?"

She didn't feel like eating, but the place was so small, they needed to order food to justify taking a table.

"Sure," she said gamely. "And a large melon drink."

He gave her a fleeting smile. "I know."

He stepped up to the counter. The tacos were made to order, and everything was fresh. Joey took a seat at the two-top. Guisados had been written up a few years before by Jonathan Gold, the late Pulitzer Prize–winning food critic for the *LA Times*, and now boasted six locations throughout the city. But this one in Boyle Heights was the OG, and it was always busy, although this far east the customers were mostly locals.

That afternoon was no exception. Every table was full, and there was a line out the door, people willing to wait on the sidewalk to order. But the counter people worked quickly, and the line moved at a good pace. All the regulars knew the drill: if you couldn't get a table, you did takeout.

Eli returned with their food, then went back to get her melon drink and plastic utensils. He sat down across from her and started to doctor his tacos with salsa.

"I didn't know I was hungry till I got here." He bit into a mole poblano taco, dribbling salsa over his fingers.

Joey looked down at her sampler platter, and her stomach did a flip. She hadn't been to Guisados since the breakup with Eli, and the situation was too emotionally charged for her to take even a bite.

"Something wrong with your food?" He stopped chewing, peering at her across the table.

"It's not that." She pushed her plate aside. "You said you wanted to talk, so let's talk."

"Always right to the point." He shoved the rest of the taco in his mouth.

"You asked me to meet you and I'm here." She took in some air. "You didn't sound good on the phone. I thought maybe you needed . . ." She shook her head. "I don't know what I thought, to tell you the truth."

"I was worried about you." He looked down at the table. "I heard the sheriffs had you in for questioning, and I'm sorry about that."

This was a detour she hadn't expected. "That's not your fault." Her breath caught and she had to swallow. "I'm the one who found her."

"Yeah, but I heard they were rough on you," he glanced up for her reaction. "Mostly because of our relationship."

"Who told you that?" she asked, more sharply than she meant to.

"Some girl reporter who's been hounding me."

"Tall thin brunette? Works for some website with a funny name?"

"That's the one." He frowned. "She talked to you too?"

"Tried to. She had me paged at LCC yesterday, but I didn't stick around to chat." Joey sat back in her chair, trying to figure out where this was going. "Wait, she's the one who told you the sheriffs were rough on me? I didn't tell her that, or anything else. I blew her off as soon as I realized what she was up to."

"She said she's got a contact inside the sheriff's department."

"Sounds like you two had quite a conversation," Joey said coolly.

He gave an impatient shrug. "I wanted to hear what she knew."

"That's how she set the hook, so she could turn around and pump you for information." Her resentment for Fuller's tactics boiled over. "You shouldn't let her play you like that."

"Give me some credit," he said. "I'm not a total idiot."

"Don't put words in my mouth," she snapped.

"Truce." He made the time out sign. "I don't want to argue with you."

She nodded, trying to compose herself. It felt so strange, but also familiar, talking to him this way, almost as if they were still a couple. *Unsettling* was the word that came to mind.

"I just don't trust that woman," she said. "She's out for blood, and I don't think she'll be picky about collateral damage."

"I hear what you're saying, but she was right, wasn't she?" He gave her another searching look. "They raked you over the coals."

"It wasn't that bad." She shook her head irritably. "They're going to talk to everybody on the movie; that's their job."

"What did you tell them?" He hesitated. "About us?"

"I told the truth," she said. "We used to be a couple, we're not anymore, but we want the best for each other."

He kept his eyes fixed on her. "What did they say to that?"

"The detective I talked to didn't say much, aside from the non-stop questions. She wouldn't tell me anything, even when I asked her directly."

"What'd you ask?" Now Eli's tone grew sharp.

Joey didn't feel comfortable going into a lot of detail about the interrogation, but she couldn't sidestep his question.

"I asked how Courtney died." She shifted in her seat, much as she had when she sat across the table from Blankenship.

"What did she say?" Eli picked up a plastic fork and started tapping it on the table.

"She asked me how I thought she died," Joey said softly.

Eli's gaze flicked to hers and held. "You know they think I did it."

Her heart skipped a beat. "Did they say that?"

"Not in so many words, but that's normal, right? The husband or boyfriend is always the one they suspect."

"I guess so." She nodded slowly. "But you didn't do it, and they'll prove that once they collect all their evidence."

"Maybe." He didn't look convinced. "I've been thinking I should hire a lawyer."

She could tell he was serious. "But she died on set, and they'll be able to narrow down the time frame. There have to be a dozen people who can vouch for you; you're always in the thick of things."

Joey tried to tamp down her own anxiety. This conversation rekindled every fearful thought she'd had since Blankenship made it clear that she was, at the very least, a person of interest in Courtney's murder.

"You're naïve about the legal system." Eli sat back and crossed his arms. "Innocent people get convicted all the time. The cops want to close cases and they're not always as careful as they should be with the facts."

His words were like knives carving up what was left of her fragile peace of mind.

"You should think about getting a lawyer too," he said.

A disturbance on the sidewalk made her turn toward the windows lining the little storefront. A crowd of onlookers pressed against the glass, some with cameras, some with cell phones clicking away, taking pictures of Eli and her.

Her throat closed in panic. The group on the sidewalk was attracting more people, and the noise swelled with the size of the throng. Everybody in the restaurant gaped at them. She stood in a rush, knocking her chair over backward.

"Is there another way out of here?" she said to one of the wide-eyed countermen.

He nodded, pointing toward the kitchen. She grabbed Eli's hand, and they dashed behind the counter, past the cooks in the tiny galley and out the back door.

"My car's on the next street over," she said. "Through the alley."

They sprinted down the narrow passageway together. She unpinned her keys from her waistband and had them ready when they pulled up beside her car.

"Get in." She threw herself in the driver's seat and jammed her keys in the ignition. Eli stood by the open passenger door, looking dazed. "It's me or them," she said and cranked the engine.

He got in beside her and she pulled out of the parking space, tires screeching.

Chapter Ten

"No way a bunch of photographers just happened to show up in East LA." Joey pushed the car as fast as she dared through the glut of surface street traffic, heading to the I-10 freeway. "You think somebody could have followed one of us?"

"I didn't notice anything on the way over." Eli cast a nervous glance at the passenger side mirror.

"Neither did I, yet we suddenly had a horde of people pointing at us and taking pictures." She frowned and checked the rearview mirror. "Maybe your reporter friend is keeping tabs on you."

"She's not my friend," Eli said through gritted teeth.

Joey automatically headed straight for the west side; her only thought was to get away from the mob scene at Guisados as quickly as possible. Once they were on the freeway, Eli pulled out his cell.

"I haven't looked to see what's online today," he said. "Didn't have the stomach for it."

Joey glanced over, but his face was bent to his phone, and she couldn't read his expression. She found it hard to believe he hadn't already steeped himself in the media coverage of Courtney's death, but who was she to say how he should deal with his loss? Maybe avoiding the news was part of his coping strategy, to keep himself on the straight and narrow, staying clean.

He was quiet as he scrolled through the information on his phone. Westbound traffic was heavy and Joey had to keep her eyes pinned on the road. After a while, he sighed and let his head drop against the seat back.

"What'd you find?" she asked.

"Trust me, you don't want to know."

She wondered if he'd seen anything different from the articles she'd been reading earlier but decided she could wait to find out, at least while she was behind the wheel of a ton of metal speeding along at seventy miles per hour. They made the rest of the journey in silence until they were on PCH, about a mile from the trailer park.

"If we see anything suspicious, keep going," Eli said. "We don't want to get trapped."

Joey's heart dropped. It hadn't occurred to her that more photographers might stake out their homes.

"Where should we go?" She flicked an anxious look at him. "If we've got company here, they'll be at your place, too."

"We'll cross that bridge when we come to it."

His response did nothing to ease her mind, but a few minutes later, they pulled into the carport next to her house without spotting anything fishy. Even so, they scurried up the porch steps like a couple of crooks on the lam.

"Make yourself comfortable," Joey said. "Can I get you anything, water or iced tea? I have some fresh orange juice if you'd rather."

This was the first time Eli had been in her personal space since their breakup. Joey was so intent on getting home safely from East LA that she didn't think how she'd feel about having him in her house until they were already there. Now she got busy in the kitchen to cover her tension, opening cabinets, setting out glasses, and checking the contents of the refrigerator.

"Relax, I'm fine," Eli flung himself down on the love seat. "I'll only stay till it's dark, then I'll call an Uber and go pick up my car."

"What if they wait for you to come back, maybe even follow you home?" Joey's mind was racing. "What'll you do then?"

"I don't think they're going spend that much time hanging around East LA." He leaned back and rubbed his eyes. "If they really want to find me, it's not that hard."

"This is serious, Eli." Between the ambush at Guisados and the weirdness of having her ex in her living room, Joey felt like a nervous wreck. "We can't just ignore the situation; we have to be prepared."

"Prepared for what?" He glared at her. "We just had to make a run for it from the zombie apocalypse. How do you expect to have any idea what's coming next?"

She turned back to the fridge, trying to calm herself. Eli's attitude wasn't the problem; not compared to Courtney's murder, Blankenship's suspicions, and all the trouble on the movie. It was a waste of energy to pick a fight over something neither of them could control.

She took out a pitcher of tea and poured some into the glasses she'd set on the counter. "You hungry? I could scramble some eggs, or I've got a pizza in the freezer."

When she crossed the room to give him the tea as a peace offering, he reached for her hand. "Listen, I'm sorry for being such a butt."

"You weren't." She tried to soften her tone. "I'm all keyed up, and I shouldn't push so hard."

"No, I mean about everything. I let us both down." He looked at her wistfully. "If I'd been a better man, who knows? Maybe none of this would have happened."

Joey knew it was never that simple. Early in their relationship, she hoped some of their issues, like Eli's chronic jealousy, would fade over time. Sometimes she wondered if their problems fed his addiction; she still didn't understand how fast and hard drugs took him down, like zero to sixty in a heartbeat. But there was nothing to be gained by rehashing that now.

"Let's just try to help each other get through this without making things worse." She gently disengaged her hand. "I don't know about you, but I'm hungry. I haven't eaten since breakfast."

"Yeah, I noticed you didn't touch your tacos." He gave her a lopsided smile. "You know me, I can always eat."

Joey got eggs, butter, and half-and-half from the refrigerator, then set a skillet on the stove. She chopped onions and a green pepper, put whole wheat bread in the toaster, and drizzled olive oil in the pan to sauté the vegetables. The homely activity helped her feel more at ease than she had since she and Eli walked through her front door together.

"Why did you take down all your artwork?" he asked, the first words either of them had spoken in ten minutes.

"Felt like I needed a change, I guess." She whisked half-and-half together with four eggs and poured the mixture over the veggies sizzling in the skillet. "I just haven't gotten around to putting up anything new."

She didn't say it was also because many of the pieces, mostly watercolors she'd done of the beach at different hours of the day and various seasons, reminded her of the time they'd been together, memories both good and bad. Somehow, she found it even more painful to remember the good times because then she was forced to think about all the reasons she fell in love with Eli, his intelligence, his dry sense of humor, his curiosity for the world, and his tenderness, especially when they were alone. It hurt to think about how much they'd both lost to his addiction.

"Are you still painting?"

His question brought her back to the present. "Who has time anymore?" she said lightly, as if that was the real obstacle.

"Do you still have them, the ones you took down?"

"They're in storage." She dragged a spatula around the pan to scramble the eggs and vegetables.

He tipped the tea to his lips, watching her over the rim of his glass. "You think I could have one of them?"

She frowned as she turned down the heat under the skillet and started buttering toast. The itchy, unsettled feeling she'd had at Guisados was back; the feeling of familiarity, fixing supper with Eli the same way they had too many times to count. But now everything had changed, and none of this felt quite right anymore.

A plaintive meow sounded outside the door to the patio.

"Would you mind getting the door?" she said, glad for the interruption. "The cat wants supper, and I've got my hands full here." She was in the middle of assembling their plates of food.

"When did you get a cat?" he asked as he crossed to the door.

"More like she got me."

She grabbed a can of Fancy Feast from the cupboard. Bigfoot scampered past Eli to the bowl Joey set on the floor.

"You didn't answer me about the painting," he said.

She knew it would be easier to just let him have one of the pictures. What did it matter? She didn't want to look at them anymore. But her paintings had a little piece of her soul embedded in each of them, and she didn't want to give that to Eli.

"Let me think about it, okay?" She set the plates of eggs and toast on the small kitchen peninsula that doubled as a breakfast bar. "Right now, let's eat."

After supper they went out to the patio to watch the sunset. Sky and water merged at the horizon in a blaze of pink as shadows stole over the shoreline. Joey switched on the fireplace to ward off the chill that took hold as soon as the sun disappeared, and they continued to sit quietly by the pale glow of moonlight.

"I'd forgotten how peaceful it is here," Eli said. "Like we're in a different world, away from all the noise and insanity."

Joey didn't know how to respond. He'd made no move to call the Uber he'd mentioned earlier, and he seemed to be making himself at home. That didn't sit well with her.

"Penny for your thoughts," he said, sounding drowsy.

She was about to suggest it was time to dial up a ride to his car, but then she saw an opportunity, with them sitting there together and no one else nearby.

"I'd like to talk to you about something that's bothering me," she said.

"Seriously?" He sat up, alerted by her tone.

"It's about work," she said. "Nothing personal."

"Okay." He leaned back on the sectional. "In that case, you've got my undivided, professional attention."

"Is Marcus Pray always such a complete dick?" she said evenly.

He closed his eyes. "Do we really have to talk about this now?"

"No, we don't *have* to," she replied, "but this job's going to be hard enough without that misogynistic jerk blowing up every time things don't go exactly his way, like he did the other day with Brooke."

"Oh, for . . ." He stood up and stalked into the kitchen. "I need some water."

But Joey wasn't willing to drop the subject.

"Somebody needs to step in and straighten Pray out," she called after him. "You can't expect the cinematographer to ride herd on him for the whole show."

She saw his face by the light of the refrigerator when he opened the door. He looked tense and angry, like a different person from the one she'd been sitting with just now. Even though she meant every word about Pray's behavior, she knew some part of her wanted to goad Eli, to lash out because of old resentments and because she didn't want to allow herself to feel close to him ever again.

"I don't know what you expect from me." He grabbed a bottle of water and slammed the refrigerator shut. "I work for the guy, same as you. I can't control him."

All at once, he sank down on his heels with his back braced against the refrigerator and dropped his face in his hands. The unopened bottle of water rolled slowly across the floor.

Shaken, Joey got to her feet and went to the kitchen. Eli crouched in the corner, weeping silently. She leaned down and put a hand on his shoulder. "Please don't cry."

"Everything's ruined." He gazed up at her, his eyes wide with anguish. "I don't know what to I'm supposed to do now."

She'd never seen him like this, not even during the worst days of his addiction—angry, despondent, remorseful, all those and more, but not broken this way, not shattered.

"Come sit back down by the fire." She knelt to help him to his feet, then guided him to the patio and lowered him gently onto the sectional.

He sighed and leaned back against the cushions. The worst of his tears had passed, and he seemed calmer. "I'm sorry, I didn't mean to make such a scene."

She shook her head, feeling guilty. "I'm sorry I upset you."

"Not you." Tears pooled in his eyes again.

In that moment, Joey understood this wasn't about Pray or the job, or their ragged history together. This utter collapse came from brutal, naked heartbreak.

"Try to relax," she whispered. "Don't think about anything, just breathe."

He nodded weakly and closed his eyes. Before long, she realized he was asleep. She watched him for a while, thinking maybe they'd all suffered enough; maybe it was time for her to offer Eli more than perfunctory forgiveness. Whatever he'd done in the past, he put in the hard work to get his life straight.

"I think you must have loved her very much," she said softly. Tears started in her own eyes. "I am so very sorry about Courtney."

This time, she really meant it. She got up to cover him with the afghan and left him dozing by the fire.

Chapter Eleven

E arly morning light showed through the bedroom windows, and the smell of fresh coffee drifted in from the kitchen when Joey opened her eyes.

Eli stood in the doorway, jingling his keys in his hand. "I'm heading out now. I need to get across town before rush hour. We're officially up and running again tomorrow at the Paradise Cove location, so I've got a laundry list waiting for me."

"Already?" She sat up, pulse drumming in her throat. "How'd you find out?"

"Had an email waiting from Gordon when I woke up. He must be pulling out what's left of his hair. The sheriffs released the scene late last night, so we're good to go."

"That was fast." The sight of him at the threshold of her bedroom gave her the same troubling sense of familiarity she'd felt the day before; it was hard for her to concentrate on what he said. "Any word about what the cops found?"

He rattled the keys like a tambourine. "Not as far as I know. I only hope I've talked to them for the last time."

"Amen to that."

He continued to stand in the doorway as if he had something more to say. She stole a look at the clock on her nightstand, wishing he would leave. She was sympathetic to his pain, but she wasn't ready for another emotional scene.

"Listen, I'm sorry about last night," he finally said, as if he read her thoughts. "I just blew a gasket, and you got the brunt of it."

She tried to hide her discomfort. "You don't have anything to apologize for. Yesterday was . . ." She cast about for the right word and had to settle for "Difficult."

"That's one way to put it." He frowned. "You going in today?"

"I have to if we're shooting tomorrow. Has word gone out to the rest of the company?"

"Gordon said production was on it. With a little luck, I'll be able to put out a preliminary call sheet by midday." He glanced at his phone. "My Uber's here." But he still didn't move. "One thing: you might want to check out some of the stories they're posting online before you go in this morning."

"Why?" She was startled by his tone. "What's wrong?"

He shook his head, looking lost. "Never mind, forget I said anything." He held up his phone. "I gotta go. Thanks for letting me crash."

Joey knew she should get on the road to the office before the freeways seized up, but Eli's warning about the online postings sent her straight to her laptop. She settled at her desk on the service porch and typed "Courtney Lisle Death Investigation" into a Google search. Her heart buckled when the light gray script at the top of the page announced, *about 875,000 results.* The story had officially gone viral.

Anxiously, she scanned the headlines until one jumped off the page: *Love Triangle Possible Factor in Homicide of Assistant Director.*

She clicked on the link that took her to an online tabloid called *Hollywood Hawkeye.* Two photos appeared above the article: the first was a shot through the window at Guisados, Eli and her sitting together inside the cafe. Both looked brooding and serious as they gazed at one another across the table. The next photo was slightly out of focus, shot on the run: Eli and her holding hands as they sprinted for the alley to dodge the paparazzi. The caption that ran under both pictures read, *On-Again, Off-Again Lovers Eli Logan and Joey Jessop Flee Reporters Two Days after the Murder of Logan's Girlfriend, Courtney Lisle.*

She hesitated with her finger hovering over the touchpad, afraid to scroll to the body of the article. The mysterious love triangle was going to be a nasty piece of fiction, but if she didn't want to walk around in a bubble . . . *Eight hundred seventy-five thousand results.*

She swept her finger over the touchpad and started to read:

Eli Logan and Joey Jessop, persons of interest in the murder of their coworker, Courtney Lisle, were spotted together at East LA eatery Guisados on Wednesday, two days after Ms. Lisle's body was discovered on the set of the new superhero movie directed by action auteur Marcus Pray.

The Los Angeles County Medical Examiner ruled the death a homicide but gave no further details. Sources within the LA County Sheriff's Department confirm Logan and Jessop were brought in for questioning on Tuesday.

Ms. Lisle was employed as an assistant director on the movie, as is Mr. Logan, who was in a relationship with the murdered woman. Ms. Jessop, who found the body, works in the costume department and also happens to be Mr. Logan's ex live-in girlfriend.

Those close to Ms. Lisle confirm she was suspicious of the friendship between her boyfriend and his ex. "Courtney was professional about her dealings with the Jessop woman," claims a friend of Ms. Lisle's, "but Jessop was always looking for ways to get Eli's attention. Courtney thought Jessop was still hung up on him."

Could a love triangle be at the heart of this crime? Investigators won't confirm or deny this as a working theory. But the exes seemed to be looking to each other for comfort following their interrogation by sheriff's homicide detectives. They had eyes for no one else at the crowded cafe on Wednesday and beat a hasty retreat, hand-in-hand, when they realized their assignation had been observed by the media.

We will update this story as it unfolds. For further details on the crime and photos of the crime scene, go to: Sneak Attack: Murder on the Movie Set.

Joey stared at the screen, stung by a poisonous blend of horror, shame, and fear; but overriding all of that was a searing sense of violation. She started to click on another link, then slammed the laptop shut. She needed to get on the road to the office where she could take refuge in a world where she understood the game, even if some of the players didn't always stick to the rules.

The first clue the day wasn't going to be business as usual at Left Coast Costumes came when Joey turned into the driveway on her way to park behind the building. Not yet eight in the morning, and a number of paparazzi already huddled near the front entrance.

A warning bell sounded at the back of her mind, though she knew some movie star might have an early fitting. Brad Pitt preferred a morning appointment, and he always showed up alone on his motorcycle, his way of getting around the city unnoticed, the helmet a perfect disguise. But after the wild scene at Guisados, she had a bad feeling about this gang of paps.

She parked as close to the loading dock as she could. A dozen or so costumers were gathered outside. Some worked at tasks like sorting shoes or lining up racks and equipment to pack onto wardrobe trailers; others were taking a break. Joey hurried toward the back door, pretending to be occupied with her phone in the hope she could dodge any questions aimed her way.

She ducked into the building without being stopped. Costumers were hard at work in the cages, kicking up a colossal racket. Her friend Kenn Smiley was the first to call to her.

"Joey, wait up."

She froze, wishing she could put off what was coming. He set down the tag gun he'd been using to size a rack of clothing and met her at the door to his cage.

"You okay?" His expression was full of concern.

"I've been better, but I'm hoping life's going to get back to normal this week."

He gave her a doubtful look. "Well, for the record, I don't believe a word of what they're saying online. But just in case, Bob and I want you to know if you need someplace to stay until things cool down, our guest room is yours."

She longed to ask what he'd read but didn't want to have that conversation within earshot of so many of their colleagues. LCC was worse than a small town for gossip.

Kenn pulled her into a hug. "Chin up. This too shall pass."

She did her best to smile. "Thanks for the encouraging words and the kind offer. I'll keep you posted."

She moved down the corridor, past the rest of the cages. Though many of the other costumers nodded in a friendly way, she couldn't help noticing the curious looks and whispered comments that followed her into the main warehouse.

Henry Burchette waved her over, but (another bad sign) had no trivia question to fire at her. "How're you holding up, darlin'?"

"Living the dream, Henry," she said dryly.

"Good for you." He gave her a broad wink. "*Illegitimi non carborundum*, I always say."

"Silver-tongued devil." She leaned down to kiss his cheek.

"Come by later, and I'll have a stumper for you."

"It's a date." She waved and continued through the warehouse, wondering if she'd find a welcoming committee camped out by the front desk.

She sent a quick text to the receptionist: *Any strange visitors lurking today?*

And got a split-second response: *All clear.*

When she stopped to say hello, the receptionist was apologetic. "I'm so sorry about that reporter the other day. She said she was doing a profile on you for her website. She made it sound like a good thing."

"No harm done," Joey said because there was no point making her feel worse. "She'd have figured out how to get to me one way or another."

"I promise that won't happen again. I already told those lowlifes in the parking lot they can't come inside the building."

"I appreciate that," Joey said, then made her way down the hall toward the *UMPP* offices. Time to face the music.

"I was about to send out an all-points bulletin," Bill said when she walked in the door. "I tried not to take it personally when you ignored my texts yesterday, but I was beginning to think you ran off and joined the circus."

"No need," she said. "The circus caught up with me."

"You could have thrown me a bone to let me know you were okay," he scolded.

She closed her eyes, at a loss. She couldn't explain how clueless she felt in this strange new reality, how confused and out of control. She couldn't even say if she hoped her coworkers already knew about the stories that were circulating, or if she preferred they were in the dark. Not a lot of upside either way.

"I've been operating on automatic pilot," she said. "I forgot I turned off my phone yesterday afternoon."

That was a white lie: she'd forgotten until this morning, then she'd been in too much of a rush to get to work. Now she scrolled through the dozens of emails and texts she had waiting.

"I don't know where to start." She groaned and dropped the phone on her desk.

"Let me jump right in then," Bill said.

As usual, they were the first ones in the office. He seemed to understand Joey needed structure and direction more than she needed his concern.

"The intel I'm getting from production says we're going to pick up again at Paradise Cove tomorrow," he said. "But that's not official. If by some chance they decide to leapfrog ahead in the schedule, we'll be in for a mad dash today."

"No kidding." She didn't mention Eli's confirmation of the shooting location because she didn't want to explain the context.

"I've alerted the troops we need all hands on deck here by nine. What have you got on your docket?" He looked at her expectantly.

Joey fumbled her notebook open, trying to sync with the workday. "First up, I've got to go for a look-see at Hammer and Tongs."

She scanned her list, feeling more confident as she slid into her comfort zone. "Gentex should have the color samples ready for the two hundred yards of uniform cordura they're dyeing. When I finish in the Valley, I'll head downtown, then come back over the hill by way of International Silks and Woolens. Safwat promised half our Eurojersey for the new superhero multiples will be in, and I need to collect some samples of silk velvet so we can choose the base fabric of that embroidered cape for Renée Zellweger."

"Good enough, let me know if you need any help." Bill's phone rang. He checked the screen, then rolled his eyes and mouthed *Gordon*. He sat down at his desk to talk to the UPM.

Joey moved to her desk and opened her laptop. She had some time before the rest of the crew showed up, and she wanted to look at a few of the stories she'd bookmarked from her search that morning, especially the one on *Popvibe.com* with Maggie Fuller's byline:

Marcus Pray Film Proves Deadly Behind the Camera

Death visited the set on the first day of principal photography for one of the biggest movies in production, the Untitled Marcus Pray Project. A young assistant director was brutally murdered, and the cinematographer for the film ended up in the hospital after sustaining life-threatening injuries. Both calamities took place last Monday during a single fourteen-hour workday on a supposedly safety-conscious, union-bonded set with a professional security detail in place. This reporter can personally testify to the last item because when I visited the set to try to get answers about the explosion that injured the cinematographer, security guards threw me out under orders from Courtney Lisle, the assistant director who tragically became the second victim of violence on set later that day.

I do not claim I could have prevented Ms. Lisle's murder by making the inquiries I was there to conduct, but greater transparency is needed when incidents like the ones on Monday occur. Although no specific cause has officially been cited for the explosion, and there are no suspects in custody for the murder, the movie company has been given the green light to continue production.

This is a prime example of the arrogant disregard for the well-being and safety of the film community by the power structure of that industry, a violation of public trust that goes largely unchecked due to the financial importance of that industry to the local and state economies.

Marcus Pray's offensive behavior on set is an open secret within the film community, along with his general indifference to the welfare of the members of his company. But to my disappointment, when I approached members of the UMPP crew, they were reluctant to speak with me, adhering to the code of silence mandated by punitive nondisclosure agreements they are required to sign as conditions of their employment. So long as people who witness acts of negligence and recklessness that put them and their coworkers at risk remain mute, the status quo will prevail.

The line between whistleblower and troublemaker is blurred by peer and financial pressure brought to bear on those within the entertainment industry. It will take people with rare courage to stand up to the challenges they will face when they finally demand changes to a system that too often proves dangerous and dysfunctional when entrusted to irresponsible leadership.

Joey sat with her chin propped in her hands, feeling conflicted. She wasn't a fan of the reporter's methods, but she admired Fuller for calling Pray out in print; and the woman clearly had some well-placed sources of information.

That reminded Joey—she had a source of her own to tap. She checked the clock to be sure it was after eight, then picked up her desk phone to make the call.

"Production," came a chirpy voice.

"This is Joey Jessop in costumes. May I please speak to Hannah?"

"Hold please."

Things had been so crazy, she hadn't spoken to Hannah, the production coordinator for the film, since before Courtney was killed.

"Girl, you still standing?" Hannah sounded more cheerful than Joey expected, but you had to be nearly imperturbable to run a production office on a movie this size.

"More or less. How are things in the eye of the hurricane?"

"I've started telling the kids in the office if they can get through this one, they can do anything." Hannah dropped her volume by half. "But I'd say the jury's still out on our chances."

"Roger that."

Hannah raised her voice to carry across the production office. "Tell him I'm on another call and take a message. Sorry," she said, coming back to Joey. "Some of these PAs are trainable, others not so much. And happy as I am to talk to you, I'm guessing this isn't a social call."

"I need a favor. Can you get me contact information for Courtney Lisle's family? I'd especially like to reach out to her twin brother, Caleb."

"Oh, Joey." Hannah's tone shifted to concern. "It's been such a madhouse around here, I almost forgot. You found her, didn't you?"

"That's right. I'd like to speak with her family to offer my condolences." She felt a twinge of guilt about her real motive for the call.

"I think they'd appreciate that." She heard Hannah tapping briskly on her keyboard. "As luck would have it, she listed her brother as her emergency contact. I have a cell and email."

"Could you please text me both?"

"Coming to you."

"Thanks, Hannah, you're the best."

Joey now had what she'd hoped for, a direct pipeline to Caleb Lisle. She pulled up the text from Hannah, then hesitated, wondering if it would be better to email first, rather than make a cold call.

Seemed like the polite thing to do. Courtesy, however, wasn't her main objective. She dialed the cell number Hannah provided.

Voice mail picked up on the first ring. "This is Caleb. Leave me a message and I might call you back."

She took a deep breath and crossed her fingers. "Caleb, my name is Joey Jessop, and I worked with your sister, Courtney. I'm the one who found her on the beach. I know this must be a difficult time for you and your family, but I'd like very much to speak with you. You have my number now in your cell, so I hope you'll call me back."

She almost ended the call, then added, "I'm sorry for your loss."

Not exactly a gracious message of condolence, but she hoped it would serve its purpose. There was no guarantee Caleb would respond to her call or the questions she intended to ask, but for now, all she could do was wait.

Chapter Twelve

The office was still quiet. Joey looked dolefully at the piles of paperwork on her desk, but she couldn't make herself focus on purchase orders and check requests. Instead, she clicked on a montage of photos she brought up on her computer, taken of Eli and her inside Guisados. A short paragraph ran under the collection of pictures, singing the same old tune:

> *Eli Logan and Joey Jessop, persons of interest named by LA County Sheriffs investigating the murder of assistant director Courtney Lisle, dined together on Wednesday at neighborhood favorite Guisados. The former lovers were brought in for questioning Tuesday by sheriff's homicide detectives. Logan and Jessop were subsequently released with no charges filed, though authorities refused to confirm they were no longer persons of interest in the death of their coworker.*

Gripped by a sudden frenzy to see everything, Joey almost clicked on another link, then dropped her head in her hands, wishing she could make it all stop.

"Don't flog yourself with that stuff." Bill stood looking over her shoulder. "You can't take it seriously."

She felt herself flush. "A lot of people who read it will."

116

"A big nothing-burger; close it out." He pointed at the screen. "And don't read any more of the drivel they're posting."

Joey turned to look at him. "You've read the stories?"

"Nobody with any sense pays attention to the tabloids," he insisted. "Everybody knows it's mostly misinformation with a sprinkle of libel thrown in, just to round things out."

Her heart clenched. "Mostly?"

"Send that garbage back to cyberspace where it belongs and concentrate on something productive." He jutted his chin at her computer. "Don't let those bloodsuckers get to you."

"Did you see the photos of Eli and me?"

Bill shook his head.

"Is that a negative or a sign of disapproval?"

"It's nobody else's business, including mine." He shrugged. "I can see why you two would want to touch base with each other."

"Misery loves company," she said sourly.

He put his hand on her shoulder. "A lot of people believe in you. Keep that in mind and let the rest of that dreck go."

She nodded, grateful for the support, though she knew many in their community would take a different view.

Zephyr walked in just then. "Oh, hi," she said. "I didn't think you'd be here today . . . I mean . . ." She stopped, looking flustered.

"Quit while you're behind," Bill said, "and check your inquiring mind at the door. We'll have a department meeting when the others get here. I'm going to tell everybody the same thing: we're a team and we're here to support each other, period."

"Right." Zephyr nodded emphatically.

"Good." He turned and went back to his desk.

"Sorry about that," Joey whispered, but the younger woman waved off her apology.

"You okay?"

"Not bad." She waggled a hand back and forth. "Glad to be at work."

Zephyr leaned close to her ear. "I'm *really* glad you're here."

Once the rest of the costume crew arrived, they sat down together to coordinate their efforts for the week. Bill closed out the meeting with a slightly longer version of the speech he'd given Zephyr and received a burst of applause that Joey found both awkward and touching.

Afterward, Malo made a point of stopping by her desk. "I just wanted to say again how much I appreciated being in your fittings the other day."

"You bailed me out." Joey sat back to give him her full attention. "You're a real asset to the crew, Malo. When all this calms down, we should talk about where you want to go from here."

"I want to do what you do," he said, then reddened with embarrassment. "I mean, someday."

He gestured to her work wall of swatches, sketches, and schedules. "This is where the magic happens."

Joey looked up at the collection of fabrics and images she posted for both convenience and inspiration, trying to see it now through his eyes. She wished she could shed her doubts about this movie and share his enthusiasm; she didn't want to rain on his parade.

"Magic doesn't have much to do with it, I'm afraid, but I think I know what you mean," she said. "And there's no reason I can see that you can't do whatever you want."

Malo beamed his shy grin. "Thanks, Joey. Coming from you, that means a lot." He slung his backpack over his shoulder and headed out the door to do whatever errand Bill had given him.

Despite the show of loyalty from her department, Joey couldn't stop thinking about the sidelong looks she'd gotten from other costumers when she walked through LCC that morning. The lurid tabloid spin on the investigation, the half-truths and outright lies, were being spewed across the internet twenty-four/seven.

Eight hundred seventy-five thousand results. That number haunted her, along with the certainty it would continue to climb. New seeds of anxiety took hold as she realized her coworkers, friends, and even her family would see the drama play out online in daily installments.

She hated the idea she'd have to talk about this with her mother, now happily settled with her new husband in Arizona; and she hated the fact her life had become the subject of common gossip, dissected and criticized in the court of public opinion. Most of all, she hated that she had to remind herself she'd done absolutely nothing wrong.

Bill was right: she couldn't let all the hype distract her or affect her work, and she refused to hide.

With that in mind, she hurried to get herself organized and on her way for the day. But when she stepped through the big loading dock doors at the back of the building, she found an unwelcome surprise. The paparazzi had figured out, or were tipped off, this was where they needed to wait. They even knew which car was hers and had it surrounded. She saw Maggie Fuller in the mix, almost a head taller than the rest of the group.

Joey dug sunglasses out of her bag and walked toward her car, head down to avoid eye contact with the paps. They didn't rush to meet her, but they started shouting questions when they spotted her coming their way:

"Joey, are you and Eli back together?"

"Was Courtney jealous of you?"

"Are you worried the producers are going to fire you if the sheriff considers you a person of interest?"

Joey shouldered them aside until one tall lean figure stood directly in her path. Maggie Fuller stuck a microphone in her face.

"Joey, if you are truly innocent, who do you believe killed Courtney Lisle?"

She drew herself up to her full height. "Let me pass," she said quietly.

"Why won't you answer that simple question?" Fuller persisted. "You found her body shortly after she was killed. Even if you had nothing to do with it, surely you have an opinion about who was responsible."

She pushed past Fuller at the same time the reporter cried out melodramatically, "You broke my toe!"

Joey was tempted to stomp on her other foot for good measure, but the crowd parted to let her through to her car. One of the photographers even held the driver's side door open.

"Good on you," he said. "Fuller's a bitch."

"Takes one to know one."

"*Touché.*" He smiled and flashed the peace sign.

His companions scattered, rushing to their vehicles.

Joey gunned her car out of the parking lot, hoping to get enough of a head start to discourage any followers. The day had taken an outlandish turn, like some kooky reality show with reporters chasing her through the warehouse district of North Hollywood.

She turned off Vanowen, a main drag that spanned the Valley, with a nervous glance at her rearview mirror, but the little side street where Hammer and Tongs was located looked all but deserted. She pulled into the parking lot next to the business and tucked her car in a space between two SUVs.

The noisy work of creation was at its usual peak levels inside Hammer and Tongs. For some reason, the welding studio opened just off the entrance. Maybe this was a bit of theater because the lights and sounds coming out of that area were certainly sensational.

Two sculptors who looked like space aliens in big welder's helmets were working on a mixed metal statue of a dragon when Joey walked in. The creature stood at least sixteen feet tall, its hide covered with iridescent purple, blue, and silver scales that flashed in the hissing light of the arc welders.

In spite of all the problems weighing on her mind, Joey felt a thrill, watching that beautiful beast take shape. *This is where the magic really happens*, she thought.

There was no formal reception area. In fact, very little was business conventional at Hammer and Tongs. A large hangout space opened off the other side of the entrance, furnished with couches, a big center table, and loads of bookshelves. A counter with three computer monitors and a couple of phones was the closest thing they had to a front desk.

Two staff members pored over sketches laid out on the big table, the shop's head cutter and a graphic artist who was a new hire.

"Good morning, is Damir in?" Joey directed her question to the cutter.

The woman glanced at her. "In his office on a conference call. Valetta?" she called over her shoulder.

A young woman materialized from one of several doorways that opened off the hangout space. Her head was shaved, and she had the build of a thirteen-year-old boy.

"Take her to Damir," the cutter said.

This was hardly necessary since Joey had been in Damir's office dozens of times, but she always rolled with the flow at Hammer and Tongs. Sometimes there'd be no one at all in the front of house areas when she arrived, and she'd find herself wandering through the back warren of rooms that put her in mind of *Alice in Wonderland*. There was always something interesting to see, works in progress both fantastic and original, and eventually she'd run into someone who might or might not be able to tell her where Damir was that day.

That's just the kind of operation he ran, creative without much structure, part of the reason it was challenging to work with him. There was no chain of command, only Damir at the top and a whole lot of worker bees. That sometimes made it difficult to shepherd finished costumes through the manufacturing process on deadline.

Joey followed Valetta to Damir's office, where they found him with several employees gathered behind the giant worktable he used for a desk. Their eyes were glued to a thirty-two-inch computer monitor.

Then she heard an angry shriek in surround sound. "You broke my toe!"

She halted in the doorway at the same time all eyes that had been fixed on the computer shifted to her. Damir glared at the hapless Valetta and dismissed the other staffers with a flick of his hand. They slunk from the room without a word.

"Well, now." Damir smiled easily. "You've had an eventful morning." He gestured to the computer. "You've become quite the

Instagram sensation in the past fifteen minutes." He clicked his mouse and checked the monitor. "More than eleven hundred views so far."

Joey couldn't believe the set-to in the parking lot was already streaming.

"How does that happen so fast?" She'd bet a week's pay Fuller was pulling a De Niro with her phony broken toe, playing it up for the cameras.

"That's how it's done, uploaded in real time. The internet's always hungry for content." Damir gave a casual shrug. "You're young and cute, which makes you ideal click bait for the online peepers and trolls."

"That's ridiculous," she scoffed.

"Don't sell yourself short." He tapped a key on his computer to close out the image. "You're a sexy girl in a sexy business, at the center of a juicy story. That's enough to make you an overnight star online."

Joey's heart sank like a stone. "Please tell me you're joking."

"Call it a reality check."

Just when she thought things couldn't get much worse. "I think I may be sick."

A grain of empathy softened Damir's angular face. "The good news is, our society is infected by cultural ADD; we're distracted by every shiny object dangled in front of us." He nodded at the monitor. "Fifty other silly vignettes will pop up in the next twenty seconds, and the freaks will move on."

Joey had a hunch he was trying to cushion the blow he'd delivered with the click bait prediction, but he couldn't unring that bell. She wasn't sorry Courtney's murder would stay in the headlines— that's how it should be, until the killer was caught. But as long as the story was front page news, she'd be living in a fishbowl.

Damir took her silence as acceptance of his counsel. "Good then. Now let me take you back to the sculpting studio. We have some beautiful things to look at and discuss."

Chapter Thirteen

"Maybe you should think about walking away from this one." Kathleen tipped the pitcher to pour tea into Joey's glass. "You can afford to; you don't live paycheck to paycheck."

"I don't think that's a smart move right now." Joey squeezed lemon into her tea. "The cops haven't cleared me yet, and I don't want to give them a reason to look at me any harder. One trip to the Homicide Bureau for questioning was enough, thank you very much."

"You're not serious." Kathleen eyed her skeptically.

There'd been no paparazzi lying in wait when Joey left Hammer and Tongs, and she managed the rest of her errands around the city without further incident. After she checked to make sure the Euro-jersey had come in at ISW and arranged for a driver to pick it up, she still had enough time for a quick trip to Hullabaloo.

Located in the trendy Silverlake district of Los Angeles, Hullabaloo was a vintage clothing store that specialized in 1960s, '70s, and '80s fashions. The place was like Disneyland for Joey: it had a festive vibe from a simpler era featuring clever displays with mannequins playing ping-pong, chatting at a linoleum kitchen table, and picnicking by a pond. All the merchandise was premium quality; plus, the store was owned and run by one of her best friends, Kathleen Quintana.

The two women sat together now on the tree-shaded patio behind the store sipping iced tea while two salesclerks wrote up the pile of clothing Joey had chosen to add to the movie's costume stock.

"That's not the only reason I need to stay put." Joey was sorry she'd mentioned the police; the subject only made her anxious. "This is a huge made-to-order show, and I'm responsible for that. If I quit now, I'll be dumping on my department. Production won't be thrilled with me either, and that won't do my word-of-mouth any good."

"Your reputation's not going to suffer because you quit one job, and it's not like you're working on some passion project." Kathleen frowned, looking thoughtful. "Considering what you've been through the past few days, no one can blame you if you take yourself off the board for a while, so you won't be such an easy target for all the wackos."

"If I had to love every movie I worked on, I'd be waiting a long time between jobs," Joey said. "I'm not going to sneak away like I have something to hide because of some feeding frenzy in the tabloids."

"But there's more to it, honey. You know that, right?" The look in Kathleen's amber-colored eyes was sympathetic. "It's bad enough to have the paparazzi chase you because you're the hot new story, but it's the social media bashing that's got me worried. Some of those people are certifiable, and I don't think we should take it for granted they won't act out."

Joey had a sinking feeling. "I've been too busy to pay much attention . . . Are you talking about Facebook and Twitter?"

"And Instagram and SnapChat. The story's everywhere, and everybody thinks they have the right to post their opinions about it."

"Are we talking death threats? Do I need to change my name and leave town?"

Kathleen's expression made her blanch. She pulled out her phone.

"Don't." Kathleen reached over to cover the screen with her hand. "It's nothing you need to see. People have a lot of pent-up rage nowadays, and they're looking for someone to unload on. Just be aware there's bad stuff churning out there and be careful."

"I can't believe this is happening." Joey felt like her brain might explode. "I understand why the police have to treat me like a suspect, but now I'm being crucified online by people I've never met. I swear, if I didn't have work, I'd lose my mind."

"This won't last forever, but please, hear me out." Kathleen peered at her earnestly. "You've worked really hard for years, so what's wrong with taking a break? It can't be a great working environment over there with that sexual predator at the helm."

"You mean Marcus Pray?" She didn't expect that even Kathleen, who was only loosely connected to the film industry, would have something to say about the director's rep.

Kathleen noticed her reaction. "Have you had trouble with him?"

Joey shifted in her seat. "He's been vile on set; went out of his way the first, and so far, only day of shooting to embarrass one of the actresses in front of the company."

"No surprise there," Kathleen said tartly.

"Honestly, I've thought about quitting, but like I said, there's more than the job at stake." She furrowed her brow. "Besides, why should I lose the work because some bully's trying to intimidate me and the rest of the company?"

"You can't win with that guy. He's a monster."

"I'll grant you, he's arrogant and rude," Joey conceded. "But if I go now, I'll leave a lot of people I care about in the lurch. I don't want to abandon my crew."

"The best thing you can do for your crew is quit." Kathleen was intent on making her case. "Trust me: Pray's dangerous. He thinks the rules don't apply to him."

Joey had never seen her friend so worked up. "I'm not defending him; I think he's a creep. But at the moment I'm also hyper-aware how easy it is to smear someone with hearsay and gossip."

Kathleen paused as though weighing her words. "I'm going to tell you something now I swore I'd never talk about with anyone."

Joey felt an undercurrent of dread. "Don't break a confidence on my account."

"I think maybe I need to. It's not my story, so I won't share her name, but I know for a fact it's true."

"Kath, I'm not sure I'm up for hearing about somebody else's pain and suffering. My head's scrambled enough for one day."

"I'll make it short," Kathleen said firmly.

Joey closed her eyes, resigned. "Okay, shoot."

"Pray cast a woman I know in a movie he was directing. Not a starring role, but a featured part, the kind that gets an actor noticed. This girl was only twenty at the time, and it was a big deal for her. She'd been on her own since she was sixteen, no family to speak of; she supported herself waitressing and shared an apartment with four other people in the same boat."

Joey couldn't help herself. "This is the short version?"

"Right." Kathleen took in some air. "This is harder than I expected. She was my friend, almost as close as you and I are."

Joey noticed the past tense and reached for Kathleen's hand.

"She was a gorgeous girl, too gorgeous for her own good, especially in this town, especially in that business." Kathleen pressed her lips together and shook her head. "It's nothing you haven't heard before, which is part of what makes it so awful. Pray hit on her as soon as they started production, but she was a savvy kid, and she managed to fend him off for a while. Made up a boyfriend, which actually didn't faze him, and made sure she was never alone with him."

A chill stole over Joey. "But."

"Yes, but. After they'd been shooting for a few weeks, he invited her to a dinner party at his house, supposedly to introduce her to some heavy hitters in the industry who could help guide her career."

"An offer she couldn't refuse."

Kathleen nodded grimly. "She shows up at his door to find she's the only guest. And she literally has a panic attack and bolts."

Joey winced. "Poor kid."

"There was hell to pay after that: Pray turned on her at work, big time. He criticized every move she made, yelled at her, made fun of her in front of the rest of the cast." Kathleen pinned Joey with a look. "Sound familiar?"

The sting of Pray's cruelty felt fresh as Joey recalled the way he treated Brooke on the first day of shooting.

Kathleen continued. "The leading man even took Pray aside at one point, but that only made things worse. By the end of the week after the un-dinner party, my friend was a wreck, completely demoralized. Then at wrap on Friday, Pray summons her to his trailer."

It was like watching a horror movie unfold; Joey already guessed the end.

"He tells her he's going to fire her unless she sleeps with him. By now she's just worn down flat by it all, and she doesn't want to lose the job, so she gets him to promise if she does it the one time, he'll let her be."

Joey slumped back in her seat and moaned. "Please don't tell me."

"Yup." Kathleen's voice turned to steel. "She did it and he fired her anyway. Said he needed to punish her for making him wait so long, and he told her she could forget about acting; he was going to blackball her with every producer in town."

"Why didn't she—"

"What? Tell somebody?" Kathleen said sarcastically. "Who was she going to tell? This was years ago when sexual harassment was still part of the regular menu. And she was a scared kid, no money, no friends, no resources."

Kathleen shrugged, her expression as bleak as her story. "Like I said, it's nothing you haven't heard before. My point is, it's a pattern of behavior: men who do that sort of thing do it over and over again. They want to control the people around them, especially women, and they're completely ruthless. Anything goes when it comes to getting what they want."

"Where is she now?" Joey was afraid to hear the answer. "Is she okay?"

"I'm really not sure. For weeks after it happened, she was practically catatonic. Her roommates got fed up and kicked her out, so she stayed with me for a while. She finally decided she had to get out of town and start over." Kathleen's eyes were dark with regret. "Wherever she is, Pray took her dreams and her confidence. In my book, that's a kind of murder."

Joey would have liked to comfort her friend, but she was too depressed by the story to think of anything encouraging to say. She hoped the young woman had managed to rebuild her life, and she wondered how many others like her Pray had mistreated over the years.

"Did the cops question Pray about the woman who was killed on your set?" Kathleen asked abruptly. "Don't look so shocked. Guys like him not only repeat; they escalate. Did you ever see the two of them together?"

"Courtney and Pray?" Joey shook her head. "Not like that; she was with Eli."

"Which would mean less than nothing to Pray. For him, it's all about the endgame. Guys like him don't have relationships, they have conquests, and getting with another man's woman is good for bonus points."

Her words sent a tingle down Joey's spine.

"I didn't know Courtney," she said. "But I'm positive Eli wouldn't care for anybody who'd be interested in that kind of action."

"That might've been the problem," Kathleen insisted. "If Pray made a move on her and she refused, maybe forcefully, things could have taken a bad turn."

"Kath, you've got to stop." Joey pushed to her feet, feeling cornered. "I can't listen to any more of this right now."

"I'd back off in a heartbeat if I didn't care so much, but you're too trusting, Joey, too willing to give people the benefit of the doubt."

"You're calling me gullible?" she said, more than a little offended.

"I'm not going to cite chapter and verse, but aside from the undeniable fact that Marcus Pray's rotten to the core, you have to face another hard truth." Kathleen got up to stand eye-to-eye with Joey. "If that girl was murdered on a closed movie set, then somebody in your company killed her. Don't dig your heels in and stay with the job because of some personal honor code that doesn't serve you or anybody else under the circumstances."

Chapter Fourteen

Joey couldn't stop thinking about Kathleen's warning as she drove home that evening. She'd known all along Courtney was probably killed by someone in the movie company, but until her friend said the words out loud, she hadn't accepted that it was the only logical conclusion.

That meant a pool of more than five hundred suspects, people she saw every day. Some she knew well, others not so much; but even so, the idea that the murderer was a coworker felt surreal and terrifying.

She had an eerie sense of déjà vu that took her straight back to the night she found Courtney's body, the same feelings of confusion and horror. But in some ways, this was worse, forcing her to look at her entire community through a lens of suspicion.

Still, she had to wonder: Why do the deed on a busy movie set? Stealth couldn't have been a priority for the killer. Was he (or she) trying to make a point or send a message? If so, to whom?

And why Courtney? From a purely practical perspective, the tragedy of her death didn't jeopardize production. She wasn't a key player, and the show would go on without her. Was she simply in the wrong place at the wrong time? Could she have seen something she wasn't supposed to, something worth killing for? Which brought Joey back to the question of whether everyone on the movie was a potential victim, as well as a suspect.

On the other hand, the motive might be personal; the sheriffs were certainly looking in that direction. She wished Caleb Lisle would return her call. Her list of questions about Courtney kept growing, and she didn't know who else to ask. Eli would probably have some of the answers, but after his breakdown in her kitchen, she wasn't going to probe that wound if she didn't have to.

He might even take offense if she started asking him questions. She thought back to their conversation at Guisados; Eli seemed almost paranoid about the murder investigation, but maybe she would be too, in his shoes. As Courtney's boyfriend, he was right to believe he'd be high on the suspect list. Joey felt like she had to be on her best behavior, and she'd only found the body.

A shiver ran through her. The plain truth was that until the sheriff's detectives cleared them, no one on the movie could be presumed innocent.

She turned on the radio to listen to NPR, hoping to silence the chatter in her brain and give herself a time out. *Fresh Air* with Terry Gross was about to begin at the top of the hour, after the news. She gave her full attention to the predictable rundown of partisan gridlock in Washington; anything for a change of pace. But the broadcast took an unexpected turn when Neda Ulaby announced:

"In other news, from the world of entertainment: a statement was issued today by producers of the embattled superhero comic book movie, *Untitled Marcus Pray Project*, which has been on hiatus following the death of Assistant Director Courtney Lisle, whose body was discovered on the film's set late Monday. On Tuesday, her death was ruled a homicide by the Los Angeles County Medical Examiner. Today's statement asserts the producers' belief that Ms. Lisle was murdered by an unidentified intruder who somehow breached security to gain access to the remote shooting location, though they acknowledge the possibility that more than one perpetrator might be involved. The studio has posted a one-hundred-thousand-dollar reward for information leading to the arrest and conviction of the person or persons responsible for the crime. Sheriff's investigators offered no comment regarding the producers' statement but have cleared the way for production on the movie to resume on Friday."

Joey hit the power button to turn off the program. She wasn't buying it. Droves of sketchy characters didn't roam the beaches around Malibu: the theory about an intruder was pure fantasy.

No doubt liability loomed large in the producers' decision to spin the publicity. But with Kathleen's ugly story about Pray and the actress still fresh in her mind, Joey found herself wondering just how far the powers that be might go to protect their cash cow.

As far as they needed to if their precious bottom line was threatened, she thought.

The answer came so automatically, it threw her. The librarian at LCC claimed the studio would turn a blind eye to Pray's shenanigans as long as he generated profits for them, and Kathleen seemed to think the man was a monster, capable of almost anything. Joey wasn't prepared to make that judgment, but now she had to ask herself: Did she really believe the studio would look the other way if that meant ignoring criminal behavior, up to and including manslaughter, or even murder?

Absolutely. At the top of the Hollywood food chain, cash trumps conscience every time.

The trill of her Bluetooth made her flinch, and the sight of the number on her console didn't help matters. She loved her mother dearly, but she didn't feel like putting on a front to keep the conversation upbeat. Still, she had to take the call.

"Mama, how are you? I've been meaning to call," she said.

"Are you all right?" Her mother sounded shaken. "Please tell me what's going on, Joey. I can't believe what I'm reading."

So much for easing into the breaking news. She wondered what media outlet beat her to the punch.

"I'm fine," she said quickly. "I guess this means the story's made the papers out there."

"I don't know about that," her mother said. "Anna Marie Baker called this afternoon to tell me she'd seen it on Facebook. She sent me a link, and I started reading about that poor girl's death online."

Joey heard the threat of tears in her voice. "Then I just had to talk to you."

Good old Anna Marie was the resident yenta in her mother's gated community. Joey could picture the little busybody humming to herself as she picked up the phone to spring the news on Helen that her daughter was featured in true crime tabloid headlines.

"I'm sorry you've been worried," she said, feeling guilty. "I should have called before now."

"The article said you were the one who found her." Helen's voice caught. "Oh, honey, I'm so sorry that happened to you. I wish I could reach out and give you a hug."

It was heart-wrenching for Joey to hear her mother so upset, especially when she was the cause. After Sergeant Joseph Jessop died in a helicopter crash during the first Gulf War, Helen devoted herself to their baby girl, named for the father she'd never know. Joey adored her mother, and right now she'd do anything to reassure her, even if that meant skirting the truth.

"Mama, we're all sorry about Courtney, but we're doing our best to keep things moving along. In fact, I'm on my way home from work," she said, trying to hit a positive note. "We've got clearance from the Sheriff's Department to start shooting again tomorrow. Now can we please change the subject? I want to hear about you and Gable."

Gable Jones was Helen's husband of just over a year, a commercial real estate developer she met at a yoga retreat in Tulum, Mexico. Joey gave her the trip as a birthday present and was thrilled when her mother returned with a new light in her eyes, brimming with energy.

Three weeks later, Helen announced she was expecting an out-of-town guest, a friend she met at the retreat. Joey assumed the friend was female and didn't give it a second thought when her mother suggested they all meet for dinner at the Water Grill. But when she got to the restaurant and found her mother nestled in a booth with a silver-haired man who was a bona fide hunk, it was a bit of a shock, the same way a 7.9 earthquake is a bit of a tremor.

Two months after that dinner, Helen and Gable married, and she moved to his home in an exclusive gated community outside Sedona. Joey worried that it had all happened too fast; her mother had rarely even dated in the years since her husband's death. But Helen remained calm and confident: Gable was the man she hadn't known she was waiting for, and she was sure Joey's father would approve.

So Joey gave her blessing, hoping for the best, hoping her mother's happiness was built on a solid foundation. In time, she developed a cautious regard for Gable, who was clearly smitten with his bride.

"Gable and I are fine," Helen said. "My husband decided he's going to retire next year so we can spend more time traveling while we're still young enough to enjoy it. His words, if you can believe it."

"That sounds great; I'm happy for you, Mom."

"Thank you, dear, but I'd be a lot happier if I could be sure you're all right. I don't like living this far apart, and that terrible story today just underlines the problem. I wish I could be there now to see what's going on for myself."

"I promise you, I'm fine," Joey said. "Glad to be working in town. That's a big plus for me."

"I know you like sleeping in your own bed." Her mother's good humor sounded forced. "But how about this: I could come visit for a few days, maybe fly in tomorrow night and out again Monday morning. That would give us the weekend together. I'd love the chance to spoil you."

Joey didn't want her mother anywhere near the front lines of the ongoing turmoil around the movie. Better for both of them to have Helen safely tucked behind security gates in Sedona.

"The next couple of weeks are going to be rough," she said. "I'd love to be able to see you, but I'm going to be working even longer hours than usual. I wouldn't feel right leaving you cooped up in my house all day."

"I wouldn't call it 'cooped up' when the Pacific Ocean's at your back door."

Half a mile ahead on PCH, Joey saw a crowd gathered under the streetlights at the entrance to her trailer park. She scanned the area for signs of an accident or some activity that might have drawn them, but she couldn't see any reason for a large group of people to be lingering along the darkened highway. Something was up, and she needed to be ready for it.

"Mama, I'm running into some bad traffic. Can we talk about this later?"

"Sweetheart, I need to see you, and I'd like to book my ticket."

Joey sighed. Tonight, she didn't have the emotional bandwidth to try to explain the situation to her mother calmly. If she started to talk about the murder investigation or the paparazzi, she'd only upset them both, and Helen would almost certainly be on the next plane to LA.

"I've gotta go now," she said, trying to keep her tone light. "Can we please talk about this later? We'll figure out a trip, I promise. Or better yet, two trips: you'll come out here, and I'll go out there to visit you and Gable, just as soon as this job is over."

"Promise and cross your heart?" her mother said.

"I promise. Sleep tight, and we'll talk in a few days." Joey disconnected, feeling worse than before, knowing her mother was worried.

She was almost at the entrance to the trailer park when her suspicion was confirmed: paparazzi, a big knot of them clustered around both sides of the driveway and spilling onto the shoulder of PCH. She thought about driving on by, but a quick flash of anger changed her mind. What right did these people have to blockade her home?

Gritting her teeth, she made a fast turn into the park's entrance. Some of the photographers recognized her and charged into the road to cut off her access. She laid on her horn and pumped her brakes, trying to nudge her car up the driveway.

A solid wall of bodies surrounded the vehicle, pushing up against the doors and leaning across the hood with their cameras to shoot through the windshield. She felt like a fish trapped in a barrel. More than anything, she wanted to scream at the top of her lungs, but she'd only be giving them the photo op they dreamed of.

Finally, she turned her head and dropped her chin, so that a curtain of hair screened her face. She sat that way, like a statue, while the photographers shouted and pounded on the car, trying to get a rise out of her.

Then came a beautiful sound. Another car started honking behind her, one of her neighbors just trying to get home, same as Joey. The next second she heard the trumpety voice of Clarice, the on-site property manager, giving the paps what for.

"Break it up! This is private property, and you're obstructing our residents' access. If you don't leave right now, I'm calling Pacific Patrol Security, and my friends, we're not talking about 'we'll show up when we feel like it' LAPD. These guys'll be here in two minutes flat."

Chapter Fifteen

"I can keep them off the property, but I can't stop them hanging around the entrance along the highway," Clarice said. "It's a public nuisance, and I can make the authorities aware. Maybe they'll step in and do something if those fools keep on with this nonsense."

Joey nodded glumly. They both knew the chances of that.

The two of them sat with Gina on Joey's back patio, watching moonlight spread across the ocean like a dark mirror gleaming on the surface of the water. Turned out, Gina was the driver who pulled in behind Joey at the entrance to the trailer park. Between her blaring horn and Clarice's threats, they managed to roust the paparazzi long enough for Joey to get past the human barricade.

"I'll do what I can to help you," Clarice went on. "But if you stay a hot commodity and they're determined to stalk you, they'll find a way. That's their bread and butter, a good-looking girl like you in the news."

Joey was tired of people telling her why she wasn't going to shake the paparazzi anytime soon, but Clarice and Gina had come to her rescue. She was grateful for that.

"I'm sorry for all the trouble," she said, "and I appreciate the way both of you showed up for me out there. I'm lucky to have neighbors like you."

Clarice stood up and stretched. "I'd best get back to the office." She turned to look at Joey, her face unreadable in the dim light. "You might want to think about finding some little hideaway where you can stay for a while, for your own peace of mind."

The irony that this was how she'd always thought of her snug beach digs didn't escape Joey. Now her tiny refuge felt flimsy and exposed, ill-equipped to weather the gathering storm.

"I'll give that serious thought." She knew Clarice was in a tough spot too, balancing the greater good with Joey's personal trouble. But it still felt like a low blow.

Clarice nodded and patted her shoulder. "I'll see myself out."

"Thanks again for your help tonight, Clarice," she said, trying to be a good sport.

Joey waited until she heard the front door close, then sat back in her chair and sighed. Any hope of reprieve from the stress of the day died with Clarice's suggestion.

"You have someplace in mind you can go?" Gina asked.

"One of my friends offered a guest room." Joey shook her head. "But how can I ask anyone I care about to take all this on?"

"Maybe if you got out of here on the down low, left your car behind and took an Uber, you could throw them off the scent."

"Maybe." Joey felt overwhelmed and discouraged. She had no idea how she was going to manage her day-to-day with the insanity that had sprung up around her.

"Look on the bright side," Gina said.

"Which would be?" She wasn't in the mood for a pep talk.

"You got through today, which means you can do it again tomorrow."

"I wish I had your optimism."

Gina shrugged and changed the subject. "I saw Eli as he was leaving this morning. He said hello and we chatted for a minute."

Joey knew she was fishing; Gina had always liked Eli. "He only stayed over because we got cornered together by the press, so he ditched his car and came home with me."

"It's an ill wind that blows nobody good, as my mother used to say. Maybe this thing will be the catalyst that brings you two back together."

The remark did nothing to put Joey at ease. Romance was the furthest thing from her mind, and least of all with Eli. A rush of anxiety made it hard for her to sit still.

"Why don't we head inside," she said. "The chill's making me antsy."

"I need to get home, anyway," Gina said. "Rocky'll be wondering if I forgot his evening constitutional."

Joey walked her to the door. "Thanks again for helping me out of that bind earlier."

"That's what friends are for, kiddo, to look out for each other."

Joey nodded, unable to trust her voice, even though she had the distinct impression Gina would prefer she decamped for the duration. Once her neighbor was out the door, she leaned her head against it and tried to empty her mind. Back in the kitchen, an incoming text chimed from her cell, probably some last-minute bulletin about the shoot resuming in the morning.

"Give me a break," she moaned.

A headache had been brewing since her talk with Kathleen, and she could tell it was going to be a whopper. She got a bottle of water from the fridge and drank half of it down before she checked the message.

She tapped her cell's screen to bring up the text, and an attachment popped up, an audio file. She checked the number: not one she recognized but a 310 area code, so probably someone in production. She clicked on the file, and a robotic voice, altered by some type of mechanical distortion, grated from her phone:

"The wages of sin is death, but you'll never see it coming."

The words hit her like a physical blow. Her eyes darted to the front door, and she rushed to make sure she'd locked it behind Gina. Even though the number was unfamiliar, she had no doubt the warning was meant for her.

What kind of freak quoted scripture to terrorize a perfect stranger? At least Joey hoped her fake-religious troll wasn't anybody she knew.

And what did they even mean, "The wages of sin is death"? Was that some twisted reference to Courtney's murder? How batty were things really getting out there on social media?

It's not going to do you any good to see it. Kathleen's advice came floating back.

Her cell lay on the kitchen counter like a snake waiting to strike, but she couldn't stop herself. She grabbed it up and opened the floodgates, feverishly scrolling through the mishmash of email and text messages, along with her Twitter and Instagram accounts. At first, she was shocked, then angry, and finally exhausted. Pledges to kill and dismember her formed the central theme in many of the posts, with the occasional marriage proposal thrown in for comic relief.

But after a time, the threats began to blur, a mountain of irrational hatred that had no meaning. Kathleen was right: People were looking for a place to park their anger and bitterness; Joey was just a convenient target. Finally, something clicked in her brain, an overloaded circuit shutting down. She rested her head on the cool countertop.

She must have dozed off, because the next thing she knew, the ring tone of her cell sat her up like a shot. She picked up the phone, ready to decline the call, but something made her press the button to accept it instead. She held the cell to her ear without speaking.

A male voice said, "Hello?"

She closed her eyes to screen out everything but the voice on the phone, waiting for more.

"Is anybody there? I'm looking for Joey Jessop." He sounded irritable, and she almost disconnected. Then he said, "I don't know what your deal is, lady, but you called me. You said you're the one who found my sister."

"Caleb?" she whispered.

"That's right. You wanted to talk to me?" His tone landed someplace between question and accusation.

"Yes, I'm sorry," Joey said, trying to collect her thoughts; she didn't want to waste this chance to speak with Courtney's twin. "I've had some strange calls lately, but I've been hoping we could talk."

"I want to talk to you too." He skipped right over the preliminaries. "What can you tell me about that night? The night she died," he added as if clarification was necessary.

That brought her up short; of course, he was looking for answers. She hadn't considered what he might want from her. Now she wished she had more to offer.

"I doubt I can tell you much the police haven't told you already."

"They haven't told me anything," he said bitterly. "They won't even say how she died."

"I asked about that when they questioned me," she said, "but they wouldn't tell me either."

"Then tell me whatever you can," he said.

Joey took a deep breath, shifting gears to concentrate on his request. She was the one who reached out, so she owed him that much.

"To be honest, I don't remember a lot myself, but I'll try." She cringed as the image of Courtney's body lying in the surf flashed through her mind. She couldn't tell him about that. "What would you like to know?"

"Do you have any idea who killed her?" Something closer to sorrow tempered the hostility in his voice.

She'd made a mistake. This man was grieving his murdered sister; she felt ashamed for exploiting his loss to dig for information.

"I don't," she said quickly. "And I'm very sorry to have bothered you."

"Wait." A command, not a request. "Do you think the police could be covering up for someone?"

Joey stopped breathing. "That's an odd question."

She'd been worried about the studio brass using their influence to limit or deflect the focus of the investigation; or (thanks to Eli) about cops who might be willing to cut corners to close the case. But the idea the police might protect a criminal from prosecution hadn't occurred to her.

"Powerful people get away with murder all the time, don't they?" he said. "Especially out there." Like California was another planet. "If they've got enough money and clout, nothing else matters."

She nodded, then realized he couldn't see her. "Sometimes, yeah, I think maybe they do."

He went quiet, but his silence was alive with questions.

Finally, he said, "Why did you call me?"

"I'm trying to make sense of things," she said. "But I feel like I should tell you, the police haven't officially cleared me as a suspect."

"Because you found her?" He sounded more curious than concerned.

"And because she was seeing my ex-boyfriend."

"Oh." She heard him exhale. "I'm not sure what to say to that."

"We'd been apart for some time before they got together. I just thought you should know, since we're talking this way."

"Full disclosure, eh?"

"You could say that, I guess." She paused, feeling awkward because she hadn't thought to offer condolences before now. "I'm very sorry about Courtney."

"My sister was her own person." There was a sharp intake of breath on his end, almost like he was smoking a joint. "She never let anybody in completely, and that included me."

Maybe because of the late-night hour or the nature of their conversation, a strange cocoon of intimacy seemed to enfold them.

Joey felt enough of a connection to say, "Were you serious when you asked about the police covering for someone?"

Caleb did another deep inhale; definitely a joint. "Specifically, Marcus Pray."

She felt her pulse quicken. "What makes you say that?"

"Because of their relationship, and the way he treated her." His tone was cold and blunt.

"You mean professionally?" she said, to be clear.

"That too, now you mention it, but I was talking personally."

She clamped the phone to her ear, concentrating now on every word. "Are you saying they had a romantic relationship?"

"I don't know if I'd call it *romantic*. They had sex, but that's about as far as it went."

Joey almost choked. "Courtney told you that?"

"She didn't have to," he scoffed. "It wasn't a big secret."

Joey tried to stay calm; she needed to be deliberate about what she said next. "Did Pray and your sister already know each other when she moved to California?"

His tone sharpened suddenly. "Why do you ask?"

"I'm just trying to put the pieces together, and I couldn't help wondering if it's a fluke they're from the same little town in Oklahoma."

"You've done your homework," he said. "I'm impressed."

"I've poked around a bit, but I still have a lot more questions than answers."

He drew on the doobie before he responded. "Oklahoma State gave Pray some bogus honorary degree a few years ago when Court was a senior there. The theater department threw a big bash for him, and she was the prettiest girl at the party. End of story." He gave a harsh laugh. "Or maybe I should say, the beginning of the nightmare."

Joey got up and hurried to the sunroom to grab a pad and pen. "Did she move to Hollywood to be with him?"

She settled back at the kitchen counter and channeled her excitement into making notes while they talked.

"My sister had her heart set on a career in film before she ever met Pray, but she was obsessed with that guy from day one," Caleb said. "So moving to California was a two-fer, as far as she was concerned. I don't think he much cared one way or the other."

"He must have given her some encouragement," Joey said. "She worked on his last four movies."

"I think he was happy to have a willing playmate standing by, as long as she didn't make too many demands. I mean, who wouldn't, right?"

"Was Courtney okay with that?" Joey felt like a Peeping Tom, but she was finally getting some of the answers she needed, so propriety could take a back seat.

"I asked her once," Caleb said coolly. "She claimed Pray promised to make her a producer, and she was getting everything she wanted out of the relationship."

Joey picked up on his skepticism. "You don't think that was true?"

"I think it's what she said to save face. She wanted to be a producer, but I don't know if Pray promised her anything, or if he'd have come through, even if he did."

It sounded to Joey as though Courtney's obsession with Pray might have been more about ambition than affection; or maybe the two were inextricably linked, a classic transactional relationship.

"When did she stop seeing him?" Joey asked.

"What do you mean?"

"Did she have any other serious relationships before Eli?"

Caleb hesitated. "I'm not sure Courtney was ever serious about anybody except Pray."

Joey felt her thought processes slow down and stretch out, like an elastic band pulled taut. "Are you saying she was still seeing Pray, even after she and Eli were together?"

"As far as I know. She said Marcus got really bent whenever she was with another guy, but it also got him hot. That was part of whatever weird chemistry they had," he said. "Made me sick, you want to know the truth."

You're not the only one, she thought. Still, she wanted to keep Caleb talking as long as he was willing. "So you're saying Pray was her number one, and she slept with other men to keep him interested?"

"And maybe to get back at him for all the other women; but she claimed they had a special bond, no matter how many people they slept with."

This conversation made Joey's skin crawl, but it brought up new possibilities she couldn't afford to ignore, particularly in light of everything she already knew about Pray.

"Did you ever spend any time with Courtney and Pray together?" she asked.

"I never wanted to meet the man, and my sister never would have agreed to it anyway."

Joey took a mental step back. "You mean, you've never even met Marcus Pray?"

From the way he talked, she just assumed Caleb was at least acquainted with the director.

"Court got very good at compartmentalizing her life once she moved to California," he said, sounding defensive. "And before that, I'd have to say, looking back on things. She had goals and she wasn't going to let anything get in her way."

Or anyone, Joey thought. She wondered how close these twins had really been. Did Caleb have a score to settle with his sister? Could that be the reason he was so willing to talk to a stranger about Courtney's sex life?

"Have you told the police about any of this?" she asked carefully. "Courtney and her relationship with Pray?"

He took so long to answer, Joey thought maybe the call dropped. "Caleb, you still there?"

"I haven't spoken to the police yet," he said. "I think they talked to my parents, but that's about it."

Joey felt blindsided: At the beginning of the call, Caleb said the police hadn't told him anything; they wouldn't say how Courtney died. That implied he'd already talked to them. Now she had to take everything he said with a big grain of salt, but she still had one more question for him.

"Do you know if your parents told the police about Courtney's involvement with Pray?"

"Court's always been their golden girl," he said quietly. "They don't know anything about her extracurricular activities, and I guarantee they'd never believe it."

"You're the one who asked if the police are covering for Pray, but what if it turns out they don't even know about his relationship with

Courtney?" Joey didn't try to hide her frustration. "Don't you think that might be important information for them to have?"

"I figured if it really mattered, they'd find out some other way," he argued. "Does that mean you think he did it?"

"I told you before, I don't have any idea who killed her," she said. "It was the first day of shooting and everything was crazy busy, and I was away from the set for most of the day, so I don't know much about what happened before I found her."

"I get the picture," he said. "The thing is, I'm the family screw-up, if you know what I mean. But my folks think my sister was perfect, and they don't want to hear otherwise. They'd cut me off at the knees if I ran my mouth to the cops about her."

Joey sighed and scrubbed a hand over her face. She was tired of thinking, and she needed to clear her head. "I've got to get up early," she said. "I appreciate you returning my call, and I'm sorry for your family's loss."

"Thanks," Caleb said curtly. "I'll pass that along to my folks."

They ended the call, but Joey had the feeling neither had gotten quite what they hoped from the conversation. Caleb wanted answers Joey couldn't provide, and for her part, she didn't trust him. He shaded the truth about talking to the police, and she was suspicious of his motives in general.

Courtney's affair with Pray was a bombshell, but if Caleb could share details of his dead sister's personal life with Joey, what was his hang-up over telling the cops about it? The line about his parents didn't ring true; she couldn't imagine they'd want their daughter's killer to get off scot-free under any circumstances. But every family had its quirks, and maybe Caleb believed they wouldn't approve of him talking to the police about his sister. Then again, maybe he had other reasons to avoid contact with the authorities.

She sat at the kitchen counter for a long time, staring at the notes she made during the call, thinking about everything she'd learned and what it might mean. It wasn't hard for her to believe a Hollywood power broker could be a murderer. Fame was no antidote for human frailty: OJ, Robert Blake, and Phil Spector were all examples that proved the point. There was a statistical reason the husband or boyfriend topped the list of suspects when a woman was murdered, and now, if Caleb told the truth, Pray was on that list.

Guys like him don't have relationships, they have conquests. Kathleen's words again, cautioning her.

No surprise, then, that Pray would prefer his women occupy a lower rung of the power structure, so there'd be no mistake about who was in control, like Kathleen's actress friend, the awful story that had never seen the light of day.

Pray must believe he was bulletproof, because it seemed he was.

"For now," she said aloud.

Like Harvey Weinstein, who was untouchable for years, until his grip on power began to slip. But how many lives and reputations did he trash in the meantime, and how many women traded their dignity for the chance at a career because that was the price he demanded, while those around him remained silent?

That brought up another troubling question for Joey. The cruelty Pray showed Brooke in front of the entire company suggested he and Weinstein were made of similar stuff. But if she were asked, would Joey be willing to go on the record about Pray's abusive behavior? She wasn't sure of the answer to that. If she wasn't prepared to speak out about events she personally witnessed, was it appropriate for her to pass along what amounted to gossip regarding Pray's involvement with Courtney, even if she meant to help the police?

From her perch in the kitchen, she could hear the drumbeat of waves on the shoreline, like a call to action. She was beginning to connect the dots, and a picture was emerging, but she wasn't sure the result would be anything she hoped to see.

Chapter Sixteen

"This is nuts." Bill Nichols gazed around the trailer at the costume crew the next morning. "The ADs called production to request additional security, but Gordon's throwing a fit about the cost. The teamsters have agreed to help secure the location's perimeter until production can sort that out, so they'll be doing double duty. But until that's settled, we're going to have to limit our in and out to base camp. It's going to be a hassle and a waste of time."

The sun was up early on Friday morning, and so were the paparazzi, in force. Joey was relieved when she pulled onto PCH at dawn without running into a human blockade, but she soon found a horde of tabloid press laying siege to the Paradise Cove shooting location. By crew call at six AM, the crowd of photographers was easily quadruple the number at the trailer park the previous evening.

"Today's going to be messy, but I have confidence in all of you," Bill said. "Stay focused, and don't be afraid to ask for help. Any questions?"

He scanned the group for signs of uncertainty. "Okay, then, let's get started and make it a good day."

The crew went back to prepping for the shoot: steaming clothing, polishing shoes, and gathering supplies they'd need on set that day. Bill caught Joey's eye and gestured for her to step outside with him.

"Let's get some breakfast."

"I can't yet," she said. "I still have fabric samples to organize for Dahlia."

"You know she won't be here till shooting call, so you've got at least an hour."

She realized this was more than a suggestion and fell in step with him, headed in the direction of the catering truck.

"I think it might be best if you stayed on set today," he said.

"But there's a lot to do back at the department," she protested.

Joey had spent most of the night lying awake, trying to decide if she should tell Detective Blankenship about Courtney's affair with Pray. But she didn't have any proof, and she still had doubts about Caleb's credibility, so she tabled the question for the time being. Today she meant to keep her mind on the job and the job on track.

"We need more background stock, and I have vendors to check on," she continued. "I told Mr. Yee at Gentex I'd swing by today to look at the two hundred yards of cordura he's dyeing. If it matches the sample, I can get it up to the workroom so they can start cutting those uniforms."

"Maybe we could send a costumer to pick up a yard for you to check," Bill suggested.

"That'll only hold us up." Joey peered at him, getting a strange vibe. "I appreciate you trying to save me the trouble of going back and forth, but I'll manage."

"It's just that the models are called in again today and that's a fluid situation, if you get my drift. Pray's going to turn that into a cluster, and Dahlia will need your help fitting and organizing out here."

"Okay, I'll stay for as long as that takes," she agreed. "What time are they called?"

"Starting at nine, we have ten girls scheduled every half hour."

"No problem," she said. "We should be finished fitting them by noon; then I can peel off and tend to the rest of my list."

Bill stopped walking and turned to her. "I respect you too much to give you the runaround. We need you here today, but we also need you to keep a low profile. No photo ops going to and from crew parking, no chances for you to get pounced on back at the costume house or at one of the vendors, not until things settle down."

Joey felt her good intentions fade to black. "Where's this coming from?"

"The producers are worried about how this is playing in the press."

"That's just perfect!" she snapped. "They blame *me* for being hounded all over town by a bunch of lunatics."

"The pictures of you and Eli at the restaurant are the real issue." His expression was serious. "The studio wants to clamp down on that kind of publicity."

"What happened to 'that's nobody else's business'? Isn't that what you said yesterday?"

"That's still my personal view." He shook his head apologetically. "But the producers want to avoid any appearance of impropriety, and we both work for them. I'm just the lucky stiff they tapped to deliver that message to you."

She could tell Bill wasn't any happier about this than she was.

"They probably think I'm a loose cannon because I mashed that reporter's toes yesterday." She raised her eyebrows. "How am I doing so far at reading between the lines?"

"They don't want this thing to get blown out of proportion." He shrugged. "It's about perception and controlling the narrative."

"That's a laugh." Her temper flared again. "They don't seem to be all that worked up about the fact they've got a sadist with a God complex running the show here. But heaven forbid two people who happen to be working together on their stupid movie meet on a day off for lunch."

He cautioned her with a look, and Joey realized she'd begun to draw the attention of passing crew members.

"I'm not claiming it's fair," Bill said. "I'm only telling you what's being discussed behind closed doors at production. Those pictures don't do you or Eli any good, especially after the sheriffs brought you both in for questioning."

"Along with everybody else on set that day," she said impatiently.

"Joey." He shook his head. "You know what I'm talking about."

She put her hands up in surrender. "If I'd known we'd be followed and photographed and chased, I wouldn't have met him. They can't blame me for that."

"No, but you've got to understand the fallout's been a problem. The press has a bead on you now, and you need to minimize your public exposure if you want to keep working here."

She felt the blood drain out of her face. "Are they talking about firing me?"

"Nobody's said that yet."

"Yet?" The earth seemed to shift under her feet.

"Don't get ahead of yourself." Bill put his arm around her shoulders. "Keep your head down and do the same great work you always do. Let's hope this thing dies a quick death."

"I need to work." She couldn't keep the desperation out of her voice. "Especially now, or I'll go crazy."

"To be perfectly frank, I told Gordon you're essential to our department if he wants us to finish this monster on time and on budget; because that's the truth of the matter."

"Thank you." She nodded, feeling faint. "I'll get with the program. There's nothing I'd like better than to have those vultures point their cameras someplace else."

"I know," he said fondly. "And I want you to know that Dahlia and I have your back on this."

Joey tried to take comfort in his reassurance, but her mouth felt dry as dust.

He gave her shoulders a squeeze. "Let's go get some chow before all the breakfast burritos are gone."

Melanie Beale, a rail-thin bottle blonde from the makeup department, gave a flirty finger wave when they stepped into the catering line.

"Hi there, Billy." Dimples showed when she smiled. She cut a look at Joey that could freeze hell over, then turned back to the gaggle of hair and makeup crew waiting for their orders to come up.

"I don't think she gets that I don't play on her team," Bill said out of the side of his mouth.

"Not to discount your masculine charm, Billy-boy, but I'd say that was more about dissing me." Joey downplayed the slight, but it confused her; even though she and Melanie weren't close friends, they'd never had any trouble.

"What's her problem?" Bill grumbled.

"Who knows?" she said. "My poll numbers seem to be trending down lately."

He leaned close to her ear. "Don't let that little alley cat get to you."

She smiled and nodded, but something told her Melanie's snub was a preview of coming attractions.

Bill wanted to eat in the catering tent. He texted Zephyr to tell the costume crew to break two at a time for a walking breakfast.

"I feel guilty sitting down while the rest of them have to eat on the run," Joey said.

"How many times have you eaten drive-through in your car because it's the only way you can get your work done?" Bill wiped his mouth on a paper napkin. "At least the crew gets to sit down for lunch."

"Apples and oranges." She hiked her shoulders. "It's a different job."

"Shut up and eat your burrito."

His phone started buzzing on the tabletop.

"Perfect timing," he muttered and slipped on his reading glasses to check the screen. "I gotta go talk to transpo."

Joey started to get up from the table.

"Finish your breakfast." Bill took the rest of his burrito and coffee to go. "I'll see you back at the trailer."

"Be there in a few."

"No rush." He waved over his shoulder.

She was about to take a bite of cantaloupe when she heard a stage whisper behind her.

"Check out the ice queen."

"I can't believe she has the nerve to show her face on set; like we're supposed to pretend nothing happened."

Joey fought the urge to turn around and bit into her melon.

"I was sure they'd fire her," someone else chimed in. "With all the bad press, you wouldn't think they had a choice."

"Karma's a bitch. She'll get hers, one way or another."

The barbs, clearly aimed at Joey, came courtesy of Melanie and her buddies on the makeup crew, like some campy high school schtick straight out of *Mean Girls*. The smart money told her to tune them out, but she couldn't eat another bite.

Crew members sitting nearby pretended to ignore the scene, and she wondered if others harbored similar feelings of resentment. Joey hadn't bargained on coworkers buying into the social media beatdown she had to endure, and she'd never felt so alone, like an exile cut off from her tribe.

Chapter Seventeen

When she got back to the wardrobe trailer, Joey found Dahlia propped against the tailgate, talking on her phone. Today the designer wore a cobalt blue silk kimono with skintight jeans, knee-high boots, and a collage of chunky amber necklaces to top it all off. The outfit would have overwhelmed a woman less sure of herself, but on Dahlia, it looked just right.

She ended the call and spread her arms. "We're keeping you right here as long as you want to stay, and I hope that's for the run of the show."

Joey accepted the hug, feeling self-conscious. "I appreciate the vote of confidence."

"You're my secret weapon." Dahlia drew back to look at her. "Without you, the made-to-order would be a nightmare. It's bad enough as it is, with this wacky schedule."

Joey knew she was right: The first four weeks of shooting were front-loaded with every one of the fifteen superhero costumes to establish. Weeks two through five included three big action sequences, each shooting for several days with hundreds of background players. No matter how smoothly it all went, the shooting company was in for a wild ride.

"With a little luck, I'll be able to get the red uniforms into the workroom later today," Joey said. "And I have the fabric samples to show you for Renée Zellweger's cape."

"Fab! Let's go in and have a look. How long do you think it'll take them to do the embroidery?"

"Sylvia said they could deliver the first cape in two weeks. Once we've fit it and made sure the pattern works, the other three will take a week apiece, or if we want to pay a big rush charge, we can get them all in ten days."

"We may have to go that route," Dahlia said. "But it needs to be a show-stopper. Are you positive these people can deliver?"

"They do beautiful work," Joey assured her. "There's nobody better on either coast."

"That's what I'm talking about." Dahlia smiled appreciatively. "Everybody told me to hire you because you know all the best sources and vendors."

As they started to climb the steps, Bill stuck his head out the door of the trailer. "We got confirmation Russell Crowe's deal is done. He's set to play Doctor Diacritico, and he's available to go to Dennis Oh for measurements today. I've set it up with his assistant to be there at two. Tomorrow he flies to New York and then on to Europe and Australia to do press for a movie that's about to come out. He won't be back in town for three weeks."

"Have you called Dennis yet?" Joey asked. "To book the time?"

Dennis Oh was the best tailor in Los Angeles, and his shop was just around the corner from LCC, on Vineland Avenue. There were a handful of freelancers who went from movie to movie whose work could give Dennis a run for his money, but for a brick-and-mortar business, Mr. Oh was the gold standard for tailoring in the industry.

"I already called Dennis and we're set with him for today," Bill replied. "But I haven't talked to Damir over at Hammer and Tongs. They're going to have to go over to Dennis's to take their own measurements."

Bill put on his best winsome expression. "You're the Damir whisperer, Joey. Can you set that up? I couldn't get Crowe's assistant to agree to make two stops."

This was a surprise to nobody. During the golden age of Hollywood, the studios required stars to be available on demand for measurements and fittings without question or discussion.

But the heyday of the studio system was long gone. These days, actors not only had a great deal more autonomy, they were routinely overbooked, often shooting more than one film at the same time they were promoting others already in release. It wasn't unusual for stars to insist costume fittings come to them, whether it be at their private residences or a remote city where they were working. Joey had been to New York, Montreal, Vancouver, and London to fit actors for various films.

"I'll call Damir now." She also made a note to call Mauricio, the shoemaker at LCC, so he could be there to trace Crowe's foot. "One-stop shopping is better for all of us. I've worked with Russell before, and he can turn cranky on a dime."

A memory from that other job came back to her: On his way to the set, Russell had kicked off a pair of custom-made boots, boots he'd pronounced "Perfect, mate" with a big smile in his final fitting. Walking on ahead in his stocking feet, he shouted at Joey over his shoulder, "Deal with it." He was all smiles again later that day, but the boots were remade for him anyway. She bit her lip now and kept the recollection to herself. No point stirring the pot.

Dahlia frowned. "I wonder if Renée knows he's been cast."

"I think they've buried the hatchet," Bill said.

"They have history?" Joey asked.

"Things got ugly between them on that Ron Howard movie, *Cinderella Man*, but that was what . . . almost twenty years ago?"

"True." Dahlia nodded. "And Russell was the big dog back then. Things'll be different since Renée got the Oscar for *Judy*, and she's a sweetheart. Still, I wish I could go to Dennis's to make a fuss over Russell for old times' sake, but I need to stay on set today to hold Marcus's hand."

"And monitor his behavior," Bill said. "Especially with the models coming in again today."

"I can't do much about that if he's in one of his moods." Dahlia wrinkled her nose. "Who knows what frame of mind he'll be in with everything that's going on."

"I'll be fine on my own," Joey said. "I'll make your apologies and chat Russell up while Dennis and Damir do what they need to do. I just have to get him talking about himself, and I'll be home free."

"Remember what we talked about earlier," Bill said quietly. "Keep a low profile."

She swallowed a comeback about whipping out her cloak of invisibility. They were all under pressure and she knew he was on her side.

Joey, Dahlia, and Christine, along with two additional costumers hired for the day, went to work getting ready to fit the models. They set up racks of clothes and a three-way mirror in a back room of the Paradise Cove Cafe.

At nine AM, the first group of professional beauties showed up, escorted by the new second AD, a fellow named Lionel Hughes. Joey had worked with him before; they'd gotten along well, and she was glad to have that position filled by someone she knew. After he introduced himself to Dahlia and the other members of the costume crew, they hugged briefly.

"It's great to see you," he said. "I don't like coming on the show this way, but I'm happy to find a familiar face."

"Same here," she said. "We need a strong second, and it's always good to have another friend on the job."

"Joey?" Christine was checking the models in. "These ladies aren't on our list."

"Do they have vouchers?" Joey asked.

"Yes, but they're not on the list the ADs gave us."

Joey turned to Lionel. "Do you know if they're replacements?"

"Sorry, I don't." He looked confused. "Let me find out."

"It's just that we don't have unlimited stock to fit them out here on location," she said mildly. "I need to know if I'm going to have to get more clothing together."

He spoke into his walkie-talkie. "Eli Logan, go to two, please."

The instrument crackled in his hand. "Go for Eli."

"Wardrobe says this group of models I brought them isn't on the list. Are they replacements?"

Several seconds of silence followed, which is a long stretch of dead air on a walkie. Lionel glanced at Joey uncertainly.

Finally, Eli said, "They're additionals, per the director."

"Copy that," Lionel said.

"Can I talk to him for a second?" Joey asked.

"Go for it." He handed her the walkie.

She pushed the button to talk. "Eli, it's Joey. Are we dressing these girls for the same scene?"

"Coming to you." He sounded annoyed.

"Okay then." She gave Lionel his walkie, resigned to the inevitable discussion and delay. "I guess there's a story."

Dahlia and the other costumers gathered round.

"I was afraid of this," Dahlia said.

Before Joey could ask, Eli appeared in the doorway. "Walk with me?" He signaled to Dahlia and Joey; they followed him outside.

This was the first time Joey had seen Eli since she'd learned about Courtney's affair with Pray, and she had a hard time looking him in the eye.

"Marcus wants this group of ladies to be dressed by your team," Eli said. "They're not to appear on camera, but he wants them to look, and I'm quoting, 'sexy as hell.'"

"I don't understand," Joey said, frowning. "Are we doing a still shoot for set dressing?"

He gestured vaguely toward the set. "They're going to keep Marcus company in video village."

Video village was the director's headquarters on set, equipped with a monitor that crew members could watch to see what the camera was shooting in real time. Hands down it was the best place to keep an eye out for any problems with the scene in progress. But there was never enough space, and certainly no room for extra people to crowd in.

"He wants them in costume to stand around in video village?" Joey looked at Dahlia, who was shaking her head. "They all have vouchers, so does that mean the movie company's paying them to be there?"

"They're eye candy," Dahlia snorted. "To keep Marcus from getting bored."

Joey stared at her in astonishment. "How can he get bored when he's directing next summer's big blockbuster?"

Dahlia looked at her, poker-faced. "He always does something like this, but I was hoping we'd get farther into the shoot before it started."

"Let me get this straight." Joey turned to Eli, her irritation starting to build. "They're not going to be on camera, but they're going to hang out with the director on set, and we're supposed to dress them?" Her head swiveled from Eli to Dahlia, then back again. "What, like hookers? Is that what he wants?" she demanded.

"Let it go, Joey," Dahlia said. "It's not worth your energy or your outrage. This is a fight we can't win."

Eli shrugged. "What she said."

"That's pathetic." Joey shook her head, then glanced back at the room they'd set up for the fittings. "Do those girls know what their deal is, or do they think they're going to be in the movie?"

"They're getting paid their daily rate, which is well above scale," Eli said. "I don't think anybody's going to complain if all they have to do is stand around for a few hours looking good for an A-list director."

"Do we know that's all he's expecting them to do?" she asked coldly.

"Above our pay grade," he said.

With Bill's warning in mind, Joey did her best to curb her temper. "This is a new one on me, but if the studio's fine with it, I guess there's nothing more to talk about."

"Come on, Secret Weapon," Dahlia said cheerfully. "Let's get back in there and sling some hooker wear on those gorgeous girls."

Chapter Eighteen

The morning left a bad taste in Joey's mouth. Once they finished tarting up the women Pray chose to hang with him in video village, she was glad to leave for Russell Crowe's measurement session. But on her way to catch the shuttle to crew parking, Eli called to her.

"Joey, hang on a second."

Reluctantly, she slowed so he could catch up to her. She still couldn't look at him without thinking about Courtney and Pray, which made her feel painfully awkward. "I don't have much time; I've got to get to town to measure Doctor Diacritico."

"I won't keep you." He glanced around them. "I just want to apologize for the position I put you and your department in this morning with the off-camera models."

"I understand it wasn't your decision to have us dress them for Pray," she said stiffly. "I don't think anybody can control that guy, and he doesn't seem to have any impulse control of his own."

He stepped closer and lowered his voice. "Just remember, money talks, and he makes plenty of it for the studio, so do us both a favor and listen to Dahlia. Don't let this get under your skin because it's not going to do any good."

"If the models don't care, I should probably let it go," she said, trying to convince herself. "But it makes me feel dirty to be part of setting up that open-air meat market for a sleaze like Marcus Pray."

"Joey and Eli!" Two paparazzi with high-speed video cameras popped out from behind one of the lighting trailers.

Eli thumbed his walkie-talkie. "Security to base camp lighting trailer number one, stat!"

One of the paps lunged at them; Eli tried to grab his camera. The guy ducked and kept shooting, so Eli went for him again, and they crashed to the ground in a tangle of arms and legs. The second pap rushed in to film the fight, just as two transpo guys hustled around the corner of the trailer, with Pete-the-Lech O'Neill in the lead.

"What's the big emergency?" he shouted.

"Eli needs backup!" Joey pointed at the paparazzi. "These guys sneaked in to film us."

The drivers moved to break up the fight, then confiscated both video cameras. The intruders lost their enthusiasm for brawling as soon as they were outnumbered, but they still had plenty of attitude.

"You got no business attacking us." The guy who scuffled with Eli had a nasty gash over his left eye. "We're only doing our job. You and your studio's looking at a big fat lawsuit."

Eli shook his head contemptuously. "You're trespassing, so good luck with that." He signaled to Pete. "Take Joey to the shuttle."

"You got it." Pete motioned to her. "You ready to go?"

"I guess so." She looked around in confusion; it felt wrong to leave, like fleeing the scene of an accident.

"Just go!" Eli yelled. "Get her out of here, now!"

"You sure got people stirred up," Pete grumbled as they hurried through base camp. "Between you and that girl who got herself killed, we got nothing but trouble."

"Her name was Courtney, and she didn't *get herself* killed." Joey couldn't tolerate his callousness. "She was murdered."

"Excuse me if I don't pretend to be all broken up about it," Pete shot back. "The whole crew hated her, so you can climb off your high horse."

Joey stared at him intently; she'd never considered how other crew members felt about Courtney.

Pete misread her expression. "Don't look at me like that. Lotta people thought she was a bitch," he sneered. "She treated us drivers like the hired help."

Joey kept her eyes pinned on him. "You think one of them might have wanted to hurt her?"

"There's a big difference between *wanting to* and *doing*." He furrowed his brow. "That's all I'll say about that. Now let's get a move on before you land me in more hot water with the first AD."

She fell in step with him, wondering if it was true that a lot of the crew disliked Courtney. Her own experience with the woman hadn't been pleasant, but she always figured that was mostly because of Eli.

When they got to the shuttle van, Pete bundled Joey into the back. He told her to stretch out face down across the seat, then covered her with a canvas drop cloth he'd borrowed from the painters.

"You think this is really necessary?" she said, her voice muffled by the heavy fabric.

"There's about twice as many of them out there as when we got here this morning," he said. "They mob us whenever they see passengers. I'll have trouble enough getting past without hitting any of those scumbags."

He fired up the van and started up the track to the freeway. It was stuffy under the canvas and Joey folded back a corner of the drop cloth to get some air. She still couldn't see anything, but as soon as they began the final climb to PCH, a free-for-all erupted outside. Bodies bumped and smacked the side of the van as paparazzi tried to get a look inside. Pete swore and planted his foot on the brakes as he revved the engine to make it growl.

"Get outta the way, you losers!" he shouted through a crack in his window. "I'm just tryin' to get out of here to gas up the van."

The noise didn't subside, but Joey felt the van inch forward, gravel crackling under the wheels.

"That's right, back up." Pete hit the brakes and she nearly flew off the seat. "I said *back up*, you jerk! You wanna get run over, I'm happy to oblige!"

He continued to mumble curses until Joey felt the van turn right, connecting with the smooth surface of the highway.

Pete let out a whoop. "We made it!"

She poked her head out. "Will they be at crew parking too?"

"Nah, they're only staking out the set." He remembered then that he was mad at her. "That's bad enough," he said gruffly.

She pushed the drop cloth aside and sat up for the rest of the short ride down PCH. The day was classic Southern California perfection, sunny with temps in the low seventies and a steady, mild breeze coming off the ocean.

But Joey was too preoccupied to notice the beauty around her. If she didn't have such tunnel vision about Courtney, maybe she'd have seen for herself the second AD had enemies on the crew; but right now, it was her own questionable conduct that bothered her most. She couldn't stop brooding over Kathleen's story about the actress Pray had victimized, and she wondered if she'd helped arrange a similar fate for one of the young women she dressed that morning to look "sexy as hell."

Pete cleared his throat. "This okay, or you want me to drop you closer to your car?"

She realized the van had stopped. "This is fine, thanks," she said briskly.

She slid the side door open and stepped down to the parking lot. The sunbaked asphalt felt hot underfoot, and she hurried to the far corner where she'd left her car.

She needed to find a way to shelve her personal problems, if only for a few hours. With three prima donnas to manage, she had to bring her A game to the measurement session. Dennis Oh had been known to refuse to make clothes for celebrities who rubbed him the wrong way, and Russell Crowe certainly had that capacity. Damir was a piece of work under any circumstances, and then there was

Russell himself, the genius talent with a mercurial temperament to match. She was going to have her hands full.

But her mind went blank when she caught sight of her car. Somebody had used a can of spray paint to send her a message. A crude skull and crossbones was splattered across her driver's side door along with a single word in bold black letters:

MURDERER

Chapter Nineteen

"Out with it." Damir appeared at Joey's side as she sat in a corner of Dennis Oh's enormous workroom, organizing her notes from the measurement session.

"I thought it went well." She looked up at him, thrown by his confrontational tone. "You had Russell eating out of your hand; he loved your ideas."

"Sure, it went well; why wouldn't it? But the whole time, you looked like you were about to lose your lunch." He peered at her. "What's up?"

She frowned and went back to her notes, hoping he'd let this go. "I'm trying to make sure this information doesn't slip through the cracks. You have everything you need from me for now?"

"A straight answer would be helpful." He reached down and picked up the notepad she was writing on. "I'm not budging until you tell me what's going on."

She blinked back tears. "Please don't be nice to me; I don't have time to fall apart right now."

"I saw your car on the way in." Damir took a handkerchief from his pocket and handed it to her. "I can have one of my people here in ten minutes to hit it with a coat of primer, then you can bring it to the shop anytime you like. I'll have my best guy repaint it and give you one of the shop's vehicles to use while it's out of commission."

Before she could respond, he pulled out his cell phone and called a number on his speed dial. "I have a job for you at Dennis Oh's."

He listened for three seconds. "You heard me right, and I need you here *now* to paint over an epithet on a car door." Another beat. "It's a bad word, okay? Just get over here with some primer."

Damir ended the call. "Not the sharpest knife in the drawer, but he's a virtuoso with a paint gun. We'll get you fixed up and have you on your way in twenty minutes. You can't be driving around the city with that filth on your door, even in LA."

Joey blew her nose. "Since when are you in the business of repainting used cars?"

"Since a friend of mine got jammed up by some dirtball."

"You're a good guy, Damir." She pressed her lips together to stop them trembling.

"If there's anything else I can do to help, I'm here for you. Anything, and I mean that." He started for the door to wait for his painter in the parking lot. "But don't let this get around. You'll ruin my reputation."

Joey watched while Damir's painter worked on her car, thinking how easy it was to cover up an ugly word with a coat of paint, but that didn't erase the ugliness that put it there in the first place.

The Tao according to Joey.

She knew it wouldn't hurt to keep that in mind as she tried to understand what was happening on the job with her coworkers, to remember appearances didn't always match up to the truth.

Before long, she was on the road with a neutral gray blotch on her driver's side door, jockeying through midday traffic from the Valley to downtown and back again as she made her professional rounds.

Against all odds, the fabric dyers had achieved the exact shade of red on the first try, so she was able to get the uniforms started in the workroom at LCC. She stopped off in midtown to buy the velvet, then delivered it to the costume shop that would cut and embroider Renée Zellweger's cape. She even had enough time to make a run through one of her favorite costume rental houses.

Chateau Costumes felt like a cross between a New Orleans bordello and the backstage of a vaudeville theater. Each room had a theme: the Victorian room, hung with vintage corsets and petticoats; the Hawaiian room, decked out with Tiki torches and grass skirts; and the Asian room, with its collection of antique kimonos. They also had the best selection of vintage jewelry for rent in the city; Joey left with several bags of 1980s necklaces, bangles, and earrings.

But when it was time to head back to Malibu, she had a knot in her stomach at the thought of returning to set. If she had to guess who'd stoop low enough to trash her car, the hair and makeup divas would top the list, but she just couldn't picture that snooty little group tottering around crew parking, brandishing cans of Krylon.

Back at base camp, she checked in with Bill and Dahlia to find that, for once, everything was running smoothly. The shooting company was on break while the grips and electricians worked to light the next setup, so she took the opportunity to pull Bill aside and tell him about the vandalism to her car.

"Eli needs to call a company meeting to get to the bottom of this." He grabbed out his cell phone, ready to hit speed dial.

"Maybe we should hold off before we make a big stink," Joey said.

"We need to shut these goons down now." Bill shook his head stubbornly. "Who knows what they'll do next?"

"I'm just saying, let's think it through before we involve the rest of the crew," she suggested. "We're all jumpy enough without pointing fingers at each other."

"Let me handle this." Bill's expression was stern. "I'm in the mood to raise a righteous stink." He stepped away for privacy to make the call.

Joey knew arguing with him was useless, and she was glad to have him so firmly in her corner. She headed up to the cafe to see how things were going on set, but the company was still on break, and most of the crew was at Crafty. Even Pray was there with his scantily clad harem in tow. Joey drifted over to check out the table of fruit and vegetables, steering clear of the director's orbit.

"Joey, right?" The craft service girl she met the day Courtney died set a plate of fresh sliced pineapple on the table.

Joey groped for her name. "Sam?"

The girl nodded and smiled. "It's nice to see you again."

"Nice to see you too, Sam."

She noticed Sam's father, Stuart, standing off to one side with a scowl on his face. Joey could see now that his left arm looked shrunken compared to his right. Just then, she felt a tap on her shoulder and turned to find herself facing one of the models she had dressed that morning. Pray hovered next to the girl with a proprietary hand planted on her shapely behind.

"Hi there!" the model chirped, then turned to Pray. "This is the woman who dressed me today."

She struck a flirtatious pose to highlight the miniskirt and crop top she wore. Joey thought she looked far too young to be pawed by anyone, let alone a middle-aged Lothario.

"Keep up the good work, wardrobe." Pray gave Joey a mock salute, then pulled the model close and started to nuzzle her neck.

"Behave yourselves!" Stuart grabbed Pray by the elbow. "Nobody here wants to see your dirty business."

"Get your hands off me!" Pray snarled.

"I'm not afraid of you." Stuart stood toe-to-toe with him. "You think everybody's going to take your guff because you're famous."

A restless murmur rose from the people nearby as they backed away from the two men.

"I'm the boss of everybody here." Pray drilled Stuart with a look. "I'm *your* boss, old man, so shut up and do your job or get out."

"Daddy, please don't spoil everything." Sam moved between them. "We've worked so hard to get here."

The fire went out of Stuart's eyes as if he'd wakened from a trance, and he took a wobbly step back. Sam leaned in to support him, then turned to Pray beseechingly.

"Please don't fire us; my father's just upset."

He focused on her lovely face. "What's your name, honey?"

"Don't talk to him," Stuart whispered urgently.

"Daddy." Sam hushed him. "My name's Samantha," she said to Pray. "We need this job."

He looked from Sam to Stuart; then his gaze slid back to Sam and lingered. "For you, Samantha, I might be willing to excuse your father's behavior."

He lifted her chin with one hand to look at Sam's profile, studying her with an intensity that gave Joey chills.

"Amazing," he said softly, as if to himself. "You have a face the camera would love."

He bent to kiss Sam's cheek, then turned and walked away, trailed by his female retinue.

Silence had fallen over the crowd at Crafty while the scene played out. Now the buzz of their chatter filled the air like a swarm of insects as they filed back toward the set.

"You stay away from that devil," Stuart hissed.

"Daddy, please," Sam's expression looked pinched, but her tone was patient. "I wish you hadn't lost your temper. Remember what you told me before we started for California?"

"I won't say I'm sorry." The fire was back in Stuart's eyes. "That animal should be on a choke chain."

He stalked off toward his truck, parked behind the craft service area.

Sam watched her father with a mixture of affection and concern, then she turned to Joey. "He was so determined to come out here, I hoped this trip would be good for him, but I think it's only making things worse."

"A movie set can be a real pressure cooker," Joey said carefully. "Maybe not the best environment if your dad's working through some issues."

"You're probably right about that." Sam nodded solemnly.

Joey was trying to think of something reassuring to say when Eli came rushing through the back door of the cafe set, looking grim.

"Where's Stuart?" he demanded.

"You're not going to fire him." Joey didn't frame it as a question. "Stuart didn't do anything wrong; he was only standing up for himself. Pray even said he might be willing to forget the whole thing."

"Guess again," Eli said curtly, then turned his attention to Sam. "I need to talk to your father."

"He's over there, in his truck." She pointed toward the pickup. "He's probably having a smoke, to calm down. You want me to get him?"

"No, I'll go to him."

"I'm sorry we've caused you this trouble," she said in a small voice.

Eli nodded, then moved off to talk to Stuart.

Sam followed him with her gaze. "Daddy's never been the same since my sister passed away."

Her manner was so matter-of-fact she might have been reporting the weather.

"I'm so sorry," Joey said automatically.

"He tries to put up a good front for my sake, most of the time, anyway. But it broke his heart." Sam smiled sadly. "Sofia was his favorite."

Joey didn't know what to say. "That must be tremendously difficult for you and your family."

She could only imagine how painful the death of a sister would be, and the heartache of knowing Sofia was their father's favorite couldn't make the loss any easier for Sam.

"Daddy always said we were the three musketeers, but it's just the two of us now," Sam said wistfully. "My sister was an actress. That's why he wanted to come out here, to try to get a feeling for what her life was like."

Joey couldn't help being curious. She wanted to ask Sam about her sister's experience in the business, but that felt disrespectful under the circumstances, like digging for gossip.

"Now I'm the one who should say sorry." Sam seemed to shake herself out of her memories as she moved to gather up discarded plates and napkins. "I shouldn't complain to you about our troubles."

Joey's heart went out to the girl; apparently, her father had made it his mission to chase after a ghost and didn't seem to be thinking about his living daughter's best interests.

On impulse she said, "I know how hard it can be starting out someplace new, where you don't know a lot of people. If you ever need someone to talk to, I hope you'll call me. You have a crew list?"

"Sure, but I wouldn't want to be a bother."

"My cell phone's on the list, and that's what I'm trying to tell you: it's no bother."

"That's sweet of you." Sam ducked her head. "Thank you for sticking up for us."

Joey reached for her hand and squeezed it. Over Sam's shoulder, she saw Eli walking toward them. Stuart remained in his truck. She didn't want to quarrel with her ex, but she didn't want to leave Sam alone to absorb bad news.

Eli read her expression and patted the air in a calming gesture. "I talked to Stuart, and I think we've come to an understanding." He turned to Sam. "Your father and I agreed to a new set of ground rules."

"You mean, we're not getting fired?" she asked, wide-eyed.

"Not today."

She gave him a tentative nod. "Thank you."

"Do what you can to help your father stay on an even keel, okay?" he said.

"I will." Her eyes flicked to Joey. "And thank *you* again, for everything."

She left them to go talk to Stuart.

Eli looked at Joey and raised his eyebrows. "You headed back to base camp?"

Joey watched thoughtfully as Sam got into the truck with her father. "Probably a good idea."

"I'll walk you to the wardrobe trailer," he said.

The tension between them had tapered off since he'd spoken with Stuart.

"Bill told me about your car." He gave her a sidelong glance. "You have any idea who might have done it?"

"Not really." Joey's throat suddenly felt tight. The conversation with Sam had driven everything else from her mind, and for that bit of time, she'd forgotten her own problems. "But I'm not feeling up to an in-depth discussion, not if I want to be able to function for the rest of the day."

"We can't let this go; Bill's right about that." Eli made a sweeping motion. "I want to find whoever did this and fire them in front of the whole company."

"I won't fight you on that." Joey sighed and shook her head.

He frowned, then nodded slowly, allowing her the breathing room she asked for. "Let me know if something more occurs to you, or if something else happens."

She shrank from the thought. "I will, but can I ask you a question now?"

"I'm all ears."

"Why didn't you just tell me you weren't going to fire Stuart when you came looking for him back there?"

"Truth?" Eli gave a wry smile. "I'm still surprised that I didn't." She perked up at that. "Why the change of heart?"

"Would you believe I listened to you?" He hiked his shoulders. "I hope I made the right decision."

She couldn't help smiling a little. "Isn't His Highness going to have a cow when he finds out Stuart remains gainfully employed?"

"I don't think that's going to be a problem," Eli said coolly. "I took care of something for him on the last show we did together, so I'm going to call in that marker to keep Stuart and Samantha on the crew."

This was news to Joey. "I didn't know you worked with Pray before."

"His last movie. I took over after he fired the first six weeks into the shoot."

"That's the favor you're going to collect on?" She eyed him skeptically. "Pray doesn't seem like the grateful type."

"You're right about that; it was a separate issue and gratitude won't be his motivator," Eli said. "But trust me, you don't want to know the specifics, and you'll never see anything about it in print."

His walkie-talkie sputtered to life. "Eli Logan, we're ready for picture."

"Copy that. Coming your way." He sent her a brief wave and jogged toward the set.

Joey watched him go, thinking about the leverage he'd earned with Pray. Whatever he did to protect the director made Eli complicit, adding his name to the long list of people who were willing to overlook the corrupt behavior of a powerful man like Pray because it was easier, safer, or somehow served their own interests. It disgusted Joey to realize her name might belong there too.

Chapter Twenty

T he walk to base camp gave Joey time to think how her world had changed in the past few days. Nothing felt familiar or secure. Her workplace, where she'd always been comfortable, had become a combat zone.

She still couldn't guess who had graffitied her car, beyond the obvious fact that it was somebody with access to crew parking, which pretty much limited her choices to the shooting company. To make matters worse, she knew Bill had a point: if some rat was willing to mess with her car, what else would they do?

On top of all that, she was worried for Sam, now that Pray had his eye on her. But Joey had to ask herself if she was part of the problem, one of the enablers who allowed Pray to create a toxic environment on his set. She was ashamed that she'd "gone along to get along" and dressed the models to please him without raising a single objection.

Then again, if she refused to toe the company line, she'd be fired. That came through loud and clear in the message the studio sent Bill to deliver. She'd be blackballed as a troublemaker, or industry code: *not a team player*. Everybody knew what that meant. She'd lose her job, maybe even her career, and certainly any chance she had to get at the truth about Courtney's death. Doubt and suspicion would follow her until the murder was solved.

Her thoughts spun on a compulsive loop until she got back to the principal trailer. Bill was the only one on board, studying the preliminary call sheet for the following day's work.

"Is Dahlia around?" Joey asked. She needed to get out of her head for a while, give her mind a chance to wind down so she could think straight.

"She's up at the set." He checked his watch. "They're on the last setup, so we should be wrapped by eight at the latest."

"Are we moving on tomorrow?" she asked.

"Tentatively is what the prelim says. Looks like we're getting all the work we need here, unless Herr Director has another idea or wants more coverage of something. The shoot's been a little hairy, to say the least, but it helps to have Bernard back behind the camera."

That got her attention. "How's he doing?" she asked eagerly. "Have you seen him?"

"Just to say hello. He looks tired, but otherwise okay. They do seem to be moving along up there."

"Do you know if they're sticking with the one-line?"

She hoped they weren't going to stray too far from the short-form shooting schedule called the one-line that boiled down each workday to the basics: number of shots, scene numbers and locations, a one- or two-sentence description of the action, and the cast members who'd be involved. Big changes to that schedule could mean big trouble for her prep calendar.

"As far as I know," Bill said, "which means we'll be exterior downtown tomorrow, unless production decides that's going to create too much of a security risk."

"I didn't have to hide under the drop cloth on the ride from crew parking when I came back earlier," Joey said. "Maybe we're old news by now."

"Yeah, the photographers cleared out around midday, but that doesn't mean they won't be on our tails again tomorrow." Bill shook his head doubtfully. "Especially if we're shooting in a more exposed location."

Her heart sank, thinking about another paparazzi blitz. All at once, she felt caged in the cramped quarters of the trailer.

"I think I'll head up to set and check in with Dahlia, maybe watch the last shot," she said. "I'd like to say welcome back to Bernard, unless there's something I can do to pitch in here."

"Go for it," he said. "We're all buttoned up until wrap."

The sun was beginning to dip in the west as she made her way to the set. A portable work light flashed outside the cafe's front entrance, signaling the company was in the middle of a shot. Joey looked out over the Pacific, where the warm colors of the evening sky began to blend with the water at the horizon.

Hoping the ocean would work its magic on her ragged nerves, she stepped down to the sand, drawn by the endless procession of waves sweeping across the beach on the incoming tide. A small red sea star rode in on a swell as Joey strolled along the water's edge. It had been days since she'd walked the shoreline, and she was thinking how much she missed the sounds and smells of the sea when a shrill voice startled her.

"Returning to the scene of the crime?"

She pivoted to find Melanie Beale standing with her legs spread, like a parody of an Old West gunslinger.

"You about gave me a heart attack," she protested.

"Except you'd have to have a heart for that."

"Seriously?" Joey bristled. "What's your problem?"

"Don't play dumb!" Melanie said harshly. "As soon as I saw you head this way, I knew where you were going."

The sun was nearly down, and now Joey saw they were standing almost exactly on the spot where she discovered Courtney's body. Horrified, she clapped a hand over her mouth.

"Save the performance for the jury," Melanie snapped.

Joey stared at her through a glaze of indignation. "You can't believe I had anything to do with what happened to Courtney."

"I got news for you, I'm not the only one."

Joey knew there was no reasoning with the hatred she saw in the other woman's eyes.

"Excuse me." She made a move to pass.

"Not so fast." Melanie body-blocked her. "Courtney was my best friend, so I'm not falling for your act. She told me how jealous you were of Eli and her."

Joey tried to keep her tone civil. "If that's what Courtney thought, it was her imagination."

"You found out she was pregnant, didn't you?" Melanie's face was a mask of rage. "You couldn't stand she'd have that bond with Eli forever, so you killed her, you evil bitch!"

"You're insane," Joey whispered.

Suddenly, she couldn't get enough air. She spun and started trudging through the soft sand that led away from the water's edge, blood thudding in her head like a hammer.

Courtney was pregnant?

"Go ahead, run away!" Melanie shrieked. "You can't go far enough. By the time I'm finished, none of the actors will want anything to do with you!"

Outside the cafe set, Joey stopped to catch her breath, still reeling from the clash with Melanie. The work light beside the front door quit flashing, the signal it was safe to go in. But in the short space of time since she'd left the principal trailer, her world had changed again. She felt sickened that Courtney's killer had taken two lives.

Eli called from inside, "Picture's up!" alerting the onstage personnel.

"Action!" Pray said to start the roll, and the work light started flashing again.

Joey's cell buzzed with an incoming text. Still dazed, she looked down at the message:

For where there is envy and selfish ambition, there you find disorder and every evil practice.

A primal scream welled up in her. She felt trapped in some drug-dream hallucination, only she wasn't going to wake up from this nightmare, and the hits just kept coming.

She glared at her cell. The text came from the same number that sent the "wages of sin" message, but this time no audio file. She had to wonder if her troll was someone on the crew, maybe the same kind soul who vandalized her car. She didn't think it was Melanie; for one thing, the makeup artist had no trouble confronting her in person. Hats off to her for that.

Whoever her digital stalker was, they had a wicked sense of timing. Joey focused on the flashing work light, and knew she wasn't strong enough to go inside the cafe. Even if Melanie spoke for a small minority, there were people on the crew deluded enough to think Joey could have killed Courtney. For those who drank the Kool-Aid, it didn't matter that she'd been a hard worker and a reliable colleague; her good name and record were meaningless.

Instead of waiting for the next break in shooting to face down her detractors, she decided to go back to the trailer. This was shaping up to be a marathon, not a sprint. She needed to save her energy and be smart about how she used it.

Chapter
Twenty-One

As she hurried through base camp, Joey couldn't help wondering why there'd been no mention of Courtney's pregnancy in the media. It was the kind of story the tabloids would be blasting from every outlet, if they had it. Did that mean the police decided not to release the information, maybe because it had some bearing on their investigation?

But how do I know Melanie's telling the truth?

Once Joey started thinking clearly, that was a logical question. And the next: If Courtney was, in fact, pregnant, and she was having relations with both Eli and Pray . . . who was the father? Did Courtney even know?

She wondered what the two men knew about the situation. Pray obviously knew about Courtney's relationship with Eli: everybody did. But did he know she was pregnant (if she was)? Joey still couldn't believe Eli was aware of Courtney's affair with Pray, but did he know about her pregnancy (ditto, with the qualifier)?

She thought about his breakdown in her kitchen a few nights before. Was he mourning the loss of his child, as well as his lover? Maybe it was time to talk to him frankly about everything, including the affair with Pray, though she dreaded the idea.

But before she got into that loaded discussion, she wanted to try to verify Courtney's pregnancy, and her options to do that were limited. Asking the cops would be a fool's errand, and she couldn't talk to anybody on the movie without firing up the rumor mill, even though Melanie didn't seem to have that concern.

There was only one choice, but it was one she didn't relish. She dug her phone out of her pocket and searched her call history for Caleb Lisle's number. Even though their first call ended on a chilly note, he was her only hope.

His voice mail picked up on the first ring, and she left a brief message asking him to call her as soon as possible. Then she pocketed her phone and continued through base camp, feeling the charge of free-floating anxiety crackling in the air around her.

Bill was on his cell when she came in the door of the principal trailer. He waved to her urgently as he spoke into the phone. "Say again?"

He ran a hand through his hair as he listened. "Okay, I'll get back to you as soon as I have all the information on my end."

He closed his eyes, his face like a clenched fist as the person on the other side of the call had the last word. "Copy that. Give me a minute to locate my magic wand, and I'll get right on it." He ended the call and sent his phone sailing across the trailer.

"Tell me what's going on," Joey said.

"They want to bring the green screen work forward on the schedule." He rubbed his forehead like he was in pain. "How soon can we get Brooke, Fiske, and Cameron's superhero outfits ready? Can we fit them tomorrow?"

She keyed into the challenge. "I'll call Damir. When do we need them?"

"Wednesday."

"As in, next Wednesday?" She stared at him in disbelief. "That only gives us four days."

"They wanted to skip over the location work and start green screen tomorrow, but I told them that's impossible." Bill shook his head, looking blank. "Even if we work all weekend, I don't know how they expect us to pull this off."

Joey's personal troubles slid to the background as she focused on the problem, automatically breaking it down into the steps they needed to take.

"How many are we talking about: the first one for each, or do we need the multiples too? And what about stunts?"

"I need to look at the sequence again, but I think we have some room to negotiate with production about the shooting order." Bill blew out a breath as he calculated. "Let's say, one for each by Wednesday, but then we should see how fast we can get everything for those three characters, at least two of the multiples, and the stunts."

"Let me get on the phone to Damir right now, and we'll see what we can figure out." She glanced at him sharply. "You know it's going to cost us."

"Sure, and production will kick about it." He spread his hands and shrugged. "All we can do is present them with the information and let them make the call."

"Understood." She nodded. "I'm on it."

She knew one of the obstacles would be the fact that *UMPP* wasn't the only movie Hammer and Tongs had in their workroom. They were also making prototypes for yet another *X-Men* sequel.

"Remember how I asked you what it would cost to get Brooke and Fiske's first costumes ready early?" Joey said when she got Damir on the line.

"I hate it when you're psychic," he said.

"Only partly. I need to add Cameron in there too—one complete costume for each of them to shoot next Wednesday."

"You've got to be joking."

"I wish." She braced herself. "And that's not all."

"We're up against the deadlines already," Damir said coolly. "You know what's required to manufacture these costumes, even if the bozos you work for don't have a clue."

"I understand what you're saying," she replied. "But before you give me a hard no, let's break it down. First, can we fit the three principals tomorrow and fast-track one complete costume for each?"

"Yes, but finished by Wednesday? Only with massive overtime, and that means through the weekend."

She stayed quiet and let him grind it down on his own.

"I'll have to back-burner everything else in the workroom, including the rest of your order for the other characters, and I'll need to bring in additional help to get it done." He paused. "Can we schedule final fittings for all three actors Tuesday evening?"

She signaled across the trailer to Bill and gave him a thumbs up. "If that's what we have to do."

"It's either that or final fits on delivery, and I don't think we want that."

"I'm with you one hundred percent." She grabbed a manila wardrobe tag and started making notes. "Can you get me the additional costs as soon as possible so I can pass them on to production?"

"Since you called the other day, I've been mulling that over, and I can tell you to pull this off by Wednesday, it's going to be double for everything, at minimum. But your producers have to understand we won't have exact figures until the work's done."

"Fair enough." She wasn't going to quibble about money, even vast amounts of it, when she was asking for a Hail Mary effort. "How fast can you have their multiples and stunts?"

"You're killing me, Joey."

"Just let me know what's possible," she said. "I'll tell production it's going to be double the cost for the three costumes we're getting for Wednesday, with the understanding that number could go higher. Then as soon as you can, get me the information about completing those three characters."

"You got it," he said crisply. "Let me get to work on this, and I'll call you back."

The shooting company wrapped while Joey was on the phone, but the costume crew still had to prep for the overnight move from the beach to the new location in downtown Los Angeles. They had to lock down the clothing racks, then secure all the boxes and drawers on the two wardrobe trailers with bungee cords to prevent any damage on the trip across town.

Once the trailers were closed up for the night, Joey walked with the other costumers to the shuttle for crew parking. As they stood waiting to board the next van, Zephyr pulled her aside.

"Can I talk to you alone for a minute?" She glanced around anxiously.

"Of course." Joey nodded. "What's going on?"

Zephyr leaned in and lowered her voice. "I heard Melanie Beale talking to Brooke earlier in her trailer."

Joey got the picture, and all the problems she put on hold when the scheduling crisis hit came back at her full force. But she didn't want Zephyr to see she was upset.

"Don't let her bother you," she said mildly. "We don't need to waste time worrying about Melanie's big mouth."

"She shouldn't get away with spreading lies about you," Zephyr fumed. "I told her that, too, right in front of Brooke."

Joey put her arm around the younger woman. "I appreciate you sticking up for me, but don't get in the middle of this. We need to keep our minds on our work and ignore the haters. Let them be the ones mucking around in the gutter."

"If you say so." She didn't look convinced. "But I don't want to see you get hurt."

"You're a good friend, you know that?"

Zephyr flashed a shy smile. "You too."

Joey tried to put the day behind her once she got in her car, but fat chance of that. Even worse, she couldn't stop thinking about Melanie and her smear campaign, as if she didn't have enough to worry about.

"That's it," she said aloud. "Practice what you preach. She gets no free space in my head, no more of my energy and attention."

She had to trust the relationships she'd built with the actors would stand up to this test. She worked with them closely and knew them even better than she did many of the crew. Trying to fight fire with fire would only make things worse, and it wasn't her style, anyway.

She switched on NPR and tried to get interested in the *TED Radio Hour* as she pulled onto PCH. It was almost nine o'clock, and though the road was still busy, traffic had eased off from rush hour gridlock.

The TED Talk was about "the next global agricultural revolution," and she was only half listening to the broadcast when a light popped up on her dashboard, the dreaded tire pressure symbol. Joey groaned and switched off the radio.

She'd had problems with the pressure calibration a year ago when she bought the car, but swapping out a faulty sensor seemed to do the trick. Whatever the issue, she was only a few miles from the trailer park and hoped she could make it home without having to pull over on the freeway, especially in the dark.

A minute or so later, she felt the tire begin to drag, so definitely a flat. The stretch of PCH where she found herself was one of those areas without streetlights or businesses strung along either side of the road. She thought about trying to make it to the next cluster of buildings, but the flaccid flap of rubber against the pavement told her she was out of time. Braking gently, she steered the car onto the shoulder of the freeway.

She turned on the dome light and was fishing in her purse to get the number for Triple A when her car was suddenly flooded with white light. Startled, she checked the rearview mirror and saw a dark SUV pulled onto the shoulder directly behind her, with its headlights trained on her car.

Joey waited, eyes fixed on the SUV. The wall of light obscured whatever was going on inside the other vehicle, and she couldn't decide what to do. She wanted to let them know she was calling Triple A, but she didn't want to get out of her car. Nobody got out of the SUV to approach her, but the headlights stayed on. The intense brightness made her feel exposed and vulnerable on the side of the darkened road, like a sitting duck.

That thought settled the matter for her. Maybe the SUV's driver was a good Samaritan who'd stopped to help a fellow traveler in need, but she wasn't going to take that chance, not after what she'd been through the past few days.

She dialed 911.

"My car has a flat tire, and I've pulled onto the shoulder of PCH, northbound near Paradise Cove. An SUV pulled in behind me, and I feel like this could be a bad situation. It's an isolated stretch of road."

"Do you feel threatened?" the operator asked.

"I don't feel safe, let's put it that way." Joey cursed the surge of adrenaline that made her voice shake. "The other car's stopped on the shoulder behind me, but I can't see who's driving. Nobody's gotten out or tried to communicate with me so far."

"Maybe they're waiting for some sign from you."

"Ma'am, I'm alone on the side of a dark freeway in a disabled car." She tried to stay calm. "I'm not going to get out to talk to some random stranger."

"Is there more than one person in the other vehicle?"

"I can't tell. They've got their brights pointed right at my car. I can't see much of anything and I've . . ." She searched for the right words. "I've had some trouble the past couple of days, and there are people who might want to hassle me."

"Then stay in your car and lock the doors," the operator said.

"You don't have to tell me twice." Joey swallowed hard, trying to steady her nerves. "How soon will anybody be able to get here?"

"We have your position, and help's on the way. You should be able to see their lights any time now."

Behind her, the driver's side door of the SUV swung open, then a man stepped out. Tall and wide-bodied, he had a dark mane of shoulder-length hair, but she couldn't see his face. He rapped on the roof of the vehicle, and the passenger side door opened on his signal. Joey sat with her eyes riveted on the rearview mirror, hardly breathing.

"They're getting out." Her own voice sounded strange to her, thin and far away. "I don't . . . I can't wait." The panic she'd been fending off choked her. "I'll drive on the rims if I have to."

Her hand shook as she reached for the keys hanging in the ignition.

"Sit tight," the operator said in her ear.

She saw the blur of lights in her mirror before she heard the sirens, syncopated dots of red and blue about a mile up the road, racing toward her through the dark.

Her followers saw them at the same time. The passenger door closed again, then the big man got back in the SUV. He flicked on his turn signal, pulled smoothly into the flow of traffic on PCH without haste and proceeded up the road.

Chapter
Twenty-Two

"I couldn't see much because he kept his headlights on, even after he pulled up behind me," Joey said.

"But you're sure it was an SUV?" The younger of the responding sheriff's deputies had sandy hair and looked like he'd be more at home on a surfboard than in a patrol car.

"Yes, I'm sure it was an SUV, but I couldn't tell you what make." Joey wondered why cops always had to ask the same questions a dozen times.

"How about the color?"

"Definitely a dark-colored SUV," she said. "Maybe black or dark gray."

"Or blue, green, even maroon?" The older deputy wasn't so patient. He hadn't been solicitous to begin with, and he became downright surly when she couldn't offer much in the way of a description of the SUV or its driver.

"I suppose," Joey said. "I only know it wasn't white or silver."

"That sure narrows it down," he muttered.

"The man who got out—what can you tell us about his appearance?" The younger fellow seemed to be trying to make up for his partner's rudeness.

"He was tall and very broad across the shoulders, like a weight lifter. Shoulder-length hair." Joey closed her eyes, trying to call up the image in her rearview mirror. "I'm almost certain he was white." She frowned. "But I couldn't see his face."

The older deputy gave a snort and headed back to their patrol car.

"I wish I could give you a better description," she said, "of the man and the car."

"Don't mind him," the younger deputy said. "He gets testy, but he's good at his job."

"I guess he thinks I'm wasting your time, but I'm awfully glad you showed up when you did. Thanks for getting here so fast."

"No worries." He looked back over his shoulder toward the patrol car. "What about the passenger in the SUV? Did you get a look at him?"

"All I saw was the door swing open when the driver knocked on the roof. I couldn't even tell you if it was a man or woman inside the car."

"I don't suppose you got a look at the license plate when they pulled away?"

"I was too rattled to think about that." Joey bit her lip, wishing she'd had the presence of mind to notice those details.

He bobbed his head sympathetically. "Could you please step out so we can see if there's any damage to your car?"

He opened the door for her and stepped back so she could get out. Her legs were rubbery, but otherwise she felt okay.

"You have any pain?" he asked.

"No, but I'm a little shaky." She tried to smile. "Nerves, I guess."

He motioned for her to precede him. "Have you had anything alcoholic to drink this evening?"

She stopped in her tracks and looked back at him. "What are you implying?"

His tone shifted to something more official. "Ma'am, it's standard procedure to ask."

The feeling of relief that had come with the deputies' appearance on the scene drained away. "I understand you're only doing your job," she said. "And no, no alcohol of any kind."

He frowned, and she knew he was trying to decide if he should breathalyze her. She could have made it easy by offering to take the test, but she clamped her mouth shut and let him make the call.

He trained his flashlight on the ground in front of her. "Be careful of your footing. This shoulder's pretty rough."

"I don't think there's any damage other than the flat tire," she said, trying to keep any emotion out of her voice.

The deputy bent to inspect the front driver's side tire and gave a low whistle. "When did you say you started having trouble with your car?"

"Right after I left work."

"You didn't notice you've got four nails punched into the sidewall of your front tire?" He focused the light on the area around the hubcap. Four shiny nail heads, neatly spaced, were embedded in the rubber.

"And what happened to your driver's side door?" He stepped back and flicked the flashlight over the splotch of gray primer, then put the light on her face. "What's really going on with you?"

She flinched, and her defenses went up. "Is that an official question?"

"Does it need to be?" His voice was stern.

"Not as far as I'm concerned." She held out her hand. "You've been very helpful and patient, but it's been a long day. I don't have anything I can add to what I've told you."

The older deputy came stalking toward them, looking even more sour than before. "Talk to you a minute?" he said to his partner.

"'Scuse us," the younger fellow said. The two of them stepped away to confer.

The older guy held out his cell phone, and they studied the screen together for several minutes. At one point, the younger deputy stole a look at her, but turned away when she caught his eye. Finally, the two finished examining the phone. The older guy went back to the patrol car without even glancing at Joey.

The younger deputy appeared to be thinking things over as he approached her again. "You've been in the news a lot lately."

Joey just looked at him without offering any comment.

"May I speak candidly, Miss . . . ?"

"Jessop." She nodded. "Of course."

"I haven't jumped to any conclusions about what happened here tonight. There's not enough information to be able to sort that out, but my partner thinks you're playing some kind of game for the attention."

She started to protest, but he held up a hand to silence her.

"If you wanted to whip up some drama, having a police report to back up your story about being stalked, or chased, or whatever, would be one way to do it, if you take my meaning." He fixed her with a hard look. "So consider this a warning. I guarantee my partner'll be keeping an eye out for anything you might post about this on social media, and if he finds you making hay online, he'll slap you with a citation for placing a false emergency call."

"You think I pounded those nails into my own tire?" Joey asked coldly.

"I'm not prepared to say that." The deputy shrugged and nodded toward the patrol car. "But my partner is."

She felt a pang of frustration. There'd be no way to convince these two she was anything but a fraud.

"What's more," the deputy continued, "he thinks you waved off someone who stopped to help so you could get your incident report on file. That way you'd have a story to tell tomorrow to keep yourself in the spotlight."

He opened the driver's side door of her car and gestured for her to get it. "I talked him into letting you slide this one time. But my advice is, call Triple A and get them to change your tire, then go home and keep this thing to yourself."

Chapter Twenty-Three

L ate that night, Joey lay in bed staring at the ceiling while she thought through the whole lousy day: Eli's fight with the photographers, the vandalism to her car, Stuart's face-off with Pray, Melanie flipping out, the mysterious SUV, and the humiliating encounter with the deputies, all in less than twenty-four hours. She dreaded what the next day might bring.

Finally, sometime after one in the morning, she gave up on sleep and sat with her laptop at the desk in the sunroom. She'd sworn off logging onto her Instagram and Twitter accounts to spare herself the social media persecution, so she needed to come up with some online alternatives to while away her insomnia.

She considered sending an email to Caleb but nixed that idea; better to let him think about the voice mail she already left before she reached out again. Then she remembered Sam's sister, the actress who'd died; that was a subject that grabbed her. If the sister did any legitimate work in film or TV, her profile should be on IMDb. Joey might be able to satisfy her curiosity without asking Sam a lot of painful questions.

But she couldn't recall the sister's name. She knew it started with an S. An S-O sound. Sonya? No, Sophia, or Sofia. Hoping the girl used her own last name professionally, she typed *Sophia Campbell* into an IMDb search and was rewarded with links to three profiles for *Sophia/Sofia Campbell*.

Joey started at the top, opening them one by one. When she clicked on the second Sofia with an *f* Campbell, she felt a thrill of recognition and knew she'd found Sam's sister. The profile page, featuring the actress's headshot, filled her laptop's screen, and the family resemblance was unmistakable.

The young woman in the photograph gazed directly into the camera as though she could see through the lens into the soul of the observer. Sofia wasn't smiling, but somehow managed to appear both worldly and vulnerable. Her dates of birth and death showed below her picture: (May 11, 2000–January 1, 2022).

The IMDb website sometimes included a cause of death, so Joey clicked on her biographical details, but she found no reference to the manner of Sofia's death on the first day of a new year, four months before her twenty-second birthday.

"Whatever happened to you?" Joey murmured as she scrolled to the actress's screen credits.

It wasn't a long list. The record of her work history in Hollywood spanned only three years, mostly one-shot day-playing roles on TV shows Joey had never heard of. But two credits at the top of the page made her sit up and take notice. Sofia had roles in two Marcus Pray films, and the order of their placement on the page meant they were the last credited film work of her young life.

Joey sat back and crossed her arms. This unexpected connection between the Campbells and Pray raised a lot of questions she wasn't sure she wanted to ask. She'd only watched a couple of Pray's films, and then only because she felt obligated before she started work on *UMPP*, so Joey wasn't familiar with these movies or Sofia's roles.

She clicked on the earlier of her two credits, released Christmas of 2019, the second entry in Pray's blockbuster *Extinction* sci-fi franchise, *Extinction: Mutant Galaxy*. She studied the lineup of the cast and read the synopsis to find Sofia's character was low on the roster, though definitely a speaking role.

Then she went back to look at the information for the other Pray film Sofia appeared in, *Extinction: Battleground Earth*. For that movie, she'd been elevated to the second female lead.

Joey wondered why Sam hadn't mentioned Sofia worked with Pray. Was that because she was shy, or was there something else that kept her from talking about it? She closed her eyes, thinking about how to dig into that question.

She logged onto Instagram. There were six accounts registered to various Sofias with an *f* Campbell, and within minutes, she pulled up the one that belonged to her Sofia. Joey was stunned by an assortment of joyful images that showed a happy young woman in love with her life and, it appeared, with Marcus Pray. For a period of six months, until a few weeks before her death, Sofia and the Hollywood mogul were photographed together at a number of public appearances and industry events, though Joey had found no record of these photos online, nor were any of the pictures posted to Pray's Instagram.

Even more fascinating were the private moments Sofia had documented and shared with her followers: selfies with Pray in the kitchen cooking pasta, walking on the beach, and snuggling together on a leather sectional with two giant brindle mastiffs lounging beside them. Sofia glowed with happiness and Pray looked more natural and relaxed than Joey would have thought possible, given what she knew of the man. Here was the appearance of a relationship in full bloom, so different from the pattern Kathleen assigned Pray as a sexual predator without the capacity for loving connection.

Was it possible he'd been a different man with Sofia?

And how had they managed to avoid public scrutiny? Cinderella stories are money in the bank to the tabloids, but Joey hadn't found any mention of the relationship when she looked for Pray's romantic history, no articles in *People*, *Us*, *TMZ*, or any other gossip outlet.

She scrolled through more of the online album but found nothing that hinted at the end of the story. The pictures were a gallery of memories frozen in time, and a profound sadness stole over her, looking at Sofia's brilliant smile as she and Pray stood with their arms around each other on the terrace of a beach house, sunlight sparkling on the ocean behind them.

Inevitably, she landed on the questions she'd been circling: How much did Stuart and Sam know about Sofia's romance with the famous director, and what did Pray know about them?

Joey hadn't seen anything to indicate Pray and the Campbells knew each other. Sam hadn't said a word about it, despite the personal confidences she shared with Joey. When Stuart confronted Pray the day before, there was no sign they'd ever met.

And yet . . . Joey closed her eyes, recalling the scene. Had Pray made the connection? Could that have been the reason he considered overlooking Stuart's defiance (if he had), even briefly? Sam was blonde, Sofia a brunette, but they had the same remarkable hazel eyes; and although Campbell was common enough, they had the same last name.

Joey remembered the way Pray studied Sam's profile and how edgy that made her feel. At the time, she thought he was doing his usual ogling routine, and his "amazing" remark was an offhand opinion. But now the episode took on new stomach-churning significance. The more she thought about it, the less she understood what was going on between those three people; she only knew it wasn't good.

The last post to Sofia's Instagram was Thanksgiving weekend, 2021. Three publicity stills from the gala premiere of *Extinction: Battleground Earth* showed her with the other leading cast members posed on the red carpet. Pray wasn't in any of the shots, and though Sofia smiled for the cameras, there was little life in her eyes.

The photos racked up over 100,000 likes and comments from her followers, but Sofia hadn't replied to any of them. Joey knew from her account activity, that was unusual for the actress. She seemed eager to engage with her fans and appeared to enjoy those exchanges.

That was it. No photos from any after-parties following the premiere, no pictures from the Thanksgiving holiday, nor from Christmas that year. No more pictures, period. Six weeks later she was dead. But how?

Joey could go to work the next day and ask Sam what happened to her sister, but she wasn't sure a direct question was the best way to handle this.

She tackled the problem by searching online obituaries for Sofia Campbell, but of the dozen or so results that popped up, none was a match. She tried again, typing *Obituary: Sofia Campbell, Los Angeles, CA*, and once again came up empty.

For about half an hour, she fiddled with her search, getting specific with publications, *Sofia Campbell Obituary: Los Angeles Times*, *Sofia Campbell Obituary: Hollywood Reporter*, *Variety*, and a raft of entertainment websites.

Nothing.

She racked her brain but couldn't remember talking with Sam about where they came from, so scratch the search for a hometown newspaper. Nevertheless, she kept at it, expanding her search to ferret out articles or public records mentioning *Sofia Campbell/death/ January 1, 2022*.

She even went through the Homicide Report in the *LA Times* for January that year. The report gives a monthly catalogue: name, age, cause, and location of death for every homicide in Los Angeles County, but there was no mention of Sofia Campbell. Joey had to wonder if she died by accident or some natural cause. That wasn't out of the question, despite her age. Of course, there was another alternative to consider, but she really didn't want to think about that.

She leaned back in her chair and stretched, feeling spent. There were other sources she could check during business hours. IMDb published the date of Sofia's death; maybe they could shed some light. And she would have belonged to SAG, the Screen Actors Guild; they'd have the name of her agent.

To be thorough before she logged off, Joey clicked once more on Sofia's biographical details to read more carefully through all the snippets of largely useless information: special skills and talents, nicknames, personal quotes. But at the bottom of the page, an item with a highlighted name, *daughter of Stuart Campbell*, snagged her attention like a flashing neon sign. How had she missed that the first time she looked?

Stuart's name in highlight meant he had his own IMDb page. She clicked on his name for the link, and presto—there he was, hiding in plain sight. In the late '80s through the early 2000s, Stuart had been a busy stuntman on a long list of TV (mostly cop) shows and a handful of low-budget features.

"What the heck?" she yelped loud enough to wake Bigfoot, who'd been sleeping near her feet.

Joey didn't believe for a minute that coincidence brought an ex-stuntman to work in craft service on a movie his dead daughter's lover was directing. That raised the question of how much Stuart already knew about Sofia's life, and maybe more to the point, her death.

Her cell phone buzzed, and she grabbed it up after she checked CallerID. "Caleb?" She looked at the clock on her computer: twenty past two in the morning. "How are you? It must be what, around four your time?"

"Yeah, it's late," he said. "But you sounded anxious on your message, so I just thought . . ."

"No, I appreciate the call," she said quickly. "I have an important question." She hesitated. "But it's uncomfortable, and I'm sorry for that."

"Ask away," he said. "Can't be any worse than what we already talked about, right?"

She nodded to herself; he had a point. "What would you say if I told you Courtney might have been pregnant?"

"Who told you that?" he asked, suddenly sharp as a razor.

"A self-described friend of hers."

"That's interesting." His tone didn't have the brotherly warmth she might have expected. "That could explain a few things."

"What things?" she asked, confused by his reaction.

"You know what? I think we should get together to talk about this in person," he said briskly. "Better than on the phone."

"Are you planning to come out here . . ." She paused to choose her words. "To take her back home?"

He ignored the question. "What's your schedule tomorrow?"

"Tomorrow," she repeated. "What time is your flight?"

"I'm already in town."

Her heart jumped. "Since when?"

"Let's talk about this tomorrow," he said. "When are you free?"

She felt like she'd been kicked in the head. "I'm working all day."

"Call me when you're done," he said. "Doesn't matter what time, I'll meet you wherever's convenient."

"Okay," she said uncertainly, but he'd ended the call.

Chapter
Twenty-Four

C aleb's strange phone call hung like a cloud over Joey's morning. His tone put her off both times they'd spoken; he just didn't sound like a grieving brother. Now she felt torn about meeting him. She wondered how long he'd been in town and why she assumed he was someplace else. For all she knew, he lived in Los Angeles, and that made her feel stupid, ambushed, and unprepared to sit down with him. But she had already agreed to the meeting, and he was still her best hope to learn more about Courtney, even though his attitude made her leery of him.

After his call, she lay awake most of the night, thinking about Stuart and Sam, trying to convince herself they were there to do exactly what Sam claimed, learn more about Sofia's life in Hollywood. But she wasn't buying that line, much as she wanted to. She suspected that Stuart, at least, had a hidden agenda that somehow took aim at Pray, and she worried that Sam could get caught in the middle. She just wasn't sure what it all meant or what, if anything, she should do about it.

Work felt like a reprieve from her doubts and speculation, even if it was a mixed blessing. First up was a phone call to coordinate with Hammer and Tongs, which Joey placed as soon as she got to the movie's base camp in downtown LA.

"Damir says they can fit all three actors any time after noon today." She switched her cell to speaker while she consulted Bill and

Dahlia. The three of them were gathered on the poop deck of the principal trailer.

"Let's do it at three," Dahlia said. "Then we'll call it a day after the fittings."

"As long as we can get those first costumes for Wednesday," Bill said.

"You hear all that?" Joey said to the phone.

"Three it is," Damir said. "And Wednesday works as long as we can do those final fits we talked about on Tuesday."

Joey looked to Bill for confirmation.

"Whatever it takes." He nodded. "Production's given the approval."

"We're good to go, then. See you at three." Damir ended the call.

"I'll contact the actors to set the time," Joey said. "I texted all three of them yesterday, and they promised to keep today open. This may work out better than we thought."

"Once we get the background and stunts dressed, we're set for the day down here," Bill said. "You can take off any time after we get the first shot if you need to get ready for those fittings."

Joey checked her watch: eight o'clock, straight up. Her job was to think ahead and be prepared, but right now, that meant she also needed to be ready to handle a slew of unpleasant possibilities that could be waiting just outside the trailer. Plenty of people seemed to think she was guilty and needed to be punished. Some confronted her openly, but others chose to operate in the shadows. She felt as though she was under siege, and both her dependable safe havens, work and home, had been breached by hostile forces.

The shooting company was set up in the gritty heart of downtown. Base camp was in one of the large public parking lots haphazardly strung along Figueroa Street like so many missing teeth. Joey stepped out of the trailer to text the actors, then spent the next hour helping to dress stuntmen and extras in their costumes. The company would spend most of the day shooting portions of a high-speed car chase. A section of Broadway was cordoned off for the movie, to the frustration of drivers already dealing with the gridlocked one-way streets in the busy hub of the city.

The day's work could have been shot by a second unit film crew. Most of the action called for trained stunt people to double for the actors, along with a crowd of regular background players who wouldn't directly participate in the choreographed stunt sequence. But Pray wanted to shoot the chase himself, so it stayed with first unit. That was the main reason this ended up being a perfect day to schedule the superhero costume fittings. No principal actors were called, so the fittings didn't conflict with the work on set.

Once all the players were camera ready, Joey and Dahlia walked east along Seventh Street to look at the primary shooting location. Off-duty motorcycle cops working security for the movie stood post at every intersection, with no paparazzi in sight.

"Looks like the studio's going all out to keep the media off our backs today," Joey said, feeling cautiously optimistic.

Dahlia nodded. "Trying to take the reins in hand. They're fine with the extra publicity, even if it's sordid; but in the end, they want to be the ones shaping the coverage."

"I haven't heard anything since the announcement about the big reward they put up for information." Joey gave her a sidelong glance. "Do you know if anybody's come forward?"

"No idea." The designer shook her head. "Between you and me, I have a feeling that was a grand gesture with very little substance behind it."

Joey raised her eyebrows. "You mean, a publicity stunt?"

Dahlia shrugged. "Potato, po-tah-toe."

Less than a block from base camp, they passed a young woman nursing a baby under a pop-up tent bleached almost white by the sun. Two other children huddled nearby, hollow-eyed and thin. Homeless encampments were now part of every street in the downtown landscape, and the sidewalk bivouacs continued to spread each year. The city center was a study in contrasts, where the very wealthy and very poor lived side by side. Luxury high-rises overlooked the ragged tent cities that squatted on the streets below.

Joey dug a ten dollar bill out of her pocket and held it out to the nursing mother, who accepted it wordlessly.

"I never give money away on the street," Dahlia sniffed.

Joey looked back over her shoulder. "Well, it's not going to change their lives, but maybe it'll get the kids some breakfast."

"Or she'll use it to buy drugs."

Joey felt a flash of irritation. "Not everybody down here's an addict; some of them are just poor and out of options."

"You're too soft-hearted for your own good."

"Funny you should say that, because lately I feel like I'm getting more cynical by the minute."

"Best to be in our business," Dahlia said lightly. "You won't get disappointed that way."

Somehow the locations department had cleared the homeless tents and lean-tos from the six blocks of Broadway barricaded for the day's shoot. Joey hoped that meant more street people were eating on the movie company's dime that morning.

Eli was talking with Pray, the stunt coordinator, and his assistant in the middle of Broadway. Picture cars, vehicles leased or purchased by production to be used in the movie, lined both sides of the street while the props, camera, and lighting crews worked on last-minute rigging to get them ready for the first shot.

Stunt players in costume began to appear on set. The set costumers weren't far behind, rolling a rack hung with clothing multiples for the featured stunts. Joey went over to make sure they had everything they needed to start the day.

Across the street, she saw Sam Campbell rushing to set up craft service behind the canopy that shielded video village. The girl looked stressed, and there was no sign of her father. Joey knew she should mind her own business, but she didn't want to see Sam struggle, so she crossed the street.

"You need a hand over here?" she said.

"What?" Sam looked up in consternation. "No, I'm fine." She frowned as she bent to lift a double flat of water.

"Let me help you with that." Joey moved to grab the other side of the case.

Lionel, the second AD, approached them. "You're going to have to move your setup," he said to Sam. "Marcus doesn't want extra people congregating behind the monitor."

"Where do you want me to go?" The young woman looked flustered. "I thought he wanted us nearby."

"But not directly behind him," Lionel said.

"It needs to be someplace I won't be caught in any of the shots," she said.

He scanned the area. "Let me figure this out and get back to you."

"You think you could get some muscle to help her make the move?" Joey asked. "She's trying to do this on her own."

"Sure, of course." He thumbed his walkie and called for the DGA trainee.

Sam blew out a breath. "Thanks."

"You okay?" Joey peered at her. "Where's your dad?"

"He'll be along," Sam said vaguely. "He had something he needed to do this morning."

Joey wanted to talk to her about the information she found online the night before, but this wasn't the time.

"Joey! Hey, Joey Jessop!"

She squinted against the morning sun to see who was calling her name. Malo stood kitty-corner across the intersection, waving to her.

"Hey, yourself," she called, a little surprised by how glad she was to see him.

He crossed the street to join her.

"Malo, this is Sam, a very important person to know on set," she said.

The boy held out his hand. "Nice to meet you, Sam."

"Likewise," she said.

"Are you busy?" Joey asked. "Sam may need some help in a minute to move her craft service setup."

"I'm available," he said. "Bill sent me down with an envelope full of paperwork for the ADs, but I think he just wanted to give me the chance to see all this."

He gazed out at the busy street, eyes wide behind the Buddy Holly glasses. "I've never been on a big set like this before."

For the first time, Joey realized she'd never asked the kid much about himself, and she felt bad about that.

"I just figured you had experience with big productions," she said, impressed more than ever by his gumption. "You always seem like you know what you're doing, no matter what we throw at you."

He hiked his shoulders. "Life experience can be a great teacher."

There was no joy in the way he said it, and she was struck by the thought that he was too young to have learned to adapt so skillfully.

"Joey!"

She looked up to see Dahlia waving to her from the other side of the street. "They're placing the background for the first shot."

"Can you stick around for a while?" she said to Malo. "I'd like to talk to you some more."

"Sure. You want me to see about helping her out?" He gestured to Sam, who was busy repacking her craft service supplies for the move.

"That'd be great if you don't mind. Then head over to video village, and I'll meet you there in a bit. We can watch the monitor together."

"Cool!" he said happily.

Joey patted him on the shoulder, then moved up the street to join Dahlia. They stationed themselves where they could check all the stunts and background players as the ADs placed them on set. Each would get a final look to make sure every detail was ready for camera. They paid special attention to the pedestrians who'd be featured in the shot.

"Will we be okay if they pull drivers from the cars to use as pedestrians?" Dahlia asked.

"We dressed them all head-to-toe for exactly that reason," Joey replied. "Whatever the day brings, we'll be fine."

"All the women have heels?" The designer pursed her lips. "And I mean good ones, nothing cheap or clunky."

"Absolutely." Joey wondered if Dahlia was feeling insecure about something, but she didn't let her thoughts linger on the topic.

The first shot up was an ambitious two-minute sequence with a Ferrari and a Maserati racing hell-bent down Broadway, zigzagging through city traffic. In addition to the A camera, both cars had dashcams mounted to film the scene from the drivers' POVs.

"Everything looks fine for now," Dahlia said. "Let's get over to video village before Marcus's B-squad gets the best seats."

Joey did a last visual sweep of the street, just as one of the stunt drivers a couple of blocks away got out of his car and motioned to a set PA for assistance. The PA got on his walkie, and Joey waited to see if a problem was brewing. Moments later, a big man emerged from behind the barricades posted along Broadway to talk with the PA and the driver—a big, broad-shouldered guy with a mane of flowing dark hair. Joey felt a tug on her visual memory.

"Hey!" She started up the street in his direction.

"Clear the set!" Eli shouted. "Picture's up!"

"Joey, where are you going?" Dahlia called.

The big man retreated behind the barricades, the stunt driver got back in his car, and Joey stopped mid-stride. A showdown would have to wait. She had nothing except her intuition to rely on, but deep down, she knew this was the guy who had pulled up behind her the night before on the shoulder of PCH.

And now she knew where he was.

Chapter
Twenty-Five

Video village was already crowded with Pray's female entourage wearing the usual—as little as possible. Most of the crew did their best to ignore the B-squad, as they'd been dubbed, short for "Wannabe," no small feat when they were constantly front and center, vying for Pray's attention.

Joey spotted Malo waiting just outside the canopy that sheltered the equipment and crew from the elements. She motioned him to join them as she and Dahlia squeezed into a corner behind the script supervisor, who sat to Pray's left, to watch the action on the monitor. But it soon became clear they'd boxed themselves into the middle of a disagreement between two B-squad girls.

"Marcus said I could sit to his right today," a sweet-faced blonde said, not so sweetly.

"You were planted there most of yesterday afternoon," complained a redhead with porcelain skin.

"And he said I'm his good luck charm because we got so much work done," the blonde replied.

Dahlia glanced sideways at Joey. "It's going to be a long morning."

But Joey was distracted, thinking about the mystery man from the SUV. He was apparently attached to the movie in some capacity, but she hadn't seen him on set before, so not part of the regular crew. She'd ask Eli at the first opportunity; it was his job to know everybody who worked on the film.

The first shot was delayed by a last-minute discussion between Pray, the DP, and the stunt coordinator, with Eli and Lionel listening in.

Meanwhile, the rest of the B-squad waded into the seating dispute, talking over each other like children squabbling on the playground:

"Some of us haven't had a chance to sit next to Marcus at all."

"It's Marcus's decision; he can sit next to whoever he wants."

"We should draw numbers and take turns so it's fair."

"You're just jealous."

"And you're annoying."

"Here he comes, so let's ask him." The sweet-faced blonde saw Pray striding toward video village. "Marcus, tell them I'm sitting by you today."

A chorus of protests burst from the other girls.

"All of you, shut up!" Pray made a slashing motion across his throat. "Get back to the trailer and wait for me there."

"But Marcus, don't you need your good luck charm?" The blonde tried a pretty pout and latched onto his arm.

Angrily Pray shook her off. She stumbled and took some B-squadders down with her as they toppled like bowling pins onto the pavement.

"I said shut up!" Pray stood over the frightened women, fists clenched.

Joey started to shoulder her way past Dahlia, but the designer grabbed her arm. "Don't you dare move," she hissed.

Frustrated, Joey snapped an irate look at her; Dahlia just shook her head. "You'll only make it worse for them."

Eli stepped between Pray and the models. "Marcus, you need to calm down," he said quietly.

"You shut up too!" Pray turned his fury on Eli. "And get those bimbos off my set. I'm sick to death of them."

"You're being a dick." Eli kept his voice pitched low, but everyone in video village could hear him. "You need to get hold of yourself."

"Don't tell me what I need to do, tweaker," Pray said scornfully.

The two men stood glaring at each other, then Eli broke eye contact.

"Come on, ladies, let's get you back to base camp." He bent to help the blonde to her feet. The girl's face was smeared with tears; both her knees were skinned and bleeding.

Lionel moved to help two of the other models as he spoke into his walkie, alerting the medic. The young women looked smaller and frailer than they had only minutes before—just girls, really. Joey felt sorry for them, and for any uncharitable thoughts she'd had about them.

"Take them to base camp," Eli said to Lionel. "Stay with them, get them cleaned up, and we'll figure this out later."

Lionel looked at him doubtfully, but he rounded up the young women and led them in a small, sad parade toward the parking lot on Figueroa.

"Show's over." Pray clapped his hands to get everybody's attention. "Let's shoot this." He put on his headphones.

Eli scanned the faces around him and caught Joey's eye. She nodded to show her support, but he quickly looked away.

Dahlia leaned close to her. "Shake it off and focus," she said coolly. "Eyes on the monitor."

Joey stiffened and didn't reply. Malo stood on her other side, his expression closed. She wanted to reassure him, but she didn't know what she could honestly say. She felt mortified that she continued to stand by silently in the face of Pray's fits of temper.

"Picture's up!" Eli called. "And . . . background action."

Joey tried to concentrate as pedestrians began to walk along the street, moving by assignment as individuals, pairs, or groups with specific bits of business and intent. Vehicles that weren't directly involved in the primary action of the stunt began to move in regular traffic patterns through the intersections within the prescribed six-block boundaries of the shot.

"And action," Pray said.

Stunt vehicles that had been specially reinforced and rigged, including four city buses, began to drive along Broadway at a workaday urban clip. Moments later, the Maserati roared around the corner of Third and Broadway, tires screeching for purchase, with the Ferrari in close pursuit.

The drivers of the hero cars gunned their engines, weaving with what appeared to be wild abandon through the lanes of vehicles packed together like a mobile obstacle course, an illusion created by precision driving that allowed the two principals to pass among the slower-moving vehicles at breakneck pace. A pedestrian stunt-woman stepped into a crosswalk just as the Maserati blew through a red light, narrowly missing her. Nanoseconds behind, the Ferrari almost pancaked her again, all part of the carefully choreographed sequence that relied on flawless timing and execution. The shot was daring and exhilarating. Joey held her breath as the two hero stunt drivers piloted their cars in a high-performance *pas de deux*.

"Cut!" Pray yelled. He tore off his headphones and vaulted out of his chair. "Cut, cut, cut!"

The AD team echoed him, calling "cut" up and down the street. Background pedestrians stopped and peered toward video village. All the cars along Broadway braked to a halt.

"This looks like a kiddie car roller derby," Pray sneered. "Every-thing needs to move faster; there's no tension in the shot."

Eli and the stunt coordinator caught up to him in the middle of the street, followed by the DP. The four men stood together, with Pray doing most of the talking.

"We need to feel the fear, feel the danger in that sequence," he said. "I want to see them move twice as fast."

The stunt coordinator crossed his arms, a stern look on his face. "That shot's already dangerous, Marcus. I think the solution is to be more creative in post with the editing."

"That's very interesting," Pray said. "But since that's not part of your job, or an area where you have expertise, please shut up and try to do the thing that *is* your job: make this stunt look like I want it to."

"I can't ask the drivers to go any faster than they already are in those conditions. Somebody's going to get hurt, and I won't be responsible."

Pray nodded and smiled. "You're fired."

"Let's take a break," Eli said.

"You want to go too?" Pray pointed at him. "Because that's strike two on you already today. Get the second AD up here and then get lost."

"Marcus, we're all trying to give you what you want," Eli said.

"Then why isn't anybody doing that? All I'm getting is excuses when all I want to hear is, yes, sir, we're on it." Pray's face twisted with rage. "This is my movie, we're going to do it my way, and anybody who's not on board with that doesn't work here anymore! Am I making myself clear?"

"We *need* him," Eli said, gesturing to the stunt coordinator.

Pray was still seething. "Nobody's irreplaceable."

"Forget it," the coordinator said. "I'm out of here. My assistant can take over if he wants to. I'll let my team decide for themselves who stays and who goes." He motioned to his assistant, a lanky fellow in sunglasses and a Dodgers cap, who looked a little shell-shocked.

"Let's get on with it then," Pray said. "We've only got this location for one day, and I want to get some work done."

"Let's give the stunt team some time to regroup," Eli said.

"Why? Nothing's changed in the past three minutes except we got rid of the guy putting up the roadblocks. Everybody's ready to go; let's get the shot."

"One second." Eli held up his index finger and started to cross the street to talk to the assistant stunt coordinator.

"Back to one, everybody!" Pray called. "We want to do this double time from the first take."

Eli stopped in the middle of Broadway, then turned to look back at Pray. Joey watched his expression shift from concentration to dismay.

"You're in or you're out," Pray said. "Your choice."

"Back to one." Stone-faced now, Eli spoke into the walkie-talkie. "Talk to me, people. If we have any problems, I want to hear about them."

"Negative," came the reply from the second-second AD, who'd stepped in to cover for Lionel. "Back to one."

Up and down Broadway, pedestrians and vehicles returned to their starting positions for the scene. Two minutes later, the message was relayed to video village that all was in place.

"All right," Eli said. "Picture's up. And background action."

"Action!" Pray said. "Fast, fast, fast!"

The scene began again. Vehicles and pedestrians were in motion on the street, just another busy day in the big city, until the Maserati and Ferrari flew around the corner and hurtled down Broadway, whipping in and out of traffic.

Joey felt fingernails dig into her arm. She looked up from the monitor to see Dahlia, white-faced, staring at the action on the street.

"I think we should get out of here," Dahlia said in a low, urgent voice.

Thirty seconds into the shot, the Maserati's timing was a split second off. It sideswiped a Volvo sedan and kept going. The Volvo banged into the back of a city bus, then came to a halt. Traffic in the two west lanes of Broadway slowed and curdled in the wake of the collision.

The Maserati and Ferrari raced on, neck and neck, when the stuntwoman stepped into the crosswalk. They would have pulled off the near miss, except for the 1982 Chevy Camaro that broke sequence and rolled into the intersection from Fifth Street right at that moment. The Maserati caught the front end of the Camaro, spun it like a top, and the Ferrari hit the back end on the spin.

All three cars skidded off in an explosion of grinding metal and shrieking tires. The Ferrari sheared off a fire hydrant, and a geyser erupted, spewing hundreds of gallons of water straight up into the air.

Chapter
Twenty-Six

"Breaking news at the top of the hour, a developing story from Hollywood: the troubled feature film directed by action auteur Marcus Pray was dealt another blow today when a stunt went terribly wrong on the streets of downtown Los Angeles. A vehicular crash has sent multiple people to the hospital. This is the same movie that suspended production earlier in the week as a result of the on-set death of an assistant director. That death was subsequently ruled a homicide by the Los Angeles County Medical Examiner. We go now to our correspondent, Arabella Muñoz, at the scene."

"Crew members who witnessed the collision of two luxury sports cars being used in a high-speed chase sequence of the Marcus Pray film slated for release next year say it's astonishing no one was killed. Four stunt players were transported to LA-USC Medical Center following the vehicular crash that left the intersection of Broadway and Fifth Street awash in wreckage and floodwater flowing from a damaged fire hydrant. The condition of the injured performers is not available at this time. A spokesman for the studio says a thorough investigation is in progress to determine the cause of the accident. This is Arabella Muñoz reporting live from downtown Los Angeles."

Joey sat in her car in the parking lot of Hammer and Tongs to listen to the NPR news brief, hoping for new information. By now, hours after the crash, it was still unclear why the rogue Camaro entered the intersection, triggering the collision. But she already had more facts in hand than the radio bulletin.

The driver of the Camaro was rushed to the hospital with a broken ankle and possible concussion. The Maserati and Ferrari drivers both walked away from their vehicles, but were also taken for medical evaluation, along with the pedestrian stuntwoman. Her injuries appeared superficial, sustained when she threw herself out of the paths of the oncoming cars when it looked like they were going to flatten her for real.

There was a fair amount of collateral property damage, starting with the city fire hydrant. A men's discount clothing store on the southeast side of the intersection had its plate glass windows shattered, with resulting water damage to the interior of the business. A coffee shop on the opposite corner also took a direct hit that demolished part of the wall facing Broadway.

Despite all the destruction and injury, Joey knew they'd dodged an even bigger bullet. It was a lucky break for the crew the crash happened three blocks north of video village, or NPR's news item might have led with the death toll.

The company was forced to wrap for the day, and rumors were already flying this latest disaster would be the nail in the coffin for the movie. Joey wouldn't shed any tears if the studio pulled the plug, but until they were told otherwise, work needed to proceed as scheduled. Better to be ready with costumes that were no longer needed if shooting was delayed or suspended than be empty-handed on set Wednesday morning if they still had a job by then, no matter that seemed like a long shot.

She had twenty minutes to spare before the first fitting. Normally she'd go into the costume house to make sure all was ready, look over her notes, talk with the artisans, that sort of thing. But today she had other pressing business and wanted privacy, so she sat in her car while she made the calls to IMDb customer service and the SAG-AFTRA union.

The IMDb people said they had no information about Sofia Campbell, beyond the details listed on her profile page, period, end of story. SAG was slightly more helpful: the rep Joey spoke with was curt, but she coughed up the name of Sofia's agent, Eva Birkus at Olympus Artists Agency. But when Joey requested the spelling of the last name, the rep hung up on her.

Still, it was more than she'd had. Olympus Artists was respectable, though not one of the powerhouse agencies. She looked up their website, then placed a call to their 800 number. When she asked to speak to Birkus, the receptionist said, "Please hold," and promptly routed her to voice mail.

"Hi, my name is Joey Jessop," she began after the beep, then drew a blank.

What could she say on a message tape that would explain her purpose, but in terms vague enough there'd be no possibility for blowback? She knew nothing about Eva Birkus. What if Sofia's agent turned out to be a friend, or a friend of a friend, of Marcus Pray's? When the voice mail genie asked if she wanted to send, rerecord, or delete her message, she picked door number three and ended the call. Then she gathered her notebooks to take inside to the superhero fittings.

The welding studio was going loud and strong when she walked into Hammer and Tongs. She moved through to the common space, but it was deserted. She'd expected to find Dahlia camped out with coffee and her phone.

Joey checked her cell: no texts from Bill or Dahlia. As a rule, she'd wait up front to greet the actors if the designer wasn't on hand, but there were construction details she wanted to go over with Damir before the fittings, so she made her way down the hall to look for him.

First up on the right was the workroom where a woman was laying out pieces of a muslin pattern on orange neoprene fabric spread across a cutting table. Her mouth was full of straight pins.

"Damir around?" Joey asked.

"Star dressing suite," the woman replied around the pins.

Joey continued along the hallway, and soon heard voices coming from the suite of rooms used for principal fittings. The space was laid out like a large apartment, with three separate dressing rooms opening off a great room that featured a small stage backdropped by a wall of mirrors. A theatrical lighting system and professional video setup were available to record the fittings. Joey heard Dahlia's voice rise above the others.

"Damir, that is brilliant!"

Expecting to find an informal show-and-tell in progress, Joey gave a quick rap on the door, then let herself into the great room. Brooke stood on the stage in costume, facing the mirrored wall with Damir and the milliner at her side. Dahlia studied the actress's reflection from her seat on a sofa across the room. The head cutter for Hammer and Tongs and two of their best sculptors were stationed nearby, ready to assist. The fitting was underway.

Joey checked her watch and frowned. "Excuse me, I didn't think I was late."

There was a moment of awkward silence, then Dahlia said, "You're fine, we just decided to get things started." She glanced at Brooke, who avoided making eye contact.

"Let's step outside for a minute," Dahlia said.

Damir was in the process of adjusting Brooke's elaborately sculpted headpiece. He cut a dark look at the costume designer. Mystified, Joey followed Dahlia back into the hall.

"You know how much I value your judgment and your input," Dahlia said when the door closed behind them. "But it seems somebody on the makeup crew is whispering in Brooke's ear."

"I see," Joey said, doing a slow burn as she collected her thoughts.

Dahlia's smile was forced. "I'm glad you understand."

"Actually, I think I should take a minute to speak with Brooke," Joey said firmly. "If she has something she wants to say, she can tell me herself."

The door to the suite popped open and Damir joined them in the hall, the look on his face even darker as he focused like a laser on Dahlia. "I don't know what that little nitwit was yapping about before Joey got here, and I don't care, but you need to understand this: Joey's my point person. She's the only one of you who knows exactly what's going on with these costumes, and if she can't be in the fitting, I can't guarantee delivery within the ridiculous time frame she coaxed me to agree to. Which, by the way, I wouldn't do for anybody else in this rotten business, and if you quote me, I'll call you a liar."

Dahlia's eyes looked big as plums. "You don't give me much choice."

"That's correct," he said. "I'll see you both inside."

He turned and went back into the suite.

"I guess we'll need to make the best of this," Dahlia said.

Joey wondered if that "we" was royal or inclusive.

"I'll only ask that you wait until we're finished here if you need to hash things out with Brooke," Dahlia continued. "For now, be discreet about offering any opinions, and make a note if it's something we can discuss after the fitting. Otherwise, let's step away and talk about it quietly without involving anyone else."

Joey was both irritated and amused that Dahlia's allegiance to her "secret weapon" was so fickle. Without responding, she opened the door and reentered the great room with Dahlia close behind.

Brooke still stood on the stage in costume, facing the wall of mirrors. Damir was beside her again, with his chief artisans, studying their work.

"I don't know, Joey," he said casually when she walked back into the room. "What do you think about the proportions of the headpiece?"

She stepped up to the stage and looked at Brooke in the mirror. The headpiece was a marvel of intricate craftsmanship incorporating both copper wire and human hair. Decorative pieces of sculpted foam painted to look like bits of precious metal were scattered throughout to catch the light, adding texture and visual interest. The result was a beautiful hybrid, something between a wig and a graceful helmet. It managed to complement the actress's delicate features yet added substance to her stature.

"How does it feel, Brooke?" she asked. "Would you like to move around, see if it's comfortable to work in?"

The actress met her gaze in the mirror, a look of doubt in her eyes. Then she glanced at Damir. "Can I do that?"

He waved his hand. "You heard the lady. Give it a go."

She did a tentative hop, then smiled. "It feels good. I can't believe it's so lightweight." She twirled with her arms over her head, then did a full leap and lunge, striking an aggressive pose. "It's great!" Her smile was even brighter. "I feel like a real superhero."

Damir looked at Joey and raised his eyebrows. "Thoughts?"

She bowed to protocol. "What do you think, Dahlia? Are you happy with the way the costume looks and moves?"

The designer smiled mechanically. "I think it's magnificent. Damir, you and your resident geniuses have done it again."

"Why don't we get it on camera, then?" Joey said. "You may want to give Marcus a preview."

"Yes, let's do that." Dahlia looked at her watch. "Fiske should be here any time. I'm going to step out for a few minutes to make a phone call. Make sure you get some profile and back view footage."

"Okay, my people, you know what to do," Damir said. "Brooke, make us look good. Do another pirouette for the camera."

He stepped off the stage with Joey to watch the shoot from a distance.

"Thanks for the support." She kept her eyes on the stage.

"We need to stick together," he said quietly. "That's the only way to make it through one of these meat grinders. It always amazes me how few people in this industry seem to understand that."

"People get scared when there's so much money on the line," Joey said. "They're afraid to make a mistake."

"If you can't stand the heat . . ." He gave an extravagant shrug.

"Easy for you to say; nothing ever fazes you."

"If only that were true," he said. "But I'm afraid this movie's coming apart at the seams, and there's only so much we can do about that."

"We've had a rough start, no question."

"There's a brilliant piece of understatement if I ever heard one," Damir scoffed. "Your company's been shooting less than a week, and you can't even get through a single day without some major catastrophe."

"The lunatic's running the asylum," she complained. "If we had a real star on set every day with enough clout to stand up to Pray, it might be a different story. But we don't have a knight in shining armor, we only have the dragon."

Damir was shaking his head. "Your department's not firing on all cylinders either, and it would be a mistake to ignore that. I meant what I said to Dahlia; I depend on you, but don't let your sense of responsibility lull you into accepting the unacceptable."

"You sound like my mother."

"Then let me say it another way." Damir gave her arm a poke. "Quit if the SOBs aren't treating you right."

Joey found herself smiling, though it really wasn't funny. "May I quote you?"

He gave her a sly look. "I insist."

The two male leads' fittings took much longer than Brooke's. There were significant alterations needed to take care of fit and function issues with their costumes. But at the end of the day, Joey and Damir were satisfied those problems could be solved within their time frame.

They agreed she'd stop by Hammer and Tongs every day, so they'd be fully coordinated for the march toward final fittings on Tuesday, their last chance to make sure everything was ready for camera Wednesday morning. Even with the pressure of that deadline, Joey felt pleased with the progress they'd made. Maybe the tide was turning in their favor.

When she left the shop, it was still light outside. The summer evening was balmy and mild for the Valley, typically so parched that time of year the air could feel dry as sand. Joey would have preferred to skip the one-on-one with Caleb, but she forced herself to switch gears.

She'd decided to ask him to meet her in the food court at Fashion Square Mall in Sherman Oaks, which she'd normally avoid like the plague. But in this instance, the bland location had a lot going for it: no self-respecting paparazzo would be caught dead at the order-up counter for California Crisp, and there'd be plenty of foot traffic with an army of shoppers crisscrossing the gigantic retail plaza to provide the anonymity of the herd.

She pulled out her cell to make the call. Her phone stayed on mute for fittings, so it was no surprise when she checked the screen to find an assortment of voice mails, emails, and texts waiting for her attention. Before she contacted Caleb, she had to make sure the decks were clear, and she started in on the texts.

The first two were blanket memos from production to the entire company, routine reminders about parking and identification policies regarding studio lot access for the green screen sequences that would begin shooting on stage the following week. But it was the third one in line that shanked her. She recognized the number and had a fair idea what was in store before she pulled up the message, which was short and anything but sweet:

All who sin apart from the law will also perish apart from the law.

Chapter Twenty-Seven

"With all the great restaurants in this town, why are we here?" Caleb glanced around disdainfully at the molded plastic tables and chairs in the Fashion Square food court. "Even Grand Central Market's a step up from this."

"Taco Bell's a step up from this," Joey said. "We're not here to eat."

"Speak for yourself." He wore his hair longish, expensively cut and highlighted, a good-looking guy if you liked the type. Joey wasn't drawn to men who were prettier than she was.

"I can see you've got a problem with me, so I'd like to start by clearing the air." He sat back and crossed his arms. "Even though I can't think what I've done to offend you."

She shook her head. "I'm not offended so much as freaked out by everything that's happened recently. I don't have the patience to be polite."

"I get it." He gave her a long, thoughtful look. "I've been living with it too."

"Of course you have." She was still sympathetic, at least theoretically. "But I was surprised to find out you're here in town."

"That's why you're giving me attitude?"

"Here's the deal," she said. "I can't afford to take anything for granted right now, so when you say on the phone, 'Oh, by the way, I'm in LA—'"

"That's not what I said."

"You know what I mean." She eyed him narrowly. "I had the impression you were calling from out of state."

"Then you jumped to a conclusion." He propped his arms on the table. "*You* called *me* out of the blue, said you were the person who found my sister and that you wanted to talk. I called you back and we talked." He looked to her for confirmation. "I didn't say anything about where I was calling from."

She felt a quick burst of temper. "Then why did you try to duck the issue on the phone last night?"

"I didn't try to duck anything." He stared at her like she had a screw loose. "I'm the one who suggested meeting in person, remember?"

His statement was technically accurate, but Joey still thought he was being evasive. "How long have you been in town?"

"A while now," he said easily.

"Do you live here?"

"Not exactly." He tilted his head, looking coy.

She didn't like him any better in person than she had on the phone, but she reminded herself they'd met to talk about his dead, possibly pregnant twin sister.

"Have you been staying at Courtney's?" she asked.

Then it occurred to her that if Caleb was staying with Courtney, maybe he visited her on the job. She focused more intently on his face, trying to decide if he looked familiar.

"Why are you staring at me like that?" he asked sharply.

She noticed he hadn't answered her question.

"Have you ever visited Courtney at work?" she asked.

"Never," he said quickly. "I think I told you when we spoke on the phone, she didn't want me anywhere near Pray."

"I remember." Joey nodded.

"You keep looking at me like I'm a specimen under a microscope," he protested.

She didn't feel the need to share her thoughts about how easily, as Courtney's brother, he might have gained access to the shooting location in Malibu.

"As you pointed out, you're the one who suggested we meet," she said instead. "I'm just trying to figure out why you wanted to."

"Okay, then." He raised his eyebrows inquiringly. "First, I'd like to know who told you Courtney was pregnant. Was it Eli Logan, by any chance?"

"No, it wasn't Eli," she said. "Now my turn: What made you say it could explain some things if she was? Pregnant, that is."

"Back and forth, like a trade." He frowned, then nodded slowly, accepting her terms. "Court was never Miss Sweetness and Light, but she was really on a tear ever since I got out here this time, like, crazy hormonal."

Joey let that pass without comment, hoping she could nail down his timeframe. "Which was when?"

"Nope." He wiggled his fingers. "Ante up. Who said she was pregnant?"

"Melanie Beale," she said, looking for any sign he recognized the name. "She's a makeup artist on the movie.

He shook his head. "Never heard of her."

"Melanie claims Courtney was her best friend."

He was quiet while he thought about that, and Joey let the silence stretch out. She still didn't trust Caleb, and she didn't feel any rapport with him, but if she was going to ask her questions, now was the time.

"I'd like to get your opinion about something," she finally said.

He turned his palms up. "Fire away."

"If Courtney was pregnant, who do you think the father was, Eli or Marcus Pray?"

He looked at her coolly. "Your guess is as good as mine."

He didn't appear eager to know the answer, and that by itself seemed odd. Joey knew that grief and loss affect different people in different ways, but she was struck once again by Caleb's apparent lack of warmth for his sister.

"Now I have a question for you." His smile was bright and empty. "Do the police still consider you a suspect?"

"I honestly don't know." The thought sent a chill up her spine. "Have you talked to them yet?" she countered.

"What do you mean?" His expression grew wary.

"The first time we spoke, you said your parents had talked to the cops, but you hadn't yet."

He frowned uncertainly. "I don't remember saying that."

Then it dawned on her: "That's one of the reasons I thought you weren't in town." She waved her finger like a wand. "But you must have been in LA before she died, or you wouldn't have said . . . how did you put it . . . she was 'crazy hormonal' since you got here this time." She pinned him with a look. "You were here in town the night she was killed, weren't you?"

"You're an even bigger bitch than she was." He glanced away, but not before Joey saw something bitter flash in his eyes. "The truth is, I hadn't seen her for days. We had a fight, and she tried to kick me out; but I wouldn't go, so she left."

Joey shook her head in confusion. "Then where was she staying?"

"What does that have to do with anything?" He glared at her resentfully. "She was killed at work, and as far as I know, you're still in the running as a suspect."

She pressed him, thinking they'd landed on something important. "After your argument, did you ever talk to her again?"

"What's the matter with you?" He stood up so fast, he startled her. "What are you trying to do here?"

"I want to find out what happened to Courtney, maybe almost as much as you do." She clapped a hand to her chest. "Caleb, I just want to understand—"

He cut her off. "Don't try to lay this on me!" He pointed at her. "And don't *ever* call me again!"

He pivoted and strode across the food court toward the escalators. Joey stared after him, wondering what he had hoped to gain from this meeting, and thinking the odds were fifty-fifty that anything he said was the truth.

Chapter
Twenty-Eight

Joey sat on her back patio later that evening, nursing a glass of sauvignon blanc. She'd turned on the fireplace, lit some candles, and set up her computer on the dining table under the vine-covered pergola, intending to organize herself for the busy weekend ahead. The company had been given only a preliminary call sheet for the next day's work, but they were scheduled to shoot downtown again, much to her surprise; and she also needed to review her notes from the superhero fittings earlier that day.

But she couldn't stop thinking about the meeting with Caleb. She still didn't know why he'd stormed off, or even why he'd suggested they meet in the first place. He wanted to talk about Courtney's pregnancy, then seemed to lose interest.

Scratch that. She remembered the look in his eyes when she asked if he thought Eli or Pray was the father. *He dropped the subject flat.*

In fact, after talking with Caleb in person, she understood less than she had before. His relationship with his sister sounded rocky, and it wasn't only that he called her a bitch or that they argued before she died. His attitude about her death was just *off*; he seemed more anxious and angry than sad.

She took another gulp of wine while her imagination spun that thought. Maybe her list of suspects should expand: *When a woman is murdered, it's likely the husband or boyfriend . . . or brother.* Caleb could have gone to the set (whether Joey had seen him or not, since she was gone most of the day Courtney died). Maybe he wanted to make peace with his sister, and they quarreled again.

That was possible, of course, but it was only speculation. The truth was, she had no real information about the quality of the twins' relationship; and besides that, she knew next to nothing about Caleb. She had no idea what, if anything, he did for a living, or where he lived, for that matter. The most telling aspect of their conversation was the fact that Caleb had been stingy with answers about everything she asked.

Joey sighed in frustration. Caleb wasn't the only reason she couldn't make herself buckle down to work this evening. The crash on set kept her from asking Eli about the big man she believed was the driver of the dark SUV. She tried to think of another way to identify him, but if he was an extra hire, he wouldn't show up on the movie's crew list, so checking any unfamiliar names on social media was likely a waste of time. She sipped her wine and decided against calling Eli that night; best to have the discussion in person, so tomorrow would have to be soon enough.

Her cell phone buzzed in her pocket, and she had to shift her position to dig it out. In the process, she managed to spill most of the glass of wine in her lap. She dropped the phone on the tabletop and hit the button to take the call on speaker.

"Hang on, I'll be right back." She hurried into the kitchen for a towel to sop up the mess. "Sorry, this is Joey," she called as she patted herself down.

"Hi, this is Malo. Is everything okay there?"

"Malo," she said, bracing for bad news. "Everything's fine with me. What's going on?"

"I'm on my way to your house, and I wanted to give you a heads-up. Dahlia asked me to bring you some things she wants you to look at tonight."

"What the . . . ?" She glanced at her computer. "It's almost ten o'clock."

"I know and I'm sorry. She said it was important."

"What is it?" She sat down at the table and refilled her wine glass. "Because if it's not going on camera in the morning, it's not that important."

"Some pictures and a piece of fabric." He sounded embarrassed. "I hate to bother you, but she insisted."

Joey was livid. There was no reason to have a PA, the lowest-paid person in the department, driving around in the middle of the night to do an errand that was really only about making Dahlia feel important.

But all she said was, "You're not bothering me. You know how to get here?"

"No problem, I've got GPS."

"Okay, my place is toward the back of the lot, and I'll put the outside light on. I'm up, so don't rush and drive safe; I'll see you when you get here."

She went back inside to turn on the porch light for Malo, then peeled off her wine-soaked jeans and changed into sweatpants. Ten minutes later, there were a couple of taps on her front door, and she heard him say, "Joey, it's Malo."

She put on a smile before she opened the door. "Come on in," she said cheerfully.

"I don't want to interrupt." He held out a large manila envelope. "Dahlia said she'd talk to you about these in the morning."

"Of course she did." Joey accepted the envelope. "But come in for a minute, unless—" She caught herself. "I don't want to impose on you any more than we already have."

"No, I was happy to do the drop-off." He followed her into the kitchen. "I don't live far from here, so it wasn't a big deal."

Except Joey knew he had to make the round trip to Dahlia in the Hollywood Hills to pick up the envelope in order to make the delivery.

"You want some lemonade?" she said. "I made some fresh."

"That'd be great." He checked out the scaled-down dimensions of the interior while she got a glass from the cupboard and poured lemonade from a pitcher in the fridge. "This place is so cool."

"It's small, but it's got everything I need." She handed him the glass, then led him out to the patio.

"Wow! It's like your own enchanted garden back here, with the vines hanging down and the candles and the fire." He crossed to the back gate. "The ocean's so close, you can almost touch it." He turned to look at her, eyes shining. "It's perfect."

She smiled at him, feeling a warm connection. "Thanks, I'm glad you like it too." She settled herself on the sectional. "Come sit down and tell me about yourself. We've never had a chance to talk much about anything except work."

"Hello?" A woman's voice called from the other side of the back fence.

Joey looked at Malo and put a finger to her lips. "Who's there?" she said.

"It's Maggie Fuller, from *Popvibe*."

"You've got to be kidding," Joey groaned.

"Don't be like that. You're going to hurt my feelings."

"I can live with that."

"Come on, open up." Fuller put on a sing-song voice. "I promise you want to talk to me."

"I promise you I don't," Joey replied.

"That's the thanks I get for driving all the way out here with breaking news about your movie?"

"Yeah, right," Joey sneered. "Climb back on your broom and go home."

"I'm doing you a favor," Fuller said. "And whether you like it or not, I have an important story to tell. That's my *job*."

"From what I've seen, your job is peddling trash to people who don't know the difference between gossip and real news."

"If you won't let me in, I'll just keep shouting over the fence," Fuller called out in a loud voice. "That way your neighbors can listen too."

An outside light blinked on next door at Gina's place. Joey was well aware she had already strained the limits of neighborly good graces. Furious now, she stalked to the back gate and yanked it open.

She scowled at the reporter. "Am I going to have to get a restraining order to shut you up?"

"Hello, don't mind if I do." Fuller stepped past her onto the patio. "What a lovely place you have here. Hi there," she said to Malo, then turned to Joey. "Who's this?"

"He's not a potted plant, and he can speak for himself if he wants," she said sullenly.

"Duly noted." The reporter took a seat at the table. "Let's quit trading insults and have a chat." She sent a smile to Malo. "Or maybe your friend here will be interested in what I have to say."

"Quit bothering him." Joey sat down across from her. "What's your breaking news? Against my better judgment, I'm listening."

Fuller gazed at her calmly. "I'd like to discuss some video footage I'm thinking of posting online that shows you and Eli Logan talking about pimping out girls in an open-air meat market for your director. Ring a bell?"

Joey rocked back in her seat. "You're bluffing."

"How would I do that?" Fuller asked. "I'd have to know about that conversation somehow, wouldn't I? And if you recall, I wasn't even there, but two of my friends were."

Joey's head was swimming, and a sharp pain in her chest made it hard to breathe. "The two paparazzi," she said tonelessly.

"Precisely." Fuller nodded. "We did some negotiating, and they turned the footage over to me. Your speech about how dirty you feel giving in to Pray's demands is clearly heartfelt. People are going to eat that up and come back for seconds."

Joey glanced over at Malo. "Why don't you go inside and get yourself some more lemonade?"

The boy stood up; his face looked pale and uncertain.

"I'll be in before long," she said soothingly.

He turned and walked stiffly into the house.

"I can tell he looks up to you," Fuller said when the door closed behind him. "That's a lot of responsibility."

"Leave him out of this," Joey said, gritting her teeth. "What is it you want?"

"The same thing you want." Fuller's expression was serious. "To see Marcus Pray go down."

Joey shook her head. "That's not at the top of my agenda."

"Then you need to get your priorities straight." Fuller's anger flared like a torch. "He's the personification of everything that's wrong with your industry—with our society when you get right down to it."

"Don't lecture me about personal responsibility," Joey said contemptuously. "You use people too; you're no better than Pray."

"I don't think you realize what's at stake," the reporter insisted. "I'm writing a series of articles that focus on the habitually abusive and sometimes reckless behavior of Marcus Pray. Based on that video, I'd say you could be a contributor."

"Nope, not interested."

"I promise you full anonymity, and I never give up my sources."

Joey glared at her. "What part of 'no' don't you understand?"

"Let's level with each other." Fuller leaned across the table. "I intend to expose Pray for the misogynistic predator we all know he is. Word's starting to get around about him, and I want to be the one to break that story wide."

Joey was silent, weighing her options, all of them bad. She had enough problems without playing Deep Throat for an online tabloid, but if that footage went public, the studio would lower the boom. She'd lose her job, and her name would be added to the blacklist of industry outcasts.

As if Fuller could read her mind, the reporter pressed her. "If I post that video, the studio will fire you in a very public and embarrassing way, to send a message. But if you help me, I can make the footage disappear."

Something snapped inside her, and suddenly Joey didn't care what Fuller said or did. She was done with lies and double-dealing; she just wanted the reporter gone.

"You almost had me there for a minute," she said quietly. "But even if I wanted to take you up on your offer, I've signed a confidentiality agreement. The minute I start blabbing about anything that touches on the movie, the studio can sue me. After they fire me, of course."

"I said I'd protect you," Fuller argued.

"And I'm supposed to take your word?" Joey asked sarcastically.

"You're making a mistake," the reporter said. "Trust me, this could turn out badly for you if you don't play your cards right."

Joey gave her a flinty smile. "That's almost funny in a very twisted way."

"I don't follow," Fuller shot back.

"You're trying to blackmail me, and I'm supposed to trust you." Joey stood up. "You can sit out here all night if you want to, but I'm going inside now." She turned off the fireplace and tucked her laptop under her arm. "Shut the gate on your way out."

Chapter Twenty-Nine

"Are you afraid she's going to post that video online?" Malo looked up from the sketch pad balanced across his knees.

"I've been trying not to dwell on it," Joey said.

He shifted his gaze back to the pad, but she could see he was worried. Joey was sorry he had to overhear her conversation with Fuller, and she was angry with the reporter for exposing the boy to that kind of ugliness.

"No matter what Fuller's decision is, I'd have made the same call," she said.

"Because of the confidentiality agreement?" His eyes flicked to her face.

"If I let her push me now, she won't stop. I'd never be free of her, so I'll take my chances." Joey shrugged. "Let the chips fall where they may."

"Even if that means losing your job?" he asked softly.

A bubble of nausea rose in her throat. "I can always get another job," she said, hoping that would still be true in a week. "Free will's a lot harder to recover, once you let it go."

Sometime well past midnight, they were settled again by the fire on the patio. Joey had persuaded Malo to stay and talk. She really did want to get better acquainted, but it was also true that she didn't want to be alone with only her thoughts for company.

She tried not to obsess about Fuller's visit, but that was easier said than done. That video was a real threat to her life and work, and there was nothing she could do about it. The reporter was a wild card, and Joey believed Fuller might just be spiteful enough to post a video that could ruin her career without a pang of conscience.

All the more reason she was glad for Malo's company. At some point, he'd fetched the sketch pad from his car. The rasp of his charcoal crayon as it moved across the paper was soothing, blended with the soft rumble of the surf along the beach. Bigfoot finally decided to make an appearance, claiming her usual spot by the fireplace.

"You mind if I ask how old you are?" Joey said.

She found it relaxing to watch him sketch by the firelight; for the first time that day, she didn't feel like a bundle of nervous energy.

Malo glanced up from his drawing. "I'll be twenty in October."

"Which means you're nineteen," she said, smiling gently. She'd guessed he was young, but she was still surprised. "You thinking about college?"

"Nope." He shook his head. "I want to be out in the world working, not stuck in a classroom for four more years."

She nodded, thinking how she'd made the same decision when she was about his age.

"So how old are you?" Malo gave her a playful look.

"Thirty-four, Mr. Smarty-Pants," she said.

"Thirty-four seems young, considering all the big movies you've done." He leaned back to examine his sketch.

She looked at him curiously. "How do you know what I've done?"

"I've seen all the movies you worked on, most of them more than once."

"I've worked on some flops I'll bet you haven't seen."

"Yeah, how much?" He held out his hand, palm up, and gave her a cocky smile.

"I'm not going to take your money," she scoffed.

"Twenty bucks," he insisted. "Name the movie."

"*Bolden*," she said. "Barely got a theatrical release."

"Saw it on Amazon." He did a fist pump. "About Buddy Bolden, the jazz trumpeter."

She had to laugh. "There's an hour and a half you're never going to get back."

"You're right, it was a dog," he said. "But not a complete waste of time. You can learn a lot by watching movies, even when they're bad."

"True enough." She admired his perceptiveness. "I've learned valuable lessons working on some real losers. Once you make a doozy of a mistake, you'll do your best not to repeat it."

Malo was quiet, eyes on his sketch pad again. "Do you think this job's a mistake?"

His question gave her pause. Fuller was right about one thing: she did have a responsibility to her young colleague. "What makes you ask?"

He looked at her solemnly. "Marcus Pray." He hesitated. "Is he always like that?" He made a slight motion with his hand. "The way he was on set today . . . with those girls?"

"I'm not sure what to say, Malo." She sighed and shook her head, feeling unfit for the role of mentor. "The way Pray behaved is not acceptable, under any circumstances."

"Are you thinking of quitting?" he asked, watching her apprehensively.

"No," she said firmly. "I'm not going to quit. I made a commitment when I signed my deal, and I love our department."

"I do too!" His face lit up. "I'm learning so much from all of you."

"Then we're doing something right." His enthusiasm made her heart clench. "Let's change the subject now. Your pick, whatever you want to talk about, but make it something fun."

"Okay." He tipped his head back and forth, game for that invitation. "Who's the nicest movie star you ever worked with?"

"Walked right into that one, didn't I?" She rolled her eyes, then reminded herself this was all new to him. "Most of them are basically nice, but they're just people, same as us. The biggest difference is their take-home pay."

"Don't get all PC on me," he said, pouting. "I'm not going to repeat anything you say."

"All right then." She didn't want to be a wet blanket. "I can't choose any one person, but I'll tell you a couple of little stories about nice things stars have done for me."

He sat up straighter. "Anything juicy?"

She shook her head but couldn't help smiling. "One of the first movies I worked as a key, I was covering the set one morning when the ADs called lunch. I grabbed the crazy big set bag that belonged to the costumer I was subbing for and started hauling it back to the wardrobe trailer."

She leaned sideways in her chair, miming the drag of a heavy load. "Crew members were flying past on the way to the lunch tent, all the grips, electrics, and camera guys. Then someone tapped me on the shoulder and said, 'That bag's too big for you. Let me carry it.' I looked up and Tom Cruise was smiling at me."

"No way!" Malo's mouth dropped open. "Tom Cruise carried your bag?"

"All the way to the wardrobe trailer, like a real gentleman." She nodded. "You want to hear the nicest compliment I ever got from an actor?"

He bobbed his head happily. "Who was it?"

"Dustin Hoffman. The day after his first costume fitting, I walked into the office I shared with the costume designer, and we each had a dozen white roses on our desks with a note from Dustin that read *You found my character for me*." She smiled at Malo fondly. "Sweet, huh?"

"Wow." He sounded wistful. "That's what I want more than anything." Even in the half-light from the fire, Joey saw the longing in his eyes. "To learn how to do the biggest movies they make, like you do."

"You've made a great start." She was glad to shift the conversation back to him. "You're already working on a major studio release, the July Fourth weekend opener next year. Doesn't get much bigger than that."

"But I've been doing the PA thing for a couple of years, and I'm feeling stuck." He frowned and looked down at his drawing. "It's tough to see how to move up the food chain."

Joey knew he was right. Production assistants were nonunion, underpaid, and over-utilized by departments that faced pressure from producers to slash their budgets. A good PA could do the work of an average costumer for a fraction of the cost. But the real problem was, after they'd worked and gained the training they needed to advance, PAs had no clear path to union membership, and the people they worked for had no incentive to help them take the next step.

A union card could be earned by working for peanuts in a costume house, but those jobs were coveted, often auctioned off (under the table) to the highest bidder. The houses generally required new employees to sign a year's contract at entry-level rate, to keep them from leaving for a higher-paying movie job at the first opportunity, so you not only had to have the cash to buy yourself a slot, you had to grind it out for a year, making minimum.

Joey leaned over to get a look at his sketch. "What are you drawing?"

"You want to see?" He passed the pad of paper to her.

She held it up to the firelight. The charcoal sketch was a beautifully rendered portrait of Bigfoot napping on the hearth. "This is lovely."

"It's for you." Malo smiled shyly.

"Thank you," she said, deeply touched. "I'll treasure this." She continued to study the sketch. "Your drawing is very accomplished."

"It's just something I've always done," he said. "I've been drawing since before I could talk."

"You have a portfolio?" she asked as an idea began to take shape.

"Nothing organized, but I have tons of drawings and paintings I've done."

"I'd like to see them sometime, if you wouldn't mind showing them to me."

"Sure, whenever you say."

Joey nodded thoughtfully. Malo had talent, and if he was as capable as he seemed, she thought she had a solution to his career dilemma. But groundwork would have to be laid; and she needed to be sure it was the right move to make, for everybody involved, so for now she kept her own counsel.

"I don't feel comfortable with many people, but I like being here with you," he said.

"You mentioned you live nearby?" For the first time she wondered if someone would worry about the boy being out so late.

"In Venice," he said. "Not that far from here, on Ocean Avenue."

She raised her eyebrows. "With family?"

"I've been emancipated since I was fifteen. I have my own apartment," he added, reacting to her look of concern. "And plenty of money; my family's good about that sort of thing."

"You're not close to them?" she asked mildly.

He glanced toward the fire. "I don't feel like talking about that right now, if that's okay with you."

"That's fine," she said, not wanting to push too hard, too soon.

He stretched his arms over his head, then leaned back against the sectional. They drifted into a tranquil silence, and Joey closed her eyes, listening to the murmur of the waves, like a lullaby. Malo mumbled something, and she looked over to find he was asleep.

"What are we going to do with you?" she whispered.

She got up, moving quietly so as not to wake him. She went inside to get the afghan from her bed, then brought it out to tuck around him as best she could. The boy was a puzzle, talented and intelligent for sure, but Joey sensed a deep sadness about him she thought would be difficult to reach, and she wasn't sure she'd be doing either of them a favor if she tried.

Chapter Thirty

J oey didn't think she could sleep, but she went in to stretch out on her bed, anyway. The next thing she knew, her cell was humming on the nightstand with an incoming text around four AM.

She blinked sleep from her eyes and stared at the phone long after the buzzing stopped. At four in the morning, she was in no mood for another stalker sermonette, but now that she was awake, she couldn't ignore it. She tapped the screen to view the text, and just like that, her morning blew up:

> *Going to cover set today. Central City Mayor's Office, Sound-stage Five at Warner Brothers. Alfred Molina confirmed as Mayor, Stanley Tucci as Press Secretary, Giancarlo Esposito as City Attorney. See attached call sheet for schedule. Costumes: be prepared to fit actors at their call times.*
>
> *Please advise with any problems/questions.*

> *Eli Logan*
> *First AD, UMPP*

Joey scanned the attached call sheet. She had plenty of questions, but no time to waste sorting through them. Going to cover set was a last resort, and generally caused by something like bad weather showing up when an exterior shot needs to be sunny or a principal cast member slated to work is sick. By definition, it's a location that's prepped and ready to go with sets, props, and costumes.

But that hadn't been possible for the costume department because casting for the mayor's office scenes was incomplete. Eli's text didn't offer an explanation for the change of schedule, but it didn't really matter at the moment; they'd all know the reason soon enough.

She hurried out to the patio to check on Malo, only to find he was already gone. On the dining table, weighted by her empty wine glass, she found a second sketch, a likeness of Joey with a peaceful look on her face, silhouetted by the play of shadows and light from the fire. It pleased her to think this was how Malo saw her.

While she waited for coffee to brew, she sent a blanket text to the *UMPP* costume crew, as well as every costumer and designer in her contacts, requesting information about sizes for her three new actors from anyone who'd worked with them in the past few months. She'd done a movie with Stanley Tucci four years ago and dug those measurements out of her files, but she hoped to get more recent stats from her colleagues.

She knew there was nothing appropriate on the truck to fit the new cast, so the next order of business was to wake Carlos, the warehouse manager at Left Coast Costumes, and get him to open stock for her. He was groggy but gracious when she called at four thirty AM, as she pulled onto PCH on her way to the Valley.

If she didn't get updated sizes, she'd pull a range of suits from 42 Regular through 48 Long, along with principal-quality dress shirts and ties. They had a good stock of men's dress shoes on the trailer, so she wasn't going to bother with those. If necessary, she could find shoes at Warner's costume department, but she couldn't bank on them having decent suits.

The actors were called for seven thirty AM, which gave her just enough time to gather everything and get over to Warner Brothers Studio in Burbank. Light was beginning to brighten the horizon at five when she came over the crest of the 405 freeway and saw the Valley spread out below, still sleeping under its blanket of early morning mist. She put in a call to Zephyr, who lived in North Hollywood two blocks from LCC. The costumer answered on the first ring.

"I was just about to call you," she said.

"You see Eli's text?" Joey asked.

"I'm still hyperventilating. What're we going to do?"

"I'm twenty minutes away from LCC, and Carlos is opening stock. Can you meet me there?"

"On my way."

Zephyr and Carlos were waiting on the front steps of the costume house when Joey pulled into the parking lot.

"Carlos, you're my hero," she said and planted a kiss on his cheek. "We'll need you to write us up as we're pulling, so we can jam out the door with the clothes. And can you please call Jack? We'll pay his overtime if he'll come in to fit our actors on set, then do the alterations for camera this morning."

Carlos had seen it all more than once and was permanently unflappable. He started working at LCC as a teenager sweeping the floors at night. Now in his mid-forties, he effectively ran the place. Nothing happened in any of the departments in the vast costume complex that he didn't know about, and he was usually three steps ahead of whatever emergency was brewing.

He smiled and held the door open for Joey and Zephyr. "Whatever you need, *querida*. Jack's ready to come in whenever you say, and he has current measurements for all three of your actors."

Joey spent the next few hours wrapped in a cocoon of busyness that didn't allow her to worry about Fuller's video showing up online. She and Zephyr pulled a solid collection of clothes, and all three actors walked into a selection of suits that required only minor alterations. That meant they were not only set for work that day, they each had a custom-fit closet of clothing that could be used for later scenes.

Zephyr shifted back into set costumer mode while Joey sorted the clothing and put alterations into work with Jack, the head tailor for LCC, who'd set up shop on the principal trailer.

At eight thirty AM she sent an email to Dahlia with the fitting photos of Messrs. Molina, Tucci, and Esposito, so the designer could choose costumes for the scene to be shot that morning. When she didn't hear back by eight forty-five, Joey texted, then called, but got no response.

She knew the designer could have her phone muted and might not be checking her texts, but Joey couldn't wait any longer to get a decision about which costumes the new cast should wear for the morning's work. She was perfectly capable of making the selections herself, but given the volatile dynamics of this set, it seemed sensible to show the options to Pray. She printed hard copies of the fitting photos, then sent a text to Eli, saying she needed some time with the director to show him the choices. A minute later, her cell pinged with his answer:

Now would be good. In his trailer.

Moments later, she got a text from Dahlia:

I need you to handle this; I'm in the middle of something. Show the pics to Marcus so he can decide. Thanks.

Joey smiled and shook her head. Dahlia might be fickle, but she wasn't mean, and they were in sync about how to proceed. She tucked the photos inside her notebook. "Guys, I'm headed over to show the fittings to Pray so we can prioritize our prep and alterations."

Jack nodded, head bent over his sewing machine, and Zephyr sent her a wave. "At least you don't have to wade through the B-squad. They got the ax yesterday."

"For real?" Joey said. "All of them?"

"Clean slate." Zephyr made a sweeping gesture.

"I hope that doesn't mean we're going to get a new group to dress," Joey said, frowning. "That's the last thing we need today."

"Haven't heard anything about that so far," Zephyr said. "Want me to check with the ADs?"

"I'll stop by their trailer after I'm finished with Pray," Joey said. She held up the photos. "Wish me luck."

She hoped Pray was in a decent mood. There wasn't much time to tweak the costumes the new day players needed to wear that morning. If he didn't like the fitting photos, she'd have a mess on her hands. She wished now the B-squadders were still in play; they could've been a useful distraction, and she wasn't thrilled about meeting with Pray alone in his trailer.

But as she crossed the studio lot, she was more focused on the things she needed to discuss with Eli (besides the possibility of a new B-squad to fit), starting with the identity of the big guy she'd spotted on set the day before, who might or might not be the phantom driver of the dark SUV. The memory of that hulking figure in her rearview mirror sent a blade of dread straight through her, but she put those feelings aside when she rapped on the door of the customized Airstream trailer Pray had stationed next to Soundstage Five.

"It's open," he called.

Joey squared her shoulders and climbed the steps to let herself in. The interior of the trailer was a midcentury modern showpiece, a vaulted open concept space of polished aluminum walls and ceilings with oak flooring throughout. The furnishings were sleek and lux. Two matching Noguchi sofas faced each other across a snowy faux fur rug. An Eames floating console that served as a bar was suspended from the front wall with a reproduction of Roy Lichtenstein's lithograph *Crying Girl* hanging above it. Joey did a double take.

Surely, she thought, *it must be a reproduction.*

But it was the pair of brindle mastiffs that really got her attention. The dogs lolled atop the designer sofas in much the same poses she'd seen on Sofia Campbell's Instagram. They bounded to their feet, barking an alarm the instant she stepped in the door.

"Welcome to my home away from home." Pray spread his arms, smiling broadly. "Don't be shy, come on in."

The enormous dogs continued to snarl, clearly doing what they'd been trained to do, and Pray was clearly enjoying her discomfort.

"Your dogs are beautiful," she said, trying to keep her cool. "But would you please let them know I'm not a threat?"

"Don't worry, they're like big teddy bears once you get to know them."

Big, for sure. Both dogs outweighed Joey by a good sixty pounds.

"I don't doubt that," she said, "but that's the point, isn't it? They don't know me, and they're waiting for a signal from you before they stand down."

Pray clapped his hands twice. "*Platz!*"

On his command, the dogs stopped barking and sat, heads turned to their master expectantly.

"*Gute Jungs,*" he said, scratching them behind the ears as their tails thumped the floor. He knelt to be at eye level with them. "My darlings," he cooed, and the dogs began to lick his face. "My good babies."

Joey was taken aback by his uninhibited display of affection. Once again, she was reminded of photos on Sofia's Instagram that showed Pray looking happy and relaxed. She couldn't help thinking anybody who loved their animals that much can't be all bad. Maybe he only tormented two-legged creatures.

Pray finally stood up and gestured with a flourish to one of the sofas. "Make yourself comfortable, Joey."

This was the first time he'd called her by her given name, and she wondered if he did it just to keep her off balance; if so, it was effective.

"I've had my eye on you," he continued. "I see how hard you work and how much responsibility you take on for your department."

Joey was flustered by the director's sudden affability; she didn't know how to respond.

"Thank you." She nodded uneasily. "I appreciate you saying that, and I don't mean to be rude, but we're in a time crunch to be ready for camera this morning."

She held up her notebook as a visual aid. "Is there someplace I can lay out the fitting photos so you can see them all together?" She scanned the room, looking for a flat surface. The only option was the narrow bar top.

"Of course," Pray replied agreeably. "Let's go into the other room. We'll have more space to spread out there."

He led the way to a heavy oak pocket door and slid it open. "After you," he said, stepping aside.

The room he revealed was dark and spacious, dominated by a king-size bed. Joey turned, but Pray already had her pinned in the doorway, his face almost touching hers. "I've been hoping I'd get some time alone with you," he said, smiling slightly.

She froze as he pressed himself against her and grabbed her breast through her shirt. His breath reeked of coffee and spearmint. Like every other woman she knew, she'd had to fend off unwanted comments and attention since puberty, but she'd never been mauled by ambush this way.

His mouth felt wet on her neck. "You know, this can be fun for both of us, if you just relax," he murmured.

Her insides were churning, but she knew she couldn't show weakness.

"Don't be ridiculous." She was grateful her voice held steady. "If you want to have something to point the camera at this morning, you need to let me go do my job."

"What are you, gay?" He drew back to peer at her.

She locked eyes with him. "That's none of your business."

His lip curled in disdain. "You've got a real stick up your rear, lady."

"Better than a knee in your groin, because that option's on the table if you don't back off."

"I could fire you for that."

Joey held his gaze. "Only if you want to make this a bigger deal than it is."

He put his hands up and backed away from her. "Get out of here. You're not worth the aggravation."

She carefully stepped around him in the doorway, her entire body rigid with tension.

Final Cut

"Keep your mouth shut if you like what you do for a living," he growled, "or you can kiss this business goodbye."

The dogs yawned hugely when Joey passed them but made no sound. Her legs felt like two blocks of wood as she climbed down the Airstream's steps. She stumbled blindly to the nearest women's bathroom, locked herself in a stall, and threw up.

Chapter
Thirty-One

An hour later, Joey watched the three new cast members, Molina, Tucci, and Esposito, running lines together on set. She stood at the back of video village where she could keep an eye on the monitor, waiting for the first shot of the day. But her composure was a false front she wore like a suit of armor.

The recollection of Pray's groping hands disgusted her. She longed to stand in a steaming shower until she felt clean again, as if that could wash every trace of him from her mind as well as her body. Bile backed up in her throat, but she managed to choke it down. She was furious that he thought he had the right to force himself on her, then compel her silence; but they were on his turf and she couldn't expect a fair fight. If she came forward now to call him out, it would turn into a he-said/she-said, and she'd be on the losing end of that one.

Still, this was a turning point for her. She felt a shift that promised aftershocks to come, but she couldn't allow herself to buckle under the pressure. She needed to keep functioning to prove to herself that he couldn't crush her spirit.

Pray appeared unmoved by their confrontation. Looking serious but calm, he huddled with the DP, discussing lighting and camera placement for the scene they were about to shoot, all business as usual in his realm.

As she watched him go about his work, Joey thought about how threatened she felt, both physically and emotionally, by this same man only an hour ago; and she also remembered the way he raged at the B-squad on set the day before, simply because they annoyed him.

Kathleen's warning came back to her: *Guys like him not only repeat, they escalate.*

Pray was a powerful, cruel man who was used to controlling the women in his life. How would he have reacted if Courtney told him she was pregnant, maybe even gave him an ultimatum? Joey felt her own rage boil to the surface and Pray shot to the top of her suspect list.

"They look great, all three of them. Those suits fit like they were tailor made."

She turned to find Eli beside her, looking energized and strangely upbeat, given everything that had happened since the first day of shooting. It was hard for her to believe that was less than a week ago.

He leaned closer and lowered his voice. "But you shouldn't make it look so easy."

Joey felt a sudden urge to confide in him, but she was barely holding it together, and she wanted to get through the day without breaking down.

"I can assure you this morning was anything but effortless," she said sourly.

"Production doesn't know that." He gestured to the figures on the monitor. "They cast actors at the eleventh hour, and now here they are as if by magic, looking like a million bucks."

"The studio'll get the general idea when the bills come in for all the overtime." She squinted up at him. "Why did we have to go to cover, anyway? Was it because of the crash yesterday?"

"We couldn't afford to lose another day." His expression turned dark. "But obviously, we need to regroup after what happened. The mayor's office was the only option that didn't require a location or green screen."

"Do they have any idea what went wrong?" she asked, seizing on a topic that actually interested her. "Was it because Pray made them speed up the action?"

"I'm sure that didn't help." He shook his head impatiently. "But the brakes failed on the bogie Camaro that rolled into the intersection; that's what kicked off the chain reaction."

Joey was surprised by that. Picture cars are generally maintained and handled with painstaking care by their owners and the transpo movie crews that use them.

"Don't those picture cars get a complete inspection every time they're sent out to work?" she said, thinking a brake failure is a pretty big gaffe.

"They tell me it was a simple maintenance error; somebody in transpo screwed up." He shrugged. "The Camaro's master cylinder was contaminated with transmission fluid."

"By accident?" She peered at him, wondering why he wasn't more upset.

"What else would it be?" He frowned and adjusted his headset. "Go for Eli." He listened, then said, "Copy that, coming your way."

He took off without another word, and Joey watched him go, thinking he seemed distracted this morning. It wasn't like him to shrug off a colossal mistake that ruined a day of shooting and sent people to the hospital. Then again, the whole company had been through a lot the past few days, Eli probably most of all. Yet here he was, still on the job; she had to admire his resilience.

She turned her attention back to the monitor, but she couldn't concentrate on the images crowding the small screen. Too many mistakes and accidents, too many important questions unanswered, including the one she'd forgotten to ask Eli: the identity of the big man she'd seen on set the day before. She shuddered, thinking back to that night along PCH; if her mystery follower was on the crew, that was need-to-know information.

After the mayor and his cronies were established on camera, she checked with Zephyr to make sure the set costumers had everything they needed. Then she walked away. Her thoughts and feelings were all over the place; she wanted some time alone to try and get a grip on herself.

Crafty was set up in a darkened corner of the soundstage, not far from the set. Joey wandered over to grab a bottle of water. For once, the area was deserted, tables littered with wadded-up paper napkins and half-eaten plates of food. The solitude felt like a refuge. She took a seat on an old apple crate and closed her eyes, grateful for the quiet of the dimly lit stage.

"The troops brought their appetites today."

She looked up with a start. Sam set down two fresh plates of sandwiches, then began to clear the mess from the tables.

"Not that I'm complaining." The girl sent her a sweet smile. "I like to stay busy, and you all need to keep your energy up. It's hard, working these long hours."

Moments before, Joey had wanted more than anything to be alone, but now Sam's face held her spellbound.

You look exactly like your sister.

She wasn't aware she'd spoken her thought until Sam said, "How do you know what Sofia looks like?"

"I saw her picture on IMDb," Joey answered automatically. "The Internet Movie Database."

"You looked her up?"

Sam couldn't hide her own curiosity, and Joey nodded slowly, as she realized this could be a chance to get some of her questions answered.

"Is it difficult for you to talk about Sofia?" she asked carefully.

"No, it's not difficult." Sam went back to her work. "I think about her all the time, but it's hard for Daddy, so I don't talk about her very often." She glanced at Joey uncertainly. "You really think we look alike?"

"Very much, especially your eyes. There's no mistaking you're sisters."

"That's nice." Sam started loading bottled water into a heavy-duty cooler full of ice. "I can't see it myself, but I always thought she had the most beautiful eyes."

Joey saw this as the opening she needed. "Sofia seemed to be having quite a bit of success in film; the credits on her IMDb page are impressive."

"I've never seen that website, but I know she worked on some big movies," Sam said.

"Would you like to look at your sister's profile now?" Joey asked, coaxing her. "I can pull it up on my phone and show you."

"Maybe in a little while." Sam looked over her shoulder. "I should finish cleaning these tables before the crew breaks again."

"I looked at Sofia's Instagram too," Joey continued. "Have you seen what she posted there, the pictures of her with Marcus Pray?"

Sam moved on to the next table, hurrying to gather up the used plates and napkins. "I don't know what you're talking about."

But her face told a different story. Joey watched her closely; if Sam sidestepped her next question, she'd back away from the subject of Sofia for now.

"You must have wondered," she said gently. "I know I would if she were my sister. What happened to her, Sam?"

The young woman set down the plates she'd been collecting and braced herself against the nearest table.

"She drowned in the ocean." Her voice was hardly more than a whisper. "They said it was an accident."

"Who's 'they'?" Joey said softly, leaning toward her.

Sam ducked her head and didn't respond.

"I'm sorry, but this is important." Joey kept her eyes fixed on Sam. "Did you know Sofia was seeing Marcus Pray?"

"Leave her alone!"

Joey twisted in her seat to find Stuart standing over her.

"Don't say anything more, Sammy," he ordered. "She only wants to make trouble for us."

"That's not true!" Joey jumped to her feet. "I care what happens to both of you, and I'm worried, especially for Samantha. What were you thinking, bringing her here? Are you using her to try to bait Pray?"

"You don't know the first thing about our lives." The look on Stuart's face was ferocious.

"I know you used to be a stuntman here in Hollywood, and I know Sofia was living with Pray before she died." Joey's heart hammered in her chest. "Does he have any idea who you are?"

Stuart took a menacing step toward her. "Shut your mouth!"

Instinctively, Joey backed away and tripped over a cooler full of soft drinks. She fell against one of the craft service tables, knocking several plates of food to the floor with a crash.

"Daddy, stop!" Sam grabbed hold of her father's arm.

"What's going on back here?" Lionel came rushing around the back wall of the set. "Is everybody all right?"

"We're fine." Joey started to get to her feet. "I tripped, that's all."

"Sounded like more than that to me," Lionel said irritably.

"We had a little mishap." Sam stepped up and offered Joey her hand. "But we're okay, like she said." Her eyes flicked to her father. "Right, Daddy?"

Stuart muttered something under his breath, then turned and headed for the stage entrance.

"Okay, then," Lionel said, frowning. "But try and keep it down. We're not recording sound right now, but the noise is distracting."

"It's my fault." Joey said. "I'll be more careful."

She waited till Lionel went back on set, then bent to help Sam clean up the mess. "Sam, you need to be honest with me," she said in a low voice. "Are you afraid of your father?"

"No!" The girl shrank from her. "Why would you say that?"

"Because he seems so volatile. I'm not saying I blame him," Joey said quickly. "The death of a child would send anybody round the bend; it's no wonder if he's not quite himself." She shook her head sympathetically. "But this is a very unhealthy situation, with the two of you here, working for Pray."

"Don't worry about us." Sam's face was suddenly flushed. "We can take care of ourselves."

But Joey couldn't let this go.

"He's angry, and my guess is he's looking for someone to answer for Sofia's death," she argued. "That could make him a danger to anybody he thinks is responsible, or even to himself."

"He'd never hurt anybody," Sam said staunchly. "He couldn't."

"I know you love him, but if he's got emotional problems, you need to speak up and get him some help," Joey insisted. "For his sake as well as yours."

"Daddy's right, you don't know the first thing about us." Sam's eyes turned cold. "I need to go find him now."

She abandoned the clean-up and started toward the stage door, then turned back to face Joey. "He's a good man and a good father. Everybody needs to just leave us alone."

Chapter
Thirty-Two

Joey felt terrible about her run-in with Stuart and Sam, though in a way it was just bad luck. She was sure Sam had been on the brink of confiding in her when Stuart interrupted them. Joey wanted to reach out to her again but thought it was probably best to give Sam time to cool off.

Despite all the ugliness and confusion of the morning, she couldn't shake the feeling that some crucial insight hovered just beyond her reach. She kept collecting information that seemed important to the investigation of Courtney's murder; she just couldn't quite see how the pieces fit together.

She wondered if the police were making progress with the case, and for one brief second she wished she could call Detective Blankenship to ask what was happening on her end. But until the cops officially checked her off the suspect list, Joey needed to keep her head down.

In the meantime, she wasn't willing to sit back and wait for somebody else to figure things out. Maybe she didn't have the big picture yet, but she believed that Pray's pattern of sexual abuse and manipulation was key, and she wanted to understand more about the nature of the relationships he had with Courtney, Sofia, and, by extension, with Stuart and Sam. The fact she despised the man wasn't the only reason she wanted to expose him, but that goal gave her a renewed sense of purpose.

As always, her sources for information were scarce. She wouldn't trust anything Caleb had to say, even if he'd take her call. He'd been evasive from the start, and if he wasn't directly involved in his sister's death (and Joey wasn't ready to count him out) there was still something shady about his attitude that made her think he had more to hide than a grieving brother should.

Given her limited options, she decided it was time to take another crack at Sofia's agent, Eva Birkus. Courtney was the second of Pray's girlfriends who'd died in less than two years. Joey wanted to know more about what happened to the first one.

The dark corner by Crafty that had been her refuge now seemed claustrophobic: Joey needed to get out into the light. She pushed through the door of the soundstage straight into a wall of heat that felt like a convection oven set to broil. In other words, just your normal summer day in the Valley. She didn't want to go back to the wardrobe trailer, where there was no privacy and her side of the call to Birkus would be up for public consumption, so she pressed herself into a scrap of shade provided by an alcove near the stage entrance.

But the Warner lot was busy and noisy, with the usual studio traffic. Trucks and equipment rumbled along the narrow passageways between soundstages, dodging trams full of tourists buzzing with excitement as their guides pointed out the buildings where beloved TV shows like *Friends* and *The Big Bang Theory* had been shot.

Joey had to strain to hear the receptionist who answered at Olympus Artists Agency. This time when she asked to speak to Birkus and was told, "Please hold," she got ready to leave a message on the agent's voice mail.

"This is Eva Birkus."

Taken by surprise, Joey fumbled her intro. "Oh, hi. I expected to get your voice mail."

"Sorry to disappoint." The agent's voice was low and gruff. "What do you want?"

"I'm calling in regard to Sofia Campbell, who used to be a client of yours," Joey said cautiously.

"I'm aware Sofia was a client. Who are you, and why are you calling about a girl who's been dead for more than a year?"

"My name's Joey Jessop, and I'm a friend of Sofia's sister, Samantha."

"Really." Her tone was steeped in skepticism. "And the purpose of your call?"

"It's a long story." Joey cringed while she gathered her thoughts; she should've had her spiel down pat before she made the call.

"I'll give you thirty seconds before I hang up," Birkus said.

"Sofia's sister, Samantha, and I are working on a movie being directed by Marcus Pray, and we've gotten to be friendly." Joey knew she was talking too fast. "But I'm worried about her; I think she took this job because of what happened to her sister."

Birkus didn't hang up, but she didn't respond either, so Joey plunged ahead.

"Sam's a sweet girl, but she's delicate, and Sofia's death hit her hard. I know this isn't your problem, but I care about her, and I'd like to find a way to help."

Joey caught her breath with a little gulp. There was a long pause, and she was afraid she'd blown the contact with her garbled explanation.

"Please tell me this is some kind of sick joke," Birkus finally said. "No way on God's green earth should Sofia's sister be working for that degenerate."

Her worries the agent might have ties to Pray disappeared.

"It's no joke," she said. "Samantha does craft service for the movie."

"Well, you don't sound like a reporter, not that a single one of them has shown the slightest interest so far." Birkus's tone softened. "If this is Samantha, I'd like to meet you, honey. I was very fond of your sister."

Joey didn't blame Birkus for doubting her story. "I'm not, but I think she might speak with you if you want. My name really is Joey, and I work in the costume department."

"All I can say is, if you have any influence with Samantha, get her out of there. You should go too, you want my opinion. Nothing good can happen with Pray running rampant."

"Then maybe you can help me," Joey said. "I've been looking for information about what happened to Sofia, but I haven't had any luck online; and when I tried to talk to Sam about it, I got the impression she may not know a lot of the details herself."

"I hope for her sake that's true," Birkus said emphatically. "If you're her friend, trust me, you'll want it to stay that way."

"I hear what you're saying, Ms. Birkus, and I don't discount your advice. I'd never want to do anything to hurt Sam."

"I'm glad to know that, young lady, so please listen carefully when I tell you again to get out of there. Take Sam with you and go."

"It's not that simple," Joey countered. "I have other responsibilities . . . other people involved. That's why I need your help to understand what happened to Sofia. I know she died on New Year's Day in 2022, and Sam told me she drowned accidentally—"

"Wrong!" Birkus said harshly.

"Excuse me?" The venom she put into that one word brought Joey up short.

"There was nothing accidental about it. She walked naked into the surf in front of Pray's Malibu beach house while he was entertaining a new lady friend or two inside, and she didn't come back out. Not alive, anyway."

Now Joey heard the pain in the other woman's voice. She swallowed hard, unable to trust her own.

"Hello? You still there?" Birkus's tone went flat again. "You see why you're not doing her sister a service by pursuing this?"

"Are you sure?" Joey closed her eyes, knowing she could never be the one to tell Sam.

"I wasn't an eyewitness if that's what you mean. But yeah, I'm sure."

"But I couldn't find a single mention of her death anywhere when I looked; nothing in any of the newspapers or the trades, not even the tabloids."

It was easier for Joey to focus on facts than the heartbreak of this discovery.

"Pray's a very powerful man in this town," Birkus said, as if the answer was obvious. "It happened on his private property, and he was able to control the flow of information from the beginning."

"Then how do you know all this?" Joey asked.

"Lots of people know, believe me," Birkus said grimly. "But they're not going to say anything because they don't want to get on the wrong side of Marcus Pray. There's no percentage in it. A jilted girl dead by her own hand isn't reason enough to make him angry."

"So why are you telling me this now?" Joey persisted. "Aren't *you* worried about making him angry?"

"Don't take this the wrong way, but I don't think you're in any position to make much trouble for a man like Pray, even if you wanted to. I'd be rooting for you if you could."

Her words were a bitter pill for Joey, especially after the scene in Pray's trailer that morning.

"The truth is, I still feel guilty," Birkus went on. "I hadn't spoken to Sofia for several months before she died. Pray convinced her to dump me and sign with his agent. I know she felt bad about it, because she was a sweet girl, and we were fond of each other. I did try to warn her about him, but she said he was a changed man."

Joey thought back to the months of happy Instagram posts. "I guess it didn't take."

"Men like Pray don't change," Birkus said. "And to answer your question, I guess I'm telling you now because you asked. Nobody cared enough to call and ask about her before. She's been tossed away and forgotten."

"You don't sound like any Hollywood agent I've ever met."

"Never fear, I'm as cold-blooded as the rest of them. I just think it stinks she got such a rotten deal."

Chapter
Thirty-Three

"You all right?"

Joey looked up to find Lionel watching her. She still stood outside the stage door with her phone clasped in her hand.

"I'm fine," she said, feeling the opposite.

He shook his head. "You've been standing there staring at nothing. What's going on?"

"I'm not sure." Frowning, she pocketed the phone.

"Listen, I'm sorry about snapping at you earlier." Concern puckered his brow. "Anything I can help with, just say the word."

"Sure, I will." She nodded woodenly. "Thanks, Lionel."

"Okay." He opened the stage door. "See you later, then," he said with a doubtful glance back at her.

Joey wished she had someone to use as a sounding board to talk through all she'd learned, but she knew her coworkers wouldn't want to be burdened with the information. Gossip was one thing, but a politically sensitive scandal that could jeopardize their jobs? Nobody wanted a piece of that. Then who could she talk to, and who could she trust? Certainly no one higher up the corporate ladder at the studio. The warning they delivered through Bill made it clear they'd shut her down as soon as they got the gist of what she had to say about their megastar producer/director.

So where did that leave her? It was no secret Pray was a sexual predator, but what if he was a killer to boot? Courtney was the second of his girlfriends to wind up dead in the past eighteen months. That should raise a few red flags if only someone with official standing would take an interest.

Anxiety gripped her. Who could say for sure Sofia's death was suicide if, as Eva Birkus claimed, Pray controlled the narrative around her drowning from the beginning? That was enough to make Joey question the cause of death, especially after her up close and personal encounter with him. The man had a taste for violence; she felt that at the cellular level, like a hunted animal senses danger. Birkus's story only confirmed Pray was a toxic menace, as if Joey needed more evidence of that.

None of these insights helped much; she still couldn't decide what to do next. She felt seriously out of her depth, with nowhere safe to turn. Even if she rolled the dice and went to the cops with the information she had, there was no reason to think they'd take her word to go after a powerful man like Pray. Nobody had so far. It was maddening, but she'd hit a brick wall.

To keep from sinking into utter despair, Joey threw herself into her busy schedule for the day, starting with her check-in at Hammer and Tongs. Damir had cast his net wide and filled every available nook in his costume house with skilled craftspeople who were frantically pumping out work to meet the Wednesday goal for camera.

From there she went on to FabricArt, a studio that was custom printing fabrics for six of their superheroes; the next stop was Sylvia's to inspect the embroidery for Renée Zellweger's cape. That's how she spent the better part of the day, making the rounds of her vendors, bouncing from one to the next with a pinball's momentum.

Glendale to West Hollywood, then downtown, the west side, and north to the Valley again, Joey crisscrossed the city. The day was another SoCal stunner, sunny with cobalt skies spreading from the foothills of Pasadena to the coastline of Santa Monica. And at each of her stops, she found the work going well: no hitches, no delays, no complaints. After the past couple of days, it was nothing short of a miracle.

Normally, she enjoyed this routine. Photos and texts could tell you only so much; there was no substitute for seeing the garments, touching the fabrics, talking with the artisans who brought the designs to life.

But even the progress with the work couldn't lift her spirits. There was no escape from the dark thoughts that trailed her like an unwelcome shadow. The rift with the Campbells was never far from her mind; and the more she learned, the more she worried for Sam in this setting with Pray in command, although (as with so much else lately) she wasn't sure what to do about that.

Pray remained an open question, and no matter how many ways Joey approached the problem, she couldn't see an effective path forward. Then there was the looming issue of the mystery man, the big guy she spotted on set. Was her follower from PCH on the movie's crew or were her fears twisting her perceptions?

As she steered back onto the Warner lot, she got a text from Dahlia:

Find me when you get to set.

The text pulled her head back into the workday. She hadn't heard from Dahlia since that morning when she sent her photos of the three new actors on set and in costume just before camera rolled. That felt like a lifetime ago. The designer replied to the message with a thumbs-up emoji, but she hadn't shown up on set to watch them work.

Now Joey decided Dahlia would have to wait. Before she did anything else, she wanted to check in with the set costumers to see how the day was shaping up. When she came in the side entrance to Stage Five, she scanned the area automatically for any sign of Pray or the mystery man. It galled her to realize this had become her first instinct when she walked onto set. All the work lights were on, and she found Zephyr reorganizing the set rack near video village.

"How's it going so far?" she asked.

"I don't want to jinx us, but it's all good." Zephyr gave her a quick smile. "We're moving fast for a change."

Around them, the stage was alive with activity as the grips, electricians, and camera crew hustled to get ready for the next shot. Joey noticed Eli standing on the sidelines, supervising the work, his expression dark and serious. She wondered if that meant more trouble was brewing.

"You doing okay with our new cast?" she asked Zephyr.

"Dreamboats, all of them, couldn't be nicer." She lowered her voice. "The set feels different today; maybe they brought us good luck."

As if, Joey thought, but she wasn't going to grinch on Zephyr. "Where's the rest of our crew?"

"Crafty and bathroom. Christine and I are spelling each other so one of us stays with the rack; I'm going to break when she comes back, and that should be any time now."

"There's my secret weapon."

Dahlia appeared at Joey's side, looking camera-ready herself in a green brocade coat and black silk trousers. Her hair was a cascade of carefully blown-out curls, her makeup understated and flawless.

"Where are you off to?" Joey asked.

"I've already been." She linked her arm through Joey's. "That's what I want to talk to you about. But not here; I only popped in to make an appearance."

"I just got back myself, but Zephyr says everything's going well, the best day so far on set."

"Even a blind pig finds an acorn every now and then," Dahlia sneered. She swiveled, looking around the stage. "Speaking of pigs, where's Marcus? I need to see him for a quick sec before we get out of here."

Zephyr cleared her throat. "I heard him tell Lionel he'd be in his trailer for the break."

"Hopefully, doing something that will put him in a good mood when he comes back to set," Dahlia said, absently fluffing her curls.

Joey couldn't help being curious about the change in Dahlia's attitude. The designer seemed almost playful, a one-eighty reversal from her chilly behavior at the superhero fittings the day before.

"Look who's here." Pray swept through the door of the mayor's office set. "I thought I heard your voice, Dahlia."

Joey had to work to keep a neutral expression on her face. She felt no obligation to acknowledge Pray, but she didn't want to give any sign that it bothered her to see him.

"There you are." Dahlia pasted on a smile as she crossed the stage to greet him. "I've been looking everywhere for you."

"You know, we have three principal actors working for the first time today." Pray's tone was brittle with false cheer. "Have you met them, by any chance?"

"Yes, and don't they look handsome?" Dahlia's smile grew even brighter, as if this were a friendly conversation. "I've been in constant touch with my crew since four this morning, and they tell me everything is running like clockwork here today. Marcus, you're a wizard."

"I take that as a real compliment, coming from the queen of the disappearing act," he snapped. "Remind me why I'm paying you eight thousand dollars a week." He took a step toward Dahlia, and Joey could see it cost her not to flinch. "I'm not in the habit of paying that kind of salary to someone who doesn't think it's necessary to show up for work."

"Marcus, I've had my fingers on the pulse of this day since before dawn," Dahlia said evenly. "The actors look great, work is going well, and if you'll remember, I am OC on the call sheet. Own call. Now, if you have anything else to say to me, we should finish this discussion in private."

Pray stood glaring at her while those gathered on stage braced for the outburst sure to follow. Instead, he lurched toward Dahlia, then staggered, clutching at her as he fell. He lay on his back, eyes bulging, clawing at his own throat.

"Can't breathe," he gasped.

Eli dropped to his knees beside the director and began to loosen his clothing. "Get the medic!"

Lionel spoke into his walkie. "Anybody have eyes on the medic? We have an emergency on Stage Five."

"She's flying in," came the response.

Seconds later a young woman rushed onto the stage with an EMT bag slung over her shoulder, pushing past crew members crowded around the fallen director.

Pray's face was red and swollen, his breathing a harsh rasp. The medic knelt beside him.

"Call nine-one-one," she said. "Can we get some more light here?"

Eli was already on his cell making the call. He motioned to Lionel. "Bring a couple work lights over."

The medic made sure Pray's airway was clear, then checked his pulse. "This looks like an anaphylactic reaction." She patted the director's face, trying to get a response. "Mr. Pray, do you have any allergies?"

"He's allergic to tree nuts," Joey blurted out, recalling Sam's words when they first met.

All eyes turned to her, and she knew from the suspicious looks of the other crew members that she could expect a fresh crop of rumors and accusations.

"You sure about that?" The medic rummaged through her bag.

"Samantha from Crafty mentioned that's why they never serve nuts," Joey replied.

"Looks like he got exposure somehow." Using an EpiPen, she injected medication into Pray's outer thigh, right through his clothing. "We'll know soon enough."

She started doing chest compressions, and within seconds, Pray's eyelids fluttered. He coughed and began to choke. The medic gently shifted him onto his side to keep his airway clear.

"Make sure all the studio gates are notified we have an emergency," she said. "And somebody needs to be looking out for the ambulance."

"Gates are alerted, and we've got a PA stationed outside," Eli said. "Is he going to be okay?"

"Thanks to her." The medic nodded at Joey. "But we still have to get him to an ER as soon as possible. A reaction this acute needs to be monitored at a hospital, probably overnight."

Pray moaned and turned over on his back. His breathing had eased considerably, but his face was still swollen and red.

"Help me up." He sounded blurry.

"You need to lie back and stay quiet until the ambulance gets here," the medic said.

"No ambulance." Pray moved to sit up, but the young woman put a restraining hand on his shoulder.

"You've had a severe allergic reaction and a shock to your system. I gave you a shot of epinephrine, but you need to go to the hospital and get thoroughly checked out."

Pray made a hissing sound of frustration, but he didn't have the strength to sit up on his own.

"You'll feel better if you try to relax." The medic patted him reassuringly. "You're going to be okay."

Eli signaled to Lionel. "Clear the stage so there's no traffic jam when the EMTs get here. He doesn't need an audience for this."

"Are we wrapping for the day?" Lionel asked.

"Let's deal with one thing at a time." Eli clapped his hands impatiently. "Listen up, everybody. Let's take a break—do whatever you want for the next twenty minutes, but do it someplace else."

Joey hurried toward the stage door, feeling more anxious than ever, but Eli intercepted her. "Why were you and Samantha discussing Marcus's food allergy?" he asked sharply.

"It wasn't like that," she protested. "Sam told me Pray's allergy was the reason they didn't serve nuts. That was the extent of it; no discussion."

He bent close to her. "Don't you find it suspicious that Marcus has an allergic attack on set when the people who handle half the food service know about his condition, and one of them was ready to jump all over him two days ago?"

If he hadn't been so belligerent, she might have opened up to him, but Joey wasn't going to make trouble for the Campbells by telling Eli about Pray's relationship with Sofia, the young actress's death, or her family ties to Stuart and Sam. He'd fire them on the spot, no questions asked; and that wasn't only unfair, it wouldn't necessarily solve anything. Joey just couldn't do that to Sam.

"Here's another good question," she said instead. "How many other people around here knew about his food allergy? Did you?"

"What's that supposed to mean?" His eyes bored into her.

She glared back at him. "My point is, anybody with access could find a way to dose him, especially if he's that allergic. And I think it's safe to say there are plenty of people who wouldn't mind taking him down, one way or another."

There was a commotion at the stage entrance, and the DGA trainee came racing in. "They're here!"

Two uniformed EMTs trailed close behind, carrying a collapsible stretcher. Eli broke away to help the emergency workers, and Joey made a quick exit. She'd deflected Eli's accusations for Sam's sake, but she worried Stuart might be responsible for Pray's attack. She didn't want to believe it, but she wouldn't be surprised. He had plenty of motive to wish Pray literally ill, and, as Eli pointed out, he had the perfect means and opportunity.

She started hiking across the studio lot, trying to walk off her tension. For once, she could almost understand Eli's former love affair with drugs. If only she could shut down her brain for a while, just to take a breather, that would feel like heaven. The relief of oblivion.

A thick blanket of late afternoon heat made the air shimmer. Up ahead, Melanie Beale emerged from the makeup trailer. Joey almost doubled back to avoid her when a big man with long wavy hair followed Melanie out of the trailer and down the steps where the two of them stood chatting.

Without a doubt, this was the same guy she'd seen talking to the PA and stunt driver on Broadway the day before. She was less certain he was her follower in the SUV, but the build and hair were a match. What were the odds? Along with the fact he was pals with the lovely Ms. Beale, another black mark against him.

"Hey!" Joey called. "Who's your friend, Melanie? He sure looks familiar."

She broke into a trot. Melanie scooted back up the trailer's steps while her long-haired friend decided it was a good idea to jog wherever he was headed next.

"Wait up! I want to talk to you." Joey picked up her pace.

Other people stared as she ran past, probably wondering what emergency called for a sprint across the studio lot in triple-digit heat. Sweat streamed down her face and into her eyes. He moved fast for a guy his size, she had to give him that, but she was gaining on him.

Right up until the moment a golf cart shot from between two soundstages directly into her path. The driver was on his phone, deep in conversation. She stumbled, narrowly avoiding a collision, and went sprawling on the searing hot pavement. He noticed her then.

"Watch where you're going," Mr. Golf Cart said indignantly.

As she lay there prone and panting, she saw the big guy loping off in the distance. And then her cell phone buzzed with an incoming text.

Something told her it wasn't good news.

Chapter
Thirty-Four

The next morning Joey went down to the beach as soon as light began to lift over the ocean. She dreaded going in to the studio. No call sheet had been issued the night before, so the company was winging it and the day was up for grabs. But that wasn't the reason she was walking the shore before dawn, trying to shake herself out of the dark blue funk that made her want to dive back under the covers.

For starters, there was the latest poison pen text, the one that came through the day before while she was laid out flat on the asphalt after her skirmish with the golf cart:

The Lord said to Moses: whoever has sinned against me, I will blot out of my book.

She'd felt so overwhelmed between the on-set crash, Pray jumping her in his trailer, his allergic attack, her worries for the Campbells, and her PCH mystery man on top of Courtney's murder that her text message bully had all but dropped off the radar. Now that her troll was back, she still wasn't willing to go to the cops, not that she wasn't bothered by the harassment. She just didn't think the police could or would do much about the texts, anyway.

The messages were creepy, but not explicitly threatening. Plus, she didn't recognize the number that sent them, and any person with half a brain would use a disposable cell. Given all the unwanted publicity she'd attracted since Courtney died, her stalker could be virtually anyone, from a crackpot with Wi-Fi access in another part of the country to someone far too close for comfort, like the long-haired guy who was so eager to avoid her yesterday. That was the trouble: it was anybody's guess.

The sun wasn't up, but her head was already spinning. She stood at the water's edge and howled in frustration, startling a seagull who'd been foraging nearby in the skeins of seaweed coiled on the sand. The big brown bird squawked at her angrily and flew off down the beach, tracing the shoreline on his hunt for breakfast. Joey thought the bird had the right idea; it would be wonderful to just fly away whenever something aggravated you.

But she didn't have that luxury, and her problems weren't going to disappear on their own. Pray's poisoning put a new light on everything. He'd damaged so many lives, maybe the attack on him wasn't all that surprising, but it was confusing to think her number one suspect in Courtney's murder was also a target. Still, that didn't mean he hadn't killed Courtney, and although things didn't look good for the Campbells, they weren't the only people who had reason to want to harm Marcus Pray. Joey could personally testify to that.

Her cell buzzed in her pocket, drawing her back to the here and now. She grabbed it out to find a blanket text from Eli to the entire crew:

Company meeting at the Studio, Stage Five, 7:30 AM.

She was startled to see she'd missed a call, and shocked that it was from Caleb. He'd left a brief voice mail: "I need to talk to you about something important, but I don't want to say more on a recording. Please call me as soon as you get this."

His delivery was clipped but not hateful. If anything, Joey thought he sounded frightened.

She called him back right away, but his voice mail picked up. Disappointed, she left her own message. "Sorry I missed you, Caleb.

Please call or text me when you can." She still didn't trust him, but she hoped he'd be in touch.

The hodgepodge of thoughts from her beach walk followed her back to the house. She told herself to open her mind, to let go of any prejudices or preconceptions. *Look at the big picture.* If nothing else, her training had taught her that was the only way to see clearly.

She dressed for work quickly, then poured the last of her morning coffee in a travel mug and hit the road feeling buzzed, but not in a good way.

"Marcus is home resting." Eli looked haggard this morning, as though he'd aged ten years overnight. "He's going to try to come in this afternoon, but in the meantime, we're going to continue with the scenes in the mayor's office, per the one-line schedule."

Murmurs rippled through the company on Stage Five. The prop master raised his voice to be heard over the chatter. "Who's going to run the set?"

"Bernard and I will, together," Eli said, nodding toward the DP. "We can't lose the day because we need to shoot Alfred Molina out by the end of the week. He has other commitments on the East Coast."

The prop master bobbed his head, but Joey heard him grumble to his assistant, "You watch; that control freak'll make us reshoot everything when he gets back."

"We'll pick up where we left off yesterday with Scene 104B," Eli said. "Any other questions?"

A few people exchanged nervous glances, but most telegraphed their readiness to get on with the workday.

"Okay then; the actors are called for eight o'clock." Eli twirled a finger in the air to signal the meeting was over. "Makeup and hair, you'll have them for one hour. Set call is nine thirty."

Dahlia was MIA again this morning, so Joey needed to stay with the shooting company until they got the first shot. She and the set costumers headed to the wardrobe trailer to prep the actors' rooms while Bill split for the office back at LCC to work on the latest version of the costume budget.

"The numbers are a fairy tale at this point," he said to Joey on his way out the door. "But I've got to go through the motions. Call me when the daily crisis hits."

His wisecrack pushed her to make a snap decision, and she turned to Zephyr. "You need my help setting the actors' rooms?"

"No, we got it, piece of cake." Zephyr peered at her. "You okay?"

"I have something to take care of, but I won't go far," she said. "Text me if there's a problem."

Joey waved and set off for craft service. Forget about waiting around for the next disaster—she meant to talk to Sam before the day got away from her. No matter what was going on with Stuart, Joey wanted to help if she could, but there was no dancing around the situation. She had to meet it head on.

Stage Five was only dimly lit by work lights, and the corner where craft service was stationed felt cold as a deep freeze. A large crowd, mostly teamsters and camera crew, gathered around the tables spread with sandwiches, deviled eggs, and pastries. Sam and Stuart were busy restocking the plates with food as fast as the crew mowed through it.

Joey hung back in the shadows, heart beating double time as she waited for the crowd to thin. She fiddled with her phone while she tried to decide what she needed to say, to choose words that would convince Sam she only wanted to help.

"Whoever took him out," one of the grips hoisted his Styrofoam cup in a toast, "they did us a solid."

"The fool could've done it himself," a camera operator said. "But if somebody helped him along, I'd like to shake his hand."

"How do you know it's a 'he'?" the grip said. "Isn't poison a woman's weapon?"

"Nuts don't count as poison," a teamster declared.

"Close enough, when they put a man down like that."

Joey keyed into their conversation as soon as she realized they were talking about Pray. She was surprised they'd trash him so openly, but it proved the point she'd made to Eli the day before: the whole crew resented Pray's brand of leadership, the way he treated them like flunkeys.

She noticed Pete O'Neill, the teamster who took care of Pray's trailer, in the mix. His head was bent over a plate of food, but she could tell he was tracking the discussion.

"Too bad they didn't finish the job," the grip went on. "But you know what they say, 'If at first you don't succeed.'" He winked at Stuart. "Right, my man?"

"Stop your nonsense." Stuart scowled as he plopped a bowl of potato salad in the middle of the table. "You're just talking to hear your head rattle."

An idea started to form at the back of Joey's mind, and she kept her eyes on Pete, watching for his reaction to the other crew members' comments.

"Whatever you say," the grip replied. "Call it a happy accident. We've had more than our share of the other kind, thanks to that lunatic. Serves him right to be the one in the hospital this time around."

Pete glanced at the grip and smiled. The hair on the back of Joey's neck stood up. Eli said someone in transpo made a mistake that screwed up the brakes on the picture car, but what if that was no accident? And when it came to Pray's poisoning, who had better access to the director and the food in his kitchen than the man who took care of his trailer? Pray surely treated Pete as badly as he did everyone else.

She jumped when her cell phone vibrated with an incoming call, and she answered without checking the screen. "This is Joey," she said breathlessly.

"That's not a very bright greeting," Dahlia said. "What's wrong with my secret weapon this morning?"

It was all she could do not to groan, but Joey wanted to get off the phone ASAP, and the trick to that was composure.

"Everybody's getting on fine," she said, adjusting her tone. "The costumers are setting the rooms, and the actors should be in any minute. We're picking up where we left off yesterday with Scene 104B in the mayor's office."

"Marcus is back already?"

"He's resting at home, but production says we can't lose the day, so Eli and Bernard will run the set."

"Good then." The designer sounded bored. "Now find a spot with some privacy where you can talk for a few minutes."

No, no, no! Joey wanted to shout, but she made her way outside, sticking close to the soundstage entrance. "Ready when you are," she said briskly.

"I'm telling you this in strictest confidence," Dahlia said. "I haven't even told Bill."

"Okay," Joey said cautiously. She needed to marshal her racing thoughts and listen to Dahlia if she hoped to cut this conversation short.

"I'm leaving the show early." The designer's voice brimmed with excitement. "I'm doing the next James Bond picture! It's more than a year of work, locations all over the world, and boatloads of money."

So that's why she was dressed to impress the day before, for a high-profile interview. But Dahlia wasn't just leaving the show early; they'd barely begun shooting. The movie wasn't fully cast yet, let alone designed. Any other time, Joey would have showered her with questions, but right now, she couldn't drum up much interest.

"I guess I should say congratulations," she offered.

"Don't sound so gloomy," Dahlia scolded. "The reason I'm calling is," she took a dramatic pause, "I want *you* to come *with* me!"

That got Joey's attention. "To do the Bond movie?"

She couldn't believe she'd heard correctly. Her relationship with Dahlia was civil, but not exactly a love fest, and it would be a double whammy to their department if both members of the design team abandoned ship. For her, that made it a no-brainer.

"I'm flattered you'd ask, Dahlia, but I think we'll be better off if I stay and finish this one."

"Here's the thing," Dahlia continued as if Joey hadn't spoken. "The climax of the movie happens during a spectacular masked ball at a castle in Monaco, and I'm going to need someone with your skills on the job because we have to make everything from scratch."

"Really, Dahlia—"

"Turns out a terrorist group planted a bomb to take out one of the guests, a sheik they have a grudge against, for some reason," she said cheerfully. "Cue Bond to save the day . . ."

Joey was only half-listening while she waited for Dahlia to wrap up her sales pitch when she noticed a motley procession of people coming her way.

Marcus Pray marched at the center of the group. Next to him was Eli, head bent as he spoke to a dark-haired woman in a business suit. Four uniformed sheriff's deputies were also part of the retinue, along with two technicians lugging cameras and bags of equipment.

"What the heck?" she murmured.

"I said, I'll give you co-design credit!" Dahlia screeched in her ear at the same time Joey recognized the woman in the suit, Detective Corinne Blankenship of the Los Angeles County Sheriff's Homicide Bureau.

"I gotta go," she said and hung up on her boss.

Chapter
Thirty-Five

J oey's eyes stayed on Blankenship and the deputies. She could see their tension mount as they approached Stage Five; heads came up, shoulders straightened, conversations ceased. One of the deputies placed his hand on his holstered gun.

They stopped a few feet from the stage door, and Blankenship turned to Eli. "Mr. Logan, I think it best if you and your people wait outside while we execute the warrant."

"No way." Pray stepped between them, glaring at the detective. "I want to see his face."

"That's inadvisable," Blankenship said calmly. "For everybody's safety, yours and ours, I must respectfully instruct you to remain outside."

"Shove your instruction," Pray snarled, and slammed through the stage door.

Eli followed him inside.

Blankenship pursed her lips, then motioned to two of the deputies. "Cabrera, you and Smith establish a perimeter and secure the entrance so nobody else gets inside."

She pointed to her other two team members. "Dillon and Murphy, come with me."

The detective and her deputies went through the stage door while a handful of the movie crew began to gather near the entrance,

272

peppering the deputies who remained outside with questions they refused to answer.

Joey scoped the area with a glance, but nobody was paying attention to her. She slipped into the soundstage. After the blank brightness of the morning outside, she had to stop to let her eyes readjust to the shadowy interior. Voices drew her to the craft service station in the far corner of the stage.

"My truck's right outside the stage door," Stuart was saying. "Go ahead and look at whatever you want. Knock yourselves out."

Joey peeked around one of the flats of scenery. The teamsters, grips, and camera crew had dispersed or been ordered off the stage. Only Stuart and Sam faced the authorities who were flanked by Eli and Pray.

Blankenship held out a document. "Mr. Campbell, I need you to acknowledge service of the warrant."

"Keep your paper." Stuart waved her off. "I already gave you leave."

"I'd like to cram that warrant down your throat till you choke on it!" Pray shouted. "You can't weasel out of this, old man."

"Please, Mr. Pray, let us handle this," Blankenship said firmly.

Tendons stood out in bands on his neck as the director lunged for Stuart. "He tried to poison me!"

One of the deputies moved to block him.

"Out of my way!" Pray roared.

"Not another word," Blankenship ordered. "I told you to wait outside."

Pray's eyes flashed savagely. "You can't throw me off my own soundstage!"

"I most certainly can, and I will. Murphy." Blankenship gestured to the deputy who stood between Pray and Stuart. "Please escort Mr. Pray outside."

"Don't try it." Pray made a wild swipe at the deputy, then jabbed a finger at Blankenship. "You're more stupid than you look, if that's even possible."

Eli stepped in to restrain Pray, but the director shook him off. "You're messing with the wrong guy!" he shouted at Blankenship. "I'll have your badge by the end of business today."

"Get out," she said harshly, "or I'll arrest you myself."

"Come on, Marcus," Eli urged him. "Let's get some air."

"Shut up!" Spittle frothed at the corners of Pray's mouth. "You're useless as the rest of them!"

Eli held up his hands as he backed away. "I'll be outside if you need me," he said to Blankenship and turned to go.

"You leave now, and you're fired!" Pray bellowed.

Eli kept walking. Joey followed him toward the stage door.

"What's going on with Stuart?" she asked anxiously. "What kind of warrant does Blankenship have?"

"Where'd you come from?" His tone wasn't friendly. "You're not supposed to be in here right now."

She quickstepped in front of him. "Is Stuart being arrested?"

"Keep your voice down." He took her by the arm and steered her to the stage door. "They've got a search warrant for his truck and his workstation, maybe his house, I don't know."

"Is this about what happened to Pray?" She shook her head, confused. "Why is Blankenship here? He's not dead."

Pray might be a Hollywood powerhouse, but she still didn't understand why his allergic reaction would bring in the sheriff's Homicide Bureau, even if someone dosed him intentionally.

"Believe it or not, they didn't take me into their confidence," Eli replied. "I know they're working off an anonymous tip of some kind. I got that much from what they *did* say, which wasn't a lot."

He propelled them both through the stage entrance, back out into the radiant, hot morning. "Now you know everything I do," he said irritably.

Word spread fast through the company, and much of the *UMPP* crew now crowded behind the perimeter established by the sheriff's deputies. They huddled in small groups, speaking in hushed tones to each other and watching apprehensively as Blankenship walked

Stuart and Sam out of the soundstage. Stuart pointed to his truck, parked only a few feet from the stage door.

While the detective and her team searched the vehicle, the Campbells stood apart from the rest of the crew, under the careful watch of a deputy. Stuart's habitual scowl was in place, but Sam looked frail and wan. Pray finally emerged from the stage. He appeared to be more composed, but still on edge.

Joey shaded her eyes. "Any idea what they're looking for?"

Eli gave her a sharp glance. "Not a clue."

Blankenship signaled from the passenger side of the truck to the technician with the cameras. She stepped aside and directed him to take pictures of the interior. When he finished, she leaned in again, then brought out an object that glinted silver in the sunlight.

Joey squinted against the glare. "Is that a flashlight?"

"Shut up," Eli said out of the side of his mouth.

She shot him a testy look, but then her cell buzzed, and after checking the screen, she quickly took the call. "Caleb?" She turned to go back inside the soundstage, but Pray stood blocking the door.

Voices rattled around her: Blankenship reading Stuart his rights over the gabbling of the crew, Samantha wailing and inconsolable, then Pray spewing obscenities as he pushed past Joey, clearing the path to the stage door. On the phone, Caleb was talking.

"I can't hear you!" Joey shouted as she bolted for the shelter of the soundstage.

Inside, she had to give her eyes another chance to adjust to the dark interior.

"I'm sorry," she said. "I'm at the studio, but I just now found a place I can talk."

"I'm leaving town," Caleb said.

She closed her eyes, the better to listen. He sounded frightened, like he had on the message he left her.

"Can you tell me where you're going?" she asked carefully.

"That wouldn't do either of us any good. I don't even know if I can trust you with what I'm about to say, but I feel like I need to tell somebody before I go." He made a thin noise in his throat. "I owe Court that much."

"Caleb, if you're in trouble, you need to tell me," she said urgently. "I'll do whatever I can to help, or help you get help."

"Just listen, then I have to go. I don't know what this means, or who knows about it already." He hauled in a breath, pulling himself together. "Courtney had a prenatal paternity test done. They can do it with a blood sample from the mother and a cheek swab from the guy, results in a week."

He was beginning to run hot again, sounding freaked out.

"I'm with you so far," Joey said, trying not to freak out herself. "Did she get the results back?"

"The day before she died. I didn't find them till last night when I was going through her desk, looking for her birth certificate. The printout from the lab was crammed in the back of a drawer."

Joey felt her heart contract. "What did the test say?"

"The only thing it can prove is whether the guy who's tested is the father." Caleb's voice was tight, and she sensed him weigh his next words. "It's not Eli; Eli wasn't the father."

Joey's mind emptied out for an instant as the realization of what Caleb was telling her sank in. Then a tiny splinter of sorrow burrowed in for the baby, and the person she or he might have become, and for Courtney, and all that had been so brutally taken from her.

But she couldn't allow herself to think about that now; she needed to focus on Caleb, keep him talking, convince him to stay and go to the cops with this. "Do you know if she told anybody?" she pressed him.

"You mean, Eli or Marcus Pray?" he said bitterly. "I don't know who else knows about this. I don't know if Court told anybody; I only know she didn't tell me."

Joey's thoughts tumbled together, but there was no way to understand what this meant without knowing who Courtney may have told. If Eli wasn't the father, would she then have gone to Pray, maybe asked him to take a similar test? That couldn't have gone well.

"There's one more thing," he said.

A tinny voice blared over a loudspeaker someplace close to him, blotting out every other sound.

"Caleb?" Joey yelled into the phone.

"Yeah, I'm here. Court went to stay with Pray. When she tried to kick me out and I wouldn't go? She went to him to get away from me," he said grimly. "If that makes any difference."

"It could make all the difference!" Joey wanted to reach through the phone and shake him. "You've got to stay and tell the police about this."

"You tell them," he said. "I've gotta go or I'll miss my flight."

"You have to turn over the pregnancy test!" She knew she sounded frantic, but she couldn't help it. "The police need to know about Courtney and Pray!"

"We're not sure the baby was the reason she was killed," he said stubbornly.

"We can't be sure it's not," she argued. "That's why the police need to know."

"I don't want to stick around. With my luck, the cops'll try to blame me, especially if they're in Pray's pocket. I'm not going to take that chance."

"Not if you tell them the truth!" She felt desperate. "I'm begging you, Caleb, please talk to the police. Call Detective Corinne Blankenship at the sheriff's Homicide Bureau. Do it for your sister."

"I don't know," he said, sounding spooked. "I'll think about it on the plane."

"Caleb, wait," she pleaded, but he was already gone.

Chapter
Thirty-Six

Joey was shaking when she got off the phone with Caleb. If Courtney was trying to confirm the identity of her baby's father, that could prove a powerful motive for her murder. Since Eli's paternity test was negative, that almost certainly meant Pray was the father, and Joey didn't think the rageaholic control freak would react with a nod and a cheerful smile to the news he was going to be a baby daddy.

She bent double at the waist, feeling light-headed. This was too much to process on her own.

"Who were you talking to just now?"

Her heart jumped when Eli stepped out of the shadows. The sight of him threw her for a second, and she hoped that didn't show on her face.

"One of my vendors." The lie rolled off her tongue. Then she remembered the pandemonium outside. "What happened with Stuart and Sam? Did the cops arrest both of them?"

He narrowed his eyes. "Never mind that. I heard enough to know you were talking to Caleb Lisle."

"Then why'd you ask?" She started to move past him; no way was she getting pulled into a Q and A about that phone call.

He stepped in front of her. "To see if you'd lie to me, and you did. Now I'd like to know why."

"Our conversation was personal." Stung by his surly manner, she looked him straight in the eye, hoping to back him down. "Excuse me, but I need to check in with my crew, then I want to go see about Sam."

He peered at her suspiciously. "Caleb's a born liar. He's a twenty-nine-year-old drug addict who's never held down a job and still mooches off his parents. Courtney knew what he was. She finally washed her hands of his poor-pitiful-me act, and you better believe he wasn't happy about that."

"I really don't have time for this." She broke off eye contact and tried to get by him once more. "If you have a problem with Caleb, that's not my concern."

"First you lie, then you try to justify it to avoid answering my question." He moved again to block her path. "What are you trying to hide?"

Fed up with his badgering, she shook her head. "You know how ridiculous you sound right now?"

He still wouldn't let her pass. "Tell me what Caleb said, or you and I are going to have a problem." His voice was an ugly growl.

She heard someone gasp and caught a glimpse of Sam Campbell over Eli's shoulder. Joey was startled by the expression on her face, the naked fear she saw there.

"It's okay," she said automatically, but Sam turned and bolted.

"Now look what you've done," she said angrily. "Quit trying to bully me, Eli. I need to go talk to Sam."

He took hold of her wrist and pulled her close. "She's upset because the cops just hauled Stuart off to question him about what they found in his truck."

The fierce look in his eyes stirred a dark memory. "Let go of me," she demanded.

He tightened his grip on her. "You don't want to hear about it?"

Blood thundered in her ears as she flashed back to a place in time she never wanted to visit again, the night she had to lock herself in the bathroom and wait for the cops.

"Stop it, Eli," she said, gritting her teeth. "Now."

"Have it your way." He let go her wrist and finally stepped aside.

Voices rose from the other side of the stage as crew members filed back into the building. Joey moved quickly in their direction; she needed to get away from Eli, and she needed time to think.

"One last thing," he called after her. "Courtney's parents are good people. You'll only cause them more pain by indulging whatever paranoid fantasies Caleb's dreamed up. Besides, it looks like the sheriffs already have her killer."

That stopped her. She took a moment to steel herself, then turned to face him again. "What are you talking about?"

"I tried to tell you. That flashlight we saw them take out of Stuart's truck? There's blood on it, and they think it may be Courtney's. They're sending it for tests, and they've taken Stuart in for questioning."

She stared at him, feeling blank as she tried to parse what he'd said. "Why would Stuart kill Courtney? That doesn't make any sense."

"Come on, Joey," he said scornfully. "We've all known since he went off on Marcus the other day, he can't be right in the head. Maybe he's even crazier than we thought."

His walkie-talkie crackled to life as Lionel's scratchy voice came through. "Eli Logan, what's your twenty?"

Eli kept his gaze on Joey as he spoke into the walkie. "Crafty on Stage Five."

"Coming to you," Lionel replied.

"How do you know all this?" Joey asked, still dazed by the news.

"The sheriff's people are in with Marcus now, taking his statement about what he consumed that might have triggered the allergic reaction." He furrowed his brow, looking stern. "They're investigating it as attempted murder, and in light of what they've learned about Stuart, he's their main person of interest."

"So now he's guilty of everything?" She felt a pang of frustration. "I hope they're not just focusing on Stuart when there's a company full of people who can't stand Pray."

"They're only doing their job." He turned his palms up. "I'm sure they'll want to talk to you too, based on what you told the medic yesterday."

Joey's stomach did a nosedive at the thought of another interrogation with Blankenship. "I'll bet you piped right up about that, didn't you?"

"I'm not the only person who heard you say the Campbells knew about Marcus's tree nut allergy, and I'm not going to apologize for telling the truth." He lifted his chin defiantly. "It's relevant information."

"What is your problem, Eli?" She swallowed hard, still unnerved by his attitude. "I'm not the enemy."

He looked at her for a long moment. "I know that," he said gruffly, then turned and walked away.

Joey passed the rest of the day in a fog of distraction. She went on putting one foot in front of the other, but Stuart's arrest together with the news about Courtney's paternity test had her spinning again. She thought it was possible Stuart crossed a line to punish Pray, but she didn't believe he was a homicidal maniac, as Eli implied, and she couldn't see any reason he'd want to harm Courtney.

Unless it was a matter of wrong place, wrong time.

She'd had that thought about the murder early on: maybe Courtney saw something she wasn't supposed to. What if she surprised someone in an act of sabotage? The idea didn't seem so far-fetched, given the explosion that sent Bernard to the hospital, the crash on Broadway, and Pray's near-fatal allergy attack, all in less than a week. Her mind snapped back to Pete O'Neill, the ugly look on his face when he bad-mouthed Courtney right after she died:

"Lotta people thought she was a bitch. The whole crew hated her."

At the time, she thought he was probably blowing hot air, but what if she was wrong? This was a guy who had privileged access to Pray's private trailer, ditto the picture cars and pretty much everything else on set by virtue of being in the transpo department. That gave him plenty of opportunity, and he worked directly for Pray, so it was a safe bet he had an ax to grind.

But she couldn't forget about the long-haired mystery man. He was right at the heart of the action for the on-set crash, and he seemed more likely than ever to be Joey's PCH follower. As far as she was concerned, that was enough to put him on the short list of suspects.

On the other hand, she wasn't ready to let Pray off the hook for the murder simply because he'd been targeted himself. The two incidents weren't mutually exclusive, and Joey could easily picture Pray killing Courtney in a fit of rage if she backed him into a corner over the paternity issue. She was sure he was capable of that kind of brutality.

Still, she only had Caleb's word the paternity test even existed, and she just didn't trust him. At this point she was less inclined to believe he was responsible for his sister's death, but she couldn't understand why he wouldn't go to the police with the test results, if he had them. Maybe he was guilty of something else, dealing drugs perhaps; or maybe if Eli was right, one of his paranoid fantasies sent him running. Then again, maybe he'd killed her, after all.

Shooting resumed on Stage Five with Pray back in control of the set; the general mood of the company was curiously subdued. To Joey, it seemed they'd adopted a siege mentality, as if the police action of the morning was only a hashtag marking some weird new normal. Bill Nichols nailed it: they all knew it wasn't *if* but *when* the next crisis would hit.

While she waited for her turn in the barrel with Blankenship, Joey stood within view of the monitor in video village and pretended to pay attention to the set, but her thoughts continued to swirl. She tried to shake off the tension she felt after her run-in with Eli; everybody was stressed out and short-tempered, herself included. You had to make allowances for that.

When she was finally called in for questioning, Blankenship surprised her. The detective only asked her to repeat the brief exchange she'd had with Sam about Pray's tree nut allergy. That was the extent of the interview.

Joey expected to be put on the block and almost opened up about everything she couldn't figure out on her own: the Pray/Courtney affair, her pregnancy and the paternity test, Pray's relationship with Sofia, her supposed suicide, and the lack of available information about her death. If only Joey had a copy of the paternity test results or she could count on Caleb to back her up, she'd have gladly dumped it all in Blankenship's lap.

In the end, she chickened out. Again. Without a hard copy of the test or a reliable witness to confirm her story, Joey still wasn't prepared to risk everything by putting herself in the crosshairs of the investigation.

Maybe the detective sensed her internal conflict because when Joey got up to leave, Blankenship held out a business card. "If anything occurs to you, Ms. Jessop, please don't hesitate to call me." She nodded her encouragement, and Joey reached for the card. "My cell number is in the bottom right corner. Any time," she added.

"Thank you," Joey said faintly, and walked out, free to get on with her day.

But she couldn't move past the chatter in her brain. At work, she was used to tackling problems head on, certain she'd make the best decision possible, given the information at hand. Now she found herself in alien territory, and the consequences of a poor decision were far grimmer than choosing the wrong fabric for a movie star's costume. Most painful of all was the haunting thought that the worst was still to come.

Dahlia texted her repeatedly about the Bond gig, but Joey responded with a brief *Will call when I can* and left it at that. When she went for her daily check-in at Hammer and Tongs, Damir took her aside.

"What's with you today?" He tapped her forehead with his finger. "And don't tell me you just have a lot on your mind, because I can see the committee's in session up there and the consensus is bleak."

Her eyes filled with tears, surprising them both. "Have you ever felt like you suddenly dropped into some alternate reality where everything you took for granted was the opposite of what you thought?"

"That is both vague and disturbingly specific."

"Don't mind me." She dashed at her tears impatiently. "It's been a hard week for everybody, and I think I'm cracking under the strain."

"You're human." He smiled. "And a pretty good specimen, at that. Why don't you cut yourself a break and play hooky for the rest of the day? Have a margarita, go home, and walk on the beach."

"I wish." She leaned up to give him a kiss on the cheek. "Thanks for listening; I feel better already."

"Liar," he said fondly.

"Cross my heart."

In the parking lot at Hammer and Tongs, she checked the crew list for Sam Campbell's cell number and placed the call she'd been hesitant to make. When voice mail picked up after the first ring, she left a message. "Sam, this is Joey Jessop. I hope your father's okay, but I'm mostly worried about you. Please call me when you get this. I promise not to ask a lot of questions, I just want to hear from you."

She pocketed her phone, feeling as if she needed to do something more, though she couldn't think what that might be. Playing hooky wouldn't cure what ailed her. With everything in a constant state of upheaval, it seemed smart to stick close to the set. Lacking direction or a better idea, she headed over to LCC to spend the afternoon updating the made-to-order bible.

The costume office was unusually quiet. Malo and Bill worked on the budget in silence, communicating by some form of telepathy, or so it seemed to Joey. Everyone else on the costume crew was at the studio with the shooting company or out in the field doing errands.

But the stillness only served as a vacuum, sealing her in with the questions she had no way to answer. Forget about compiling the details of costume construction, she couldn't concentrate on her work.

"They've wrapped for the day."

Joey looked up from the fabric samples spread across her desk. Bill was on his way out the door, a computer bag slung over his shoulder.

"Shoot." She ran a hand through her hair, irritated she'd lost track of the time. "I meant to go back to the studio to help the costumers wrap."

He waved his hand in a *let it go* gesture. "They only had three actors to watch."

"But it's been an awful day for everybody, Bill. I don't want them to feel abandoned."

"They're adults, Joey, and professionals." He took a closer look at her. "Are you all right?"

"Of course." She glanced at her desk with a frown. "But I didn't do half what I'd hoped with the extra time I had this afternoon."

"It'll still be there tomorrow." He motioned to her. "Let's get out of here."

Malo appeared next to Bill in the doorway. "Cage is locked up in back."

"Then we're all set. I hope you're hungry." Bill looked back at Joey. "I'm taking Malo out to dinner to thank him for the extra work he's been putting in with the budget. We'd both be happy for your company."

"That'd be awesome." Malo nodded enthusiastically.

She was touched by the invitation, but she'd never be able to make polite conversation over dinner. "Can I have a rain check?" She tried to smile. "I'd like to, but I'm not fit company this evening."

"Okay, but let's make it soon." Bill adjusted the bag on his shoulder. "Don't stay too long. The shooting company's done for the day, and we should be too. It's not going to get easier anytime soon."

He and Malo waved their goodbyes, leaving Joey alone in the silent office. She stared dispiritedly at the small mounds of fabric on her desk. These were her tools, as familiar and useful as her own hands. When she worked with them, it was almost as if they spoke to her, a dialogue that helped guide her through the creative process, from concept to image to clothing as the designs took shape. But tonight they were just piles of lifeless scraps with nothing to say.

When her cell phone buzzed with an incoming text, she closed her eyes and sighed. Probably Dahlia again. Maybe this was the time to bite the bullet and finish the conversation about the Bond movie once and for all. She pulled up the message with half an eye on the stack of fabric swatches she needed to organize for Neptune Girl.

Vengeance is mine and retribution. For the day of their calamity is near and the impending things are hastening upon them.

Chapter
Thirty-Seven

Joey wanted to throw her phone against the wall, or better yet, flush it down the toilet. Just her luck to pick up a cyberbully who browbeat her with sanctimonious sound bites. This time she blocked the number, even though the action felt pointless. But the text was the last straw for the day; she left her book work open on the desk, picked up her bag, and headed for home.

The long drive to the west side through the teeth of rush hour not only trapped her behind the wheel for the next two hours, it plunged her back into a death spiral of obsessive thinking. A pall of gloom enveloped her. Even with the bits and pieces of information she'd spent so much energy collecting, she was still floundering when it came to putting them together to make sense of the nightmare her world had become. But a new feeling of dread was building that sickened her to consider. By the time she got home, she felt a migraine brewing.

The sun was down, but the moon was out; a ghostly halo of light bled through feathery clouds floating across its pale face. She bypassed her house and headed straight for the beach.

At the water's edge she took a deep, cleansing breath, inhaling the sharp nighttime scent of the ocean, so different from the sun-warmed fragrance of the day. The onshore breeze was brisk, but she didn't mind the chill, even when a sturdy wave splashed over her feet. The sting of the cold water revived her, but tonight she couldn't tap into the comfort she usually found in the natural world.

When her phone began to ring, she was feeling so depressed and confused, she almost burst into tears. She pulled the device from her pocket, checked CallerID, then did her best to collect herself before she answered.

"Hi, I was about to call you," she lied.

"Didn't you see my last text?" Dahlia complained.

"When did you send it?" she asked to buy time while she checked her inbox.

She'd stopped looking at Dahlia's messages after receiving more than a dozen variations of *We need to talk* and *Call me when you can*.

"About ten minutes ago, when I managed to peel myself off the ceiling," Dahlia sputtered. "They gave Bond to some Brit with a BAFTA."

Joey closed her eyes and groped for something to say that wouldn't betray her complete lack of interest in the topic.

Dahlia saved her by rushing on. "They promised me the job, and then I find out this evening they've signed some dinosaur who belongs in a museum. On Twitter, mind you, not even a peep from my agent."

"That's terrible; I'm sorry, Dahlia," she recited.

"Yes, well, I hope you haven't given your notice," the designer said sullenly. "That would really put us in a pickle."

"No, I haven't." Joey didn't see any need to tell her the idea never crossed her mind. "I thought it best to wait until we spoke again."

"That's something, anyway," Dahlia said. "One less knot to unravel. Now I have to find a way to smooth things over with Marcus."

"Did you tell him you were leaving?"

"No, but he's got some ruffled feathers I need to tend," Dahlia grumbled.

"I'm sure you'll work it out." She hoped the designer had someone else she could call to pour out her heart to.

"There's one thing I need you to do for me, though." Dahlia shifted back into command mode. "For tomorrow."

"Sure, if I can."

"I left some fabric samples at the office. That batch from your kit, the silks and voiles from Europe?"

Joey racked her brain; it was hard for her to focus on the everyday details of the movie. "The Hopkins collection?"

There was a brother-sister team in England that manufactured the most exquisite reproduction antique fabrics, and they had them in long yardage runs that made them viable for film. The samples were part of Joey's regular kit of supplies, research books, and equipment that she brought along on every job. Dahlia had fallen in love with the beautiful vintage look-alikes and was determined to find someplace to use them, even on a superhero movie.

"I think so," Dahlia said. "Anyway, they're right beside my desk. I need them first thing tomorrow morning. Can you stop by our office and pick them up on your way to set?"

Call waiting beeped through on Joey's phone, and she checked the screen. Sam Campbell. *Hallelujah.*

"Dahlia, I've got to take this other call," she said hastily. "I'll bring the samples to set tomorrow." She clicked the keypad to switch lines. "Hey, I'm glad it's you. How are you doing?"

"Okay, I guess." Sam sounded shaky, which was no surprise. But there was no resentment in her tone, and Joey was happy about that.

"How's your dad doing?" she asked.

"I'm not sure." Sam hesitated. "I need your advice."

"About Stuart's situation?"

"Partly." The one-word response was freighted with doubt.

"I can refer you to a good lawyer if that's what you need," Joey said. "He doesn't do criminal law, but he'll be able to recommend somebody very capable."

"It's nothing like that." Sam took a sharp breath. "I don't think I can talk about this on the phone."

Joey's caretaker instincts kicked in. "Do you want to meet someplace?"

"Would you mind coming over here? I hate to ask, but . . ."

"No, it's fine," she said, relieved to have something useful to do and somebody else's problems to think about. "Where do you live?"

"We're renting a house on Clybourn Avenue in North Hollywood."

Joey was in the kitchen now, dishing out dinner for Bigfoot. She glanced at the clock: nine thirty PM. North Hollywood was easily an hour's drive, even at this time of night.

"I'll get on the road as soon as we hang up, but it'll take me a while to get there," she said. "Will you be okay in the meantime?"

"Yes." Sam still sounded anxious.

"We can stay on the phone if you want," Joey suggested. "We can talk while I'm driving."

"No, I'll be fine as long as I know you're coming."

"Hang in there, Sam. Whatever it is, we can figure it out."

Joey hoped she could keep that promise. If legal representation wasn't the issue, what else might be so urgent? But she'd given her word to lend support, and she'd do the best she could.

Away from the coastline, light pollution from the urban sprawl overpowered the gentler glow of the moon and stars. Traffic on the 405 heading into the Valley moved at a good clip, but there was still plenty of it. Driving along with dozens of other vehicles left Joey feeling isolated in the bubble of her car, a reflection of the city's inherent duality. Strange how a person could feel so separate and apart, alone in the midst of millions.

The block on Clybourn where the Campbells lived was lined with modest World War II–vintage bungalows surrounded by postage stamp–sized yards. But given the location and attendant skyrocketing real estate values, the tiny two-bedroom houses would doubtless fetch north of $700,000 apiece in the current market. It was only a matter of time before some developer bought up the block to raze it and build three or four McMansions in place of the dozen houses that stood there now.

The address Sam had given Joey belonged to a gray stucco cottage that could have used a fresh coat of paint but looked otherwise neat and in good repair. It sat back from the street at the end of a narrow brick walkway.

Nearly eleven o'clock and the heat of the day hadn't loosened its grip on the Valley. The warm night wrapped itself around Joey when she stepped from the car. As soon as she started up the walk, Sam appeared at the front door, looking pale in the dim light that spilled from the bungalow's interior.

"Did you have any trouble finding it?" She glanced past Joey to the street as if someone might be waiting in the shadows.

Joey looked over her shoulder, but all was quiet on Clybourn Avenue, the neighborhood tucked in for the night. She turned back to Sam, who shrank from the doorway, beckoning to her.

"Please come in."

She hurried inside and Sam shut the door behind her. "I can't thank you enough for coming."

Up close, the young woman's eyes looked red-rimmed, her skin drawn tight over the delicate bones of her face.

"You need to sit down," Joey said gently, alarmed by Sam's appearance. "Have you eaten anything today?"

Sam shook her head. "I can't."

They stood just inside the doorway, in the living room of the little house. Joey took her by the hand and led her to an overstuffed beige sofa that had seen better days but looked comfy enough.

"On second thought," she said, "why don't you lie down here for a while and rest your eyes. How about I fix you a cup of tea, maybe something simple to eat?"

"No, thank you." Sam gestured to the sofa. "Please, I need to talk to you."

Joey took a seat, feeling the weight of Sam's anxiety. "I'm here to help any way I can." She nodded reassuringly.

Sam remained standing. "I saw something." She frowned. "More like I heard something the night Courtney died . . . in Mr. Pray's trailer.

Joey's heart starting thudding, but she made herself go very still. She'd found Courtney's body on the beach. This was the first hint of direct contact that evening between the second AD and Pray.

"I know I wasn't supposed to be there, but I saw him leave with two of the women." Sam spoke quickly, as if she needed to say this as fast as she could. "Nobody else was around, so I waited until they drove off."

"You saw Pray drive away with two women," Joey repeated, to be clear. "Did you recognize them?"

"Not that night." Sam shook her head. "But I saw them with him again on set the next day."

So two of the models who'd been "auditioning" for Pray in his trailer on the first day of shooting.

"Okay." Joey clasped her hands tight in her lap, working to stay calm. "What happened then?"

"As soon as they'd driven off, I went into his trailer." Sam seemed surprised by her own audacity. "I don't know what I was looking for; I didn't even stop to think about it."

But Joey thought she understood. Sam uprooted her life to follow her father on his quest for answers about Sofia. Pray's trailer wasn't exactly ground zero, but it was as close as she was likely to get.

"The place was a mess; bottles and dirty glasses and dishes everywhere." Sam wrinkled her nose. "Smelled terrible, too. I opened a window and went back into the bedroom, but I'd only been there a minute or two when I heard someone come in the door up front; so I quick, hid in the bathroom."

She closed her eyes, remembering. "I was scared to death, trying not to make any noise. Then she started moving through the front room, banging around like she was mad or something."

Joey couldn't stop herself asking. "Could you tell who it was?"

"Not till she got a call on her walkie-talkie." Sam pitched her voice lower. "'Courtney, what's your twenty?' She didn't answer them, but she started swearing." She looked at Joey and nodded. "That's when I knew for sure it was Courtney."

"Did you recognize the voice on the walkie?"

"Only that it was a man."

Joey felt a hollow place open in the pit of her stomach. "Then what?"

"I heard her working her way toward the back. I just knew she was going to find me, and what could I say? There wasn't any reason for me to be in that bathroom."

Sam started to pace. "Another voice came up on the walkie and said, 'Courtney was headed to Marcus's trailer when I talked to her a few minutes ago.' She moved back up front in a hurry then, swearing the whole time."

Joey's jaw clenched as she pictured the scene, knowing how it ended for Courtney.

"The front door opened and closed." Sam sent Joey an anguished look. "I thought she was gone. Then I heard a man's voice up front, but I couldn't make out what he said."

The hollow place inside Joey opened wider. She willed herself to concentrate on what Sam was saying.

"Then Courtney said, 'You can't tell me what to do.' And you could tell she was pissed."

Sam stopped, transfixed by the memory. "I heard this awful voice, like a growl, 'You don't get to make that decision alone.' And Courtney said, 'It's not even yours.' Just like that—real cold."

Her eyes flicked to Joey again. "It all happened so fast. Courtney screamed, and I knew she was hurt, but she fought him. I think she whacked him with something and managed to get out of the trailer, but he went after her."

Joey stood, heart racing, her eyes locked on Sam; needing to hear the rest of it, wishing she didn't have to.

"I didn't know who it was until I heard him on stage today." Sam covered her face with her hands. "That same awful voice, arguing with you."

The room spun, and Joey thought she might faint. She braced her hands on the girl's shoulders. "Breathe," she said, as much for herself as Sam. They stood that way, leaning on each other, until Sam said very quietly, "I should have tried to help her. If I'd done something, maybe she'd still be alive."

"You must have been afraid for your life," Joey managed to whisper.

Sam eyes were swimming with tears. "So was she."

Joey couldn't think of anything to say to that. She felt a terrible sadness for this fragile young woman, and for Courtney. "Come sit down with me."

She guided Sam to the sofa. She needed to stay in the moment, or she'd be paralyzed by what she just heard. "Did you tell any of this to the police?"

"I know I should have, but . . ." Sam shook her head, shame-faced. "There's something else."

"I told her not to."

Stuart stepped through the front door into the living room.

Joey bobbed up from the sofa like she was spring-loaded. "The police let you go?"

"That's none of your business." His eyes glowed with hatred. "Why the devil are you here, hounding my daughter?"

"I invited her, Daddy." Sam got up to stand as a buffer between Joey and Stuart. "I asked her to come talk to me."

"We don't owe these people anything," he said angrily. "What they do to each other doesn't concern us."

"I can't do this anymore." Sam put her hands over her ears. "It's got to stop."

"You're too young to understand," he argued. "You haven't seen enough of the world to know who to trust."

"I know you're trying to protect me, but you're not thinking straight!" Sam cried.

"Don't you dare talk to me like that!" he thundered.

"Somebody's got to before it's too late." Tears washed Sam's face. "I know you're the one who's been sending Joey those texts about vengeance and death."

He reared back as if she'd slapped him. "Don't you see, she's one of them, the people who hurt your sister and let her die alone! She's even worse because she keeps trying to cozy up to us."

"No, Daddy." Sam shook her head resolutely. "She's my friend."

He stared at her, a look of despair in his eyes. "This is an evil place, Sammy. It's a mistake to open your heart."

"We couldn't help what happened to Sofia, but we can't let it spoil the rest of our lives, or use it as an excuse to keep the world at arm's length."

Stuart's face twisted in pain. "I only want you to be safe."

"I know." Sam reached for his hand. "But we can't keep living in a house filled with so much hate. Sofia wouldn't want that; and she'd want us to do what's right."

"Oh, Sammy." Stuart gathered her in his arms.

She clung to him, weeping like a child with a broken heart.

He pinned a furious gaze on Joey. "Haven't you done enough here for one night? Have the decency to leave us in peace."

Chapter
Thirty-Eight

D espite the warmth of the night, Joey shivered as she hurried to her car. She sat behind the wheel for some time before she put the key in the ignition, wrapped in a kind of leaden shock that blunted her pain.

Intellectually, she knew how odd it was that discovering the identity of her cyberstalker felt anticlimactic; couldn't hold a candle to finding out the man she used to live with was a murderer. Now she understood why she couldn't get the pieces of the puzzle to fit. The truth had been laid out like a road map from the beginning, a map she was uniquely qualified to read, but she'd been blind to the possibility of Eli's guilt because she wasn't willing to see it.

A sob caught in her throat as heartache punched through her shock. What was she supposed to do now? She reached for the door handle, then stopped herself. There was no reason to go back inside. Sam was a wreck and Stuart had ordered her out of the house; they couldn't help her, anyway.

Blankenship said to call any time.

Joey grabbed onto the thought like a lifeline: that's what she needed to do, right this minute, no matter it was almost midnight. She dug into her pockets, then tore through her bag, looking for the card the detective had given her earlier that day, but came up empty.

She squeezed her eyes shut, trying to remember what she'd done with it. Maybe she'd chucked it in the catchall drawer of her desk at Left Coast Costumes. That's what she usually did with a card or button or some such thing she didn't want to throw away but had no immediate use for.

At any rate, it was the likeliest place to look. If she couldn't find the card, she'd sit at the desk and work her phone until she convinced somebody at the Sheriff's Department to contact Blankenship for her. LCC was only a few blocks away, and she had the entry codes for both gates and the back door. She fired up the engine and headed for the costume house, desperate to reach the shelter of her own personal port in this storm.

Eight minutes later, she pulled into the parking lot behind the building and sprinted to the back entrance. Now that she'd made the decision to call the detective, she felt like she was on the clock, playing catch-up. Her hands shook as she tapped in the code on the keypad by the door and let herself into the shadowy area by the loading dock and cages. Work lights placed near the top of the thirty-foot ceilings sent wan cones of light to the floor but did little to illuminate the vast space.

She made her way through the massive, darkened warehouse with its multitiered racks of clothes hanging like so many silent ghosts from past eras in history. But Joey had often been here at night, and the place felt like home, comforting rather than eerie.

Up front, she unlocked the door to the costume office and repinned her keys to her waistband, then flicked on the lights. Her desk was just as she'd left it, spread with fabric swatches for the bible. She rushed over to look for the card and pulled the catchall drawer so hard it almost flew out of its slot. When she saw Blankenship's card on top of the scrap heap she hoarded there, she let out a yelp of relief.

She placed the card in the center of her desk and pulled out her phone, but before she sat down to make the call, she really needed to pee. There was a ladies' room up the hall, just a few steps from the office, so she laid her phone next to Blankenship's card and went to take care of her business.

The harsh fluorescent lighting in the bathroom didn't do her any favors, and she made her ablutions quickly, avoiding her reflection in the mirror. Goose bumps prickled her arms as she hurried back down the hall. She walked into the office, thinking about what she'd say when she got Blankenship on the phone, but she couldn't get past *I know who killed Courtney.*

"Hi, there, Joey." Eli sat at her desk. He held up her cell phone. "Hope you don't mind; I was playing solitaire while I waited for you to get back."

She stood in the doorway, still as a block of ice. "How did you get in here?"

"That doesn't sound very friendly." He leaned back in the chair, eyes shining with that vacant light she recognized as the glaze of a cocaine binge. "You gave me the codes, remember?"

He made a rolling motion with the hand that held the cell phone. "That time last year I came to pick you up after hours and you weren't quite ready to go?"

Joey's heart pounded like a jackhammer as she nodded dumbly, tracking the revolutions of her phone in his hand. She'd given him the codes for the gates to the parking lot and the back door, done it without a second thought.

"I didn't know you kept them." Her mouth felt dry. He continued to sit in a pool of light at her desk, as if they'd decided to meet this way, maybe go out for a quick drink. And then the obvious question presented itself. "How did you know I was here?"

"First I have a question for you," he said. "Why are you here in the middle of the night?"

Waves of tension poured from him like a storm surge battering the shoreline. She wondered how high he really was.

"I worked late." She gestured to the stacks of fabric samples on her desk. "I have a big clerical backlog to get up to speed."

He sighed and shook his head like he was sorry to deliver bad news. "You've only been here about twenty minutes, and you came straight over from the Campbells' house on Clybourn."

She felt her legs turn to water. "Have you been following me?"

"Not exactly."

"What does that mean?"

"You should see your face," he said. "When that brain of yours starts clicking away, it's really something special."

"What do you want?" She tried to sound natural, but it didn't quite work.

"I thought we should have a talk," he said mildly. "Someplace quiet, where we wouldn't be interrupted."

She tried to match his tone. "Why the urgency?"

"I didn't want to let the issue linger."

"What issue?"

He indicated a folding chair nearby. "Why don't you take a seat? You're making me nervous, standing in the doorway."

"I'm good." She flicked a glance over her shoulder, working up an exit strategy. "I didn't realize how late it is, and I still have a collection of fabric samples at home to organize. Dahlia asked me to bring them to set in the morning, so is there any way we could talk about this tomorrow?"

"No, it needs to be tonight." His smile was more of a rictus. "Don't look at me like that; I'm not as high as you probably think. Matter of fact, I've been high a lot since Courtney died, just enough to take the edge off."

But his voice was tight as a wire pulled taut.

Her phone began to ring in his hand, and he watched her eyes zero in on the device.

"This time of night, it must be something serious," she said. "Go ahead and answer it for me, if you like."

He checked the screen. "We can let this go to voice mail." He pressed the power button to turn the phone off. "Now, where were we?"

Fear choked her as she tried in vain to think clearly.

"Things have been strained between us the past few days," he finally said. "So I came over here tonight to hash things out, and I found Detective Blankenship's card sitting in the middle of your desk, which seems strange." He kept his eyes fixed on her as he tapped the card with his finger. "Then you tell me you've been working, and I know you haven't."

He raised his eyebrows, inviting a response.

Joey tried to steady her breathing, afraid her voice would betray her. "Eli, I think we're both tired. I know I am, and the stress is getting to us."

"You're trying to humor me now, and that's not like you." He propped his elbows on her desk, resting her phone against his cheek. "Makes me even more curious about what you're up to."

She forced herself to stand there and look at him, pretending they were still friends and colleagues, hoping she could bluff her way out the door.

"You're reading too much into a cross word or two," she replied. "I'm sorry if I've upset you, and I think we should call it a night."

"Soon." He nodded, his eyes holding on her face. "But I still want to know why you went to the Campbells'. What's so important you had to rush over from the beach tonight?"

Her mind was racing. "How do you know so much about where I've been this evening?"

He gave a casual shrug. "I put a tracker on your car."

Joey felt like she'd been doused with a bucket of cold water. "Why on earth—?"

"Not recently," he said, as if that made all the difference. "You know I like to keep tabs on my girls, and the model I buy . . . let's just say it holds up over time. But don't worry." He shifted so he could dig into the pocket of his jacket. "I removed it on my way in here tonight."

He pulled out a small black rectangle, no more than three inches by two inches, and laid it on the desk next to Blankenship's card. A short bundle of wires stuck out from one end of it like a tail.

"I hardwired it inside your car, so I'm afraid I had to jimmy the lock on your driver's side door." He shook his head regretfully. "But no serious damage done."

Joey stared at him, trying to recognize the person she'd known and loved in the man sitting at her desk. But they were only shadow images, like a double exposure, neither distinct nor complete.

"I'm not your girl anymore," she said tonelessly.

"But you were." He made the shrug again. "So I knew you came over the hill tonight the same way I knew Courtney was sneaking off to Marcus's house at odd hours a few times every month."

His words sliced through Joey, and all pretense was abandoned. The ghastly truth lay between them like a piece of bloody meat.

"She was a fool, but Marcus was the one with the power, so he's the one I blame. It's his fault she's dead." Eli's jaw set in that stubborn look Joey knew so well. "Everything that's happened since day one is his fault."

In a flash of insight, she understood, and the rest of the puzzle fell into place: Eli was behind all the trouble from the beginning. He'd known about Courtney's affair with Pray and decided to take revenge, to torpedo Pray's next big blockbuster. So he rigged the power outage that exploded the light on set, sabotaged the brakes on the picture car, and poisoned Pray.

Maybe he didn't plan to murder Courtney, but their jealous confrontation in Pray's trailer had spiraled out of control. After he killed her, he had to cover himself, so he planted the flashlight in Stuart's truck to throw suspicion on the older man. Eli didn't like leaving things to chance, so the anonymous tip to the cops made sense.

If she hadn't been so frightened, sorrow would have flattened her; it was all such a tragic waste.

"What do you want from me?" Her voice sounded as hollow as she felt.

"I told you, I want to know why you went to the Campbells', but we can come back to that." He held up her cell phone like a prop. "I'm even more interested to hear what you and Caleb Lisle talked about this morning."

She still hadn't moved from the doorway. Despite the civil tone of their conversation, she hadn't misunderstood the underlying menace. But whatever playlet they were performing for each other, she didn't want to be the one to break character.

"There's really nothing to tell. I said I was sorry about Courtney, and Caleb thanked me for the call." She watched him, wondering what he'd do if she simply turned to leave. "May I have my phone now?"

He looked at her coolly, then at the phone in his hand. She read the expression on his face and knew what he was thinking, and what she had to do.

She took a step back and slammed the door to the office, then charged down the hall, legs pumping at top speed. She sprinted through reception past the main entrance, secured at night by a padlocked grate, and hooked a right down the side hallway.

Eli would be on her tail in no time. If she could make it into the main warehouse, she'd have the advantage of knowing every inch of the humongous space like she knew her own home. With its narrow aisles and towering racks stuffed with costumes, it would give her plenty of places to hide and achieve her immediate goal: survival.

She flew through the women's stock of clothing, past the crinolines and hoop skirts, heading for the men's section on the other side of the building. She dove under a rack of clerical vestments like a rabbit into its burrow and pulled the long skirts of the robes around her for a curtain. So far, she hadn't heard a sound from Eli.

Doubtful he'd give up that easily, but he'd have his work cut out for him, trying to search every nook and cranny of the costume house. In addition to the central warehouse, there was a labyrinth of smaller storerooms, toggling erratically off the main space. There were endless corners and cubbies; the place was just too big.

Then again, maybe he'd decide to wait for her outside, stake out her car. If that was the case, she could stay put. People would begin to arrive for work by seven AM. All she had to do was spend a few hours breathing years of accumulated dust trapped in the hems of the garments providing her shelter. Not a bad trade-off. The rest she'd think about later. For now, she was safe, and she had to be grateful for that as she settled in to wait out the night.

Then she heard a noise. She knew from experience the building was full of sounds at all times, day and night. There were creatures that made their homes by tunneling into the walls or nesting in the wooden storage bins overflowing with shoes and accessories. She also knew these permanent residents were most active when they had the place to themselves.

She listened, hardly daring to breathe. Then she heard it again, closer this time. A soft sound, but not the skittering of small claws across the cement floor: this was a bigger rat on the prowl.

"Joey, whatever's upset you, come out, and let's talk about it. I swear, that's all I want to do, just talk to you."

He was getting warmer. Panic swelled in her chest, sending her heart rate through the roof. The urge to move, to flee, was almost unbearable. Moments later, she saw a ray of light move past her cocoon, tracing a narrow path on the floor, a small keychain flashlight he was using to try to ferret her out. It took every drop of willpower to remain still. The point of light disappeared, and she allowed herself to breathe again.

Sweat pooled at the small of her back. She had no sense of how much time had passed, but she didn't dare make even the slight movement required to look at her watch. Maybe the building wasn't big enough, after all. He'd already come so close to her hideout.

Why hadn't she taken her phone to the bathroom? That trifling choice could seal her fate. There were landlines stationed throughout the warehouse, but most were mounted in the open to provide easy access. She couldn't risk that kind of exposure. Even if she went for the phone in Henry Burchette's cubicle, the cover would be minimal, and if Eli found her there, she'd be trapped.

Then she heard him again. "Joey, come on. Give me a chance. We've always been there for each other. Nothing's changed; we're still the same people."

His voice was getting louder. She wanted to scream with frustration—tens of thousands of square feet of real estate to search, and he was doubling back. Because he was smart and playing the odds, knowing she was terrified and hadn't had much time to find a place to hide, and that she'd want to stay in an area where she wouldn't be cornered, where she could still run for it and have a shot at reaching the back door.

All was quiet for a time, and Joey rested her cheek on the stone-cold floor, trying to find a more comfortable position. Even if he'd killed Courtney by accident in a jealous rage, now the die was cast, and she had no illusions about Eli's intentions. He didn't have any options unless he chose to give himself up, and that didn't seem to be part of his playbook.

She shuddered, remembering the wild look in his eyes that awful night she locked herself in the bathroom before he went to rehab. She'd caught a glimpse of that same look when he grabbed her wrist on set, triggering her suspicions about the truth she didn't want to see. That wildness was in his eyes again tonight—it's what sent her running from the office. She knew he wouldn't hesitate to hurt her, just as he'd hurt Courtney.

"This is it, Joey. If you won't come out and talk to me, I'm done."

His voice hit her like an electric shock, the plaintive tone he aimed for earlier replaced by irritation.

"I tried to do this the easy way, but you wouldn't listen, so this is on you." He sounded aggrieved, as if she was at fault.

She closed her eyes, trying to get a bead on his location. Her best guess put him near the threshold that served as a boundary between the men's and women's sections of the main warehouse, smack in the middle of the space. She strained to hear any sound that would provide some clue about what he was up to.

Then, just as she was about to risk a peek from under the rack of clothing, she caught a whiff of something pungent, a stench that bit the back of her throat.

She smelled smoke.

Chapter Thirty-Nine

S he poked her head out from beneath the curtain of vestments. Sharp snapping sounds from the flames floated through the air as she lay there, rigid with fear. The sheer recklessness was beyond belief. Coils of smoke began to gather around her; the acrid stink was stronger now and building fast. Time to move; if she stayed where she was, she risked suffocation by smoke inhalation or even worse, being trapped by the fire.

But the idea of running blindly through the maze of clothing toward the back door filled her with dread. The pale glow from the work lights scattered throughout the warehouse did little more than cast a tangle of shadows, and Eli could be hiding anyplace among them, waiting to intercept her.

There was one other possibility: the catwalks, the grid system of metal bridges suspended high above the warehouse floor, used to reach the uppermost racks of costumes.

Best case, she'd climb up without being spotted and make it to the back door before he even knew she was there. It would also give her a bird's-eye view of the warehouse below, so she wouldn't have to worry about him leaping out at her from behind a rack of clothes. She'd caught a break because one of the ladders that accessed the catwalks was located at the end of the row where she lay, only about twelve feet away.

She scooted from under the row of heavy garments and popped up into a squat to balance herself, then dashed to the base of the ladder. She scaled the metal rungs that tinked softly with her climb. In a few seconds, she reached the network of narrow bridges twenty-five feet above the warehouse floor and felt a surge of relief. For the moment, she was beyond his reach.

The distance she had to travel to the back door was roughly two hundred yards, just two football fields, not so very far to go. She kept her focus on her immediate path to be sure of her footing in the dark; a stumble could be deadly. The racks of clothing provided her some peripheral cover until she reached the end of a row. Then she'd pause to gather her courage before moving through the no man's land between racks that left her without any screen except the open metal structure of the catwalk.

After what felt like an eternity but was closer to two minutes, she came to the end of the main warehouse where all the clothing was stored. The walkways extended over the cages and shipping area at the back of the building, but from this point forward, she lost her cover. No more racks of costumes to hide behind.

The air was now thickly clotted with smoke. She tore a man's peasant shirt from a hanger and wrapped it across her nose and mouth before starting across the exposed metal track above the cages.

She dared a look across the top of the rack beside her, searching for any sign of Eli, but there was no way for her to see past the billowing curtain of smoke and flames spreading across the warehouse. The masses of vintage clothing provided excellent fuel, and fire jumped up the full height of the racks with alarming speed. Terror gripped her as she realized the smart play would be to stake out the back door and wait for her there.

But she had no choice.

She couldn't see the back wall through the smoke. It occurred to her that might be an advantage, screening her from view as she crossed the final span. And the full-throated roar of the fire should cover the clatter of the metal walkway under her feet.

A thunderous crash sounded in the women's section as part of the roof collapsed, and she launched herself onto the open catwalk as if she'd been shot out of a cannon. Below her, the cages were filled with smoke, but she didn't see any flames. Within seconds, she covered the distance to the back wall and the access ladder that led down to the door.

She paused to get her bearings. Behind her, smoke poured from the main warehouse into the back of the building. Through the enormous doorway she saw towers of fire twenty-five feet high lick across the roof in a rush to consume the acres of clothing hanging on the multitiered racks, waiting to feed the beast. Some piece of her deep inside hurt over the loss she was witnessing—the history, the beauty and cultural artifacts from other periods that were being destroyed. But there was no time to stop and grieve.

The shirt she'd tied over her face was gone. The air around her was hot and dense, blistering her lungs with every breath. Tears stung her eyes as she squinted through the veil of smoke, searching for Eli. If he wasn't below, he'd be waiting outside for her unless he'd gotten careless when he set the fire. Part of her wished for that.

And then there he was, gazing up at her from the shadows at the base of the ladder.

"Joey, come on." He beckoned to her, extending his hand.

She shrank from the edge of the catwalk, but there was nowhere to go. Her shoulder banged up against the back wall, connecting with something sharp.

"Don't be stupid." Eli stepped onto the bottom rung of the ladder. "We need to get out of here." He began to climb toward her.

"Stay back!" She whirled, desperate for escape and saw she'd slammed into a metal bracket that held a fire extinguisher.

In one swift movement, she pulled the cylinder free and hurled it down the ladder as hard as she could. It caught Eli square in the chest and sent him pitching backward, arms flailing, to the warehouse floor.

Without thinking, she vaulted down behind him, taking the rungs two at a time. He lay sprawled on his back at the base of the ladder, gasping for breath. She used the last rung as a platform to leap over his body, clearing him like a hurdle, and hit the back door at a dead run.

She gulped fresh air like a drowning victim, then doubled over in a spasm of coughing as her smoke-filled lungs worked to expel the poison. Flames spouting from the roof of the building lit the night sky, the giant facility now fully engulfed. Any second she expected to hear the wail of approaching sirens.

Feeling dizzy and spent, she limped across the parking lot to her car, unpinned her keys, and then saw the signs of Eli's tampering with her driver's side door. The lock was broken. She couldn't even work up the energy to be upset about the vandalism; she was just glad to be alive. She felt a shred of remorse that Eli was still inside the burning building, but she couldn't bring herself to feel sorry about anything she'd done to put him in that position. She pulled the driver's side door open and dropped into the front seat of her car to wait for the fire department. If they didn't show up in the next five minutes, she'd drive to the nearest gas station and place the call herself.

A fog of smoke hovered above the parking lot. The power of the fire blew out windows as it ripped through the costume house. Then, like a phoenix literally rising from the ashes, Eli stumbled out the back door and fell to his knees.

Backlit by the inferno, he dragged himself across the asphalt, then staggered to his feet. He looked as if he'd been through a battle, his clothing torn and stained with soot. Joey could hardly believe her eyes, and she didn't know whether to feel relieved or frightened.

She watched as he stood swaying like a punch-drunk fighter, gazing at his handiwork while the blaze devoured the building. Finally, he seemed to come back to himself and turned to stare directly at Joey sitting in her car. The look in his eyes settled the matter of how she should feel. She fumbled her keys into the ignition and dropped the car into gear, tires chirping as she sped out of the parking lot onto Vineland Avenue.

Still no sign of emergency response. The costume house was located at the intersection of two major surface streets; she couldn't understand how the huge conflagration had gone unnoticed. There was a twenty-four-hour off-brand gas station/convenience store combo on the southwest corner of Vineland, and Joey braked, wondering if she should stop to put in a call to 911.

Bright light flashed from behind, and she reached up to adjust her rearview mirror. A set of headlights was gaining on her, high beams that caught the mirror and bounced straight into her eyes. Eli's black Range Rover. Joey flinched and gave the gas pedal more pressure, but the high beams kept coming and sat on her tail, bathing the car's interior with a harsh, flat glare that made her eyes water.

"Hey, where are we going?" A sleepy voice called from the back seat.

She swerved and almost lost control of the car when Malo's head popped up. She gaped at him in the rearview mirror. "Where'd you come from?"

"I must've fallen asleep." He picked up on her distress. "What's going on? Are you all right?"

"No, I'm not all right!" she fumed. "What are you doing in my car in the middle of the freaking night?"

"I wanted to see if you were still at the office . . . Then I saw your car was broken into, so I decided to wait." He turned to look through the back window. "Why is that car—"

"Sit back and buckle your seat belt," she snapped. Suddenly she was glad to see him. "Do you have your phone with you?"

"Well, sure."

"Call nine-one-one."

At that instant, they felt a solid bump from the rear. Malo made a sound that was part protest, part shriek. The car did a little shimmy but kept to the road. Joey flicked another look in the rearview mirror; all she got was another blinding eyeful of headlights.

She heard Malo scrabbling around in back. "Operator, we've got an emergency. We're heading south on Vineland Avenue in North Hollywood, and there's some crazy person ramming us with their car."

"Tell them the other driver is Eli Logan!" Joey shouted.

"For real?" Malo cried.

"Tell them!" she insisted.

She leaned over the steering wheel, straining to scan the road ahead. There was little traffic on the big thoroughfare, but she worried about the intersections. She couldn't afford to stop at the lights.

"The other driver is Eli Logan," she heard Malo say. "He just slammed into the back of us on purpose."

A pause, then he wailed, "No, we can't pull over!"

Joey pressed down on the gas pedal, but the Range Rover stayed with them and bashed them again, a little harder this time. The bone-jarring jolt threw her against the steering wheel and sent the car sailing through a red light at the big intersection of Vineland and Victory. Malo moaned in the back.

"Are you okay?" she called to him frantically.

"I dropped the phone. I think it bounced under your seat." He sounded foggy.

"Forget the phone and buckle your seat belt," she ordered.

She kept her hands clamped on the steering wheel, heart in her throat as she checked the speedometer: seventy-two miles an hour and climbing; insanity on a surface street, even at this time of night. They flashed through the red light at Vineland and Burbank, narrowly missing a Pepsi delivery truck. Joey wished she could signal the driver.

Please, please, please call the cops on us.

Then dead ahead, a waking nightmare: a homeless woman pushing a shopping cart loaded with her possessions entered the crosswalk at Magnolia and began to make her way at a snail's pace to the other side of the four-lane road. Joey laid on her horn. The woman finally looked up to see two cars speeding right at her, and ran for her life, abandoning her cart in the middle of the crosswalk.

"Malo, hold on!" Joey yelled, wondering if he was conscious, hoping he'd strapped himself in.

She hadn't been able to do that for herself, so she braced for another impact and tapped the brakes. The Range Rover rammed them again. She tasted blood and knew she'd bitten her tongue.

Then the SUV swooped around and pulled even. Eli spun the wheel to smash them with a glancing blow from the side, trying to force them off the road.

Her car shuddered and veered to the right. She sheared a driver's side mirror off a pick-up parked on the street but kept control of the car. And then, like an answered prayer, flashing lights caught her eye in the rearview mirror.

She stomped on the brake at the same time Eli swerved to hit them broadside. He caught her front fender and spun out, pinwheeling into the six-point intersection where Vineland, Lankershim, and Camarillo converge, just as the crosstown bus barreled through.

Joey screamed as the bus hit the Range Rover with a crash of screeching metal. She yanked the steering wheel to the left and felt something snap in her neck when her car hit the median and went airborne. The car bounced once, then landed upright in one of the northbound lanes and stalled. She pushed against the driver's side door, but couldn't get it to open.

"Malo, talk to me." She struggled to look over her shoulder, but it hurt too much.

"That was awesome." He poked his head over the front seat. "You should be a stunt driver."

"You're not hurt?"

He toggled his head back and forth. "I don't think so."

She wanted to slap him and hug him at the same time. "What were you doing back there?"

"You seemed so down this evening, I went by your house," he said. "Then I called, and when you didn't answer, I figured you might still be at work, so I came back to LCC."

Her mystery midnight caller. She flashed on her cell phone ringing in Eli's hand. Maybe it was a good thing he hadn't let her answer. Her mind began to wander.

Malo was still talking. "I couldn't get into the building, but then I spotted your car and saw somebody messed with the door, so I tried calling you again. When it went straight to voice mail, I decided to wait." He shrugged. "I must've fallen asleep."

"You could have been killed," she murmured.

The first emergency vehicles screamed into the intersection, sirens blaring. Malo said something, but she couldn't hear him over the noise.

"You could have been killed," she said again.

All at once she felt tired, so tired she could hardly keep her eyes open. She shook her head to rouse herself, which proved to be a mistake. Malo peered at her over the seat.

"You don't look so good," he said. "I'm going to hop out and get one of those guys to come over here."

"Stay in the car," she tried to say.

But he was already out the door and scrambling across Vineland, a gangly scarecrow of a kid bobbing through a sea of flashing lights, waving his arms at the paramedics.

Chapter Forty

Joey knew she was truly on the mend the day she couldn't stand to wear the neck brace anymore. The darned thing was hot, itchy, and generally uncomfortable, especially during the dog days of summer in LA.

The tipping point came about two weeks after she and Malo went airborne on Vineland Avenue. Although the headaches hadn't completely disappeared, they came less frequently and hung around for shorter periods. Her neck was still stiff, but it was better, and when she pleaded for mercy, Dr. Yacoubian gave the okay for her to ditch the plastic collar.

The day felt auspicious for a couple of reasons: she was also getting her wheels back. Much like its owner, her car wasn't totaled by the smashup, but needed time in the shop to replace the oil pan and muffler, which were basically ripped apart when it jumped the median; and there was body work required to repair the damage inflicted by the Range Rover.

All in all, she and the car were both lucky to be in one piece.

They certainly fared better than Left Coast Costumes. Joey was still in mourning, along with her entire professional community. Designers and costumers from around the globe sent condolences and posted tributes on social media worthy of the passing of a revered public figure. Which was, in fact, the case.

LCC wasn't just a repository for the best collection of costume rental stock in the world; it was the hub of the costume universe, the nerve center of a highly specialized society, a touchstone of creativity, a multifaceted resource of incalculable value. Its loss was devastating.

But that morning, Joey's thoughts were elsewhere. The sun was out early at the coastline, and the air looked clear as blown glass over the ocean, which sparkled like a string of semiprecious stones stitched along the horizon. She had an important appointment in the Valley, and after she Ubered to the dealership to get her car out of hock, she headed over the hill. The guys in the dealer's service department always switched her radio settings, so news at the top of the hour was almost over by the time she tuned in to NPR:

"Four more women came forward yesterday to add their names to the class action sexual harassment lawsuit filed earlier this week in Los Angeles County Superior Court against Marcus Pray and MP Productions, alleging a pattern of misconduct by the producer/director spanning two decades. The legal action comes in the wake of an exposé by investigative journalist Margaret Fuller that chronicles in exhaustive detail the accusations of six women who claim to have been assaulted and/or harassed by Mr. Pray at various points in time over the past twenty years. Originally published by the website *Popvibe*, the story was subsequently picked up by mainstream media outlets. The Los Angeles County District Attorney's office is said to be considering an investigation into specific allegations that have surfaced in conjunction with the civil suit that could result in criminal charges against Mr. Pray. This is Mandalit del Barco reporting from Los Angeles for NPR news."

Joey switched the channel to a classic rock station, but the damage was done. Now she couldn't think about anything except the phone call from Maggie Fuller she'd been trying to forget for the past two days. The reporter slammed her with a gut punch of an opening salvo:

"I have a source who tells me you had a close encounter with Marcus Pray. You were observed stumbling away from his trailer early one

morning on the Warner studio lot, looking like you'd been through the spin cycle. Do you have any comment?"

She should have hung up on the spot, but she waited a beat too long. Encouraged, Fuller pushed forward.

"Don't you see, this is why he's gotten away with it for all these years? Because people like you keep quiet."

Joey's temper flared. "And people like you think it's that simple: black and white, good and evil."

"Don't try to tell me there's a gray area when it comes to Pray's treatment of women."

"That's not what I'm talking about," Joey said impatiently.

"Then I give up, because you're not making much sense. What are you talking about?"

"I'd feel like a hypocrite if I came forward now pointing fingers, because I've been part of the whole rotten system." Her anger gave way to shame. "I turned a blind eye and kept my mouth shut for years to keep my life and career on track."

"I think I understand what you're saying," Fuller replied. "The whole culture turned a blind eye until recently."

"I'm saying a lot of people have been hurt," Joey swallowed to clear the knot in her throat, "and I don't feel it's appropriate for me to whine about behavior I've tacitly condoned. Compared to what other women have been through, my experience was a walk in the park."

"Okay, I get it." Fuller's tone was gentler. "But this is a story I care deeply about, and I'm sticking with it for the long haul, so there's time if you change your mind. It's never too late to start listening to your conscience."

On the radio Joni Mitchell was singing "Free Man in Paris" and Joey turned up the volume. She realized that despite all the darkness of the past weeks, there was a part of her that was straining toward the light, unfettered and alive, just like Joni.

A brush with catastrophe can do that when you come out the other side.

She knew it would take time to come all the way back, to feel completely safe again, and maybe she never would. If that was the case, she'd learn to live with her personal new normal.

Because she believed we're resilient, we humans. Bad things happen and more often than not, we find a way to take our licks in stride. After the initial shock, we adjust, even when our lives are changed forever.

The welding studio was going great guns when she walked in the door at Hammer and Tongs. Heavy metal music blasted from an old-school boom box as two sculptors worked on a giant centaur that looked like it was molded from strips of copper. The sight of the magical creature gave Joey a childlike thrill as she waved to the artists, even though this was the first time she'd visited since the studio pulled the plug on the movie, and she felt a little weird about being there without a job and work to bring in the door.

But when she entered the common area, there was Malo, and she felt her spirits lift. He'd gotten there early, and even better, he and Damir already had their heads together as they looked at Malo's drawings spread out on the big table in the center of the room.

"I guess you guys don't need me here, after all."

Their heads came up in unison, then both jumped to their feet.

"Joey, you're not wearing your brace," Malo said.

"Got sprung this morning." She leaned into a quick hug.

He drew back in alarm when she winced.

"I'm still a little sore, no big deal," she said, smiling brightly.

"You're looking very snappy for a recently concussed woman," Damir said. "Malo and I were just getting acquainted while we waited for you. Come join us."

He indicated a spot on the sofa. "What can we get you to drink? Water? Iced tea? Shot of whiskey?"

"I'm good." Joey gingerly lowered herself to the sofa. "Thanks for seeing us today."

"I'm glad you finally returned my calls." Damir took a seat beside her. "And that you brought this talented guy to see me. His work is impressive." He smiled at Malo, who looked like he was ready to burst with excitement. "How would you feel about coming to work here?"

Malo stared at him. "For real?" He turned to Joey.

"Don't look at me," she said. "He's the boss around here."

"We're a union signatory house, so you'll have to work the first thirty days at an entry-level hourly rate," Damir explained. "After that you'll be eligible to join seven-oh-five, the costumers union. Once you have your membership, you'll get a big bump in pay plus benefits—health insurance and contribution to your pension fund."

"That would be totally awesome!" Malo was beaming.

Damir held out his hand. "We'll talk about the particulars in a while, if you can stick around."

Malo took his outstretched hand and pumped it enthusiastically. "Thank you so much! This is incredible."

"You're very welcome, but you should thank Joey. She's the one who got you in the door."

Malo turned to look at her again, eyes shining. "You're amazing."

"Back at you," she said. "Make us both proud."

"Sesu," Damir called to an androgynous youth lounging nearby. "Could you show Malo around, introduce him to the others?"

"Sure." Sesu stood up.

"Come on back after, and we'll get some start paperwork going," Damir said to Malo. "If you want, your first day can be tomorrow."

"I can't believe this is happening." Malo shook his head in wonder. "It's like a dream."

"Come on." Sesu beckoned to him. "What's your name again?"

Off the two of them went down the hall, Malo peppering Sesu with questions a mile a minute.

"Thank you for this," Joey said when they were out of earshot.

"The kid has talent, and as long as he puts in the work, we can train him." Damir shrugged. "Other people took chances on me when I was about his age. I'm just paying it forward."

"We both know not everyone's so generous. I appreciate you giving him the opportunity. From what I can glean, he hasn't had an easy time of things, and he deserves a break."

"Happy to do it, especially since it got you up here so I can see for myself how you're doing." He leaned toward her, frowning. "So, how're you doing?"

She tipped a hand back and forth, spirits plunging as the focus turned to her. "Some days better than others."

"I'm glad to see you looking so well. I didn't know what to expect." He paused. "It's been hard to sort truth from fiction with all the media hype. I'm sure you've had a rough go."

"The press has kept their distance the past few days, and that's been a relief. For the most part," she amended, thinking again about Maggie Fuller. "Or maybe they've moved on to the next big thing. I'm trying very hard not to pay attention to any of it."

"Not even the *meshugas* around Marcus Pray?"

"I wish." Joey sighed. "I got a call from one of the lawyers handling the class action suit. Several calls, actually. And there's a reporter who's still hassling me about that. I'm ducking them all for as long as I can."

"Good luck with that."

"I know, but I need a minute to clear some head space before I can face it."

"Does the lawyer want you to testify?"

"The message didn't say. I'm assuming a deposition at the very least."

"There's more, though, isn't there?" He sat back, watching her carefully. "What's really bothering you?"

"So much for being inscrutable." She had to look away. "I've watched guys like Pray operate since the day I started in the industry, and I never made any waves. For fifteen years I told myself to just keep my head down and do my job."

"Hey," he said mildly. "You know, you weren't alone in that."

"But I'm the only one responsible for my behavior, so who am I to judge?" It pained her to think how she'd set aside her own values.

"It's not about judging, though, is it?" he said. "It's about bearing witness."

"Feels like I'm letting myself off the hook." She glanced at him, embarrassed. They'd never talked about these things so openly. "I dressed those girls up for Pray in miniskirts and tube-tops, just like they told me to, and now I'm supposed to claim some sort of moral superiority?"

Damir shook his head. "You're too hard on yourself."

"Anyway," she rolled her shoulders, trying to work out her tension. "I should talk to a lawyer before I do anything, to see what my exposure is, given the confidentiality agreement I had to sign for the studio when I did my deal memo."

"From what I've heard, the studio's cut Pray loose since the class action was filed," Damir said.

"They were probably looking for some way out of his pay-or-play contract once they decided to shut down the movie."

"You'd think the sexual harassment charges would be enough to do that," he said tartly. "More women came forward yesterday to accuse him on the record, and there's even talk about criminal charges being filed."

"I heard about that on NPR, and I've gotta say, even with #MeToo making some progress in terms of industry policy, practical application's another matter. I'll be amazed if he actually goes down." She knew there was a long road ahead before Pray faced any serious consequences. "Cash is still king in Hollywood. I thought he'd be untouchable until his movies started to tank at the box office."

"Systemic change is a slow process." Damir nodded sagely. "The movie industry's been around for more than a hundred years, and even though it's a world of its own, it's also a reflection of the society that spawned it."

"I suppose you're right," she conceded. "Everybody's feeling their way along now, trying to sort out the new boundaries. Nothing's quite the same, but it's not a magical transformation."

"And Pray's not out of it yet." He puckered his lips suggestively. "Did you hear he pulled a Weinstein last week and checked into sexual addiction rehab?"

"That's why I'm boycotting the news." She almost wished she'd stayed home today, after all. "I don't even want to hear about that stuff."

"Okay, my bad. But can I ask—?" He stopped, his brow furrowed.

"You can ask anything you want."

"What's going to happen with Eli?"

"Good question." Joey closed her eyes, skewered by guilt.

The pain didn't surprise her anymore when it came, and she knew there would always be part of her that mourned for Eli and the lives he destroyed, including his own. But she couldn't forgive her own willful ignorance. If only she'd been smarter and quicker, more objective, she might have headed off some of the damage he'd done. Left Coast Costumes might still be standing.

"You may be avoiding the media coverage," Damir went on, "but they're all saying you're a hero for flushing him out so the cops had enough evidence to arrest him."

"Talk about fake news." Joey shook her head scornfully. "The sheriffs had him as a person of interest from the get-go, and they had to be closing in, especially since they'd eliminated Stuart Campbell as a suspect that very day."

"Who's Stuart Campbell?"

"Our craft service guy on the movie." She rubbed her eyes. "It's a long story, but they had him in for questioning about Courtney's murder, mainly because Eli set him up to look guilty. But the cops realized Stuart couldn't have killed her. She was stunned by a blow with a flashlight, then she was manually strangled, and Stuart's got a bum arm."

"None of that's been in the news, the part about her being strangled, not even on Twitter."

"I'm surprised they've been able to keep it quiet this long," she said wearily. "Or why they even need to at this point. I hear Eli made a full confession in the hospital." Damir reached over and took her hand. She gazed at him, dry-eyed but solemn. "Truth is, he almost killed me, and I barely got away. If it hadn't been for Malo and the cops, I wouldn't have made it."

"Malo?" Damir looked at her in confusion.

"I told you he's special." Tears pooled in her eyes. "Someday we can talk more about that night if you want to, but not today."

He squeezed her hand. "Whatever you say."

"I don't know if I'll ever be able to trust my own judgment again." Her voice sounded harsh and flat. "In the end, I think that's the worst of it."

"Everybody feels like that sometime in their lives."

"Don't try to sugarcoat it. I was so sure Eli was a good guy at heart. There was a time I even thought I was in love with him." She took a shaky breath.

"We're hard-wired as humans to assume the best about the people we know. It's a scientific fact."

"Says who?"

"A shelf of books have been written on the subject." Damir brushed a strand of hair from her forehead. "He fooled a lot of people, Joey, and nobody's just one thing. Maybe he changed . . . or snapped."

She dipped her head, acknowledging his point.

He put an arm around her shoulders. "You need to try to forgive yourself for not having all the answers, for being human; because I guarantee you'd do that for anybody else in your position."

She looked at him sideways. "You sure about that?"

"Look at what you're doing for Malo. You're helping that kid change his life. Don't let this dark moment consume you. Follow the light because that's who you really are."

His words, so closely aligned with her thoughts only a short time before, struck a hopeful chord in Joey. "How'd you get to be so smart?"

He leaned over and kissed her cheek. "I hang out with a superior class of people. Now, what's next on your agenda?"

"You mean, today?"

"I was thinking more along the lines of the near future."

"I'm going to visit my mom and her husband in Arizona for a few days." She hiked her shoulders. "After that, who knows? I can't look too far ahead right now."

"Go with the flow?"

"Something like that," she said softly.

Malo came back from his tour wreathed in smiles and plunked himself down on the sofa beside Joey. "This place is awesome!"

He bounced up again like a jack-in-the-box, too excited to sit still. "I can't thank you guys enough."

"Hey, Malo," she said. "I just had a thought. How would you feel about house-sitting for me at the beach for a few days, taking care of Bigfoot?"

"Seriously?" He looked ready to break into song.

His joy was infectious, and Joey felt grateful to be sharing this moment with her friends, when all at once, she knew what she wanted to do.

She turned to Damir. "Why don't you two get his start work filled out, then I'll take you gentlemen out for lunch to celebrate."

"Sounds like a plan." Damir stood up. "Malo, follow me and let's make it official."

Malo squeezed his eyes shut and stood at attention, arms tight at his sides.

"Are you okay?" Joey asked.

He nodded and his eyes popped open. "I wanted to memorize this feeling, so I'd always be able to remember the very best day of my life."

Damir clapped him on the shoulder. "We won't be long."

Calm settled over Joey as she watched them walk down the hall together. She smiled to herself, then pulled out her cell phone and brought up Maggie Fuller's number.

Her fingers hovered over the keypad as she thought about what it means to bear witness, to tell the truth, even when that's uncomfortable. She tapped out a text.

We should set up a time to talk.

Acknowledgments

N o book is solely the work of one person. It requires the dedication and labor of an array of talented people to bring any book to publication. I have so many to thank for their generosity and important contributions to the production of this book. I am also grateful to the wonderful people with whom I share my life and who have supported me in countless ways for years to make it possible for me to realize this dream.

Thank you to my literary agent, writing coach, tireless advocate, and friend, Ann Collette. I dedicated this book to her, but she deserves thanks wherever I can offer it. Many thanks also to two gifted editors who provided invaluable encouragement and guidance, Toni Kirkpatrick of Crooked Lane Books and Jennifer Hooks. Toni, your unflagging support and intelligent counsel have meant the world to me. Jennifer, your perceptive and thoughtful suggestions, coupled with your patience, talent, and skill greatly enriched both the book itself and the process of editing it. I have great respect and appreciation for the whole team at Crooked Lane Books, especially Madeline Rathle and Rebecca Nelson; they are a fine group of hard-working professionals. My heartfelt thanks and admiration to Madeira James and her associates at Xuni.com who created a beautiful website for me that is even better than I'd hoped it could be. Maddee, your artistry and ingenuity never cease to inspire me. And I consider myself very fortunate to be working with Holly Watson of

Acknowledgments

Holly Watson PR. Thank you, Holly, for your resourcefulness, hard work, attention to detail, and delightful good humor.

Endless thanks and love to my amazing family: Jeff, Christy, Marianna, Jeffrey, John, and Anna McCown; Frances Bridges; Rich Gialluca; Chris and Joe Lange; Lorien, Chris, and Julian French; Jasmin, Nick, and Zora Nelson; and my precious Buck and Kitty Jones.

I am blessed with incredible friends whom I love dearly and who make my life better: Kenn Smiley and Bob Mathews, Daniel Orlandi, MJ McGrath, Bobi Garland and Ned Albright, Mari Grimaud, Heather Bridges, Cy Bridges, and Kathleen Troy.

There are a host of people who have been both friends and colleagues in the film community with whom I worked for so many years. I owe them all a debt of gratitude for the experiences we shared and the kindnesses they showed me.